More Than a Duke

Heart of a Duke Series

Christi Caldwell

SPENCER
HILL
PRESS

More Than a Duke
Copyright © 2015 by Christi Caldwell

Please visit www.christicaldwellauthor.com

First Edition: January 2015
Christi Caldwell

More Than a Duke: a novel / by Christi Caldwell—1st ed.
ISBN: 978-1-63392-104-7
Library of Congress Cataloging-in-Publication Data available upon request

Summary: Polite Society doesn't take Lady Anne Adamson seriously. However, Anne isn't just another pretty young miss. When she discovers her father betrayed her mother's love and her family descended into poverty, Anne comes up with a plan to marry a respectable, powerful, and honorable gentleman—a man nothing like her philandering father.

Armed with the heart of a duke pendant, fabled to land the wearer a duke's heart, she decides to enlist the aid of the notorious Harry, 6th Earl of Stanhope.

Harry, the Earl of Stanhope, is a jaded, cynical rogue who lives for his own pleasures. He's come to appreciate that all women are in fact greedy, title-grasping, self-indulgent creatures. And with Anne's history of grating on his every last nerve, she is the last woman he'd ever agree to school in the art of seduction. Only his friendship with the lady's sister compels him to help.

What begins as a pretend courtship, born of lessons on seduction, becomes something more, leaving Anne to decide if she can give her heart to a reckless rogue, and Harry must decide if he's willing to again trust in a lady's love.

Published in the United States by Spencer Hill Press.
This is a Spencer Hill Press Contemporary Romance.
Spencer Hill Contemporary is an imprint of Spencer Hill Press.
For more information on our titles, visit www.spencerhillpress.com

Distributed by Midpoint Trade Books
www.midpointtrade.com

Cover Design by: The Killion Group, Inc.
Interior layout by: Scribe Inc.

Printed in the United States of America

Heart of a Duke Series

TO MY READERS

Thank you for your beautiful support and the laughter you bring into my life. And an extra special thank you for all the times you "kick me off" social media so I can keep telling my stories! Hugs.

Contents

Chapter 1

*I*n a Society that placed such value upon honor, respectability, and virtue, Lady Anne Arlette Adamson came to a very interesting revelation. A young lady would discard her self-worth and sense of decency . . . all for a glass of champagne.

Or more precisely, *two* glasses of champagne.

The full moon shone through the Marquess of Essex's conservatory windows and splashed light on the two sparkling crystal flutes. Drawn to them, Anne wet her lips and did a quick survey of her host's famed gardens, searching for any interlopers. Lured by the forbidden liquor, she wandered over to the table strewn with vibrant pink peonies and blush roses and picked up a flute. She angled her head. Eying the pale, bubbling liquid contained within, a sudden desire filled her, to taste the fine French brew.

Of course, young, unwed ladies did not drink champagne. At least that was what Mother was forever saying. A mischievous smile tugged at the corners of her lips. Then, she'd never been lauded as the obedient, mild-mannered daughter. Anne raised the glass to her mouth . . . and froze. An *honorable* young lady however didn't drink champagne belonging to two other people.

She sighed and set the glass down.

With a frown, she began to pace the stone floor. Where was he?

She'd heard rumors of his notorious assignations, knew he planned to meet . . . she wrinkled her nose, *some* widow or another, in the marquess's conservatory.

Perhaps the rumors were just that, mere rumors. Perhaps . . .

The click of the door opening sounded off the glass walls of her floral haven. Anne jumped. Her heart pounded hard and she raised a hand to her chest to still the sudden increased rhythm.

For the first time since she'd orchestrated this madcap scheme involving Harry Falston, the 6th Earl of Stanhope, she questioned the wisdom of such a plan. Enlisting the aid of one of Society's most scandalous rogues would hardly be considered one of her better ideas. The ladies adored him, the gentlemen wanted to be him, the leading hostesses frowned at him from one side of their fans and tittered behind the other.

He also happened to be the gentleman who'd tried—and failed—to seduce Anne's twin sister, Katherine.

For all Anne's twenty years, she'd forever been considered the more spirited, imprudent twin sister. Of course, being the more sensible of the twins, Katherine had not fallen prey to his devilish charms. However, in a wholly *insensible* thing to do, her sister had befriended him, a rogue of the worst sort who didn't even have the decency to respect Katherine's marriage . . . or *any* marriage, for that matter.

The door closed. With breath suspended, she slipped behind one of her host's towering hibiscus trees.

Good, respectable young ladies, marriageable young ladies at that, should have a care to avoid Society's most notorious rogue.

Her nose twitched and she widened her eyes in attempt to hold in a sneeze. Then, she'd not paid too close attention to the *ton*'s rigid expectations for a young lady.

The tread of a gentleman's footsteps echoed off the glass windows. "Hullo, sweet."

Oh, by Joan of Arc and all her army. *Hullo, sweet?* That was the kind of claptrap this rogue was known for? His husky baritone however, well, that was better suited for the Gothic novels she'd taken pleasure in reading before her mother had gone and stolen her spectacles. But "Hullo, sweet"? She shook her head. It would take a good deal more than an unclever endearment to earn her favor.

The bootsteps paused. She peeked out from behind the tree.

Her breath caught. The moon bathed the lean, towering gentleman in soft light. The earl's gold locks, loose and unaffected, gave him the carefree look of one who flouted Society's rules. But then, isn't that what the Earl of Stanhope had earned a reputation for? Which made him perfect. Perfect for what she intended, anyway.

The sweet fragrance of the hibiscus tickled her nose yet again. She scrubbed a hand over her face hard and drove back a sneeze.

The earl cocked his head, as if he knew she stood there secretly studying him, quietly admiring him. It really was impossible not to. His black-tailed evening coat clung to sculpted arms. Anne continued to scrutinize him with objective eyes. Gentlemen really shouldn't have sculpted, well-muscled arms. Not like this. Why, they were better suited to a pugilist than a nobleman.

A grin tugged the corner of his lips up in a hopelessly seductive smile. She fanned herself. Well goodness . . . mayhap it wasn't the champagne flutes after all but the pirate's grin that made foolish young ladies toss their good names away.

She stopped midfan. Not that she would be swayed by such a smile. No, the gentleman she would wed was serious and respectable and obscenely wealthy and unfailingly polite and just enough handsome. Not too handsome. Not unhandsome. Just handsome enough.

The earl shrugged out of his coat. He flipped it over his shoulder in one smooth, graceful motion. The effortless gesture jerked her from her musings.

Anne swallowed hard. Yes, he was entirely more handsome than any one man had a right to be. She supposed she really should announce herself. Especially considering his . . . er . . . arrangements for the evening.

"You do know, sweet, if you're content to stand and watch me remove my garments, I'd be glad to provide you such a show. I would, however, vastly prefer you allow me to slip the gown from your frame and . . ."

She pressed herself tight against the tree. Her arm knocked the branch of the hibiscus and wafted the cloying, floral scent about the air. "Achoo!" Blast and bloody blast.

The earl's grin widened as he yanked a stark white kerchief from his jacket and wandered closer. He extended the cloth. "Here, sweet—"

Anne stepped out from behind the tree. The earl froze, the stark white linen dangled between them. His hazel eyes widened. She plucked the kerchief from his fingers and blew her nose noisily. "Thank you," she said around the fabric.

"Bloody hell, Lady Anne," he hissed. "What in hell are you doing here?" He shrugged into his jacket with the speed surely borne of a man who'd clearly had to make too many hasty flights from disapproving husbands.

She frowned. "You really needn't sound so . . . so . . ." Disappointed. "Angry, my lord."

He took her gently by the forearm. "What are you thinking?"

She tugged her arm free. "I require a favor—"

"No." He proceeded to pull her toward the front of the conservatory.

She frowned up at him. "You didn't allow me to ask—"

"No." He shook his head. "Mad," he muttered to himself. "You're completely and utterly mad. And maddening."

"I am not mad," she bit out. She really wished she was as clever as her eldest sister, Aldora. Aldora would have a far more clever rebuttal than "I am not mad" for the scoundrel.

His mouth tightened. And she swore he muttered something along the lines of her being the less intelligent of her sisters.

Anne dug her heels in until he either had to drag her or stop. She glowered up at him, this rogue who'd tried to earn a spot in Katherine's bed. Alas, Katherine loved her husband, the Duke of Bainbridge, with such desperation the earl hadn't had a hope or prayer.

He folded his arms across his chest. "What do you want then, hellion?"

She gritted her teeth, detesting his familiarity that painted her as the bothersome sister. Still, she required something of him and as Mother used to say, one can catch more bees with honey than . . . she wrinkled her nose. That didn't quite make sense. Why would anyone want to catch a bee? Unless—

The earl took her, this time by the wrist, and began tugging her to the door.

"I need help," she said and pulled back.

To no avail. He held firm. The man was as powerful as an ox. "No."

Most gentlemen would have inquired if for no other reason than it was the polite, gentlemanly thing to do.

Anne at last managed to wrest free of his grip. "Please, hear me out, my lord."

He took a step toward her. "By God, I'll carry you from the room this time." The determined glint in his eyes lent credence to his threat.

She danced backward. "Oh, I imagine that would be a good deal worse." He narrowed his eyes. "Your carrying me," she clarified. "Imagine the scandal if—"

Lord Stanhope cursed and advanced. "You risk ruin in being here, my lady," he said, his voice a satiny whisper that sent warmth spiraling through her body.

She shook her head. People might believe her an empty-headed ninnyhammer, but she was not so foolish to be swayed by a crooked grin and a mellifluous whisper. She took another step away from him. Her back thumped against their host's table. It rattled and one of the champagne flutes tipped over. She gasped as the pale liquid spilled across the wood table and threatened her skirts.

Lord Stanhope yanked her away from the dripping champagne and tugged her close. "Tsk, tsk, my lady." He lowered his lips to her ear. "However would you explain returning to the ballroom with your skirts drenched in champagne?"

Anne glanced up. And wished she hadn't. *Really* wished she hadn't.

The earl's impossibly long, thick golden lashes were enough to tempt a saint, and after more than twenty years of troublesome scrapes, Anne had earned a reputation amidst her family as anything but a saint.

A lock toppled free from the collection of ringlets artfully arranged by her maid. She brushed the strand back. It fell promptly back over her brow.

The earl collected that single curl between his fingers and studied the strand bemusedly. "A ringlet," he murmured. His lips twitched as though he found something of the utmost hilarity in her gold ringlet, immediately snapping her from whatever momentary spell he'd cast.

She swatted at his fingers. "What is wrong with my ringlets?" She knew there was a more pressing matter to attend. But really, what was wrong with her ringlets?

He tweaked her nose. "There is *everything* wrong with them."

Well! Anne gave a flounce of those ringlets he seemed so condescending of. "I've not come to speak to you about my hair."

The earl narrowed his gaze as he seemed to remember that one, they were shut away in their host's conservatory one step from ruin and two, she was the sister of the twin he'd once tried to seduce. And more specifically, the sister of the twin who'd looked down a pointed nose at him whenever he was near.

With trembling fingers, she righted the upended flute. "I require but a moment of your time."

"You've already had at least five moments."

Distractedly, she picked up the crystal flute still filled to the brim and eyed the nearly clear contents of the glass. It really did look quite delicious. "Do you mean five minutes?"

Because there really wasn't such a thing as five moments. Or was there? She raised the glass to her lips.

With a growl, he snatched it from her fingers with such ferocity the exquisite liquor splashed her lips.

"What are you doing, Lady Adamson?" he asked, his voice garbled.

She sighed. She really should have tried the bubbly drink before he'd arrived and gone all serious, disapproving-lord on her. "If you must know, I'd intended to sample—"

"You are not *sampling* anything, my lady." He set the flute down so hard liquid droplets sprayed the table.

Yes, it seemed the roguish earl had gone all stodgy. She released a pent-up sigh of regret. What a waste of perfectly forbidden champagne.

Footsteps sounded outside the door and her head snapped up as suddenly, the ramifications of being discovered here with the earl slammed into her. She felt the color drain from her cheeks and frantically searched around.

The earl cursed and taking her by the hand, tugged her to the back of the conservatory. His hasty, yet sure movements bore evidence of a man who'd made many a number of quick escapes. He opened the door and shoved her outside into the marquess's walled garden.

"You really needn't—"

"Hush," he whispered and propelled her further into the gardens. From behind the marquess's prize-winning gardens, the moon's glow shone through the clear crystal panes and briefly cast the earl's partner in a soft light. The tall, voluptuous lady walked about the conservatory.

"The Viscountess of Kendricks?" Shock underscored her question. "But she is recently widowed." Granted she'd come out of mourning, but that was neither here nor there. Oh, he had no shame.

Lord Stanhope clamped his hand over her mouth. He glowered her into silence and pulled her back, before the viscountess caught sight of them.

Oh, the highhandedness! She'd never been handled thusly in her entire life. She glared up at him.

At long last he drew his fingers back. She continued to study the lush creature, a recent widow with a hopelessly curvaceous figure.

Anne frowned. Mother said gentlemen didn't desire ladies with well-rounded figures but Anne quite disagreed. All the well-rounded ladies seemed to, for some unknown reason, earn the favor of all manner of gentlemen. The respectable ones. The less respectable ones. Even the old ones with monocles.

A sly smile played about the viscountess's lips as she paused beside the table. Even with the space between them, Anne detected the viscountess's lazy yet graceful movements as she picked up the still full glass and took a slow taste of the bubbling champagne.

Envy tugged at Anne. He really should have allowed her just a small sip. Surely there was no harm in a mere taste of the French liquor. And now this blousy creature with her . . . She wrinkled her brow. "Has she dampened her gown?"

The widow froze midsip and glanced around.

Lord Stanhope cursed softly, clapped his hand across Anne's mouth yet again, and whispered harshly against her ear. "Hush, you silly brat, or you'll see the both of us ruined."

Anne pointed her gaze to the moon above. As if a rogue, especially this particular rogue, could be ruined. She, on the other hand . . . She swallowed hard. She, on the other hand, danced with disaster.

With good reason, of course. But still, disaster nonetheless.

"Hullo, my lord," the woman called into the quiet. A smile played on her too-full lips. "Are you teasing me, Lord Stanhope? I'm eager to see you. Will you not come and see how eager I am?"

Anne glanced up the more than a foot distance between her and the earl to gauge the gentleman's, er . . . eagerness. He appeared wholly unmoved by the woman's none-too-subtle attempt at seduction. His narrow-eyed gaze remained fixed on Anne. Annoyance glinted within the hazel-green irises of his eyes.

"Lord Stanhope?" the woman called again.

Oh, really. She tapped a foot and wished the bothersome baggage would be on her way already. As charming as the Earl of Stanhope seemed to most ladies, she was quite confident that no gentleman could manage to lure her away from polite Society—for any reason.

Lord Stanhope reached down between them and through the ivory fabric of her satin skirts, wrapped his hard hand about the upper portion of her leg, effectively stilling her moments.

Anne's breath froze and she looked at him.

Be still, he mouthed.

Her throat convulsed. Odd, they were just fingers on just a hand, so very uninteresting, something possessed by everyone. And yet, her skin thrummed with awareness of his touch. She swallowed again. There was nothing *uninteresting* about his fingers upon her person.

"Stop tapping your foot," he whispered against her temple. His words had the same effect as a bucket of water being tossed over her foolish head.

"She's not going to hear my foot," she shot back. "It is more likely she'll hear your constant haranguing."

He closed his eyes and his lips moved as if he were uttering a silent prayer. Which was peculiar, because she'd not ever taken him as the religious sort.

"Lord Stanhope?" the woman called again, impatience coating her words.

Anne sighed. She'd had this all planned out. She'd speak to the earl. Enlist his help and be gone before his trysting partner had arrived. That had been the plan. Then again, a lifetime of scrapes that had gone awry should have prepared her for how this evening would likely turn out. "Oh, for goodness sake, will she not go already?" she muttered. "Whyever is she so insistent on seeing y—"

The earl cursed under his breath. "For the love of all that is holy." And then, he kissed her. Hard.

Anne stiffened and leaned back a moment, eyes opened, studying his impossibly long golden lashes. She trembled under the heated intensity of his kiss, a kiss that drove back all logic. He slanted his lips over hers again and again and she moaned, but he only swallowed the desperate sound. He slipped his tongue between her lips and boldly explored the contours of her mouth.

The tension she carried inside slid down her body and seeped from the soles of her passion-weakened feet as she went limp. He caught her to him and cupped her buttocks in his hands, anchoring her body to his.

Then he stopped.

She blinked up, dazed, waiting for the world to right itself. *Goodness . . .*

She tugged her hand free and fanned herself.

Goodness . . .

So *this* is what young ladies threw away their reputations for. It would appear it had nothing at all to do with the wicked smiles. Or even the forbidden champagne. She'd venture the champagne was merely a little extra sin for a lady's troubles.

Anne stole a glance up at Lord Stanhope and her eyebrows knitted into a single line. The bounder had his gaze trained on the conservatory windows, looking . . . looking . . . wholly unaffected. Impossibly composed. And horribly disinterested. He released her so quickly, she stumbled backward, catching herself before she made a cake of herself and fell at his feet.

She frowned as he turned abruptly and walked away. "That really wasn't well done of you, my lord."

He swung back around and took a step toward her. "Do you know what was not well done, my lady?"

"Uh, well . . ." She retreated and then remembered herself, angling her chin up. After all, there could very well be any other number of offenses she might hold him responsible for. She ticked off on her fingers. "There was the hand over my mouth." She shook her head. "Not at all well done of you. Then there was the kiss." Her cheeks burned with embarrassment. "Certainly not well done of you." Definitely pleasurable, however. "Or you setting me aside so—"

By the saints, he mouthed, appearing more and more religious. "I referred to *your* actions, my lady. It wasn't well done of you to drive away my company for the evening, Lady Adamson."

Humph. "Oh." She wrinkled her nose. That wasn't at all gallant.

His golden lashes swooped downward as he peered at her through a narrow-eyed gaze. "Now, say whatever it is you've come to say so I might be rid of you." He folded his arms across his chest.

Why, with his clear desire to be free of her, she may as well have been the gorgon Medusa with her head of serpents. She bristled, all foolish desire replaced by annoyance. How dare he? How dare he kiss her and remain wholly unaffected by that soul-searing moment? She shook her head once. No, that was not quite right.

"Lady Anne," he said again, this time with even more annoyance.

How dare he kiss her, *period*. No further outrage needed. How dare he kiss her? Rather, that is what she'd meant. "I need help."

He scoffed. "Yes. So you've said. Four times now."

"Oh." Had she? She really didn't remember . . .

He gave her a pointed look and she jumped. "As I was saying, before I was interrupted." She gave him a pointed frown. "I require a bit of help."

"Five times," he muttered under his breath. He really was quite infuriating.

"I am—"

He drummed his fingertips upon his coat sleeves. "If you say you're in need of help, I'm leaving without a backward glance, Lady Anne," he said drolly. He rocked on his heels and she suspected his words were no mere idle threat.

Anne smoothed her palms over her skirt and drew in a steadying breath. With the time and care she'd put into her plan, she had imagined this conversation would go a good deal more smoothly than this botched attempt on her part.

The earl cursed and spun on his heel.

"Wait!"

He continued walking toward the glass door back into the marquess's conservatory.

Her foot snagged a particularly nasty root in the ground and she cursed. She pitched forward. Lord Stanhope swung back around and closed the distance between them in three long strides, catching her before she hit the ground. The breath left her on a swift exhale. "Oh." The touch of his hand burned through the modest fabric of her satin gown. "Thank you," she said breathlessly.

He grunted and set her on her feet. Humph. Who knew the Earl of Stanhope did something as barbaric as grunt? He resumed his hasty exit, wholly unaffected. *Well!*

"Stop," she cried softly into the quiet. Her voice echoed off the brick walls.

His broad shoulders tightened under the folds of his black evening coat. He changed direction yet again and advanced on her. Fire snapped in his eyes.

Anne stumbled backward. A friend of Katherine, Anne knew little of the Earl of Stanhope beyond the roguish reputation he'd earned amongst the *ton*. She couldn't be altogether certain he'd not hurt her. She swallowed hard and continued to retreat. And her slipper caught that blasted root again.

This time she landed with a solid thump on her buttocks. "Ouch." She touched a hand to her bruised derriere and then remembered herself.

He froze above her with a glower on the chiseled planes of his face. "Are you trying to compromise your reputation, my lady?"

"No." *Not per se.*

He stretched out a hand. "Because I'll not be caught in a compromising position and forced into a wedded state with one such as you."

She ignored his offering and shoved herself to her feet. "With one such as me?"

"An impertinent, empty-headed young lady without a serious thought in—"

She jabbed a finger into his chest. He winced and she delighted in that slight twinge of discomfort from him. *The cad.* "I've had quite enough of your insults. I don't like you any more than you like me, my lord." She'd long tired of Society, her family, everyone's rather low opinion of her. But she required his assistance and when one required help, it behooved them to set aside their pride.

"You have two minutes, my lady," he bit out.

Her mind raced. How did a lady ask such a question as the one she'd put to him. There was no polite way to make a request as the one she intended to make—

"Your first minute is up, my lady," he said, his voice heavy with annoyance.

Anne took a steadying breath and opted for direct honesty. "I'd like you to teach me how to seduce a man."

Chapter 2

*H*enry Falston, the 6th Earl of Stanhope, known to polite
Society *and* impolite society as Harry, had never considered his hearing faulty, and expected at thirty years of age
he had a good many years before his ears began to fail him.
He stared at Lady Anne Adamson, the tart-mouthed miss
he'd gone to great lengths to avoid this past year, certain he'd
heard her incorrectly.

"Not just any man," she went on, her cheeks turning pink.
Did the chit wear a perpetual blush?

"I'd like you to teach me how to seduce a *specific* gentleman."

He scrubbed a hand over his face. Yes, it seemed he had
heard the young lady right, after all. Harry studied her objectively. With Anne's golden ringlets, fair skin, and blue eyes,
she easily fit with Society's standard of a perfect, English
beauty. She did not however, fit with the beauties he'd come
to appreciate through the years, including her sister, the dark-
haired, brown-eyed Lady Katherine, Duchess of Bainbridge,
whom he'd tried to seduce last year. Tried and failed.

The gossip sheets reported Lady Anne to be both proper
and pretty and not much more than that. In other words, a
tedious bore he went to great pains to avoid.

Not that he wasn't above a good flirtation, but not with
this pert baggage.

"Will you not say something?" She stomped her foot more
like a child in the nursery than a young woman he'd just
kissed senseless.

A kiss that, if he were being truthful, had been somewhat captivating, and if he were to be entirely truthful with himself, a kiss he'd like to further explore. He violently shoved back such dangerous thoughts. "No."

She frowned, seeming displeased with his curt reply.

He went on before she could continue pestering him. "One, as a friend of your sister, I'd never dare assist you in this mad scheme to trap some poor—"

"Not trap," she said, shaking her head.

"—gentleman," he continued as though she hadn't spoken. "Two," he proceeded to tick off on his fingers. "You like me even less than I like you."

"Ah, yes," she wagged a finger under his nose. "But I'm reasonable enough to put aside my personal differences on matters of importance."

"Three," he caught her wrist. His large fingers encircled the delicate flesh. "Though you are passably pretty, I couldn't even begin to drum up interest enough to help you."

Hurt flashed in her eyes. "Pleasantly." She wrenched her hand free.

He furrowed his brow. What was she on about?

"The papers have called me pleasantly pretty." Something in her tone hinted at a young woman who desired more than being gossiped about and ascribed labels by a judgmental *ton*.

He dragged a hand through his hair. "Bloody hell," he cursed. The little termagant brought out the worst in him . . . and ladies didn't ever bring out the worst in him. Not the young debutantes, not the eager widows, not even the frowning dowagers. Lady Anne, with her usual, reserved-for-him frown and often-harsh words, on the other hand, did. "Forgive me," he said. "That was uncalled for."

She waved a hand. "You needn't apologize for being truthful, my lord," she said with far more somber maturity than he'd imagined her capable of. She held up her palms. "But I need help and I decided to enlist your aid first."

First.

Which, of course, implied there'd been a second gentleman whose aid she intended to seek out if, nay, *when*, he refused to take part in her imprudent plan.

If he'd been any other rogue, Harry suspected she'd be ruined by now with her skirts up, bodice lowered, as he instructed her on all the ways to seduce *whomever* it was she wanted to seduce.

Anne spoke softly, pulling him back to the moment. "You have a notorious reputation and I . . ." Her gaze skittered to a point beyond his shoulder.

Harry told himself not to ask. He really should send her on her way, back to the ballroom and forget she'd ever put the scandalous proposition to him. "And you what?" he asked tersely.

She jumped. The color in her cheeks deepened. "And I thought as Katherine's friend I could trust you with my request and also trust that you wouldn't, er . . ." She fanned her cheeks. "*You know.*"

No, he really didn't know. He recognized the perils in acknowledging as much. He eyed her warily. "What wouldn't I do, Lady Anne?" And then promptly wished he'd never fed his curiosity.

"Why, you wouldn't take liberties with any inappropriate embraces." Her pink cheeks burned red.

"As opposed to the more appropriate embraces?" Droll humor underscored his question.

Anne nodded once. "Er, yes, I do suppose I see your point," she conceded.

He'd intended to send her away with a curt rejection, back to her protective, but not protective enough, mama's side. Except, she'd mentioned Katherine and as a friend, he could not in good conscience let her go without talking some sense into her senseless head. He'd wager his entire landholdings that if he sent her back to the evening's festivities with a simple no, she'd surely find the second someone on her list to help her with this *plan*. He balled his hands into fists. "Who do you intend to seduce?"

Hope flared in fathomless depths of her eyes. "I can trust you?"

"Really, my lady?" He scoffed. "You'd ask me to teach you how to seduce a man but you'll withhold his identity?"

"I suppose you're right." She caught her lower lip between her teeth and nibbled the plump flesh. "To be skeptical, that is."

His gaze went to her mouth. Heat surged through him at the innocently erotic movement. And then he remembered the sweet taste of her, orgeat and honey. His fingers twitched with a sudden urge to pull her back into his arms and avail himself to . . . "Christ." The angry entreaty burst from him.

She jumped, clearly misinterpreting the reason for his annoyance. "Forgive me. The Duke of Crawford. I'd like you to teach me the skill of seduction so I might . . . er . . . earn the duke's affections."

She'd clearly mistaken the reason for his frustration. He imagined the fun Anne would have at his expense if she gleaned his sudden desire to kiss her senseless until she was moaning in his mouth once more.

Then her words penetrated the mad haze around him. "The Duke of Crawford?" he repeated.

She nodded.

Crawford. The thirty-year-old duke who'd inherited his title nearly ten years back was rumored to be in the market for a wife. Obscenely wealthy, coolly proper, company desired by all, Lady Anne could not have set her marital sights on a more sought-after bachelor.

Harry's lip curled back in a sneer. Surely a title-grasping miss should no longer take him aback. Not after Margaret Dunn's betrayal all those years ago. As long as there was an unwed duke about, there would be a scheming miss at hand. Lady Anne Adamson could not be more different in appearance than the woman who'd broken his heart many years back, but she was remarkably similar in her goals and desires.

Lady Anne waved her hand in front of his face. "Lord Stanhope?"

He squared his jaw. "So, you'll trap poor, unsuspecting Crawford?"

She patted the back of her head. "I've already said I do not intend to trap His Grace. I intend for you to teach me how to teach him to desire me." Another blush. "For a wife," she said hurriedly.

He folded his arms. "Why Crawford?"

"Well, if you must know—"

"I must." Though he already strongly suspected not much more than the man's old, revered title most accounted for Anne's interest in the duke.

She gave a slight shrug. "He's pleasantly handsome."

He snorted.

Anne bristled. "And he's unfailingly polite." She gave him a pointed look.

"I gather that's because you've never insulted the gentleman," he muttered. Unlike Harry, who'd become something of an archery target for her well-placed barbs since their first meeting. Though, in fairness, at this particular moment he quite deserved the lady's displeasure.

"I suppose you are correct," she surprised him by concurring. Her next words ended all such shock. "But then, the duke has never done something as reprehensible as trying to seduce my sister."

A dull flush climbed up his neck. And when put in those blunt terms, he did feel properly chastised.

She continued either uncaring or unaware of his discomfiture. "He's wealthy and in possession of one of the oldest titles." Ah, there it was. "And he doesn't even know I exist," she finished on a dramatic sigh.

Harry tugged at one of her golden ringlets. "It is your ringlets—"

"Oh, do hush." She slapped his fingers again. "It is not my ringlets."

"Then, what is it?" he asked in a lazy whisper as he laid claim to the silken strands once more.

Anne froze, her mouth screwed up in concentration. He used the momentary quiet to study her. Though not the lithe, exotically dark beauties he generally preferred, she really was quite lovely; in an unsophisticated, English-lady type of way. "I don't know what it is," she said at last. Her shoulders rose and fell. "I've tried to capture his attention."

He swallowed a chuckle, imagining just what *that* had entailed.

Her face set in a familiar scowl. "Don't laugh at me."

"You need my help," he reminded her and released the satiny strand.

She squared her shoulders. "I'll still not humble myself and be mocked by you because I've *sought* your help."

Good for the young lady. With her steely strength, Anne rose in his estimation. Oh, he'd never admit as much to the spitfire. He drummed his fingers upon his thigh. There was no helping it, he really must know. "How have you gone about trying to capture Crawford's notice?"

She gestured to her skirts. "My gowns."

He looked at her wildly gesticulating hands. "What about your gowns?"

"I've worn my finest gown."

It would seem Harry was more a gentleman than even he believed because he managed to resist pointing out that her ivory ruffled skirts wouldn't manage to stir interest from even the most staid, respectable lord in the market for a wife. Instead, Harry mentally stripped the proper gown from her lean, lithe frame and replaced it with the gold, water-dampened skirts the Viscountess Kendricks had worn. He must have had too many spirits to even be considering such an outlandish thought involving the tart-mouthed Anne Adamson. "Hmm," he said noncommittally.

"And I've dabbed lavender oil behind my ears." She recoiled. "What are you doing?"

He froze, his nose a breath away from her ear. "I'm smelling your lavender-scented skin, my lady."

Color stained her neck. Harry inhaled the sweet, fragrant hint of lavender that clung to her and started. He'd never found the innocent scent to be the least enticing and yet . . . "Well?" Anne prodded.

"Yes, certainly the scent of lavender, there . . . ow . . ."
She jammed the heel of her slipper into his toes. He'd always
taken her for a bloodthirsty creature. With that disagree-
able attitude the young lady stood little hope of snaring the
sought-after Duke of Crawford.

"Oh, hush. I'm speaking of the duke. *Not* about my skin."
My skin.

Something sultry and spellbinding held him captive as he
considered the delicate, satiny softness of Lady Anne's skin.
When she'd been in his arms, he'd appreciated the silken feel
of her, smoother than the finest French fabrics. Christ, he
must be going mad to notice such things as—

Anne jammed her heel into his foot yet again.

He grunted in surprise. "What the hell was that for?"

"Er, you seemed distracted. That was merely to obtain your
attention. Will you help me attain the duke's affections?"

He snorted. "Title grasping and fortune-hunting, my dear?"
Just like Margaret. His humor fled as with Anne's scheming,
she dragged him back into a past he'd buried long ago, and
forgotten—until now. Until Anne and her talk of wealthy,
powerful dukes. "I must say not wholly unexpected for one
such as you."

She folded her arms across her chest once more, and drew
his gaze to her plump breasts. He angled his head. How had
he failed to note her rather enticing décolletage? "Why must
you use that 'one-such-as-you' phrase? It's rather insulting."

"Are you trying to seduce a gentleman for his title?" He
shot back.

Her color deepened to the red of a sun-ripened straw-
berry. "It's . . . I . . . you wouldn't understand."

Harry thought back to a different woman. A young lady
he'd been reckless enough to waste his heart upon. He thrust

thoughts of her from his mind. He lowered his head so his lips nearly brushed Anne's. "No, you are correct. I wouldn't," he whispered. "Nothing can ever merit seducing a gentleman for his wealth and title."

She angled her head back and withered him with a glare. "No, but seducing a woman for her . . . female attributes is entirely honorable, my lord?"

Touché. And, hell, when she put it that way . . .

She tapped his cheek. "Will you help me or not?"

Most any other young lady would be fluttering her lids and using a honeyed tone to convince him to do her bidding. Anne, however, was immune to his usual charm. "I cannot, my lady." In spite of Society's low opinion of him, he still had some sense of honor. Honor enough to not teach a marriage-minded, innocent miss the art of seduction.

She sprung forward on the balls of her feet as if prepared to launch her whole self into the protest on her lips but then sank back on her heels. "Very well." She gave a flounce of her curls and started for the door.

He crossed his arms and drummed his fingertips on his forearm. He knew from those mere two words and the steely resolve in her tone that the young lady had already moved on to the alternative in her plan to ensnare the duke.

Do not ask. Do not ask. Do not ask.

Her fingers touched the handle of the conservatory door.

"Who do you intend to seek out next, my lady?" Because a lady as resolute to snare the duke, a lady who'd crafted this ill-advised plot had surely already considered the course of action after his inevitable refusal.

Anne spun back to face him. "The Marquess of Rutland."

Bloody hell.

She tipped her head. "What was that?"

Of all the men in the whole damned kingdom, she'd picked Rutland. He fisted his hands at his side. "What was what?" His question emerged as a steely whisper.

She glanced about, seeming wholly unaffected by the inner turmoil raging through him. "Er, nothing, I'd believed I'd heard—"

"Do not try and change the subject, madam," he bit out.

She waved her long, graceful fingers breezily about. "No matter, then."

He stared transfixed at her elegant fingers and unbidden thoughts entered of the innocent Lady Anne Adamson using those hands upon that bastard Rutland, using them for things no proper lady should ever do. The irony in her selection for tutor was not lost on him. Nearly ten years ago, he'd battled Rutland for the avaricious Miss Margaret Dunn's hand. His lips twisted in a humorless smile. In the end, they'd dueled and she'd chosen neither of them. Since then, Rutland, with his shocking proclivities for bondage and riding crops behind chamber doors, had earned a reputation far blacker than Harry's.

And Rutland wouldn't hesitate to *assist* Lady Anne and introduce her to the art of seduction.

"Good evening, my lord," Anne's parting greeting yanked him back from the hell of his past. The click of the door opening sounded like a shot in the night.

He imagined her slim body stretched out, bound to that bastard's four-poster bed. A cold chill snaked through him. "Stop," he said quietly. He must be going mad. There was no other explaining the fact that he now seriously contemplated her proposal.

She spun around yet again and all but sprinted across the expertly manicured grounds. "Have you reconsidered, my lord?" Hope danced in her eyes.

"Quiet. I'm thinking." He stared out at the Lord Essex's meticulous grounds. He fixed his gaze on the massive rendering at the farthest corner—a life-size stone Hercules with his spear thrust toward two lions reared in battle. Harry would be wise to seek out Lady Katherine and let her know just what request her sister had put to him. And yet . . . He glanced at Anne.

She studied him with a somber expression.

Perhaps it was boredom on his part. He looked back at the vicious stone lions. Or perhaps he and Rutland were not unlike those primitive beasts. He'd be damned if he allowed Rutland the upper hand in this matter. Not when it affected Katherine's sister.

Something compelled him to help her. To protect her from not just Lord Rutland but also any of the other reprehensible rogues who would gladly take advantage of her naïveté. Yes, if he were any kind of friend to Katherine, he'd throw Anne his support.

Her blue eyes sparkled. "You'll do it," she breathed, having clearly followed the silent direction his thoughts had traveled. She excitedly clapped her hands. "You must—"

He held a hand up and effectively silenced her. "Let us be clear, Lady Anne, I'm doing this merely to protect you from yourself."

Her mouth formed a small moue of displeasure.

He took a step toward her. "I've no intentions of touching you." Did she appear crestfallen? "I'll help until he makes you that offer." And Harry had little doubt under his tutelage, the haughty duke would be offering for the infuriating Lady Anne well before the end of the Season. "I'll instruct you on how to entice a gentleman but beyond that, do not expect anything else of me."

She spoke on a rush. "Of course not, my lord." A golden ringlet fell over her eye.

Harry brushed the silken tendril back. "Harry," he corrected. For many years, he'd detested the nickname. It held reminders of the empty promises on Margaret's lips as she'd breathed his name. He lowered his lips close to Anne's ear. "If I'm to teach you the art of seduction, then I imagine you should use my Christian name." Now he embraced the sobriquet for it reminded him of the perils in loving another.

With their closeness, he detected the audible inhalation of breath, the rapid rise and fall of her chest. She trailed her tongue over her lips. So the minx *wasn't* immune to him. Harry reveled in that slight attestation of her feminine interest. Harry dropped his gaze lower as he once again appreciated the creamy expanse of her full breasts. He nearly choked. What in hell was he doing ogling Lady Anne's charms? Hadn't he just stated in no uncertain terms he'd not, in any way, touch her?

She squared her shoulders as if bracing for battle and said, "Very well, then." She paused. "Harry." All antipathy for that name, Harry momentarily lifted. There was a husky, almost sultry quality to Anne's voice. It filled him with a sudden urge to hear it upon her plump, red lips once more.

She stuck a hand out. "Then you must call me Anne."

He stared blankly down at her outstretched fingers. "What in hell is that?"

"What is what?" She looked around and then followed his gaze to her hand. "This?" She waggled her fingers. "This is a hand, my lord." Confusion tinged her reply.

"Harry," he corrected and sent a prayer skyward in search of patience. "And what are you doing with your hand, Anne?"

"I'm offering you my hand, Harry." She smiled.

He counted to five. "For what purpose?"

"Well," she screwed her mouth up as if pondering his question. "It seemed like a kind of an introduction between us and then I thought we might shake hands to seal our agreement."

The young lady intended to enlist his tutelage in the art of seduction and she thought to seal that with a bloody handshake? His lips twitched.

She lowered her hand back to her side. A frown chased away her cheerful smile. "Have I said something to amuse you, my lord?"

Why did he suddenly mourn the momentary camaraderie between them? The curl fell back over her brow. She blew it back. Harry caught the sun-kissed lock between his thumb and forefinger. "You have."

She gave a flounce of her curls and spun on her heels. "Oh, do forget I ever mentioned anything. I don't need your help. I'll speak to Lord Rutland. I certainly don't need—"

The hell she would.

She gasped when he settled his hands upon her shoulders and slowed her steps. He placed his lips a breath away from the long, graceful stretch of her neck. "Lies," he breathed. "You do need me, sweet, or you wouldn't have set aside your dislike, risked your reputation, and put such an offer to me."

It didn't escape his notice that she didn't contradict his claim. It shouldn't matter whether or not she disliked him. After all, the imp had hardly endeared herself to him this past year. Except, he loathed the idea of her seeking out Lord Rutland or any other nameless bounder. But especially Rutland.

Anne gasped and arched her neck as though tickled. "S-stop," she whispered. She didn't make to pull away and he was encouraged.

He ran his hands from her shoulders, down her forearms and wrapped his fingers loosely about her wrists. "You mistook the reason for my amusement, sweet Anne," he breathed.

"D-did I-I?" she angled her head and looked back up at him.

"I laughed at the idea of shaking on an agreement. I imagine our agreement would best be sealed with a kiss." Only what had begun as a game in teasing now became something all too real. He dropped his gaze to her lush lips and groaned.

With the pink tip of her tongue, she traced the seam of her lips. She raised her gaze to his mouth and for a moment he believed the bold vixen intended to lean on tiptoe and brush her lips against his. "B-but I believed you'd said you had n-no intention of touching me." Then, a slow, knowing smile wreathed her cheeks. "Oh." She swatted at his hands. "You're teasing me."

No, no he hadn't been. He really should let her go. They flirted with disaster. Someone would surely notice the young lady's absence and if he were discovered with her . . . He shuddered at the prospect of being saddled with marriage to the insolent baggage.

Anne danced out of his arms on a small laugh. "It is settled then." She placed her fingers in his and gave a firm shake.

It certainly wasn't. "Not quite, sweet."

"Don't call me sweet." She frowned with all the stern disapproval of a woman vastly older than her twenty years.

He propped his hip on the wrought-iron bench behind him. In his experience, ladies loved all manner of endearments. Sweet. Dear. Lovely. The only one he took care to avoid at all costs was love.

Anne took a step back toward him. She squinted as if trying to study his features in the moonlight. "What is it you want?" she said with a world-wise wariness. Perhaps the first sensible thought from the lady all night.

He shot his hand out and pulled her lazily toward him.

A squeak escaped her lips as she tumbled awkwardly into his arms. He righted her. "I'm to set the rules for your lessons. When I feel you've been successfully schooled in the art of seduction, I'll end them. And at no point are you to fall in love with me."

Laughter exploded from Anne's lips. She laughed so hard, tears seeped from her closed eyes. She emitted little snorting sounds from her nose.

He didn't know if he should be insulted or endeared by the unladylike noises escaping Anne's too-kissable lips. He folded his arms at his chest and glowered.

"Oh, that is rich," she said on a gasp, when her laughter had subsided. She dashed a hand across her tear-stained cheeks. "You may rest assured, I've no intention of falling in love with you, my . . . Harry," she said with mock solemnity. She patted his hand like he was a small child. "What else do you require?"

Harry tightened his jaw, irked by the lady's effortless promise. "Nothing." Something of a rogue for a good many years now, he didn't like to believe his charm was failing him. Even if it was only with the bothersome Lady Anne Adamson.

She gave a pleased nod. "Very well. You may begin courting me tomorrow, then." Anne spun on her heel and stared back toward the front of the gardens.

He stared unblinking at her swift-retreating back. He shoved himself off the bench. What in hell? He quickly and efficiently closed the distance between them then placed himself between her and the door, effectively blocking her exit.

"What?" Impatience threaded her one-word question.

"What did you say?"

"I asked, what."

He scrubbed his hands over his face. "No. Before that." He could practically see the wheels of her mind spinning.

"Oh, I merely said you may begin courting me tomorrow," she said sunnily.

"There was no mention of courting you." The last thing he required was Society believing he had honorable intentions for a proper, English lady—particularly *this* genteel, English lady. "Bloody hell," he muttered to himself.

"You know you really shouldn't curse, Harry. It's not at all proper."

"Nor is it proper to request a gentleman to school you in the art of seduction."

She nodded. "Er, yes, I suppose you're right." She let out a beleaguered sigh. "But really, how else do you expect to begin instructing me? And," she pressed, "I imagine the duke will become outrageously jealous when he sees you're courting me."

"You said he's not even paid you any notice," he said bluntly.

"That is rude of you to mention, but yes," she said hurriedly before he could speak. "He hasn't noticed me, but attention from you might make me . . . make me . . ."

He quirked an eyebrow.

"More desirable." Another one of those becoming blushes stained her cheeks. "Do you see?"

The moonlight bathed the high planes of her cheekbones in a pale glow, giving her the look of a veritable Athena. He sucked in a breath. Bloody hell. He'd had too much of his host's champagne. There was nothing else to account for this madness. But he did see something that until this very moment had escaped him. She really was quite lovely.

Anne touched a hand to her hair. "What is it?"

"I'll pay you a visit tomorrow." He thrust his finger toward the door. "Now, go."

With a jaunty wave, she all but skipped toward the front of the gardens. "You'll not regret this, my . . . Harry," she whispered loudly.

He shook his head. *I already do.*

Chapter 3

*A*nne bit her lip and stared down at the array of ribbons strewn about the table. The thin and thick strips of cloth covered her copy of *Lady Wilshow's Midnight Danger*, a Gothic novel she'd borrowed from her sister Aldora.

She leaned forward and picked up a black-striped pink ribbon. She laid it atop a small pile of other similar-colored ribbons. One. Two. Three. Four. Five pink satin ribbons in total. Anne reached for a dear orange satin ribbon. She held up the sole scrap she'd retained from her girlhood, during a time when every last shred of her ribbons, gowns, and everything in between had been carted off by merciless creditors.

She turned the ribbon over in her hands. The light reflected off the shiny strip, giving the prized scrap an almost iridescent effect. If she were permitted to wear a gown other than the pale hues insisted upon by Mother, she'd have the finest French modiste design her a gown to match this very shade.

The butler entered. "My lady, you have a caller."

Startled by the unexpected intrusion, the ribbon slipped from her fingers and fluttered in a whispery dance to the floor.

The older servant who'd been with them since she was just a girl cleared his throat. "The Earl of Stanhope," he introduced, admitting Harry.

She leapt to her feet as he stepped into the room like Michelangelo's *David* come to life. Impossibly tall and sinfully handsome with his thick, unfashionably long golden hair, he cut quite the figure. Anne dipped a curtsy.

He grinned. Then he glanced at her pile of ribbons.

Heat blazed in her cheeks. The butler ducked from the room. "Er . . . Mary," she called softly. "Would you see to refreshments?"

Her maid hurried from the room.

Harry beat his hand against his large, muscular thigh. He sketched a deep bow. "My lady," he drawled.

Anne motioned for him to sit. She sank into the gold-brocade sofa. "My lord," she murmured as he sat in the giltwood open armchair beside her. He stretched his long legs out in front of him and hooked them at the ankles. Anne angled her head. Hmm. She'd never before noticed anything about the Earl of Stanhope other than the fact that he infuriated her with his roguish grin. After all, rogues were unreliable, and unreliable gentlemen did unreliable things. She'd learned as much after her father's betrayal. Since then, she'd developed a new appreciation for staid, respectable gentlemen. And wealthy gentlemen; that mattered, too.

Harry drummed his fingers on the arms of his chair. "Perhaps Crawford's disinterest stems from a lack of conversation?" His amused baritone jerked her from her melancholy.

She kicked his ankle with the tip of her slipper. "Oh, do hush."

He continued to study her through thick, hooded, golden lashes.

Anne sat, perched at the edge of her seat. She folded her hands in her lap and glanced down at the forgotten orange ribbon in her fingers. Her fingers curled reflexively about the satin strip that represented her past, and now her present-day goals.

Harry leaned over and plucked the precious fabric from her grip. "You've quite the collection of ribbons, Anne." He trailed his forefinger down the stretch of material and she studied that oddly sensual movement.

Her cheeks warmed. She said nothing, praying he'd move the topic to far safer grounds.

Alas, God appeared otherwise busy. "It seems like a rather exorbitant amount," he said.

Anne bristled at the mocking edge to his words. She didn't expect he'd understand. She reached for her fabric. He held it just out of her reach. She gritted her teeth. "Give me back my ribbon." She made another unsuccessful grab for it. With an indignant huff, she settled back in her seat.

Harry shoved himself up and claimed the seat beside her.

"What are you . . . ?" She swallowed hard.

He touched his fingers to her hair and claimed a single lock. With an expert precision a lady's maid would have admired, he wove the ribbon through that lock, knotting it, and draping the tress over her shoulder. "There," he said softly. "This is how you use a ribbon to attract a gentleman's notice." Something dark and indefinable glinted in his eyes.

She followed his gaze to the point where the fabric nestled between her breasts. "Oh." She'd scandalize the matrons at Almack's and every other polite member of Society if she arrived at any event with her ribbon displayed so. Anne frowned. "I'd not have a roguish gentleman." She would not settle for a gentleman who'd be so easily, so *improperly*, swayed.

He ran his thumb over her lower lip. "Ah, yes, Crawford. The ever proper, unfailingly polite duke."

Harry really needn't make the Duke of Crawford's properness sound so very awful. "The duke would not be lured by such shamelessness on a lady's part."

"Shamelessness?"

Anne gulped at the silken edge to his hushed tone but refused to be cowed. "Yes. *Shamelessness*. As in, without shame."

He continued to toy with her lower lip. "If you knew how to bring the gentleman up to scratch then why did you enlist my support?"

She tried to focus on his question, she really did. But his teasing caress made it quite difficult to so much as remember her name, let alone process his question. His smirk indicated he knew as much.

Blast him. "A gentleman has different expectations of his prospective wife's behavior," she managed, proud of the steady deliverance of those words.

He continued stroking her lip in that way that sent little shivers from the point of his touch. "You're wrong, sweetheart. A gentleman wants his wife kissable and seductive and all things inappropriate."

Her body burned with the memory of his embrace, and she decided she would like her *husband* to be kissable. "D-does he?" And proper, as well. Certainly both would be quite splendid.

Gold flecks danced in the hazel depths of his eyes. "Oh, yes."

She longed for a loyal, honorable gentleman who desired her and only her, but also a man who respected her mind. "I do not want a rogue." Were those words spoken for Harry? Or herself?

He moved his gaze over her face. "Surely you see the imprudence of your plan," he said softly.

The breath left her as it occurred to her . . . "Why, this was all an attempt to sway me in my goal." He didn't speak, confirming her suspicions. She rose in a flurry of skirts to stand over him. "I told you last evening I'd find another willing to help me."

He leaned his head back. "Rutland?" he drawled.

She nodded once. "Yes, Rutland."

Harry scoffed. "If you are outraged by my actions with your ribbon then you'd have the ladylike shocked out of you by Rutland's tutelage."

Anne bit the inside of her cheek. Something hard and dark in his eyes gave her pause. He might attempt to deter her, but in this, he spoke the truth. She held her palms up. "Will you help me or not, Harry?"

He opened his mouth.

"I need to know why a gentleman wants to marry a young lady."

Ah, this was very different indeed. With her ladylike indignation and talk of marriage, she'd deviated rather a lot from lessons on seduction.

In fact, had she mentioned the words *wedded*, *marriage*, *bride*, or any variation in between in Lord Essex's conservatory, Harry would've had a good chuckle and advised her to avoid him, Rutland, and all the other useless rogues in Society. After all, if he'd known the precise answer to her question, he'd have managed to win Margaret's hand all those years ago.

"A gentleman desires a woman's body and not much beyond that," he said with a bluntness that snapped her mouth closed.

That hadn't always been the case. Once again, he shoved aside thoughts of Miss Margaret Dunn and buried her where thoughts of faithless creatures bent on nothing but title and wealth deserved to be buried. Unbidden, his gaze went to Anne. His lips pulled back in a sneer. They were all alike.

Color filled her cheeks. "What of love?"

A half-laugh, half-groan lodged in his throat. God help her.

"Why are you looking at me in that manner?" she spoke with candidness not common among ladies of the *ton*.

"In what manner?" he asked, his tone harsher than intended.

"Like you detest me."

His loathing was not reserved solely for her but rather all women who'd trap a man for his wealth and title alone. Only Katherine possessed an integrity not commonly found in women. He stood and his rapid movement forced her to retreat. "Do you know why, sweet?" he asked quietly.

"Don't call me sweet," she ordered automatically. In her haste to be away from him, she bumped into the Hepplewhite pier glass table. She winced, but continued moving backward. "And why?"

He forced her across the room until her back collided with the white-plastered walls. Harry braced his elbows alongside her head and framed her within the confines of his arms, ignoring the heat of her lithe figure. "Because you are no different than every other self-centered, title-grasping lady. You speak of love." He shook his head. "Yet you'd ask a notorious scoundrel to school you in the art of seduction. You'd put your material pleasures above all else?" He chuckled. "And for what?" He lowered his brow to hers. "More ribbons."

She jerked as though he'd struck her.

For one slight, infinitesimal moment guilt slammed into him. He felt like a bastard who'd bullied a small child into turning over their bag of peppermints.

She wet her lips in a way he'd come to learn, just in this past day, of Lady Anne's nervousness. "You don't know me,

Harry." Accusation blazed from the blues of her eyes. "You judge me as being, what did you say? Title-grasping and self-centered? But you don't *truly* know anything about me."

He scoffed. Really, what more was there to know? Only . . . his biting response died on his lips. Something indefinable, an uncharacteristic somber glint in her eyes gave him pause. Something that hinted there was more to Lady Anne than he or any of polite Society had ever suspected. Her chest rose and fell heavily with the force of her breath. He swallowed hard.

Anne hurried to collect her stack of ribbons, wholly unaware of the effect she had on him. "Here." She thrust them toward him.

He eyed them as though she'd handed over a pile of snakes. "What is this?"

"They are my ribbons. Take them. They are yours." She touched the piece he'd woven through her hair. "But this, this one is mine. This is the only one that matters."

If he were a complete bastard he'd point out that the last thing he wanted or needed of her was her fripperies.

"Material possessions do not drive me. If that is what you think of me, then you're greatly mistaken." She jerked her chin toward the ribbons. "Accept them as a kind of payment for your efforts."

He rubbed the ribbons between his fingers a moment. Soft. Silken. Like the feel of her lips beneath his. "Then what does drive you?" Wealth, power, a grand title—just like Margaret. "I'll not take your ribbons." Not when they seemed to mean a good deal to her, for reasons he did not know or understand and reasons he likely *would* never know or understand.

Anne soberly shook her head. "The only thing you need to know is how to help me."

It was highly foolish to keep any of the lady's things. He set her scraps of fabric down. The sooner he aided her efforts, the sooner he could end his connection to the infuriating Lady Anne Adamson with her too many ribbons. "You want my guidance, Anne? Then wear the damned ribbon when you see Crawford." The stern, proper duke would forget propriety and spirit her off to Gretna Greene for the plump mounds of her cream-white breasts alone.

Anne touched her fingertips to the satin ribbon, eliciting all manner of sinful thoughts he should never have about this hellion. With long, graceful fingers, she stroked the flesh of her décolletage. "This is silly." She looked pointedly at the ribbon. "It's not even properly placed."

He choked. "Trust me, it is properly placed," he said, his voice garbled. The young lady didn't realize that if she were to use her clever hands exactly as she was now in the presence of the duke, she'd find herself a proper duchess faster than she could say marital bed.

She eyed him skeptically. Little did the lady know she was mistrustful for all the wrong reasons. Anne reclaimed her seat and folded her hands on her lap. "What else is there, my lord?"

"Harry," he insisted, his tone harsh, but damn it, for some inexplicable reason he craved the sound of his name on her lips.

"Harry," she murmured.

He glanced over his shoulder. He should leave. He should forget his offer to assist her. Then, he'd been a rogue for longer than he remembered. He took the seat beside her. So close their legs brushed. He shot a sideways glance to determine if the lady was suitably shaken by his body's nearness.

Anne wet her lips.

He brushed his fingers along the nape of her neck and she angled her head, leaning into his touch. "I think the rule of ribbons is enough for the day," he murmured.

Anne blinked but did not pull away from his caress. "I've just the remainder of the Season to earn the duke's notice."

Annoyance filled him at her ability to speak so effortlessly about Crawford with Harry's hand upon her person. "I'll set the rules of our arrangement." She opened her mouth to protest. "You are free to reject the rules, but if you do, then you'll have to enlist Rutland's support."

She cocked her head, a baffled look in her eyes. "Rutland?" Her eyes went wide. "Er . . . yes, uh, Rutland."

He narrowed his gaze. Why, the lady had never intended to seek out Rutland, or probably any other gentleman for that matter. Anne could out wager the most experienced of card players at the seediest gaming hells. He made to rise.

She scrambled forward in her seat. "Don't." She sighed. "Very well, I'll agree to whatever terms you set." She swatted his hand. "Though I don't understand why you're not eager to impart all your lessons immediately and be done with me. You no more want to be in my company than I yours," she muttered more to herself.

Indeed, she was correct. Why didn't he merely provide his roguish suggestions and be on his merry way? He'd never wanted to know a thing about Lady Anne. Hell, he'd never even wanted to be in the same room with the spitfire. What manner of question to ask the lady? "Why a duke?" he asked suddenly.

She wrinkled her brow at the unexpected shift in conversation. "Every young lady desires a duke," she said at last. Still, she'd hesitated and he'd detected the slight heartbeat pause.

"That isn't much of an answer," he made to rise again.

Anne touched her fingers to his hand, stilling his movement.

He stiffened at the innocent, yet enticing pull of her fingers upon his person.

"I . . . I . . ." She slid her gaze away from his. "It is not merely for his title." Harry strained to hear those faintly spoken words.

He scoffed. "It is *always* about the title, my lady."

She gave a toss of her golden ringlets. "In this instance, it is not." She flattened her lips, indicating she had nothing further to say about her selection of Crawford for her future bridegroom. "Did you know," she said, her voice whispery soft, "my sister Aldora and her friends once met a gypsy. The woman provided them a pendant and promised whoever wore the necklace would win the heart of a duke."

Ah, so the lady didn't just want Crawford's hand and name. She wanted his heart. His lip curled back in an involuntary sneer. "I imagine the wearing of the pendant is an essential part to your plan." It was never about love. Ultimately wealth and power drove all.

She chewed her lower lip, ignoring the sarcastic twist to his words. "You're right." She leaned over and picked up a gold pendant on top of the forgotten book on the table before her. Anne studied the inexpensive-looking bauble. The chain danced and twisted in her fingers. "Katherine *did* find the heart of a duke by wearing it."

He expected a pang of envy at mention of Katherine. She'd been the first woman to rebuff his advances and instead repaid his heavy dose of charm with an impressive facer. Somehow, they'd still found friendship. All the while he'd believed she'd tire of the husband who'd not deserved her. In the end, the duke and duchess had found love and she and Harry had never become anything more. He took the locket from Anne's fingers then unhooked the simple clasp at the back. "I imagine if you're to land Crawford we should begin by keeping this on," he said.

"Are you making light of me?" She turned her head in a clear attempt to gauge his reaction.

He grinned. "Just a bit," he said.

"Tonight, when I see you at Lady Westmoreland's recital you may evaluate my use of the ribbon."

He blinked. When he saw her at . . . ? He laughed. "I've no intention of attending Lady Westmoreland's recital for her daughters." And his lack of interest in attending had little to do with the rather deplorable reputation her daughters had earned as wretched singers and everything to do with it being a respectable venue he'd not be seen at.

"But you're courting me," she blurted.

Since he'd agreed to aid Anne, he felt the first stirrings of unease. "It is a pretend courtship," he said dryly.

"I know that." She colored. "I'm merely pointing out that if you're to make the duke outrageously jealous then you'll surely have to attend and—"

"No."

"But—"

"No," he said, this time more firm in his tone. Anne fell silent. He would not feel guilty. He'd already been far more generous with Lady Anne Adamson than the little termagant deserved.

Footsteps shuffled in the hall. The young maid reappeared with a tray of tea and biscuits. Egad, tea and biscuits? Recitals? He tugged at his cravat. What was next? Attending an infernal event at Almack's? Harry stood quickly and started for the door.

Anne tilted her head at a funny angle. "Where are you going?" she called after him.

"We've concluded your lesson for the day," he said, not breaking his stride.

"When will I—?"

He sidestepped the maid and stormed from the room leaving Anne's question unfinished.

The last thing he could afford was to attend Lady Westmoreland's recital. As it was, his "courtship" of Anne would be construed as an attempt on his part to find the next Countess of Stanhope. No, to attend recitals and other like events would send a message to Society that the Earl of Stanhope was in the market for a wife.

Which he unequivocally was *not*.

At least, not anytime soon.

And most certainly not to a tart-mouthed young lady who approached rogues and demanded lessons on the art of seduction.

Chapter 4

Anne touched the edge of the sapphire-blue satin ribbon twined through a deliberately placed curl. She peeked down at the fabric. It seemed rather silly. She knew Harry had insisted it be worn so, but she still didn't quite understand how a strategically and *improperly* placed frippery would do anything but shock the matrons.

Seated in the last row of the recital hall, she peeked about for her mother. Mother remained in conversation with the hostess, Lady Westmoreland. Anne considered her mother a long while. The tight, white lines of a mouth that no longer smiled, the hard set to her eyes. Mother had given her heart to a wastrel and scoundrel and all she'd received from Father was heartbreak. His betrayal had turned her into a bitter, hardened creature. Anne squared her jaw. The powerful and dignified Duke of Crawford, purported to value respectability and propriety, would never forsake his family and fortune for the pleasure of his lovers. Confidence in that truth had guided Anne in her scheme.

Forcing her attention away from the saddened sight of her mother, Anne absently surveyed the assembling crowd; never more lonely than she was in this moment. She tapped her slippered feet on the marble foyer. Her twin had been wed nearly a year and here sat Anne, the one daughter Mother had so much hope for, unwed for a third Season, helplessly hoping for the hand of a proper duke.

A slight stir went through the crowd and she craned her neck in attempt to see who'd attracted the small party's notice. The Duke of Crawford entered. Impossibly tall and surprisingly broad, he was perfectly pleasing. He skimmed the hall and his serious blue-eyed stare moved through the crowd.

She fingered the ribbon at her shoulder and continued to study him. Young ladies dropped deep curtsies and peeked at him from under their lashes, while their mamas pushed them closer to catch his eye. Anne chewed her lip. She expected she should feel a thrill of excitement at seeing the man she'd selected for her future bridegroom. She twined the blue ribbon about her finger. So why did the sight of him not stir the faintest frisson of warmth within?

Just then, from across the hall, the duke froze midstride. His gaze caught hers a moment and then followed the sapphire ribbon lower to where it rested between her breasts. She widened her eyes. Well by Joan of Arc and all her army, Harry had been correct. The duke glanced up and looked at her.

Anne mustered a small smile and then gave thanks for the commotion at the hall's back entrance that snapped the duke's attention elsewhere. Which really made little sense. She should be quite honored and fortunate the Duke of Crawford had briefly fixed his attention upon her. But she wasn't. Instead, she'd foolishly been wondering why his stare hadn't heated her skin the way it did with a certain rogue.

Shocked whispers and loud murmurs rolled through the crowd. Again, she tilted her head in an attempt to catch sight of the latest source of interest. She damned her diminutive five feet, nearly nothing frame. Why couldn't she be one of those tall, graceful, willowy creatures? Then Harry would notice—

Her thoughts came to a jarring halt.

Harry? That is, then the Duke of Crawford would notice her. She'd meant . . . *Harry.*

She stood so quickly, her mother paused midconversation with Lady Westmoreland and looked at Anne. Whatever was Harry doing here? He'd been adamant that he'd not attend the Westmoreland recital.

A familiar figure stepped into her line of vision and interrupted her thoughts. She let out an excited squeal and greeted her sister Katherine and her brother-in-law, Jasper, the Duke of Bainbridge. Her sister and husband did not come to Town. Instead, they spent most of their time with their young son in the cottage the duke had purchased for his beloved wife. Anne ached to throw her arms around her sister. "Katherine," she said softly.

"Anne," Katherine said with a smile. She took Anne's hands in her own.

Since before they'd even drawn breath, they'd shared a special bond and Anne's life had been so very lonely after Katherine had wed. They exchanged a look no one else present could possibly understand. A look that asked questions and conveyed emotions all at once.

She squeezed Katherine's fingers and gave the duke her attention. "Hello, Jasper."

He inclined his head. "Hello, Anne," he greeted, still laconic as he'd been since she'd first made his acquaintance. Yet, gone was the harsh, hard-hearted gentleman who'd whisked her sister away immediately following their wedding. In his place was this kinder, gentler, though still gruff man.

She eyed them wistfully. Love tended to do that. Or so all the Gothic novels she squinted her way through seemed to indicate.

Unbidden, she sought out Harry in the crowd. He moved with a long-legged elegance that earned sighs—from young ladies and old ladies alike. He offered the occasional roguish grin to certain women. Anne frowned and wondered at those particular smiles. Had those ladies once dampened their satin skirts and met him for champagne in certain conservatories? A dark, ugly niggling clutched at her. Hard and cruel and ugly. And something she didn't wholly understand or care to evaluate in the moment. But she detested the memory of Lady Kendricks and all the other simpering beauties who'd surely held a spot in his bed.

All the dislike she'd carried for the roguish Lord Stanhope surged through her and she welcomed the familiar sentiment to the burning red emotion that felt a good deal like jealousy.

Her sister's gasp pulled her back to the moment. She swung around and followed Katherine's stare.

A frown marred Katherine's lips. "I recognize that look in your eyes Anne Adamson and if Mother were smart she'd recognize it too." She shot a pointed look at her husband. "I told you she required my assistance."

Since she'd been a girl, her sisters and mother had gone to extraordinary efforts to keep Anne from pain, treating her no different than her young brother Benedict. As much as she appreciated and loved them for their devotion, she'd forever resented that everyone saw her as nothing more than an empty-headed silly child.

Just as Harry did. The idea of that dug at her. She peeked around her brother-in-law's shoulder.

"Do not encourage him," Katherine said warningly.

She gave a flounce of her curls. "I don't know what you're talking about."

Her sister snorted. "Mother informed me he's paid you a morning visit. She fears Harry will ruin your reputation with a single look," her sister spoke in hushed tones.

Guilt settled like a stone in her belly. "Don't be silly." What would her mother and sister say if they knew Anne had all but asked the earl to ruin her? Only with instruction, of course, and no physical acts of intimacy. *What of his kisses, Anne?* a jeering voice needled. "Do you truly have such a low opinion of Lord Stanhope?" she shot back.

Katherine and Jasper wore matching frowns. "Yes," they answered in unison.

Humph. Well, then. "Rest assured, the earl doesn't have any interest in me." No, he'd been very clear on that score. Not that she desired his interest. After all, she'd set her marital hat upon the Duke of Crawford—a vastly safer, more respectable match than Harry. She looked to Harry once more. Her heart fell somewhere in the vicinity of her soles.

His gaze remained fixed on Katherine's back. The expression in his eyes inscrutable. The pain of his interest unbearable. She didn't know why after more than a year of them needling one another, she should care that he desired her more serious, more interesting twin sister. Harry stopped beside them. "Bainbridge," he drawled lazily.

"Stanhope." The duke stiffened. It was clear to all that Jasper had little fondness for the rogue. After all, what sane gentleman would care to keep company with the scoundrel who'd tried to seduce his wife? Nonetheless, the duke sketched a deep bow.

"Lord Harry," Katherine said with a more waspish tone than Anne ever remembered her sister using.

Harry murmured a quick greeting and then shifted his focus to Anne.

Heat unfurled in her belly. He had a way of making a lady feel like she was the only woman in a room, which was all rather silly because Anne well knew how very many ladies present in this *particular* room had been the recipient of that intense scrutiny.

Katherine's lips tightened.

"May I?" he motioned to the empty seat beside Anne's chair.

"Yes."

"It is occupied." Katherine glared. "Er . . . that is to say, it *was* occupied."

Anne reclaimed her chair.

Katherine made to take the seat alongside Anne, but Harry only sat in the vacant seat, a delicate Egyptian-style Klismos chair at the end of the row—the direct opposite side of Anne. He sat so close his oak-hard thigh brushed her ivory satin skirts. Warmth radiated at the point of contact. Her skin tingled with an awareness of his long, powerful leg. She swallowed hard.

The duke stood above them, a black scowl on his face, and then with something akin to reluctance, sat beside Katherine.

Her sister leaned around her husband and if glares could kill, then Harry would be a smote pile of tinder upon Lady Westmoreland's recital hall floor. "What a lovely surprise seeing you here. This is not your normal evening enjoyment."

Anne gasped at her sister's boldly impolite charge.

Ever the consummate rogue, a lazy grin formed on his hard, sculpted lips. "I wouldn't dare miss the recital. Lady Anne and I have discovered a shared love of music." He laid his hand alongside the back of Anne's chair. "Isn't that right, Lady Anne?"

She managed a jerky nod. "Er . . . yes." Her sister snapped her eyebrows together menacingly and Anne sat up straight in her chair, affecting a whole I'm-singularly-unmoved-by -Harry's-attempt-at-charming-me. "Yes, that is quite true," she added. "Lord Stanhope has a deep appreciation for . . ." Three pairs of eyes looked to her. "Music," she finished lamely. *She* had a love of all things music. Well, mayhap not the ladies Westmoreland's singing. Still, she couldn't quite say with any real degree of confidence whether Harry loved music.

Her twin's brown eyes became narrow slits that fairly shouted liar at the affable earl.

An awkward pall of silence descended as the guests hurried to claim their seats. Anne registered the exact moment Mother returned and realized just who sat alongside her daughter. Her thin eyebrows shot to her forehead and she sputtered like a trout tossed ashore.

Katherine all but yanked their mother into the vacant seat beside the duke.

"She appears thrilled," Harry drawled into her ear.

Anne nudged him with her knee. "Do hush," she whispered. What mother would be thrilled at the most notorious rogue in England's attention being fixed on her daughter? Of course, the same mother would never suspect the same daughter had enlisted the rogue's attention in garnering the notice of a duke.

Lady Westmoreland's daughters trotted down the long center aisle, onward to the front of the hall like a gaggle of geese meandering through Hyde Park. The eldest daughter claimed the pianoforte bench while her sisters took their position at the front of the dimly lit hall.

The crowd politely fell silent. A discordant key resonated through the hall. As the young woman launched into song, the audience seemed to flinch in unison.

"You owe me, Anne," Harry murmured against her ear.

"Hmm?" She arched her neck and strained to see the front of the room. She cursed her diminutive frame and the far-away seating Mother had insisted upon. *Last row sees all*, she'd insisted. Except the blasted instruments being played by the young ladies. What make of pianoforte did the lady play? She squinted into the distance; it appeared to be a Broadwood—

"Never tell me you're enthralled by this show," Harry continued in that devilishly silken whisper that tickled the shell of her ear.

She continued to study the rosewood-and-brass instrument. Then froze. Harry's teasing voice came as if down a long corridor. The vivid blue of the jasperware cameo adorning the magnificent piece and the faint *AA* etched into the pianoforte so very familiar. Too familiar. The air left her on a swift exhale. She curled her fingers along the edge of her seat.

Anne drew in a shuddery breath. She'd not really spared a thought as to where all her worldly possessions were taken. Thinking of someone playing with Benedict's soldiers or wearing her ribbons or reading Katherine's books had been too painful. But the extent of her father's betrayal was so much greater in this, in knowing he'd cared so very little he'd wagered away the one possession she'd loved more than all others . . . and that now some other man's daughters stroked the same keys Anne herself had, once upon a lifetime ago, dug at her.

Harry glanced down at her and his body went taut. He moved an intense gaze over her face; all earlier teasing replaced with concern. "What is it?" His soft-spoken whisper thrummed through her.

Anne managed to shake her head and looked up at him, *really* seeing him perhaps for the first time. Her breath caught. She'd always taken Harry as an indolent rogue, and yet this man, a stranger mere days ago, was so aware of her body's nuances he could detect her upset, challenging every notion she'd carried of him—before this moment. Harry, who delved enough to see hurt when everyone else remained unaware, making her feel something she'd only dared to dream of within the pages of her books—cherished. Warmth spiraled through her; it drove back the pain of her father's treachery. She managed a smile. "I'm all right," she mouthed. Because she was. The pianoforte, a token from a lifetime ago, was really just a material object, transient and fleeting. Here one day. Gone the next in a game of faro.

Harry brushed his fingertips over the exposed skin of her shoulders. "I detest your frown, Anne."

She frowned. What a horrid thing to say.

His lips pulled at the corners. "Not this displeased little frown. The other, forlorn one from a moment ago."

Her mother leaned across the seat and glared at them.

Harry promptly removed his arm from behind the back of Anne's chair and she mourned the loss of that closeness. The countess returned her attention to the performance. He returned his hand to its earlier position, and briefly brushed his knuckles along her exposed shoulders.

Anne shivered at the spiraling heat that coursed through her. She glanced around to see if anyone had noticed his deliberate touch. All the guests in front remained with their gazes trained forward. She could ill-afford the scandal of

Harry intimately touching her in public, yet she craved his expert caress.

His grin widened, as though he knew the very effect he was having on her. "Now that I have your attention, sweet." His whisper fanned her ear.

"Behave," she scolded. She leaned forward in her chair determined to put aside thoughts of Harry's touch, or his heated gaze, or well, anything and everything him. She leaned sideways in attempt to gather a better view of her beloved pianoforte around Lord Cumberland's, well his, er, cumbersome frame.

"Anne," Harry whispered.

Warmth unfurled in her belly at the hot intensity of his bold stare.

"It is time for your next lesson, sweet."

She gulped. With his thick, golden lashes he made her forget the plan that had brought him into her life. "Here?" God help her, she was as weak as her now heartbroken mother.

"Here," he said quietly. He leaned down, closing the distance between them. "Music. It is the food of the soul."

She blinked several times. This is what he'd speak of? Not forbidden kisses and heated caresses. "I thought that was poetry," she blurted. Katherine and her mother shot her a glare. Anne sat back in her seat, cheeks ablaze.

"Music, poetry. It is all the same, sweet," he continued, either unaware or uncaring of the disapproving stares trained on him by her family. Knowing Harry's reputation as she did, Anne ventured it was the latter. He pressed his thigh against hers. "You *do* know how to sing?"

The great, big lummox. She pursed her lips. "Of course I do."

He removed his hand from the back of her seat. "Not the soft, lyrical soprano type of voice, sweet, but rather the husky whisper of song that makes a man think of bedrooms and bedsheets and all things forbidden."

She should be scandalized by his outrageous words and yet, she'd never thought of music as a tool of seduction. Through the years, music had been the small pleasure she'd allowed herself in life. Something she was tolerably good at in a world where people didn't see her as very much good at anything. It seemed inherently wrong to use song to earn a gentleman's affection.

The crowd erupted into applause as Lady Amelia Westmoreland's piece abruptly ended. Anne clapped her hands until Lady Ava Westmoreland stood and approached the pianoforte. The plump, bespectacled young lady launched into song two.

She winced at the high-pitched squawk of the woman's voice, and stole an upward glance at the chandelier, fearing for the well-being of the crystal. The young woman's somewhat dismal performance, however, gave her something to focus on other than Harry's clear attempt at shocking her.

Alas, Harry was relentless. "Will you regale the duke with a song this evening, Anne?"

She scowled. "Do hush."

He leaned ever closer, so close the scandal sheets would have had quite a bit to print the following morning if Anne and Harry weren't seated at the back of the hall with only the servants as their witnesses. "You'll sing," he commanded. "And you'll remember my lesson. You'll sing in a husky—"

"A lady cannot determine whether she is a contralto or soprano, my lord," she interrupted. He might know all manner of things about seduction, but was remarkably ill-advised in matters of music.

"Sultry, contralto, Anne."

"Humph." She folded her arms across her chest and stared at the back of Lord Cumberland's baldpate, determined to ignore the rogue at her side.

The young lady thought to ignore him. Unfortunate for Lady Anne Adamson, as she'd yet to learn it was nigh impossible if Harry wanted a lady's attention.

Not that he *wanted* her attention, per se.

He stole a sideways glance at the proper English miss beside him with golden ringlets and . . . that single curl wound with a ribbon, nestled between her plump breasts. He swallowed hard. When he'd agreed to school the termagant Lady Anne Adamson on the art of seduction, he'd never for a moment considered that he himself would be tempted by the young lady who'd been quite rude to him since their first meeting. Even with her curved-in-all-the-right-places figure, Anne would never be the manner of miss to tempt him. Her tongue was too tart. Her frown of disapproval too deep. There were enough sweet-lipped, sultry-eyed beauties that Harry wouldn't bother with the Lady Anne's of the world.

Yet, something about her intrigued him. Perhaps she represented a diversion from the *ennui* that had plagued him for these months since Katherine had left London and returned with her husband. Mayhap it was the thrill of teaching a young lady the art of seduction. Whatever it was, she'd drawn him into her siren's net and he was loath to shake free of her hold.

The crowd broke into a smattering of applause as Lady Ava concluded her piece that might have been one of Shield's works, but Harry certainly would never make any significant wagers on the actual composer of the song. He hooked his ankle across his knee and continued to eye Anne. She pursed her lips and stole a quick glance up at him and then promptly returned her attention to the front of the hall. His lips twitched. Yes, the lady might attempt to ignore him, but she was little match for his charm.

"Don't you know it's impolite to stare?" she whispered from the corner of her mouth.

"Yes," he said on a grin.

Anne pointed her gaze skyward and returned her attention to Lady Caro Westmoreland, the next Westmoreland girl to take the floor. The young lady could have sprouted wings and joined the heavenly choir of angels amidst Lady Westmoreland's recital hall and Harry would still be unable to look away from Anne's breasts. The pale creamy white of her modest décolletage evoked all manner of sinful thoughts that involved her on her back and . . .

He groaned.

Concern replaced the earlier annoyance in Anne's pale-blue eyes. "Are you all right?"

Harry waved a hand. "Fine, fine," he said quietly, his voice garbled. Really, far from *fine*. Because by God, Harry did not desire proper, marriage-minded misses. Even if they did possess lush forms to rival the fabled fertility goddesses. More specifically, he did not desire Anne.

She was cheeky.

And rude.

And condescending.

To him, anyway.

And he'd enough ladies clamoring for his notice that he didn't need or want the attention of an impudent creature like her. She craned her long, graceful neck around Lord Cumberland's *cumbersome* frame in attempt to view the front hall, her attention on Lady Caro now singing her off-key tune.

"She's wearing a pale-yellow satin gown with white lace trim," he said from the corner of his mouth.

Anne blinked. She looked around.

He gestured to the front of the hall. "I gather you're trying to see the young lady's gown?"

She furrowed her brow. "Why would I care about the lady's gown?"

Anne's family glared as one at the two of them.

Harry grinned in response and continued. "Isn't that what you have, my lady? A keen appreciation for fashion and—"

She snorted. "Lord Harry, I wear white and ivory satin ruffled monstrosities. Do I take you as one to spend the evening mooning over a pretty gown?"

"Quite the reason *to* moon over a pretty gown," he amended.

Her mouth screwed up. "I suppose." She shook her head. "But I'm not staring at her gown. I'm watching the performance," she spoke as if scolding a recalcitrant child.

Lady Katherine frowned at the two of them. Harry winked and the Katherine he'd come to know as friend gave her head a disapproving shake.

"Oomph."

Anne jabbed an elbow in his side, a frown on her plump lips.

Bloody hell. The chit had sharp, daggerlike elbows. "What was that for?"

She opened and closed her mouth several times like a trout plucked from a well-stocked lake. "You weren't paying attention." He cocked his head. "To the recital," she clarified.

Lady Caro concluded her song and thunderous applause filled the hall, applause that likely had a good deal more to do with the actual end of her piece than anything else. The next Westmoreland lady stepped forward to wound the ears of those present. She eyed the crowded room with something akin to horror, and Harry suspected this particular Westmoreland was well aware of her precise level of talent. She opened her mouth and another off-key song resonated throughout the marbled space.

He sighed. "Another lyrical soprano," he said, knowing it would infuriate Anne.

She jabbed an elbow in his side. Again.

Harry winced. He was going to have a vicious bruise to his ribs by the end of the evening's performance.

"I've already told you, a lady can no more determine the pitch quality of her voice than she can . . ."

He arched an eyebrow.

She frowned. "Than she can . . . well, I don't know. But I do know a lady cannot simply decide if she is a soprano or contralto. It is something she's born with and not something she can or for that matter should"—another jab—"*want* to change, all to earn the affections of a man who'd have her with a husky singing voice."

"Sultry."

She cocked her head.

"Husky *and* sultry. You forgot—"

"Will you two hush?" Katherine whispered.

Color flooded Anne's cheeks and she gave a curt nod.

Lady One-of-the-Westmorelands at last concluded her piece, ushering in a brief, and much needed intermission. A loud buzz, like a hive he'd once knocked down as a boy, filled the room as the members of the *ton* present gossiped and chatted.

Harry tilted back on the legs of his chair and yawned.

"I imagine you may leave now," Anne murmured.

He glanced at her. "Trying to be rid of me, hellion?" He didn't know why the thought should chafe.

Her cheeks blazed red in a familiar blush. "No. No, not at all," she said hurriedly. *Too hurriedly.* He narrowed his eyes. Which seemed to indicate Lady Anne did care to be rid of him after all.

Hmm, well this was not common for the Lord Stanhope, rogue and charmer of dowagers and debutantes alike. "I think I care to stay the remainder of the performance," he lied. He didn't give a fig about the current show. He did, however, give a fig about Anne's sudden desire to send him on his way like a nursemaid giving her charge a pat on the head and smile, before hurrying them off to bed.

Anne glanced around, and then looked back to him. "I truly appreciate your being here, Harry," she said, her words so soft they barely reached his ears. "But I'd not impose on you any further than I have. Your presence has been noted. I'm sure there is any number of"—she colored—"places, you'd care to go."

What did a young, innocent lady like Anne know of the places he frequented? If she knew a hint of what occurred in those very *places*, she'd have swooned right there. Anne's supposition would have been true two days ago. Two days ago he'd have been at one of the less-reputable gaming hells or in some notorious widow's arms. Now, for reasons he didn't understand, nor cared to consider, he wanted to be here.

Just to help the young lady, he assured himself. Why did that feel like a lie?

"Lord Stanhope, how unfair of you. Occupying the attention of the most lovely lady present this evening."

Harry stiffened. He stood and greeted the *pleasantly handsome and unfailingly polite* Duke of Crawford.

Chapter 5

*T*he only silence amidst Lady Westmoreland's entire hall happened to be with the five people seated in the very last row.

Mother broke the awkward pall. She rose in a flutter of silvery-grey skirts. "Your Grace," she tittered behind her hand. "What an absolute pleasure."

Anne winced and reluctantly came to her feet wishing she could dissolve into a puddle of embarrassment at Mother's clear grasping.

Polite greetings were exchanged between Katherine's husband, the Duke of Bainbridge, and the young Duke of Crawford.

She waited for a hint of jubilance at the duke's seeming interest, yet as she studied him conversing with her brother-in-law, she felt only a bored disinterest in what matters the two young dukes cared to discuss.

The heart of a duke. *This is what you want. You've dreamed of the title of duchess and with it the security and stability represented in that lofty ascension of rank.*

With pleasantries aside, the Duke of Crawford turned the full force of his ducal regard on Anne. She shifted at his intent scrutiny, while fingering the ribbon woven through her hair. The duke's gaze drifted lower and her cheeks burned.

She released the satin striped fabric. "Your Grace," she murmured and sank into a deep, respectful curtsy.

The duke claimed her hand. "Lady Anne," he said quietly. His lips hovered above the inner portion of her wrist and he raised it to his mouth.

Disappointment surged through her at her body's total lack of awareness of that slight caress. He released her hand and she fisted the fabric of her skirts. From the corner of her eye she detected Harry's hot, furious stare. What did he have to be angry with? He was the cad who'd been eying her sister in the midst of the recital, which *only* mattered because he was supposed to be feigning interest in Anne.

The Duke of Crawford looked between them.

Liar.

He settled his autocratic gaze on Harry. "Not your usual entertainments for the evening, Stanhope, eh? I thought you made it a rule to avoid all respectable events." He chuckled at his own charge.

Annoyance churned inside her. She knew the man was a duke and surely had been reared to believe he could say anything without fear of rebuke, but really, his words were borderline crass.

Harry's hard muscles went taut, straining the fabric of his expertly tailored black coat. But then his firm lips turned up in a half-grin, an insolent smile for the other man, proof that she'd merely imagined his reaction to the duke's words. "Some rules are meant to be broken. And"—he looked to Anne—"some people are worth breaking rules for."

Her breath caught. And she knew his words, the look in his eye was merely part of his efforts to help her secure the duke's hand, yet, in that moment everything, everyone melted away so that just they two remained.

"Indeed," the duke murmured. He shifted his attention to Anne, promptly dismissing the earl. "My lady, may I request the pleasure of calling on you?"

Anne looked around, uncertain why her sister, mother, and Harry were staring at her. Then it occurred to her. "You want to call on me?" Embarrassment twisted in her belly. "I . . . that is—"

"What my daughter means to say, Your Grace," Mother interjected with a pointed glance for Anne, "is that she would very much welcome your visit. Isn't that right, Anne?"

Anne managed a jerky nod. "Er, yes." This is exactly what she wanted. "I would welcome a visit, Your Grace," she finished lamely. Perhaps Harry would need to instruct her on the art of communicating with an eligible lord on the marriage mart, as well.

The duke appeared amused by her confounded response. His lips twitched and he captured her hand. "Until tomorrow then, my lady," he murmured. He placed a final kiss on the top of her hand.

Couldn't there be shivers of awareness, like she felt at Harry's touch?

Couldn't there be the warm fluttery sensations in her belly she'd read about in her Gothic novels?

Couldn't there be—*something*?

"I look forward to your visit," she said softly. All the while, Harry's hard gaze fairly burned a hole into her person.

The Lady Westmorelands returned to the front of the hall, signifying the beginning of the next set of performances was to begin.

The duke released her hand after a longer than appropriate amount of time. "Stanhope," he said, his tone harder than before. He bowed to the other gentleman and then bid the remainder of her party a good evening.

"Well," Katherine said, a smile on her lips.

Anne sank back into her seat. "Well, what?"

Her sister sat and whispered, "The heart of a duke. It appears you are on your way to the title of duchess, sister." She made a face. "Oh, dear. That sounded rather mercurial. I'd not have you wed a duke unless your heart is engaged. Nor any gentleman for that matter or—"

"Hush, Kat. This isn't the place." Her sister appeared ready to launch a full-defense of her earlier words. Then something only twins shared passed between them and Katherine gave a solemn nod.

As she settled into her uncomfortable chair, she thought she should feel a giddy sense of victory, yet all she felt at the duke's interest was oddly hollow. He did not know her. He'd not even spoken but a murmured greeting at all the functions they'd attended together. Until the ribbon.

Until Harry and his blasted advice.

Advice she'd sought.

And welcomed . . .

But . . . She didn't want the duke to want her for her . . . her . . . *endowments* alone. "Silly," she mumbled.

"What was that, sweet?"

"Don't call me sweet, Harry," she said, not taking her gaze from the front of the hall where Lady Leah Westmoreland claimed the pianoforte bench.

"What would you have me call you? Duchess?" Thick sarcasm underscored his question.

She flinched at his deliberately placed barb. "Must you be so odious?" She blinked back foolish tears of hurt and glared at him.

Instead of being properly chastised, Harry quirked another golden eyebrow. He leaned close so his brandy-scented breath fanned her lips. "Isn't that what you want, sweet?" he said, almost tauntingly. "Title of duchess and by Crawford's interest in that"—he jerked his chin at her satin ribbon—"golden ringlet—"

"Which is not silly," she cut in.

"Which *is* silly. Well, then I'd wager all my coffers in the book at White's that you'll be carrying the duke's heir by next Christmastide season," he said, a biting edge to his prediction.

She gasped. Her fingers twitched with the urge to slap his smug, rude, arrogant, condescending face. Katherine looked over with a question in her eyes. Anne shook her head and her sister returned her attention to the performance.

A spark glinted in Harry's hazel eyes.

With his roguish cynicism, Harry judged her interest in the duke and sought to taunt her for those efforts. She'd not allow him that satisfaction.

Anne relaxed her fingers. "Then your lessons on seduction should come in quite handy, my lord." She sat back in her seat and promptly dismissed him.

At Anne's rebuttal, fury thrummed through Harry's veins, hot and volatile. By God, that he should school her in the ways in which to use her body and charms to catch another gentleman while he himself remained ignorant as to the color of the nipples atop those generous swells, or the pleasure of her touch, or the sound of her damned laughter, infuriated him.

He steeled his jaw. This sudden, inexplicable interest in Lady Anne was merely about sex. He'd never before noticed her lush form and now, well hell, now he did, and he wanted to know all of her. In the physical sense. Margaret's deception had shown him there was nothing else to know of a woman outside of the pleasure to be had in her arms.

He might mock Anne's efforts to land Crawford, but the reality was Harry had well learned the way of their calculated world eight years ago. He'd given in to the emotion of love, given his fool's heart to the sweetly innocent, beautiful Miss Margaret Dunn. He'd risked his very life, his reputation in a duel against Lord Rutland for the honor of the lady's love. In the end, she'd chosen neither of them. She'd chosen wealth and status. And Harry? He had pledged to neither love nor feel again.

He didn't care about the damned Lady Anne, tempting vixen with her sharp tongue. He pulled out his watch fob and consulted the time. He should leave. Hell, he should have left when Anne herself had made the suggestion a short while ago. A steady staccato pierced his thoughts. He dropped his gaze to the floor.

The tip of Anne's slippers peeked out the front of the gown and beat a rhythm in time to the current song selection. All the hardened anger he'd carried since Crawford had come over and interrupted whatever this was between him and Anne, lifted. An odd shift occurred. There was something so whimsical, so endearing in Anne's innocent gesture.

The lady enjoyed music.

Other than the fact that silver flecks danced in her eyes when she was annoyed and that a little muscle ticked at the left corner of her lip when she frowned, Harry knew next to nothing about Lady Anne Adamson. But with her talk of contraltos and lyric sopranos, and her fixed interest in even the horrid performance of the Westmoreland girls, he found she cared about music.

He who made it a habit of not learning anything about a lady's interests, outside of the bedchambers, that is, knew this of her. When one knew a lady's likes and dislikes and what made her smile or laugh, and even frown, then one could no longer see merely a supple body to bed.

Christ. What was next? He'd begin sprouting sonnets about the sun-kissed golden hue of her silken ringlets?

He gave his head a hard shake and stood.

Anne looked up at him with a question in her wide blue eyes.

He gave a curt bow and without a backward glance took his leave. The echo of his boot steps blended with the squawking squeal-like song of Lady Marissa Westmoreland. When at last he exited the palatial townhouse, he tugged at his cravat and sucked in a much-needed breath of air.

His driver hopped down from atop the black lacquer carriage and opened the door.

Harry strode over as fast as his bachelor legs could carry him and leapt inside. "To my clubs," he said curtly.

The driver closed the door behind him and then the carriage shifted as he scrambled onto his perch.

Harry pulled back the black curtain and peered at the white stucco townhouse bathed in candlelight, unable to account for this desire to return to the too-small, prim Klismos chair beside Lady Anne. The carriage sprung forward and he let the velvet fabric flutter back into place. He drummed his fingertips on the tops of his thighs, suddenly reminded of a different tapping. Specifically, two delicate slippered feet beating away a staccato rhythm upon the Italian marble floor.

He dragged a hand across his eyes. Slippered feet did not earn his notice. Bare naked toes used for wicked deeds, however, did.

As his carriage approached the front of Forbidden Pleasures, one of the most disreputable of the hells in London, Harry exited the coach resolved to put the innocent Anne from his thoughts once and for all. He strode up the three stone steps. The majordomo pulled the door open and Harry swept inside.

Raucous laughter and a cloud of thick cheroot smoke hung over the crimson-red establishment. Harry eyed the room a moment and then moved deeper into the club.

He strode over to an empty table and sat, absently viewing the debauchery before him. A liveried servant rushed over with a bottle of brandy. Harry accepted a glass and waved the man off. He splashed several fingers into the tumbler and then filled it to the brim, determined to get well and fully soused. He took a sip and when that did little to diminish Anne's disapproving eyes from his mind, he downed the entire contents.

"Well, well, Stanhope," a voice drawled. "I thought you'd never arrive."

He glanced up.

Lord Alex Edgerton grinned down at him. He and Edgerton went back to early days at Eton and Oxford. Theirs was the manner of friendship in which they would risk their life for the other. Harry should know. When he'd fought that foolish duel, Edgerton had been his second. Known for carousing, gaming, and overindulging in spirits and ladies, the two were remarkably similar and good friends for it. "May I?"

Harry motioned to the chair opposite him.

Edgerton, the second son to the Marquess of Waverly, tugged out a seat. A servant rushed to set down a glass for the other man. The liveried footman reached for Harry's bottle, but Edgerton waved him off. He poured himself a glass and shoved the bottle toward Harry. His friend quirked an eyebrow. "Lady Anne Adamson?" he drawled without preamble.

Harry grabbed the bottle and poured himself a second glass. He'd not come here to discuss Lady Anne but rather to bury thoughts of her in the arms of some nameless beauty with sweet lips and a clever tongue.

"Well?"

"I didn't think there was a question there," Harry said over the rim of his snifter.

"Oh, there most certainly is a question. First Lady Katherine, now the lady's sister." Edgerton chuckled. "I am, of course, imagining all manner of delicious ways to entertain twin sisters."

Harry's fingers tightened almost reflexively about the glass, so hard he threatened to shatter the thick, crystal tumbler. "Don't be crude, Edgerton." He eased his grip. After all, would he not have had similar, outrageous thoughts if they'd involved anyone other than Anne?

"Crude?" Edgerton guffawed. "Never tell me you've gone all priggish on me." Harry lifted one finger in a vulgar gesture. His friend laughed. "No, I suspect one wouldn't fear you'd go all proper." He set his elbows on the table in front of him and leaned close. "Rumor has it you were at Lady Westmoreland's musicale."

Rumor traveled faster than a purebred stallion on an empty Roman road. He took another sip. With Edgerton's unwavering loyalty there was little Harry kept from him, and yet something froze all discussion of Anne on his lips. Sharing his pledge to help her felt like a betrayal of sorts.

"Tsk, tsk," Edgerton mocked. "Attending dull, societal recitals to see an innocent miss with ringlets and ruffled white skirts?"

What is wrong with my ringlets?

A growl rumbled up his chest at those mocking words. There was nothing wrong with her blasted ringlets. They suited her well. Too well. Whatever the hell *that* meant. They just did. He really wished Edgerton would close his blasted mouth. "Go to hell," Harry muttered. He took another sip and set the partially drunk brandy down with a thunk.

His friend drummed his fingertips on the mahogany table. "Or is it merely that you have seen a hidden diamond ready to be plucked by an eager lord?" He chuckled. "It hardly matters if a lady is as empty-headed as Lady Anne when you have her underneath you."

Harry's legs jerked reflexively, knocking the table. The abrupt movement rattled the glass and sent brandy spilling onto the smooth wood surface. A servant rushed forward to clean the mess. He supplied Harry with a new glass.

Lord Alex stretched his legs out in front of him. "Ahh, you must have been soused *before* you attended Westmoreland's."

He didn't bother to correct his friend's inaccurate assumption that he was tap-hackled. Though he'd consumed several glasses, Harry was still dead sober. Certainly sober enough to feel the chill of rage run through him at the other gentleman's disparaging of Anne. Instead, he said nothing. He reached for the bottle and sloshed several fingers, thought better of it and filled the glass to the rim.

"I'm not in the mood for company," he said curtly. He passed a glance around at the tableau of sin unfolding before him. Young, scantily clad women on the laps of some of the leading members of Society. Nubile females bent over the tables while others slapped at their well-rounded buttocks. He frowned. Once enticed by such depravity, Harry now battled a sense of tedium.

His friend followed his stare. "Ahh, so that is why you've come this evening."

Harry reached for his glass.

"That is a good deal more reassuring than imagining you've become a stodgy chap at recital halls courting the vain Lady Anne."

He knocked over his second tumbler.

Edgerton cursed and jumped back in his seat as liquid spilled onto his breeches. "Bloody hell, Stanhope. I never imagined I'd say this, but you've indulged in enough spirits for the evening." He yanked his chin in the direction of a blonde vision eying Harry through sultry, interested eyes. "Time to lose yourself in a lush beauty." He motioned the woman over. "You're in a foul mood, which I gather has much to do with that recital you attended," he said as the tall, Spartan-like vision sidled up to Harry.

He stiffened. His foul mood, as his friend referred to it, had more to do with the gleam of interest he'd detected in the bloody perfect Duke of Crawford's eyes earlier that evening. The bastard had eyed Anne as if she was a berry dipped in champagne and he wanted to lick every last drop from her delectable frame.

He dimly registered an expert set of hands moving from his shoulders, over his chest. He blinked at the golden-haired angel. With her skin flawlessly white and her body curved in all the places he liked his women curved, he should be eager for her attention.

She layered herself against him. "Hello, my lord," she whispered into his ear.

Only her voice lacked the cultured tones of a certain refined young lady. "Hello," he said at last. Her blonde hair lacked the vibrant gleam of a scorching summer sun.

She smiled, taking that simple greeting as an invitation and trailed her fingers between the deep crevice of her breasts.

He jumped up.

Edgerton looked up at him with a quizzical expression. "Are you all right, Stanhope?"

No! "Fine . . . just too much drink," he lied.

The young beauty shifted her attentions to Edgerton, climbing onto his lap.

Harry raised his hand in salute and hurried from Forbidden Pleasures. What madness had Lady Anne Adamson wrought upon him? In a handful of days he'd gone from a carefree rogue who lived for his own pleasures and the pleasure he could give any woman, to this snarling, snapping, furious beast enraged at the thought of Crawford and Anne together.

He made his way out the black double doors of the establishment and paused at the threshold, absently staring out the darkened, seedy streets of London's underbelly. The sooner Anne could bring her duke up to scratch, the sooner he could be rid of her and return to his uncomplicated, blithe lifestyle.

And by the look in Crawford's eyes at the Westmoreland recital, it really would only be a matter of days.

Harry growled, abhorring the idea for reasons he didn't understand.

Chapter 6

"*The* gall of that man!"

Anne glanced up from her stacks of ribbons on the rose-inlaid table before her. Mother stood in the doorway, brandishing a paper like it was a weapon of old and she the knight defending his keep. Fury snapped in her melodramatic mother's eyes. She bit back a sigh. "Mother," she greeted. With both her sisters gone and married and her brother away at school, Anne found she far preferred her solitary company and collection of ribbons to her mother's hysterics.

Her mother sailed into the room. "The gall of him," she seethed. Just in case, Anne assumed, she'd failed to hear the same utterance mere moments ago. Mother paced. "Gentleman," she scoffed. "Why, how loosely that term is applied. To bounders and scoundrels and rogues."

A momentary twinge of pity struck her. She imagined the pain of Father's betrayal would forever turn a woman bitter as it had Mother. This is what marriage to a scapegrace would do, and a fate Anne now actively sought to avoid.

Her mother launched into a tirade that involved mention of dastards and their dastardly deeds. Anne shifted her attention back to her meticulous stacks of ribbons. She picked up an ivory satin strip and laid it carefully atop the others. Six. Six white ribbons. She rested her chin in her hand. Which seemed rather silly, as Harry had pointed out. All this white and ivory business. She glanced down at her ruffled skirts, also of ivory. After all, a lady who'd seen two Seasons should certainly have the luxury of . . . She picked up the aqua-blue ribbon, a luxuriant color that might make a gentleman think of ocean waters and—

"Have you heard a single word I've uttered, Anne?" Mother cried.

She dropped the ribbon. "Uh, yes." She waved a hand. "The whole dastardly behavior business." Which seemed rather close to whatever Mother had been carrying on about, for the older woman gave a pleased nod. Anne reached for another blue-green ribbon.

"And to do so after he'd spent the evening expressing a clear interest in you."

She froze, her hand poised over the pile. "What?" she blurted.

Mother let out an exasperated sigh. "Do try to keep up." She waved the paper in front of Anne's eyes, which did her little good. Unless squinting and angling the page just so, it was nigh impossible for her to make out a single word. "That bounder."

Her heart hammered. "What bounder?" She really wished she'd been paying closer attention.

Mother tossed her hands up. "The Earl of Stanhope. First, he sought your sister's favor." She snorted. "As though your *sister* would ever be so foolhardy as to toss away her affections on such a cad." Her pointed look, a damning statement more powerful than words, spoke volumes of her opinion on Anne's discernment.

She frowned. She'd never been considered the intelligent one of the family. Her family, polite Society, they all failed to realize Anne was a woman who saw much, heard more, and had actual thoughts inside her head beyond the fabric of her gown or the *ton's* gossip. "Mother, what is it?" she asked, impatiently.

Mother tossed the paper onto the table. The faint breeze stirred the pile of white and ivory ribbons. Several strips of satin sailed onto the floor. Ribbon piles forgotten, Anne picked up the copy of *The Times*. Her mother leaned over her shoulder and jabbed her finger somewhere in the middle of the page. "There. Read that."

Anne held it up. She tried. She truly did. She squinted hard. If she blinked in rapid succession and the light was just right, she could make sense of the blurred words.

A certain Lord HS was . . .

Her eyes flew wide and the page blurred out of focus. She wanted to stomp her foot. Blast! Lord HS was what? Smitten? Enamored? Captivated?

"Oh, do give me that." Mother snatched it from her fingers. "'Lord HS abruptly fled a certain Lady AA's side.'" She glanced up from the page. "That is you," she said as if Anne were a simpleton.

"Undoubtedly." A pressure tightened about her heart. It shouldn't matter what Harry did after he'd left her company, and yet . . . it did. Unwilling to let her mother see the effect her words were having upon her, she yawned into her hand. "He's a rogue, Mother. Why should we care about his goings on?"

Her mother continued as though she hadn't spoken. "'At which point he sought out . . .'" A shudder wracked mother's frame. "I'll not even say it. After his express interest in you last evening—"

"It was not an express interest in me." It had merely been part of their overall plan to secure the duke's notice. And really, what, or worse, *who* had Harry sought out? Her heart kicked up a frantic beat, consumed by a desire to know the blasted woman's identity.

"Do you know how this appears to the *ton*?"

She could wager any number of ways, none of which were kind or pleasant. "How?"

"As though you are a young lady unable to hold the attention of a gentleman who previously expressed an interest in you."

Her heart tugged at those bluntly spoken words. Mother, often wrong, happened to be very close to the mark in this regard and the truth of that pierced the foolish organ.

"Now the duke will never pay you a call." Her plaintive wail was as aggrieved as if she'd learned doomsday was nigh.

The duke? She cocked her head. Oh, yes. As in the Duke of Crawford; the real reason she'd sought Harry out.

"Whatever shall we do?" Mother wailed. She tossed the paper down where it landed on the floor, disrupting the pile of purple-pink ribbons in its wake.

Anne stared emptily down at the ribbon mess, a multicolored confusion not so very different from what her life had become. "Whatever *can* we do?"

Another cry split the Ivory Parlor. Alas, Anne only seemed incapable of the wrong answers where anyone was concerned. "Oh, why can you not understand, Anne? The earl's clear disinterest matters a good deal. You might find him a clever, charming rogue, but he's disgraced you." Her mother pressed her palms against her cheeks as though shamed by her outburst. She drew in a breath and when she spoke, icy resolve steeled her words. "I've had grand hopes of the match you will make."

"Thank y—"

"I am not finished," Mother snapped. "I never dared imagined Katherine would wed a duke, though this family could certainly have done without the scandalous past of Bainbridge."

Anne tightened her lips to keep from pointing out Katherine was hopelessly and helplessly in love with Jasper, and that nothing else should matter but the young couple's happiness and the happiness of their beautiful babe, Maxwell.

"Do you remember my expectations for Katherine?"

There really were too many expectations for each of the Adamson daughters for Anne to remember a specific one. She gave her head a slight shake. It was often easier to allow Mother her rant.

"I expected one of my girls would wed Bertrand Ekstrom."

She stifled a groan. Mr. Bertrand Ekstrom. Their odious second, or was it third, cousin? Mother had planned on wedding Katherine off to the miserable bugger. A man Anne had heard faint whispers of. Something pertaining to Mr. Ekstrom's perverse fascination with riding crops and violent lashes. She wrinkled her nose in distaste. What manner of gentleman abused his horseflesh? *The miserable bugger.*

"And I never imagined it would be you."

Anne blinked. "Never imagined what would be me?" she blurted, trying to recall her mother's previously spoken words, wishing she'd been paying closer attention.

Her mother threw her hands up in exasperation. "I never imagined you would wed Bertrand."

She scratched her brow. "Why would I wed Mr. Ekstrom?" She wouldn't. Ever. Not unless she was in the habit of sacrificing her very own happiness, which she wasn't. She quite enjoyed being happy.

"Because you are now on your third Season, Anne." Her mother gave her head a pitying shake. "You are unwed."

Anne moistened her lips, knowing when Mother sank her teeth into an idea she was worse than one of the queen's terriers with a bone. "Hardly on the shelf," she said, defensively.

"But certainly not married, either." Mother claimed her hands. "This is not a threat. This is me speaking to you with direct honesty. A young lady must wed and have security; for herself, her family. And if you are unwed, well, we cannot afford to risk something happening to your brother and the most logical plan . . ." Her words trailed off.

The most logical plan was to forego Anne's happiness for their family's security. *In trying to earn the duke's favor, isn't that what I'm doing?* For somehow, Mother desired another ducal connection since the one to Katherine's duke was apparently not enough. Her mother squeezed her hands. Anne's fingers twitched with the desire to yank free of her grip. "I'll not wed Mr. Ekstrom," she said quietly.

Mother inclined her head. "Do not be silly, my dear." The corners of her lips turned down ever so slightly. "I'd rather you not wed Bertrand." She released her hold on Anne. "Unless you have no other option." She gave Anne a long, pointed look, and then sailed from the room.

Anne folded her arms across her chest and attempted to rub warmth back into the chilled limbs. She'd known through the years that making advantageous matches for each of her daughters was the Countess of Wakefield's ultimate goal. Anne mattered so little that she'd be wed off to her corpulent, oft-rude cousin? A man so very different than the gentleman who now taught Anne the art of seduction.

The thought of Harry slipped in and then memory after memory of the dashing earl poured over her. Her mother, sister, and Society on the whole would call her all kinds of fool for desiring him as she did. After all, she very well knew the kind of charmer Lord Harry Stanhope happened to be—the manner of gentleman who placed two crystal glasses of champagne in his host's conservatory and almost partook in a scandalous assignation.

The muscles of her stomach tightened as her mother's earlier allegations about Harry surfaced. The mysterious woman mentioned in the papers. She'd expected such roguish behaviors from Harry, the man who'd tried to seduce her twin.

Yet . . . She eyed the forgotten paper at her feet. She'd not thought the Harry who arrived to musicales and joined her for the evening would then do something as appalling as to visit . . . She wrinkled her nose. Whoever it was he'd sought out after he'd left her side. If he'd taken himself off to some soiree or another with some scandalous widow, she would, well, she would tell him exactly what she thought of him. Even if it was a pretend courtship. She should be a good deal more concerned with Mother's threat of wedding her off to Bertrand Ekstrom, yet she could not muster the suitable outrage when compared with the hurt fury thrumming through her at the idea of Harry with . . . with . . .

Anne swiped the paper. She angled the page in a way that the stream of sunlight shone off the central part of the copy and scoured the page in search of his name—and hers, of course. She squinted hard. *Lord HS*, some word, some word, *Lady AA*. Another blurred word. *Forbidden* . . . "Forbidden, what?" she muttered under her breath.

Footsteps sounded outside in the hall. Blast and double blast. She'd had enough of her mother to last her the remainder of the Season and all the next combined. "I'm reading it, Mother," she called. Or desperately trying to, anyway. "I see the reason for your outrage, of course." Which she didn't fully see, necessarily. She saw, however, just enough words to understand what had roused her mother's displeasure. "He really shouldn't—"

"The Earl of Stanhope, my lady."

Chapter 7

$\mathcal{A}$ nne jerked her head up hard enough that she wrenched the muscles along the back of her neck. The paper slid from her fingers and took with it her stack of yellow ribbons whereupon they lay scattered like slashes over the other colors just as her thoughts. "Um, well thank you, Ollie." For absolutely nothing. "That will be all."

The ancient butler shuffled off.

Harry's tall, broad frame filled the doorway. He leaned against the doorjamb more tempting than that tantalizingly succulent apple in the Garden of Eden. "What has captured your attention, Anne?"

Embarrassed heat burned her entire body. If it were possible for one to die of humiliation she'd have been a useless heap at his glorious feet. She jumped up. "My attention?" Her mind raced. "My ribbons," she blurted, and then said on a rush. "I was paying careful attention to organizing my ribbons." Because her silly habit with the ribbons was only slightly less mortifying than admitting to her wounded hurt over his evening's *enjoyments*.

The earl shoved away from the wall and strolled over. His gaze fell to the floor. To the damning piece of evidence. "May I?" he murmured.

She opened her mouth, but he'd already bent to scoop up the copy of *The Times*. Anne planted the sole of her slipper upon the center of the page. "You may not," she said between clenched teeth.

He tugged.

She held firm.

Harry yanked once more. She teetered backward and would have toppled onto the cream-and-white upholstered sofa, but Harry shot an arm around her waist and caught her to him. Her heart thumped wildly. "Careful, sweet," he murmured and suddenly released her.

Anne screwed her mouth up, uncertain whether she was more annoyed by his high-handedness or his seemingly total lack of interest in their body's positioning. She settled for a healthy combination of the two.

As he read, she shuffled back and forth on her feet, while studying his bent head. A golden lock fell across his brow and gave him an almost boyish look. Only she'd venture Harry, the Earl of Stanhope, had never been a boy. Instead, he'd been a man sprung from the earth to torment poor, senseless young ladies.

He finished reading and picked his head up. "Hmm."

She knew he expected a reply to that dangling "hmm" and loathed feeding his amusement. Anne sighed. Mother had forever lamented her dangerously insatiable curiosity. "Hmm, what, my lord?"

"What should this nameless *he* not have done?"

Anne cocked her head. "Nameless *he* . . . ? Oh . . ." Her words trailed off with the agony of humiliation. He'd of course heard her call out when he'd entered the room. And now, having read the paper, he'd clearly made the correct supposition that *he* was the nameless someone she'd spoken of. She toed the Aubusson carpet and studied the poor, until-now-forgotten ribbons on the floor.

Harry touched his fingers to her chin and forced her gaze to his. "I gather you read the section about a certain Lord HS and a certain Lady AA?"

She managed a tight nod. She'd read bits of the piece. Most of which she'd learned, however, had come from Mother's squawking.

"And?"

"And, what?" she said on an exasperated sigh.

He stroked her chin with his thumb and forefinger. "I imagine a lady such as you would have questions for me?"

She frowned. "A lady such as me?" She rather disliked the whole "lady-such-as-you" nonsense.

"A clever, inquisitive miss with lots of questions."

Anne touched a hand to her heart. No one in her life; not Aldora, Mother, not even her twin who knew so very much of her soul, found Anne in any way insightful. They failed to see she had opinions on matters of actual significance; on life, love, happiness. "You think I'm clever?" she asked softly.

Harry worked his gaze over her face.

If he teased her, she'd slap his hands and hate him forever. "I do," he said solemnly.

And a small sliver of her heart would forever belong to Harry, the Earl of Stanhope for such an admission.

"Well?"

Her mind spun as she tried to recall his earlier question. Only she remembered Mother's outrage and then the blurred words about a forbidden someone or another. All her earlier hurt and annoyance melded to create a potent blend of fury, the easiest emotion to decipher from the swirling confusion roused by this new, startling awareness of Harry. She settled her hands upon her hips. "Who is this woman?" She gestured to the copy of *The Times*. "This *forbidden* woman." A forbidden woman he'd abandoned her for. She gave her head a shake. *Rather*, the forbidden woman he'd left Lady Westmoreland's recital for. Their arrangement was strictly a matter of business. He had no obligations to Anne. None at all. Why did that thought rankle?

Amusement flickered in the green-gold flecks of his hazel eyes. "Jealous, sweet?"

She swatted at him. Had she really just thought a mere moment ago, she'd dare love anything about the outrageous scoundrel? She spun away from him.

"You didn't read the story," he said as though with the surprise of one who'd just discovered the New World.

"I did," she said, defensively. "Or I intended to," she groused.

"Here." He slapped the wrinkled paper into her hands. "Read your gossip, my lady, and then ask your questions."

Her mouth went dry as she studied the page, and then she shook her head. "No, I don't believe I shall." She pushed back at his hands.

"I insist," he said, pressing.

On a sigh, Anne took the paper and made a show of smoothing it out. She carried it over to the window for better illumination and read. Or attempted to. She squinted at the blasted, blurred words.

A sharp bark of laughter burst from his chest. "By God."

She glowered. "What is it?" Did he expect her to be a woman who cared about the blasted comings and goings set out in the gossip rags? When in truth, her real concern was the mention of a certain Earl of S.

"You can't see the damned words, can you?"

She bristled with indignation and gave a flounce of her golden ringlets. "I can see them. *Some* of them," she amended. "And you really shouldn't curse in front of a lady." Though that was likely one of the lesser charges she could level at the dashing earl.

His long, powerful legs ate up the distance between them as he strode over. "You need spectacles," he said.

"I don't." With him finding it a matter of such hilarity, she wouldn't dare admit that truth to him, not when he'd already had such a laugh at her expense.

"You do," he spoke with a finality that suggested he considered the debate ended.

"I don't." She held the copy of *The Times* protectively in front of her. "This isn't about what I can see or not see, Harry. This is about your behavior last evening with . . ."

He arched another quizzical eyebrow. "With?" he prodded.

"Oh, hush, you very well know I didn't read—"

"Because you couldn't see it."

"—the entire article," she finished. She tossed aside the paper and once more settled her hands on her hips. "Did you leave me and go see one of your fancy pieces?" His lips twitched. She narrowed her eyes. "This is not a matter of amusement."

"Yes, I do believe you *are* jealous, sweet."

She widened her eyes and opened her mouth. She closed it. She tried again. Words failed her. "I am *not* jealous," she managed after a long, uncomfortable stretch of silence. In spite of everyone's low opinion, she had enough good sense to avoid any emotional entanglements with Harry. He snorted. "I'm not," she insisted. Anne began to pace. "As Mother said, it reflects all rather poorly on me." She slashed the air with her hand. "Society will speak about how I'm unable to hold your affections—"

He grinned. "My affections?"

She nodded and continued pacing. "They'll wonder at what flaw I possess, failing to realize the truth." She paused midstride and met his gaze squarely. He really did have splendid eyes. The flecks of gold put her in mind of the fabled pot at the end of a rainbow.

"And what is the truth, Anne?" he asked, jerking her back to the moment.

She pursed her lips. "That my inability to hold your affections is through a detriment of your own character, my lord. You are unable to love anyone. Not just me," she hurried to clarify when his eyes narrowed.

Harry wandered close. She retreated. He continued until the backs of her knees thumped against the King Louis XIV chair and she tumbled into the seat. She craned her neck to look at him and swallowed, resenting his height. It hardly seemed fair she should be a mere smidge in his commanding shadow. "You're wrong. I tried love once before. I'll not give myself over to weak sentiments."

His admission sucked the breath from her lungs. Harry, the Earl of Stanhope, unrepentant rogue, scoundrel, bane of every innocent young lady's existence had been in love? Why did envy knife her heart? "Oh," she whispered. Because really, what else was there to say to the staggering realization—Harry had buried truths of his own.

He placed his hands on the gold arms of her chair and leaned close. His breath fanned her cheek, a delicious blend of mint and lemon. "Won't you ask questions, sweet? Don't you want to know the story of Miss Margaret Dunn?"

She furrowed her brow. No, she really didn't care to hear one bit about this Miss Margaret someone-or-another who'd held his affection.

They studied one another in stony silence. With mention of some faceless young lady, Harry suddenly belonged to another. Anne frowned, regret turning inside her belly. She, for some inexplicable reason, preferred a world in which he was the grinning, teasing gentleman who courted her—if even just to school her on the art of seduction. "What happened?" Did that whispery soft question belong to her?

"She possessed a beauty men waged wars for."

Anne's stomach twisted into a thousand pained knots. With her silly gold ringlets, she'd never inspire that level of passion and devotion in him. She blinked. Anyone. She'd meant she would never inspire that level of passion and devotion in *anyone*.

"She was a baronet's daughter," he carried on, and she prayed he remained unaware of the envy sluicing through her. "She had a gentle voice, a clear laugh, and I was captivated the moment I first saw her." Unlike Anne, who'd nearly driven him to madness since *their* initial meeting. A hard smile curved his lips. "And men clamored for her. Dueled for her even."

The scandal. She dug her fingers into her palm so hard she nearly drew blood. "You fought a duel for her," she whispered. Oh, the fool. She imagined a world with him no longer in it, all for a woman undeserving of his love and loyalty. Agony wrenched her heart.

"I was a callow youth. Just twenty-two years."

Not so very young. He'd been a man who surely knew his own heart. After all, at twenty, nearly twenty-one years, she very well knew *her* heart.

"I fought the Marquess of Rutland for the right to the lady's affection."

Rutland. Her eyes slid closed. Oh, God. The very same gentleman whose name she'd bandied about to enlist Harry's aid. What must he think? "I didn't know," she whispered.

He waved her off as though her apology was nothing more than a fleck of dust upon his sleeve. "It was long ago. Eight years," he added. "I was young." His lips turned up again in that mocking smile. "Young and foolish. We fought to first blood." He touched one of her golden curls. "You don't seem surprised by my admission."

There was the hint of a question in there. She tipped up her chin. "It will take more than mere mention of a duel to scandalize me. My brother-in-law, Aldora's husband, Michael, he fought a duel as well." She sighed. She'd never understand the foolish ways men sought to settle disputes. Even with her desire for stability, she ached to know love. But she'd not ask, expect, or *want* any man to risk his life upon a field of honor for her. "You'd have died for her?"

"I would have." His automatic response gutted her.

Silence fell between them. Pain pulled at her heart as she studied him, considering the story he'd shared. He'd not always been this affable rogue. He'd become this after his heart had been broken. He had risked all for love and in the end . . . She cocked her head. "What happened?" In the end, neither Harry nor Lord Rutland had earned the lady's fidelity.

A taunting smile pulled at his lips. "She craved a lofty title and wealth, Anne."

She frowned. The only word missing from that pronouncement was, *too*. The manner in which he made that last admission bore an almost accusatory edge, as though he'd judged her and found her as guilty as the woman who'd broken his heart. And Anne loathed being placed in that same, damning category as his past love. She folded her arms and unable to meet his eyes, looked at the expert lines of his immaculately folded white cravat. *I am not that woman. I am not that woman.*

But aren't you?

Harry went on, relentless. "She pledged her love, I pledged mine."

Anne glanced at him once more and wished she hadn't.

He'd fixed his gaze to the top of her hairline and in that moment she was forgotten to him. His disregard wrenched at her. He continued, driving the daggers of pain all the deeper. "I intended to offer her marriage." Her heart spasmed. "I arrived with a bouquet of flowers and a silly sonnet in my hand, to speak first with her father." A cold, humorless chuckle escaped him. "Her father laughed. Why would he accept the hand of an earl for his daughter when she could have a duke?"

Anne drew in a slow, shocked breath under a staggering truth. Even as she craved the stability and security the Duke of Crawford represented, she wanted love. Wanted it more than anything, and knew if she'd secured the heart of a good, kind gentleman who penned her sonnets and loved her with his whole heart, she'd have traded all the titles of duchess in England. She pressed her eyes closed. God help her, she was as imprudent as her mother and terror gripped her at how easily she might allow herself to become an equally shamed creature betrayed by love.

"What? Nothing to say, sweet?" he asked, his tone, harsher than she ever remembered.

In this very moment, Anne despised herself for having involved him in this scheme that had resurrected the pain of his past. "Perhaps she had her reasons," she said softly, wishing she could spare him the agony of his lost love.

He shoved away from her chair. "Only a mercurial lady with"—he slashed his hand in the direction of her piles of ribbons—"a love of material possessions and a vain sense of her beauty to fear being a bespectacled miss would say as much."

His words held her frozen. She stared blankly down at the stacks of ribbons upon the floor, seeing them the way he must surely see them; an endless pile of fripperies belonging to a self-indulgent young lady. He could never realize the irrational fear that still kept her awake at night, of a day when the creditors would come calling. The world was an unkind one to women. It was even more unkind to women left in dun territory. Her collection of ribbons didn't represent a love of the material. Rather, they represented her fear of living in a state of destitution once more. Yet . . . she couldn't tell him this, for it would only serve to make her less desirable in his—or any man's—eyes. "Is that what you see?" she asked softly. "A selfish creature living for material comforts?"

He scoffed. "How else should I see it?"

His condemnation, this same low opinion he carried of her, shared by everyone, burned, and that which she'd buried long ago, boiled over. "How dare you?" she asked, feeding the faint stirrings of fury because it dulled the ache of knowing just how little Harry thought of her when he so revered dear Katherine. "My father was a wastrel." She took a step toward him, suddenly wanting him to understand, *needing* him to understand. "A drunkard, Harry. A profligate gambler, a man who betrayed his wife." Though Mother had never dared breathe the words aloud, Anne had heard the hushed rumors when she'd made her Come Out. "He had a mistress whom he loved and kept comfortable." Her throat worked spasmodically. "Even while he wagered away his own family's stability and security."

"Anne, I didn't—"

She took another step closer, her abrupt movement cut into his gruff words. "What? You didn't know?" He'd merely assumed like everyone else that her life had been one way when in actuality it had been quite another. His expression grew shuttered. "You didn't know that my family lost everything because of my father's wagering?" Anne looked beyond his shoulder, her throat working painfully. "The staff was the first to be let go." Individuals who'd been with her family as long as Anne could remember. "Then the creditors took everything. They even took my ribbons." Her voice broke and she hated the sign of weakness. Surely he mistook it as a love of her, as he'd called it, material possessions. Except, it had been easier to focus on the loss of ribbons than the loss of servants who'd been more like family to the Adamson siblings over the years. She forced herself to look at him. "With the exception of one orange scrap, they claimed every last silly strip. It will forever remind me of the perils of giving my heart to a roguish scoundrel." She would *never* make her mother's mistake.

The harshness within the angular plains of Harry's face softened. He held a hand out, his silence more powerful than any words he might have spoken.

She felt bare before him. Splayed open for him to see the secrets she carried, many secrets not even known by her family, and yet she wanted to turn over the burden of her past to another.

Nay, not just anyone. Harry. She needed to share this piece of herself with him, so mayhap he could understand she was not the vain creature he'd taken her for. "When I was a young girl I couldn't fathom what value there was to be had in the silly scraps of fabric." Anne bent down and retrieved the forgotten satin strips. She rubbed them in her hands. The glaringly bright, cheerful colors mocked her with the reminder of her past. A bitter laugh bubbled past her lips. "As though they could have managed to cover any of Father's colossal debt." Through the years, those inexpensive fripperies had come to represent more—the necessity of having a steadfast, unwavering husband who'd never betray his family in the manner her own father had. She folded her arms and hugged herself. "They took Katherine's books and my brother's toy soldiers, but for the handful I buried in the gardens." She came to stand before him, so close the tips of their toes brushed. "The memory of that loss and fear didn't die with my father as you might expect."

"You're wrong," he said, his voice husky. "I didn't imagine that wouldn't shape you."

"Yes, everything we experience in life shapes, us, doesn't it? It forges us into the people we are today." Anne glanced at her useless ribbons and recalled Lady Ava Westmoreland's fingers dancing upon her cherished pianoforte keys. "And I"—she looked back at him—"I live with the constant reminders of that past. I have to see it, witness it, remember it at recitals where other women play my instrument, won for them by their f-father . . ." She paused to collect herself, hating the manner in which her voice broke, almost as much as she loathed the flash of pity in Harry's eyes. "I would have traded that pianoforte and every last ribbon for a father devoted to his family."

"I'm so s—"

Anne held her palms up, not wanting his pity, rather wanting him to understand. "I'll not be destitute again. Not because I'm avaricious, as you've accused me, but because I knew the terror of lying awake and wondering what is to become of my family. So don't you judge me, Harry. Don't you—"

He folded her in his arms and kissed the remainder of the words from her lips.

Chapter 8

*H*arry kissed her. He'd only intended to silence her. Cowardly bastard that he was, he'd needed to bury her words that forced him to imagine Anne as a small girl with great, big blue eyes and golden ringlets lying in bed, staring up at the ceiling hiding a single scrap of orange satin, while her scapegrace of a father wagered away her ribbons. He wanted to cut the flow of words from her sweet lips, because he preferred to think of her as a cold, calculated miss in search of a lofty title, who fit neatly into a category alongside the Miss Margaret Dunns of the world.

With her admission, however, she'd forced him to recognize the fear that drove her marital aspirations. Most young ladies craved flowers and sonnets, but his Anne, she craved security.

And God help him, in that moment she made him wish he were the kind of man she deserved. A man who'd give up his clubs and drink and the strings of mistresses to make her his wife. But he could never be that man. He'd given away his heart and he'd not do so again. Not when there was nothing left of the useless organ.

So, he kissed her. Kissed her so his blasted heart didn't ache in remembrance of the forlorn frown on her lips at Lady Westmoreland's recital that now made sense. Kissed her until she twined her long fingers about his neck and moaned into his mouth. Kissed her until his body hardened against her belly. Kissed her until he knew from her gasping pants that desire replaced despair.

He slanted his lips over hers again and again as he longed to learn the taste of her. A hint of berry, a hint of lemon. She was a veritable dessert a man could feast on for the remainder of his days, and just then, he wanted to be that man.

"Harry." His name escaped her lips; a desperate entreaty that jerked him back to sanity.

He pulled back and she made a sound of protest. Harry pulled free the neat combs that held her hair in place. Her golden tresses tumbled around her shoulders and back like a waterfall of pure sun. His gut clenched as he imagined the satin strands fanning his pillow while he came over her and laid claim to her. He kissed her eyelids, her cheek. He trailed his lips lower to the elegant line of her neck where her pulse beat wildly. He nipped and sucked at the smooth flesh until her knees collapsed and he caught her against his chest.

Harry planted a hard kiss at the corner of her temple. "This is how you should wear your hair, Anne. Not in tight ringlets," Though, those ringlets he'd once thought silly now seemed to suit her. "Beautiful and free, just as you are. They should caress your shoulders and breasts." He brushed his hand over her modest décolletage.

She blinked and shoved him. He stumbled at the unexpectedness of the movement. Anne dragged her fingers through a mass of golden curls with frantic movements, restoring her hair to rights. "Is that what this was, Harry?" she asked, her words bleeding hurt. "Another lesson on the art of seduction?"

He stiffened. Despite her charged accusation, it hadn't been. His kiss had begun as something far more, when he, Harry, the Earl of Stanhope, never *gave* more. What had been an attempt to drive the sadness from her eyes and the damned ache in his heart had become . . . *this*.

And he'd not regret having taken her in his arms but he would never forgive himself if Anne came to believe there could ever be more between them. Not when she'd stated in no uncertain terms the respectable, flawless gentleman she desired.

He forced a grin to his lips. "Isn't that what you sought me out for, sweet?" She recoiled at his deliberately cruel and mocking tone. "For a lesson on how to seduce Crawford?" he asked, all the while knowing his words would only drive her away from him and into the duke's arms. His gut clenched at the mere thought of the other man. In thinking his name, in being Crawford and not a mere title, he became somehow more real and Harry detested him for it. The proper, staid Duke of Crawford was what Anne deserved and not a man such as Harry, too much like her shameful father.

She searched his face. "Why are you doing this?" She stuffed her curls back behind her ears in an attempt to put her hair to rights.

He cursed and spun her around.

"What . . . ?"

Harry quickly tucked her golden ringlets into the delicate butterfly combs at the base of her head. He shifted her around and studied his work. She no longer appeared as though she'd been one kiss away from a thorough bout of lovemaking on the parlor sofa. What a travesty.

Anne turned back; a pinched set to her mouth. "You're very proficient with a lady's hair."

Again, her words bore the faintest traces of jealousy, that dangerously dark emotion that had no place between them.

He arched an eyebrow. "You sound disappointed, sweet—"

"Stop calling me sweet," she bit out.

"Most women appreciate my—"

She slapped him. Hard.

Harry flexed his jaw. Christ, the woman was far stronger than most gents he'd faced in Gentleman Jackson's ring. He rubbed the wounded flesh.

"You don't have to be crude," she said, backing away from him. He took a step toward her. She held a hand up. "D-do not, H-harry."

"Do you think I'd hurt you?" he snapped. The idea she should fear him burned like acid thrown upon an open wound.

She wrinkled her brow. "Of course not." She gave a toss of her ringlets. "I'm cross with you."

"Cross?"

She nodded. "Cross." The tension eased from her taut frame. "You needn't worry I've come to care for you," she said with a remarkable insight. She caught a loose tress and gave it a distracted tug. "I would never be so naïve as to believe a kiss from you would mean anything more."

Harry jerked erect. Her words, intended to reassure, instead ran through him with a savage intensity. He remained silent.

She leaned over and patted his hand. "I've enlisted your support to garner the duke's affection. I understood your rule, Harry." He started, having forgotten he'd put any rules to her madcap scheme. "I'm not to fall in love with you." Had he said that? Anne continued, unaware of his inner strife. "So you needn't be crude or ungentlemanly or condescending," she added that last under her breath.

He bit back a smile. "You'd have me teach you the art of seduction in a way that is gentlemanly and polite, then?"

She nodded again. "Precisely."

He opened his mouth to point out that he was the last person to instruct her on anything proper or polite.

A knock sounded at the door. They looked as one to the doorway to where the butler stood with a familiar, increasingly loathsome, ducal figure. Harry fisted his hands at his side.

The servant glared at Harry as though he recognized a scoundrel in his midst. He cleared his throat, and gave his attention to Anne. "My lady, His Grace, the Duke of Crawford."

The duke swept in as if he was the King of England coming to call. He glanced around the room, and then he fixed a frown on Harry. The message clear. *I've selected my duchess.*

"Crawford," Harry drawled.

Anne dropped a deep, deferential curtsy. A becoming pink blush stained her cheeks and her eyes darted about the room. Standing as close as they were, he heard her slight sigh as her maid appeared.

"My lady, forgive me." A young maid swept in. "I retrieved your book." She held up a copy of *Mrs. Deerlander's Guide to Decorum.*

If the Duke of Crawford believed one, that a passionate spirit like Lady Anne would spend even a moment reading even a word of that drivel; two, the maid's ruse to explain away the lack of chaperone; and three, that Harry would interfere in the other man's courtship, well, then he was as mad as a Bedlamite streaking the halls of that infamous hospital.

Anne rushed forward. "Thank you, Mary," she said quickly. She took the book in her hands, hands that mere moments ago had twisted and twined about Harry's neck like a tenacious vine of ivy. She shifted under the duke's scrutiny, the leather volume held almost protectively to her chest.

Crawford walked over to her, placing himself between her and Harry. He claimed her hand and raising her fingers to his lips, brushed his mouth over the inside of her wrist.

The pink hue of her cheeks blazed a bold red.

Harry clenched his hands into tight balls at his side, filled with an inexplicable urge to separate the bastard's fingers from his person. Over the duke's shoulder, Anne met his gaze.

The tall, commanding duke with ice in his eyes followed the direction of her stare. He arched a ducal eyebrow at Harry.

Harry tugged at the lapels of his coat. It was on the tip of his lips to order the other man to hell and claim a spot beside the scattered pile of ribbons. Except, something flashed in Anne's eyes. An entreaty. A plea. Her meaning could not have been clearer than if she'd clambered onto the sofa and shouted the words. *Go.*

He gave a quick bow. "Lady Anne, Crawford. I'll leave you two to your visit." He spun on his heel and beat a hasty retreat. Ultimately, Anne seemed to remember what he'd allowed himself to forget. Their every interaction, their every meeting was a ploy to garner Crawford's notice and prompt an offer on the other man's part.

It would seem the lady's plan had worked brilliantly. Harry would soon be well-rid of the tart-mouthed Lady Anne Adamson.

Harry cursed under his breath, and took his leave. He should be elated with the rapidity of Crawford's interest.

So why was he so bloody miserable?

Anne stared at Harry's swift-retreating back and resisted the urge to call out, ask him to stay. Despite of all her earlier, preconceived notions about the roguish Earl of Stanhope, he'd proven himself to be kind and decent. She stared down at her palm, the skin still stinging from the slap she'd dealt him. Regret tugged at her. God help her, she enjoyed being with Harry. *Missed* him, even now with the illustrious Duke of Crawford in her parlor.

"My lady? I trust you are well?"

She jumped, pressing her hand to her heart. "Er . . . uh, yes . . . most well," she said on a rush. Her maid gave her a pointed look from across the room and from over the duke's shoulder gestured to the sofa.

Anne motioned to the seat. "Would you care to sit, Your Grace?"

Mary nodded.

The duke inclined his head. "I would," he murmured, coolly polite.

From across the room, Mary held up an imaginary glass and raised it to her lips.

"Refreshments!" The single-word utterance burst from her lips. The duke quirked an eyebrow. She fanned her hot cheeks, and then remembered herself. "That is," she said, her tone even, "would you care for refreshments, Your Grace?"

"I imagine I have all I need in terms of sustenance for the day with your company, my lady."

Anne's mouth pulled and she buried the grimace in her fingers. Egad, had she really desired a silly sonnet penned on her behalf? Harry's face flashed into her mind. With his bold assertions and his unrepentant words, she found she preferred the honesty in his responses than in the duke's overdone compliments. She sat in the King Louis XIV chair and rested the book on her lap, wishing for the uncomplicatedness of life before Harry when there was nothing more than the dream of security and stability to be had in the role of duchess.

The duke sat at the edge of the sofa so that their knees brushed. "And what does a lovely young lady take enjoyment reading, Lady Anne?"

Scandalous Gothic novels. Shameless tales of unrequited love and gentlemen vying for a lady's hand. With someone ultimately always meeting an untimely, ugly demise. She glanced down at the book her maid had brought her and silently cursed the excuse orchestrated by Mary to explain her absence during Harry's earlier visit. She handed the leather volume over to the duke.

He examined the title. "I imagine a lady such as you wouldn't need the help of anyone to maintain proper ladylike decorum."

One of Mother's favorites: *Mrs. Deerlander's Guide to Decorum.*

Did she imagine the hint of rebuke buried in the duke's words? "Oh, quite the opposite, Your Grace," she said blandly, disabusing him of any notions he carried about her suitability as his future duchess. "It is likely why my mother is insisting I read it."

A half-grin pulled at his lips. If she were being perfectly honest with herself, she'd admit he was a rather handsome gentleman. Even more than pleasantly handsome. With thick chestnut hair, fashionably cropped, and a powerful blue-eyed stare that could bore into a person's soul. When most of the other dukes were doddering old letches with monocles held to their eyes, His Grace possessed a tall, well-muscled form. His smile deepened, though it never quite reached his eyes. "You're a delight, my lady."

His platitudes set her teeth on edge. Confectionary treats and ices from Gunter's were a delight. People were not. "Oh, not at all. I'm the bane of my mother's existence," she said, with the lack of appreciation that had made many a wall-flower into spinsters. *Stop talking, immediately, Anne. You'll drive him away.*

"Oh?"

She angled her head, wagering he'd perfected that haughty ducal eyebrow-arching business as a small boy. "She claims I'm too spirited," she went on. From across the room, Mary groaned.

"Is there such a thing, my lady?"

And in that moment, the proper, respectable duke who'd paled in the shadow of Harry, rose in her estimation. She leaned over and dropped her voice to a low whisper. "I imagine a duke would expect a lady to be perfectly proper and not at all spirited." Her words seemed to carry over to the maid for Mary dropped her head into her hands and shook it forlornly back and forth.

The duke either failed to notice or care about the beleaguered servant in the corner, for he said, "I imagine a demure, too-proper lady would make for a very dull duchess."

"Which is how most gentleman would prefer their wives," she rejoined.

He leaned down. "I assure you they do not, my lady." His breath fanned her ear.

"Oh."

He sat back in his chair, a challenge in his eyes, daring her to ask questions about what type of lady gentlemen, in fact, preferred. Only, such an intimate topic was not one she'd care to discuss with the duke. Even if she would have him as her husband, she could not boldly engage in his repartee. Not in the way she did with the charming, affable, Earl of Stanhope.

The duke drummed his fingers on the arms of the sofa, cutting into the awkward stretch of silence.

She detested this newfound preference for charming, affable gentleman.

Anne mustered a smile, and shifted the discussion to safer, more appropriate topics. "I imagine it would gall my mother if I were to fail and initiate proper matters of discourse. May I?"

He tipped his head. "Please, do."

She glanced to the window. "We're enjoying splendid weather, Your Grace."

He lifted his head, his gaze fastened to her. "We are."

Anne tapped her feet distractedly upon the floor. "You're to respond with some comment about the sun or the rain."

"The sunlight pales when compared with your beauty."

She wanted his words to wash over her with warmth and send fluttery little sensations spiraling through her being. She truly did. Alas, they stirred not even the faintest hint of awareness. She slid her gaze off to the opposite end of the room.

What am I?

A clever, inquisitive miss, with lots of questions . . .

"Do you play, my lady?"

She froze midtap. "Do I play what?"

He waved a hand in the direction of her beloved piano-forte, a gift given her by Aldora and Michael, the obscenely wealthy second son of a marquess, who'd saved them all from certain ruin.

"I do," she murmured.

"Would you do me the honor of playing for me, my lady?"

Anne paused. Part of her longed to resist the ducal command contained within that question. If her mother ever discovered such a slight, she'd have Anne wed to horrible Mr. Ekstrom by special license that next morning.

With a curt nod, she came to her feet, wandered over to the instrument, and ran her fingertips along the ivory keyboard. She slid into her seat and stared blankly down at the keys. What song did a young lady sing when attempting to ensnare a duke?

You'll sing in a husky, sultry, contralto . . .

She opened her mouth and proceeded to sing him Dibdin's *A Matrimonial Thought* in her pure contralto. As the duke's eyes widened with appreciation, she wished she sang in a sultry, husky contralto for an altogether different gentleman.

Chapter 9

*H*arry stared into his partially filled tumbler of brandy. He rolled the amber brew around in his glass and ignored the casual greetings tossed at him from gentlemen at White's.

My father was a wastrel, Harry. A drunkard. A profligate gambler, a womanizer . . .

He set his glass down with a hard thunk and shoved it aside. The image he'd earned in Society as an unrepentant rogue was one he'd welcomed, or even appreciated. The *ton* recognized in him a gentleman who'd not become embroiled in emotional entanglements. Ladies vied for a place in his bed, knowing because of that reputation there was little hope of attaining his heart; a heart he'd carefully protected after Margaret's betrayal.

Margaret had opened his eyes to the truth—women were parsimonious, indulgent creatures and he'd neatly placed Anne into the category of grasping young ladies.

Until now.

After baiting Anne about her collection of satin ribbons, he'd learned there was, in fact, a good deal more to the young lady than beauty with a mercurial desire for material possessions. In just a handful of days, she had shattered all the notions he'd carried of her as an empty-headed, self-indulgent, title-grasping miss.

Instead, he saw a woman who'd braved great trials in her young life and had been shaped by them. She was a lady who'd be the arbiter of her own fate, and in a world where women were considered mere property of their husbands, Anne would find security where she could.

She'd selected her duke, enlisted Harry's aid to attain that duke, and in that, would steal what freedom she could as a woman in a world dominated by men who'd wager the happiness of their wives and daughters on a game of chance.

Since leaving her, he found he rather hated himself for the hard-won reputation that placed him into the class of cads like her father. The world of black and white he'd lived in after Margaret's betrayal, and before he'd truly come to know Anne, ceased to exist, ushering in a less certain shade between.

"Tsk, tsk. First courting proper, English misses, and now visiting White's instead of Forbidden Pleasures. The lady has quite the hold over you, doesn't she?"

Harry glanced up. His friend Lord Edgerton grinned down at him. He sighed. "Edgerton. Don't you have a sister to escort around?"

"Two of them to be exact," his friend muttered. "At Lord and Lady Huntly's soiree." He hooked his foot under the chair opposite Harry and tugged it out then settled into the seat, just as a servant rushed forward with a glass. Without asking, he picked up the bottle and sloshed several fingers into his glass.

"Perhaps you should get yourself there," Harry drawled. All he knew was that he preferred his solitary musings to his friend's company this evening.

Edgerton grinned. He raised his glass in salute. "Then, one of the benefits of being the spare is being absolved from most responsibilities."

Harry wouldn't know much of it. As the only son of the late Earl of Stanhope, he'd never had a sibling and both of his parents had died when he'd been in his early days at university. His responsibilities through the years had been to the title and his own self-comforts. And for a very small while—Margaret. He expected the familiar rush of hurt bitterness—a bitterness that did not come.

"I imagined with your courtship of a certain creature with golden ringlets, you'd be at the lady's side."

He eyed his barely touched brandy, filled with a longing to drink until he was bloody soused so he wouldn't have to think about the agreement he'd entered into with Anne. Considering Crawford's early afternoon visit, Anne was one near-offer of marriage away from ending Harry's role in the whole blasted scheme. He gripped the edge of the table so hard his knuckles turned white. "I intend to put in an appearance at Lady Huntly's later this evening," he said at last. After all, he'd pledged his support.

Edgerton took a sip of his brandy. "I'd venture you'd be better served going to Huntly's sooner rather than later, chap." His friend dangled that damned bit, attempting intrigue.

Harry swallowed down a curse. "What are you on about?"

Edgerton waved over to the betting book at White's. "Wagers have been placed that the young lady will find herself the next Duchess of Crawford. And you, my good friend, are already at a great disadvantage with a mere earldom."

Harry growled. He'd not let his friend bait him.

"Rumors have it, Crawford is quite taken with the young lady." His lips turned up in a wry smile. "Though I must say I don't see the fascination with a proper English miss with those silly ringlets—"

Taken with the young lady. "They are not silly," he mumbled under his breath. And why shouldn't the spirited beauty charm Crawford?

"Crawford was seen with the young lady at Gunter's yesterday afternoon."

After Harry had taken his leave of her. His body went taut.

Edgerton chuckled, seeming unbothered by carrying on a conversation with himself. He settled his elbows on the table and waggled his brow. "The gossip sheets report the duke didn't remove his gaze from the lady's—"

Harry surged to his feet. He started for the door. As he wound his way through the club, past throngs of dandies and crowded tables, he dimly registered his friend hastening to match his step.

"What in hell is the matter with you, Stanhope?" Edgerton groused.

"Nothing," he bit out.

The majordomo pulled the door open and they took their leave. His friend scratched his brow. "Is this about Crawford and your Lady Anne?"

He peered around the crowded street for sign of his carriage. "No." *Yes.* "And she is not *my* Lady Anne." He took a step toward the street as his driver wound through the clogged roadway. Filled with a restive energy he strode onward toward his conveyance. His driver hopped down and opened the carriage door. Harry climbed inside.

Edgerton followed suit. "She is clearly something to you, Stanhope," he said with far more solemnity than Harry remembered of his friend.

He clenched his jaw hard enough that pain shot up to his temple. "She is not."

Edgerton rested his ankle over his knee and tapped his foot. "I certainly hope you'd not be fool enough to toss away wasted emotion on a woman such as her." He knew of the empty shell of a man Harry had become immediately after Margaret's betrayal. They'd drank together until the liquor had dulled Harry's pain. And the day she'd wed her lofty duke, a doddering old letch from some far-flung corner of England, Harry drank some more. Then when he was bleary-eyed with too much liquor and a broken heart, Edgerton got him home, and restored him to the carefree rogue he'd been before Margaret.

"I assure you, Edgerton, there is nothing more there. The young lady enlisted my support on a matter." A matter he didn't intend to discuss with even his friend. "And as a friend to Lady Katherine, I've agreed to help her." His involvement with Anne had begun as a kind of unknowing favor to the young duchess who'd captured his attention last Season. Only, since that scandalous proposal Anne had put to him in Lord Essex's conservatory, some great shift had occurred—a desire to help the young minx who'd once been nothing more than a bother.

His friend studied him. He appeared ready to say an additional piece on Harry's succinct admission, but the carriage rocked to a halt in front of a pale-yellow townhouse ablaze with candlelight, cutting into the other man's words.

The driver pulled open the carriage door. Harry leapt out and started for the handful of steps leading into the luxurious Mayfair townhouse. His friend hastened to match his stride. They entered the palatial townhouse and made their way to the now empty receiving line. From his vantage at the top of the ballroom, he scanned the dance floor and frowned.

"Are you, perchance, looking for a particular young lady?" his friend asked with entirely too much humor. "Perhaps, a young lady who means absolutely nothing to you?"

"Stuff it," Harry said as the host and hostess rushed forward to greet the two newly arrived gentlemen. He stalked off just as the couple reached him. Lady Huntly rocked back on her heels with an indignant huff. Edgerton, ever the charmer, remained behind to speak to the couple with matching stark-white hair and wizened cheeks.

Harry walked the perimeter of the ballroom. A servant stepped forward. The liveried footman bore a silver tray with bubbling French champagne. Harry rescued a glass and continued his search. Where in hell was she? He paused beside a Doric column and leaned against the white, towering structure, scanning the rows of couples performing the lively steps of a reel. He'd taken care to find out the precise details of the lady's plans for the evening. Perhaps the information his servants had obtained from her servants had been erroneous.

The music came to a rousing conclusion, followed by a wave of applause and laughter from the crush of dancers upon the dance floor. He sipped his champagne as gentlemen escorted their respective partners back to their chaperones, methodically running his gaze through the crowd for the ringlet-wearing, cheeky young miss.

"Lord Stanhope," a sultry voice purred.

He froze as a figure sidled up to him. He glanced down disinterestedly as the Viscountess Kendricks brushed herself against him. The generous swells of her breasts crushed hard against his arm. She peered up at him through sooty black lashes.

Harry yawned. "Lady Kendricks." Had he really once desired the overblown, pinch-mouthed viscountess?

A catlike smile turned her thin lips up at the corners. Though, if she knew the exact direction of Harry's thoughts, she'd be spitting and hissing like a wounded feline. "Are you bored, my lord?" She stroked a bold finger over the sleeve of his coat. "I can imagine all manner of delicious ways to drive away your tedium."

Three days ago, he'd have jerked his chin toward the back of the ballroom and led the scandalous widow to one of the rooms in his host's home. He'd have tugged up her skirts and made fast and hard love to her and then returned to the ball with a still-bored grin. Now, he shrugged free of her touch and continued to survey the milling guests.

"I missed you the other night, my lord."

"Did you?" he murmured.

"Have you heard a word I've said?" she snapped, the wasp-ish bite to her question at odds with the husky, sultry tone she adopted in most of her exchanges.

"No," he said. He beat a quick bow. "If you'll—" The air exploded from his lungs on a rush. The viscountess forgotten, he took a step forward. Then another. And froze.

An Athena with hair dipped in pure gold stood at the edge of the crowded dance floor. She tapped a hand against her thigh as if in time to the one-two-three beat of the orchestra's tune.

Close your mouth. Breathe. Do something. Do anything.

The glorious beauty, somehow familiar, and yet not, brushed back a long wisp of honey-blonde hair away from her cheek. Glorious tresses hung in loose waves about her cream-white shoulders. Athena stiffened. She angled her head as if aware of his scrutiny. Or mayhap she registered the interest of every single gentleman with red blood coursing through his veins, fixed on the perfection of her body, bathed in the soft candlelight.

Then their gazes caught and held.

Harry jerked, as if Gentleman Jackson had delivered a swift, well-placed jab to his midsection.

The pale-blue irises of her fathomless eyes danced with fury.

Anne.

If Anne was perhaps as good with words as Aldora, she'd have something far more potent, more powerful than "spitting mad." But blast and hell . . . she was spitting mad. She yanked her attention away from Harry.

The blighter.

First, there was the whole business at his club, the Forbidden Pleasures, two nights past. It had taken her the better part of the afternoon following her trip to Gunter's with the Duke of Crawford to squint her way through the page about just how Lord Harry had spent his evening after he'd left the recital. Then, if that wasn't enough to boil a lady's blood, he'd not come 'round for the whole of a day. She tossed her loose waves. Waves not ringlets. As *he'd* suggested.

The bounder.

And the only reason she cared about his absence was the whole business of his lessons on seduction. A lesson each day, he'd pledged. Well, now he owed her two lessons for this nearly completed day.

Only . . . she looked back to the spot he'd been a moment ago, now vacant. He was assuredly with that scandalous Viscountess Kendricks. The very same woman whose assignation Anne had interrupted five days ago.

She bit the inside of her cheek hard enough to draw blood. She gasped and slapped her hand to the injured area.

"Is there a problem, my lady?"

At the dry, far-too amused baritone she bit down hard on the same poor piece of wounded flesh. She gasped again. "Blast, don't you know to not sneak up on a lady?" She despised the manner in which her heart sped up at Harry's sudden appearance.

He'd not followed his viscountess. Instead, he'd come to Anne. Why should that cause this fluttery warmth to unfurl inside her belly, she did not know. Anne continued to study the couples as they performed the delicate steps of a quadrille. "And there is no problem," she said as an afterthought to his earlier question. *There are several problems, you rogue. Your absence, your interest in the viscountess, your promise to school me in the art of seduction, your—*

"You're frowning," Harry pointed out, a smile in his words.

"Am I?" Which meant he studied her, at least enough to notice whether she frowned or smiled.

"You are. As is your mother. In fact, she has a rather nasty glower trained on the both of us."

"With good reason," Anne muttered under her breath. "You're an unrepentant rogue."

He grinned as though she'd handed him the finest compliment. Which she hadn't. She'd intended her words to sting an apparent conscienceless gentleman. "Shall I wave to her?"

Anne stole a glance at her mother, who stood conversing with the Marchioness of Townsend. "You'll do no such thing." Though there was some merit to Harry's observation about Mother. The truth of the matter was that the countess had been furious since Anne had appeared in the foyer with her golden ringlets gone and her loose tresses partially pinned up, the other locks draped about her back and shoulders. The black look in her mother's eyes suggested she knew very well who to blame for the scandalous arrangement.

And it *hadn't* been her maid, Mary.

In fact, if they'd not already been extremely late to Lady Huntly's soiree, Anne suspected her mother would have ordered her abovestairs and stood over Mary until each strand of hair was restored to a proper ringlet.

She fingered one of the flowing locks. *This is how you should wear your hair, Anne. Not in tight ringlets, but beautiful and free, just as you are. They should caress your shoulders and breasts . . .*

Her mouth screwed up. Yet, for all his opinion of her silly ringlets, he'd not made a mention of her hair. Not that she cared about Harry's opinion of her ringlets or lack thereof. After all, her intention was to secure the Duke of Crawford's hand. She merely wanted to know whether she'd affected the appropriate look.

Liar.

Harry leaned ever closer and whispered into her ear. "What has so captivated you, sweet, that—?"

"Do not call me sweet. *Especially* not here."

All traces of his relaxed humor fled. "You won't even deign to look at me?"

She clasped her hands primly in front of her and stole a peek at him from the corner of her eye. "I'm merely trying to better study . . ." He quirked a golden eyebrow. "The dancers," she finished lamely. The set concluded.

Lord Forde, a pleasantly handsome, young viscount rumored to be in the market for a wife came forward to claim his set. A waltz.

"Forde?" Harry drawled, the single word a lazy whisper close to her ear.

"Lord Forde is an entirely congenial, *honorable*"—his eyes narrowed at her deliberate emphasis—"gentleman who would make a—"

The tall, lean gentleman in a sapphire coat drew to a stop before them.

"Get the hell out, Forde," Harry snapped, not so much as sparing a look for the viscount.

The other gentleman opened and closed his mouth like a fish plucked from a pond. He tugged at his lapels and spun on his heel. "Well," he mumbled.

Anne closed her eyes. "You cannot go cursing in the middle of the ballroom and running off my dance partners."

"The hell I can't," he muttered.

The orchestra struck up the beginning chords of a waltz. Harry held out his arm.

She stared at the corded muscles that tightened the black fabric of his coat and blinked rapidly. "What are you doing?"

"Claiming your next set. You don't have a partner."

Anne pointed her gaze to the ceiling. "Because you ran him off, my lord." Goodness, the unmitigated gall of him. He'd avoided her for days, brazenly seduced the viscountess in the midst of Lady Huntly's ball, ran off Lord Forde, a perfectly respectable partner, and now demanded her waltz.

"Anne?"

"Yes?"

"Take my arm," he commanded through gritted teeth.

"Charming," she muttered and placed her fingertips along his coat sleeve.

"What was that?" he asked as they reached the dance floor. He guided her hand to his shoulder and placed his long, powerful fingers at her waist.

Her skin burned at his touch upon her person. Her mouth went dry. "I merely was wondering that you'd ever be considered charming. Boorish. Rude. Pompous."

His gleaming white teeth flashed in a smile. The orchestra plucked the beginning strands of the waltz and Harry guided her through the ballroom in long, sweeping circles.

She directed her gaze to the folds of his cravat, determined to not let him bait her. Something that he seemed remarkably proficient in doing in the year they'd known one another. He applied a gentle pressure to her waist, forcing her stare upward.

"You seem more surly than usual, Anne."

"I'm not pleased with you, Harry," she said between gritted teeth.

"I gathered as much," he said dryly.

Suddenly, his high-handedness and worse, his singular lack of interest or notice boiled like a fresh-brewed pot of tea. "You did not come 'round." She curled her toes into the soles of her slipper at the revealing admission. And promptly stumbled.

Harry easily caught her. He righted her in his arms. "It's been a day." A gentle admonition underscored his response.

Pain slapped at her heart. Fool. Fool. Fool. *Why should I care about his singular lack of notice when he should be so indifferent toward me?* But blast and double blast . . . she did care. And she hated that she cared. She dipped her gaze to his cravat. "There are my lessons," she said. "You pledged to help me—"

He nudged her chin up. "And I am—"

"Each day."

He shook his head ruefully. "Did I truly say every day?"

Anne nodded solemnly. "Oh, yes. I'm certain of it." Though in actuality, she couldn't remember whether they'd settled on a specific number of visits or lessons. She pinched his shoulder. "You owe me a lesson"—she dropped her voice to a hushed whisper—"on seduction, Harry."

Chapter 10

You owe me a lesson on seduction, Harry . . .

Harry swallowed a groan as her huskily whispered words conjured all manner of delicious images that involved Anne Adamson spread out in all her naked glory in his bed, atop satin sheets, with her golden hair a silken waterfall about them. He strove for the indifferent, affable grin he'd perfected through the years.

Anne frowned. "Why are you grimacing?"

Apparently, he failed in his attempt.

She pinched his arm again. "You didn't grimace with your viscountess," she said, voice as tart as if she'd sucked on a slice of lemon peel.

"My—?"

"You know," she said on a furious whisper. "The lovely widow you're too busy carrying on with to honor your obligations to me. The one with the dampened gown. And your glasses of champagne."

So, Anne had noticed his exchange with the young widow? His lips twitched. "I—er, gathered which particular . . . uh viscountess you spoke of." The same woman he'd left furious at the edge of the ballroom, all to seek out Anne. He'd never been filled with this desperate hungering for the viscountess. "And how was your visit with Crawford?" he asked, turning the questions back on her.

She blinked. "Crawford?"

He angled her body closer to his and dipped his head down. "As in the Duke of Crawford, your future bridegroom."

"Oh, do hush." She pinched him again. "You'll be overhead by someone if you're not careful." A beatific smile wreathed her cheeks. "You were correct."

He quirked an eyebrow. "I'm correct on any number of scores. Which matter do you refer to?"

Anne laughed. "Oh, you're insufferable. I referred to your lesson on song."

She may as well have drawn back her leg and kicked him square in the gut. She'd sung to the duke. Her bow-shaped, red lips had parted in song for the damned, pompous prig, Crawford. An image wrapped its tentacle-like hold about his mind. Anne's lovely mouth open as she sang to a captive audience in the Duke of Crawford. The other man's eyes trained on her mouth and lower . . . Harry wanted to hunt him down and shred him with his bare hands for knowing whether Anne possessed a light, airy, lyrical tone when singing or the sultry, husky timbre that men waged wars over, when Harry himself did not.

He fixed his gaze on the top of her lush, golden-blonde curls, only to recall every blasted word he'd uttered about her luxuriant tresses being arranged exactly as they hung about her shoulders and this moment. And hating he'd ever dared such a seductive coiffure that now earned the attention of every living, breathing man in the room—from footmen to gentlemen.

"Is something wrong with my hair?" Anne continued. She touched the side of her head searching for wayward strands. "I'd thought, that is, you'd indicated . . ." her words trailed off on a sigh. "I thought you might like it." She gave him a small smile. "No more of my silly ringlets."

Had she been any other woman, he'd have believed her grasping for pretty compliments. With her matter-of-factness about everything from marriage and security to those neat little rows of ribbons she stacked, she continued to defy every idea he'd carried of her.

"There is nothing silly about you," he said quietly.

Anne snorted. "Now, you've gone all serious on me. Is this part of your next lesson?"

For the closeness between them these past four days, she still believed his every thought, his every action driven by the damned scheme to bring her duke up to scratch. He'd embraced the image of rogue, worn the societal label with a good deal of pride, for it sent a clear message to all—Harry, the Earl of Stanhope, did not possess a heart that could be broken. He'd embraced the image.

Until now.

She waggled an eyebrow, unaware of his inner strife.

"Smile with your eyes," he said when it became clear she saw in him nothing more than a means to a duke, "and your lips as one. A sultry, sweet smile, Anne. A smile that convinces a man he's the only one in the room. And eyes that beg to know all the forbidden things a lady has no right knowing."

Anne tipped her head. Her smile slipped and something passed between them. Something charged and volatile. With a life-force.

He sucked in a breath as the implications of his role truly registered. Or worse, the perils in teaching her to seduce another man when Harry himself would be left to wonder the color of her nipples, or the downy softness betwixt her thighs. And more . . . the sound of her laughter through the years. "You sang to Crawford, then?" he said quietly.

"I did."

He tightened his grip upon her person. She winced and he lightened his hold. "And did he appreciate the quality of your voice?" Never did he want to hear an answer less.

Anne ran her gaze over his face. "I don't want to talk about the duke, Harry."

His heart lifted in the oddest fashion. He blamed his reaction on too much liquor and remembered he'd not touched more than a glass of champagne the whole of the evening. "What do you want?" *Let the answer be me, and I will show you the true meaning of seduction.*

"I want my second lesson for the evening."

The chords of the waltz drew to a finish. Harry and Anne stopped amidst the politely clapping couples, gazes fixed on one another.

If he encouraged her bold proposition, he flirted with the parson's trap, a snare he'd no intention of succumbing to. "Meet me in Lord Huntly's conservatory," he said quietly. He bowed low at the waist and spun on his heel.

Anne's heart thudded painfully as she stared at Harry's powerful, now-retreating form.

Fingers touched her arm and she jumped. "What are you doing, sister?"

Anne's cheeks blazed and she turned to greet her sister. "Katherine, what are you doing here?" she blurted. First the recital, now a ball. Katherine and her husband made it a point to avoid nearly all societal functions. Their sudden appearance had Mother's hand over it more than the floral embroideries she'd stitched and displayed throughout their townhouse.

Katherine angled her head. A flash of hurt shone in her brown eyes. "You're not happy to see me." Dismay and shock blended together and underscored her words.

"No. No, that isn't true at all," she said hurriedly.

Too hurriedly.

She fisted the fabric of her skirts, knowing she was surely the world's worst twin. For instead of the usual joy she found in Katherine's company, she resented the reminder of her relationship with Harry. An unspoken communication passed between them. An apology. Forgiveness.

And then the determined warrior her sister had always proven herself to be, replaced the wounded figure who'd eyed Anne with accusation. Katherine guided her from the floor with all the precision of Lord Nelson leading his men at battle. "You have made some truly deplorable decisions through the years."

Anne bristled. "I have not."

"Hiding Father's ledgers. All of them."

She frowned. "It seemed like a good idea at the time." As a girl, when she'd first heard whisperings of their father's financial woes, Anne had believed if Father's business documents were lost, then he'd not be able to continue wagering away their family's wealth. Then, that had been the foolishness of a child's naïveté.

Her sister's mouth tightened and she continued to steer her through the crowd, onward past smiling couples.

"Where is your husband?" Anne ventured, wishing for her still terrifying brother-in-law's presence if for no other reason than to be spared from her sister's haranguing.

"Then there were the letters to that publisher."

When their family's circumstances had become truly dire, she'd penned her own Gothic novel and intended to seek publication as Mr. Robert Robertson. Alas, Mother had discovered her plans and tossed every last page of Mr. Robert Robertson's work into the fiery hearth.

Katherine gently squeezed her arm and forced her to a halt beside a removed alcove. "Then there were your plans for us to attend the Frost Fair. Unchaperoned."

And no one would have ever learned a hint of what had transpired upon the frozen Thames—if Katherine hadn't gone and fallen through the one patch of soft ice. "Need I point out that you'd not have met your husband? A duke, whom you very much love, if it weren't for my bad idea?"

Katherine pursed her lips in that disappointed way she'd done as a child when Anne had bested her at spillikin. "Very well. I'll concede you were correct on that particular score. However"—she cast a discreet glance about, and then looked to Anne once more—"dancing and flirting shamelessly with Lord Stanhope can never be considered a good idea."

"Whyever not?" He'd proven himself to be kinder, more patient, more *everything* than she'd ever before considered of the legendary rogue.

"I've seen the way he studies you, Anne," she said bluntly.

Her heart sped up.

"And do wipe that pleased little smile from your face. No good can come of anything with Harry."

Anne's stomach tightened at her twin's inadvertent use of his Christian name. Her gaze skittered away from her younger sister, who through the years seemed to believe she was the one a whole six minutes and seventeen seconds older.

A resigned sigh escaped her sister's lips. "I do not want to see you hurt. I know him," she said, her tone far gentler. Gone was the motherly, patronizing tone, replaced by this kindred spirit who'd shared nearly everything through the years with the exception of that first breath drawn as babes.

Prior to enlisting Harry's aid, she'd taken him for a carefree, indolent, conscienceless rogue. Now she knew him to be a man who'd had his heart broken by a title-grasping young woman, foolish enough to let him go. "I'll not be hurt, Kat. I'm not the empty-headed ninny you or Aldora or Mother or anyone else for that matter believes I am." There could never be anything between her and a man like Harry, whose heart would forever belong to another.

Her sister winced. "Surely you know I think you beautiful and kind and intelligent and . . ."

Anne laughed. "Oh, do hush. I know what I'm doing." A familiar figure pulled into focus across the ballroom floor. Even with the space between them, she detected the flash of gold in his hazel eyes. He inclined his head as if knowing just what, or rather, who, she and Katherine now spoke of. She winked at him. Harry's sharp bark of laughter carried through the ballroom, the low rumble moved through her and she smiled. There was something so very empowering in making a sophisticated gentleman like Harry—

"Are you listening to me, Anne?" her sister chided.

Anne took her twin's hands and gave them a squeeze. "I love you. I know you mean well. But I'd ask you to trust me."

As she took her leave, in search of Lord Huntly's conservatory, her sister's groan followed her. "I have heard that too many times before Anne Arlette Adamson."

Chapter 11

$\mathcal{A}$ nne imagined Mother England had faced lesser challenges than she had this evening trying to be rid of her quite obviously overprotective family members so she might meet Harry. After their set, Mother and Katherine had maintained a resolute presence at her side, until Anne began to feel like one of the heroines in her Gothic novels constantly trying to escape the vile clutches of an evil guardian.

After tearing her own hem, she'd at last managed to sneak off to see to her *gown*. Instead, she now made her way down the corridor of Lord Huntly's home. Heart pounding, blood racing, she braced for inevitable discovery. She came to the end of the hall and paused to peek around the corner.

She didn't know how Harry carried on this way. This clandestine business was enough to streak a young lady's hair with grey. She tapped her foot and considered which corridor to turn next. If she were Lord Huntly, where would she have a conservatory? It couldn't be at the left portion of the palatial townhouse as it—

Quiet whispers sounded down the corridor behind her.

Decision made. She sprinted down the right corridor and walked onward toward the back of Lord Huntly's home. Anne shook her head. She intended to ask Harry just what in thunderation the appeal was of all this furtive sneaking. She'd far prefer a proper picnic in Hyde Park or in some tucked-away copse in Kensington Gardens. Anne had a rather unromantic tendency to sneeze whenever a bloom was near. Which was rather unfortunate. Pale-pink peonies really were quite beautiful. Even with the cluster of ants that tended to make the unfurled bloom their home.

She drew to a halt. A thrilling sense of victory filled her as she stared at the clear, double doors leading to a final room. The conservatory.

Anne stole a quick glance around, and then tiptoed forward. The soft tread of her satin slippers was somehow thunderous in the empty space. She reached for the handle and paused. There would be two crystal champagne flutes. Just as there had been for his viscountess in her dampened gown.

Her feet twitched as a sudden urge to flee coursed through her. She stared at her fingers upon the brass handle as though they belonged to another. She didn't want to be Harry's scandalous lady in the conservatory, sipping on fine, French champagne. She didn't want that, because that is what every single lady to come after Miss Margaret Dunn had been to the hopelessly handsome Earl of Stanhope.

And the moment she pressed the handle, entered the room, sipped the champagne, and partook in his kisses, she would be nothing more than the viscountess. She pulled her hand back and touched the ribbon woven through a loose strand draped over her shoulder.

The satin fabric served as an aide-mémoire of the perils of gentlemen who sipped too much brandy and collected mistresses like she amassed ribbons. In a handful of days, Harry had charmed away nearly every unfavorable opinion she held of the roguish gentleman. Ultimately, however, he would always be the seductive scoundrel meeting his lady-loves in the midst of his host's soiree. Some poor, unfortunate miss would wear the same pasted smile Anne's mother had affected through the years.

"Are you having second thoughts, Anne?" a husky voice sounded against her ear.

She shrieked, the damning sound swallowed by a familiar, large hand.

Harry pressed the handle and gently propelled her forward. He took his hand away and closed the door quietly shut then turned the lock.

Anne took a step backward. "H-harry." She detested the tremble underscoring her greeting that sent one of his golden-blond eyebrows upward.

He leaned against the door and folded his arms across the broad expanse of his chest. "Have you reconsidered the wiseness of your plan in enlisting my help, sweet?"

She had. More times than she could count on her toes and fingers combined. The moon's light slashed through the clear ceiling and cast a white glow about the room.

Harry shoved away from the door and wandered closer. "Or is it that you no longer need my help? That you've already garnered an offer from Crawford?"

He tugged at her orange ribbon. She swatted his fingers. "Don't be silly."

"About the necessity of my help or Crawford's offer?"

"Both," she said with a weak smile. The papers had remarked upon the duke's seeming interest. However, ices at Gunter's and an afternoon visit hardly equated an offer of marriage.

She wandered deeper into the room, trailing her fingertips over the Calamander wood table only to pause beside a single potted rosebush. The sweet fragrance of the pinkish-red bud hung in the air like a heady reminder of the past. She brushed her knuckles over the satiny softness of the bloom. Before she'd lost her ribbons, Katherine her books, and Benedict his toy soldiers, there had been Mother's gardener. One of the first *expenses* to go.

The quiet tread of his steps filled the otherwise silent conservatory.

She glanced up. "Where is the champagne, Harry?"

He furrowed his brow. "The champagne?"

Anne gestured about the room. "Isn't that part of your rules for seduction, my lord?" Regret tinged her words. She'd become any other woman to Harry. "Two crystal flutes filled with bubbling champagne?" Then, had she ever really been anything different?

A cloud passed over the moon and sinister shadows descended over the room. A dark look glinted in his hazel eyes, but then moonlight lit his face and she realized she must have imagined anything more serious from the affable rogue. "Ah, but you've requested *lessons* in seduction. Two champagne glasses would indicate my intentions of seducing you. Which I don't intend to do. Seduce you, that is."

Humiliated shame blazed up her neck and burned her cheeks. She yanked her gaze away, knowing she should feel a small measure of relief she didn't have to muddle through dangerous sentiments for a rogue like Harry. So, why did the relief not come? "Er, perhaps we can be on with this seduction business then," she said with a wave of her hand. She strove for nonchalance. His amused grin indicated her grand failure.

She gasped as he snaked his arm around her. "Wh-what are you . . ." Her words died on a breathy whisper as he touched the pad of his thumb to her lips.

"I'll teach you anything and everything you desire to know about seduction *within* reason," he amended, correctly interpreting the inappropriate question that sprang to her lips. He gently squeezed her waist, as if familiarizing himself with the curved contours of her body. Which was really a silly thought, when he'd been abundantly clear for more than a year now he desired her no more than he might desire Lady Jersey's prize pug.

"Oh," she said lamely. "Then what . . . ?" He pulled her into the vee of his legs. Her body burned at the point of contact. She couldn't string together a single syllable or a bout of sustained airflow to form a suitable word. *Words, Anne Arlette Adamson. Words.* She cleared her throat and tried again. "Then what is my second lesson for the day, Harry? What sage words on the art of seduction do you have?"

After Margaret's betrayal, Harry had perfected the art of seduction. Yet, suddenly the idea of imparting a single lesson more for Anne to employ all to snare Crawford burned like fire in his gut. Lady Anne Adamson was worth more than all the dukes in the English kingdom. She deserved more than a portentous bore who'd keep separate chambers for propriety's sake.

He cupped her cheek, cradling the silken smoothness of her creamy-white skin. "You want advice. You want guidance." She nodded. If any Society matron knew she came to him for any form of assistance, the lady's reputation would be shredded beyond repair. All sensible members of the *ton* knew Lord Stanhope to be beyond redemption.

He moved his hand to the graceful line of her neck. "Allow him"—Crawford or the nameless bastard who'd inevitably take her to wife—"to know just how clever and spirited and quick-witted you are. Allow him to appreciate you for more than your golden tresses." Which should be memorialized in poem. "Or your lush body." Which he'd barter his soul to explore. "You deserve a man who'd have you for who you really are." A woman who'd completely and utterly captivated him, when he'd sworn to never be so enthralled.

"For who I am?" she whispered. And because but the span of a finger separated their persons, he detected the manner in which her throat bobbed up and down.

He set her back. "A woman of intelligence, Anne," he said bluntly. "Do not be one of those simpering debutantes prattling on about the weather." Red color suffused her cheeks. He burst out laughing. "You've spoken to Crawford on the topic of weather already, have you?"

She tossed her blonde tresses. "I may have." His laughter doubled. "It is an entirely suitable matter of discourse between a lady and a gentleman."

He snorted. "An entirely *dull* matter of discourse." He sighed. "I see, I must guide you on topics of discussion, then, as well? I imagine you also sang to him in a sweet, lyrical soprano some of Dibdin's work and he showered you with praise on your trip to Gunter's."

"First, I'll have you know I quite enjoy Dibdin's work. He's a grand storyteller. Secondly, a lady cannot simply alter the quality of her singing voice. I've told you as much," she scolded, sounding remarkably out of patience with him.

Which still didn't answer what in hell her singing voice sounded like.

He straightened his back. He'd yet to hear her sing. Crawford had. Now, Crawford knew whether she possessed a lyrical soprano or a contralto; while Harry remained wholly ignorant, left to wonder, left to imagine—

Anne jabbed a finger at his chest. He winced. "Furthermore . . ." She angled her head, her words trailing off.

Feigning nonchalance, he quirked an eyebrow at her. "What is it?"

"How did you know the duke escorted me for ices at Gunter's?"

His mind froze. How, indeed? "The papers," he said entirely too quickly.

She wagged her jabbing finger under his nose in a disapproving manner. "I didn't take you as one of those to read the gossip columns."

"I don't," he said with a frown. He'd not have her thinking he was one of those dandified fops who gave a fig for the scandal sheets. Except . . .

"Then however did you discover about my trip to Gunter's?"

Harry tugged at his uncomfortably tight cravat. He really must speak to his valet about the knot. Odd, he'd not noticed just how damned tight the blasted fabric was—until now. Which presented the even odder possibility that Lady Anne Adamson was responsible for the tightened cravat. "I'm fairly certain you mentioned the ices at Gunter's."

She shook her head, a mischievous grin on her lips. "No. No, I didn't Harry. I never uttered a single word." She took a step toward him. He retreated. "Do you know what I believe?"

He backed up again. "What is that, sweet?" He shot a glance over his shoulder at the locked door, eager for escape. She continued her forward approach until his legs knocked against one of the Italian gold rope stools. He fell into the seat.

She stared down at him victoriously. "I believe you've come to care for me," she whispered with a mischievous glimmer in her eyes.

His heart paused midbeat. Anne's voice came as if down a long, muffled corridor. Her bold words echoed around his mind. Could he have come to care for Lady Anne Adamson, the termagant who'd peered down her insolent nose at him since their first meeting a year ago? He, who'd sworn to never care for another woman, not when it was so bloody dangerous?

"Harry?" She waved her hand in front of his face. "Are you listening to me?"

His heart resumed its normal cadence and his hearing restored itself. He shook his head.

"You needn't look so horrified." She cuffed him under the chin. "I was merely teasing."

Most ladies, from debutantes to dowagers, clamored for a place in his bed. Not once in all his thirty years had a single lady cuffed him under the chin as though he were a naughty child. He wrapped his arms loosely around her waist and pulled her between his legs.

Her eyebrows dipped. "What are you doing?" Nor did young ladies speak to him in this waspish tone. She shoved against him, but he held firm.

"I'm kissing you, sweet."

She edged back. "You most certainly are *not*."

"I'm not?"

She shook her head quite emphatically and, as though she didn't think him capable of understanding the significance of that shake, added, "You are not to kiss me. Not anymore. There have been far too many kisses, Harry."

He grinned lazily up at her. "There is no such thing as too many kisses." He leaned up to claim her lips. His mouth collided with her cheek.

"Now, that isn't true." She inched a hand up between them and ticked off on her fingers. "There are the kisses of married women." She shook her head. "Even a single one of those types of kisses would be too many."

He made it a point to avoid dalliances with married ladies—well, with the exception of the unhappy ones with miserable, philandering blighters for husbands. Those women were perfectly appropriate ones to partake in too many kisses with.

Her eyes narrowed at his guilty silence. "Humph," she muttered. "Then there are the kisses stolen from unwilling women."

He gently squeezed her trim waist. "I assure you, I've never encountered an unwilling woman." Her expression darkened. "I'd never force my . . ." His words trailed off. A black haze descended across his vision.

Anne winced. "You've hurt me."

"Forgive me, sweet," he murmured. He lightened his grip but retained his hold on her person. "Has there been a gentleman who forced his kiss on you?" If there was, God help the bastard, Harry would separate his limbs from his person and tuck them into the blighter's bedsheets with him.

A rush of pink flooded her cheeks. "No," she said quickly.

By God, he'd kill the bastard. Kill him dead.

"It matters not. We're not discussing the gentlemen who've kissed me."

Which suggested the young lady had kissed *more* than one gentleman. Fury licked at his insides.

"Rather . . ." she wrinkled her pert little nose. "What were we discussing?"

He really didn't remember much beyond the fact that there had been another man who'd tasted and explored her plump, bow-shaped lips. He growled. One other man who'd done so against her will. "We were discussing the gentleman who stole your kiss."

She tapped his arm reproachfully. "We weren't."

He pulled her closer. "We are now."

She sighed. "Very well. Lord Ackland." Her lips pulled into a grimace. "Lady Lettingworth's masquerade. He tasted horrid." So, the bastard had dared put his tongue inside the warm, moist cavern of Anne's mouth. "Like cardamom and brandy and . . ." She tapped a finger against her lower lip. "Well, you taste of brandy but it isn't all that unpleasant when I've kissed you, then cardamom doesn't quite blend the—"

"I'll kill him," he muttered to himself. She winced and he realized he'd tightened his grip. Again.

"You'll do no such thing," she chided. "And . . ." She swatted his chest. "Regardless, Harry. This was about the types of kisses that would be too many." So, she remembered. She invariably remembered everything, it seemed. She was far cleverer than Society credited her with being. She resumed ticking off her list. "Then there are the kisses meant to distract a lady."

"All kisses are intended to distract." Distract a woman with the thrill of a hot touch. Distract a gentleman from the pain of a wounded heart. Yes, a distraction was a distraction. And just now, he wanted Anne's kiss not merely for a scandalous diversion away from their host's soiree but because he'd not leave this damned conservatory until he drove back the taste, scent, and feel of Ackland from her memory. Harry lowered his mouth to hers to prove his very point.

She gave him her other cheek. "That is my point exactly, Harry. Kisses shouldn't be used as a distraction."

"They shouldn't?" He quite disagreed.

"No," she said emphatically.

He dragged a hand over his eyes. "Anne?"

"Yes?"

"If you consider yourself so well-versed on the art of seduction, then why did you seek out my assistance?"

She promptly closed her mouth. A frown played on her lips. He pressed his hands against her hips and drew her close. She dropped her head and his kiss fell somewhere in the middle of her brow. He sighed. "What is it?" She had the stubbornness to drive a vicar to drink during Sunday sermon.

Anne gave him a searching look. "Kisses shouldn't be used to weaken someone. They should be used to convey a gentleman's unwavering love for an equally unwavering woman."

Ah, his beautiful Anne. The hopeless romantic, who squinted her way through the pages of *The Times*, still believed in that foolish sentiment called love.

She touched her fingers to his cheek. "You don't believe in love," she said softly. Her words, both matter-of-fact and sad all at once.

Giving up on the hope of a kiss from her tempting red lips, he sank back into his host's work stool. He pulled her onto his lap. "I don't, Anne. Not in a world where ladies would trade their very happiness for the hand of the most advantageous match." Or where a title came before a name, a heart, and all else. "Do you imagine to earn Crawford's heart?" He couldn't bite down the mocking edge to that question.

Anne shifted in his arms and frowned up at him. "I believe the duke could love me," she said softly.

And, if he still believed in the sentiment of love, then he'd venture a woman such as her could certainly earn the heart of Crawford and any other gentleman she'd set her marital sights upon. He stroked the pad of his thumb along her full, lower lip. "What of you, Anne? Do you fancy yourself in love with Crawford?"

He didn't realize the vise that had squeezed off his airflow until she said, "Of course not." The pressure about his heart lessened and he could breathe yet again. "But that doesn't mean I won't come to love him," she added.

He set her from his lap with such alacrity she stumbled backward. "Then, I imagine, you shouldn't be stealing away with unrepentant rogues in the middle of your hostess's ball." He took her by the shoulders and gently propelled her to the door.

Anne frowned over her shoulder and dug in her heels, until he was forced to stop or continue dragging her along. "But you promised—"

"A lesson. And I've given it. Show him your clever, witty self. Do not bury your intelligence for his favor because such a man would never be worth having." He placed a hard kiss on her lips. "Now, go." Emotion blazed to life in Anne's soft, blue eyes. She arched her neck back as if hungering for his kiss, and before he did something like make love to her mouth, then lift her skirts and make love to every last silken inch of her, Harry affected a half-grin. He patted her on the cheek. "Go, sweet."

Anne gave her head a shake and then wordlessly ran down the length of the conservatory, unlatched the door, and fled.

Harry stood there long after she'd left. It appeared he wasn't the total dishonorable scoundrel he'd taken himself for these past years. He scrubbed his hands over his face.

Damn it.

Chapter 12

*A*nne depressed a single key of her pianoforte. She studied her fingertip upon the ivory key and remembered back to a different instrument. Remembered the moment it had been packaged up and carried off by servants and sent wherever it was lost belongings went to cover a man's debts.

There had been a time when she'd lay abed well into the early morning hours, staring at the canopy overhead, worrying. Worrying about her poor mother's breaking heart. Worrying about her twin sister losing the one joy she had in life—her volumes of poetry. Worrying about the loss of Benedict's games and toys and more—his innocence. Worrying about Aldora having to forsake a dream of love all to make a match to save.

Security had been a beacon. A talisman of hope she clung to. She had longed for the day she'd make her Come Out. Only, she'd entertained the most foolish of girlish musings that included security, a handsome gentleman, *and* love.

But first and foremost had always come security.

Now, the Duke of Crawford, with his increasing interest, represented the pinnacle of that great beacon. As the Duchess of Crawford, she'd never worry about material comforts, or more importantly, the comforts of her future children. There had always been the expectation, both real and self-imposed, amongst her family that Anne would make an advantageous match.

In her third Season, no longer a girl, Anne foolishly held onto hope for that last elusive dream—love.

She touched her fingers to the keys.

"The Duke of Crawford will make you a splendid match, Anne."

Her fingers slipped and the dissonant chords echoed through the spacious parlor. "Mother," she murmured.

Her mother sailed into the room. The firm set to her mouth, the fire in her blue eyes spoke of a determined point to her visit. She stopped at the edge of the ivory upholstered sofa and planted her arms akimbo. "Well?" She motioned to the seat beside her.

For one, infinitesimal moment, Anne thought of sticking her tongue out and banging an obscene ditty on the keyboard. "Well, what?"

"Don't be insolent, Anne," she snapped.

Reluctantly, Anne shoved to her feet. The delicate bench scraped the hardwood floor. She wandered over to the King Louis chair and sat, hands folded demurely upon her lap. Ever the dutiful daughter. The daughter Mother hung all her hopes upon, who in spite of that faith remained unwed.

After two Seasons and a bit of a third.

Mother carefully arranged her skirts. "You know, of your sisters and brother, only you really know the truth of your father." She directed that statement down at her pleated satin skirts.

Yes, her siblings had somehow remained insulated from that truth of their vile father. "Mother?" she asked, cautiously. But for the handful of unkind matrons when Anne had made her Come Out, little was said of the philandering late earl. She'd smiled brightly through all the impolite whispers.

Her mother snapped her head up so quickly Anne imagined she hurt the muscles of her neck. "It is, of course, no secret your father didn't love me." Bitterness made for an ugly smile on the countess's face.

Anne's heart ached for the pain her mother had known— still knew. She reached for her hand.

"Bah, do not give me your pity, Anne," she said with a wave.

Anne pulled her fingers back.

"If you don't have a care, you'll become me."

She wrinkled her brow.

"I see the way you stare at Stanhope," she hissed. "Stare at him when you can have Crawford."

Anne stiffened. "How very mercurial you make it all seem." She wondered if this was how Harry and her sisters saw her—cold and calculated, counting ribbons and dreaming of the title of duchess.

Her mother bristled at Anne's terse words. "Were you mercurial when you cried about your ribbons?"

She winced at her private shame being tossed in her face by her mother.

"Was it mercurial when they took your sister's books?" her mother continued, relentless. "Or when Aldora chose to marry for—"

"Aldora married for love." Even as Mother would have had Aldora wed the Marquess of St. James or some other lofty lord.

Mother colored. "Fortunate for you all, Lord Knightly was obscenely wealthy and generous with you."

How neatly she excluded herself from that general "you." Anne glanced away, knowing there was more to Mother's displeasure. Knowing it stemmed from Harry.

"Do you love him?"

She blinked several times. "Do I—?"

She scoured Anne's face. "Love him," she repeated. "Do. You. Love. Him?"

Anne shook her head. "No." She opened her mouth. Words wouldn't come. She shook her head again. "Certainly not." She was considered the fool of the family, but she'd never dare anything so mad as to fall in love with Harry, the 6th Earl of Stanhope who'd attempted to seduce her sister, and loved his Miss Margaret Dunn, and saw Anne as nothing more than a termagant. Or hellion. The moniker varied on a given day.

Mother studied her in silence as though seeking for truth in her answer. "He'll not wed you," she said at last, the matter-of-factness of those words more painful than if they'd been jeeringly flung.

Anne curled her nails into the skin of her knuckles. "I am not thinking he will, Mother," she said between gritted teeth.

"Nor should you hold out hope he would," she continued almost cruelly. "You'll always merely be second to the sister he truly desired."

She curled her fingers into tight balls, her nails leaving crescent marks upon her palms. Now, that was *indeed* cruel. Particularly in the truth to those handful of words. If she'd not begged and pleaded, Harry wouldn't have bothered to even help her in the first place. He'd have sent her to the devil with a harsh kick to her derriere and not a single backward glance.

"I always desired more for you than Mr. Ekstrom."

Anne attempted to follow the abrupt shift in conversation.

Mother slashed the air with her hand. "Katherine, well, as you know. I expected a marriage between her and Bertrand.

Benedict, why he's just a child and anything can happen to a child. Then where would we be?"

"Mother," Anne said on a gasp.

Red fanned Mother's cheeks as she appeared properly shamed at the coldness of her words. "I did not mean to sound avaricious. I love all my children," she said defensively. "But I worry for all of us. All of us," she repeated as though Anne hadn't heard her clear enough the first time.

"Neither Jasper nor Michael would allow us to become destitute."

"And what of the connection to the Wakefield line?"

Well, Anne could imagine a good many greater travesties than the loss of connection to her dastardly father. She held those words back, knowing they'd only cause her mother further pain.

"I would not see you do something reckless with your reputation and lose the duke's favor. If there is no Crawford, or some other lofty title, there is the assurance of Mr. Ekstrom."

What was she on about? She didn't want to think about horrid Mr. Ekstrom, the man Mother had tried to have Katherine . . . Her heart sank slowly into her belly.

"I see you follow my thoughts, Anne."

Anne jumped up. She glared at her mother's immaculately arranged curls. "Is that what you'd do? Threaten me with marriage to Mr. Ekstrom?" Somewhere in her mother's loathsome scheming and vile threat she'd lost sight of the fact that Harry's presence in her life came from nothing more than her goals to ensnare the Duke of Crawford's attention. "I'll not wed him."

Mother rose, slowly. She smoothed her skirts. "No. I daresay you shan't. I'd much rather you have the Duke of Crawford." She crossed over and took Anne's cheeks in her palms.

Anne yanked her face away, much the same way she'd done as a small girl when her nurse had attempted to rub lemon juice over her freckled skin in attempt to rid her of the marks. Mother took Anne's face in her hands once more. "Look at me," she said softly. This kind, tender tone—the one she remembered of the Mother who'd praised her and found pride in her playing and embroidery skills. Likely more the woman she'd been before the extent of Father's betrayal had ruined her. "I want to see you happy. You call me mercurial. Mayhap you think me cruel." Tears filled her eyes, the first crack in her indecipherable mask. "Do you know the fear I carried in my heart for not only myself but for each of you?" She blinked back the crystal drops.

"Mother," Anne said gently.

She wiped her cheeks. "Bah, silly tears. A waste they are." She drew in a shuddery breath. "I loved your father, Anne. But sometimes love isn't enough. Not when a gentleman's heart is otherwise engaged."

A faceless Miss Dunn flashed to Anne's mind. She tried to call up a clear image of a woman who possessed the beauty men would wage wars for. Surely, no silly gold ringlets there.

"Your Lord Stanhope is not without a scandal."

"I know that," she murmured, giving her head a shake. "And he's not my Lord Stanhope," she added as an afterthought.

"There was a woman, a . . ." Mother paused, seeming to search her memory.

Miss Margaret Dunn. Oh, how she detested that name.

"It escapes me now. Nearly ten years ago, I believe."

Eight years. Harry had indicated eight years had since passed. Anne would have been just a girl of twelve or thirteen around the time. She imagined Harry, unjaded, just out of university. She didn't want to ask her mother questions.

She was content to bury her curiosity and not know Mother's twisted version of the story. "I don't need to hear this," she said firmly. She would not betray Harry with Society's gossip.

Her mother rushed over and claimed her hands. "You do, Anne. Do you understand me? You need to hear this, when I myself refused to listen to the whispers surrounding your father's offer for me all those years ago. You represent nothing more than a diversion to the earl."

Anne's lips twisted ruefully. Considering the terms of their arrangement, she represented a good deal less than that to Harry.

"He can't have honorable intentions toward you."

The whole lessons in seduction business aside . . . why not? He was not the heartless rogue she'd once taken him as.

"Because he will always love another," her mother said, seeming to follow Anne's unspoken question. "I would see your life be different than the one I've lived."

Anne imagined herself thirty years from now a bitter, empty, angry shell of the woman she'd been. For everything wrong and flawed in her mother's thinking, she would be correct on this. Harry would break some woman's heart. And if Anne weren't careful, she would be that poor, unfortunate soul. Her heart twisted. She tugged her hands free. "Please be assured, Mother. I know that. I do." She slid her gaze over to the pianoforte.

Mother touched Anne's chin. "Learn from my mistakes. I loved your father enough, *so* much that I foolishly believed I could teach him to love me." Her voice broke and she coughed in an apparent attempt to hide her uncharacteristic show of emotion. "You can't teach the heart to know that which it already knows."

Oddly, those words made sense to Anne. She wandered back over to the pale-blue upholstered pianoforte bench and sat. "I understand, Mother." She raised her hands, poised above the keys. "I'll not do anything foolish where Lord Stanhope is concerned." If one could exclude enlisting the rogue's assistance on matters of seduction . . .

Anne began to play a polite, if clear, dismissal. She'd had enough of her mother's rain upon her happiness. She buried thoughts of Harry, and Mother's aching reminder of a too-sad past, and the Duke of Crawford's intentions, in the strands of John Dowland. She lost herself in the haunting melody and sang.

Not to seduce.

But merely because it was a singular pleasure she could allow herself. Her books, she could barely see. Her ribbons were empty fripperies. In the strands of song, she could drift off and be someone other than empty-headed, pleasingly pretty Lady Anne Arlette Adamson.

And Anne sang.

"Weep no more sad fountains. What need have you flow so fast . . . ?"

As Harry trailed behind the butler through the Countess of Wakefield's townhouse, the haunting melody soared from the room at the end of the corridor and danced around the plaster walls. He froze midstride. His heart pounded loud and hard in his ears.

A contralto.

The whisper of song that makes a man think of bedrooms and bedsheets and all things forbidden . . .

The butler paused and looked back at him questioningly. Harry told his mind to tell his legs to tell his feet to move. And so he moved. Onward to the husky contralto. They paused beside the parlor. The butler cleared his throat. "The Earl of Stanhope . . ."

Anne's song broke into a sharp shriek and her fingers slid along the keyboard in a discordant tune that echoed around the room. She jumped to her feet, high color on her cheeks. "My lord."

For a quick moment, Harry wasn't sure if hers was a greeting or a skyward prayer.

Her gaze met his and then wandered off to the young maid who hurried past him and advanced deep into the room. Out of the way. But certainly not forgotten.

He damned propriety to the devil. Harry beat his hand against his leg. "My lady."

Anne fiddled with her satin skirts.

"Should I . . ."

"Would you . . ."

They fell silent. He motioned for her to continue.

Anne cleared her throat. "Would you care for refreshments?" she asked loudly.

He cupped his hands around his mouth. "A seat should suffice," he returned.

Her lips twitched and she motioned him forward. The butler hurried off and Harry entered the room. "Please, sit," Anne murmured. She hovered beside the rose-inlaid pianoforte.

He claimed a seat on the sofa. He narrowed his eyes at Anne's unexpected show of hesitation. For the tart, biting hellion she'd proven herself to be since they'd met, she'd never been timid around him. And he rather found he disliked it. Disliked it, immensely.

She hurried over and sat in the mahogany ladder back armchair across from him. *Not* on the sofa directly beside him. Or even the bloody chair directly *next* to his. Across. She shifted in her seat. "Are you certain you wouldn't care for tea?"

He looped his ankle across his knee. "Quite certain. But please do not let me discourage you."

Anne glanced at her maid. "Mary, will you call for refreshments, please."

The servant hopped up from her seat and rushed to do Anne's bidding.

Silence reigned between Harry and Anne. He drummed his fingertips on the edge of his boot. What accounted for the suddenly mute version of Anne's usually vibrant self? She studied the tips of her ivory satin slippers with the attention she might show a fireworks display at Vauxhall Garden. He leaned back in his seat. Alas, it would appear the charm he usually evinced failed him whenever Lady Anne Adamson was near.

Crawford. Surely the duke's sudden interest accounted for this heightened tension. He curled his fingers into tight fists. In attempt to shake her free of this cool shell she'd affected, he whispered, "It would seem you're a sultry contralto, Anne."

Her cheeks blazed the red of a ripened berry and he suddenly had a taste for sweet fruit. "Er . . ." she plucked at the fabric of her skirts. "Uh . . . yes." Her blush deepened. "That is, I possess a contralto. Without the sultriness," she said on a rush.

He leaned forward in the sofa and lowered his voice. "With the sultriness." And now he loathed even more the idea of her singing for that bastard Crawford. The other man had the privilege of sitting as a solo audience to her performance, had likely conjured wicked thoughts of Anne, all wicked things Harry himself longed to do to her. "Sing for me," he commanded hoarsely.

She tilted her head. "My lord?"

And furthermore, what was this, "my lord" nonsense? "Sing for me." This time, he gentled his voice, used his most seductive tone that had found many ultimately well-pleasured ladies a place in his bed.

Anne wrinkled her nose. "I abhor that tone, Harry."

Ah, of course she did. Odd how this spirited beauty had sought him out, asking him to school her in the art of seduction, yet she spurned each one of those lessons as they were turned upon her. The tension in her bow-shaped lips, the frown at the corners of her riveting blue eyes bespoke annoyance. He rose and walked around the small marble-top table between them and dropped to a knee beside her.

"What are—?"

Harry took her smaller hands in his. He tugged off her white kidskin gloves and set them aside. "Will you sing for me, Anne?" He raised her naked wrist to his mouth and placed his lips along the inside, where her pulse beat hard and steady. "Please," he added.

"Oh," she said on a soft sigh. "A-are you m-making light of me?"

"No." He'd never again be able to manage such a feat. Not knowing her as he now did.

Anne glanced at his hand upon her wrist and with reluctance, he released her. She ran a suspicious gaze over his face. "And you'll not tease me for—?"

He marked an X over his heart. "On my word."

She continued to study him with an intent seriousness in her blue eyes and then stood. "I'll play, Harry." From the place she occupied at the far end of the room, Anne's maid coughed. Anne's eyes went wide. "Er, that is, I'll play, my lord." She waggled her golden eyebrows at him as she settled into her seat. "Though I imagine you'll merely be bored with Dibdin."

From his spot kneeling, he grinned at her. "I assure you, I'll not."

Her fingers danced upon the keyboard with an expertness the master Dibdin himself would have applauded, the jaunty, uplifting melody of the former resident composer of Covent Garden's *The Lass that Loves a Sailor*. Her contralto filled the parlor; the beauty of the husky, emotion-laden tone could rival the most lauded opera singers upon the Continent. Yet, he'd instructed to use her voice as a tool of seduction. Now hearing her, witnessing the depth of her instrument, he recognized the travesty in merely seeing such beauty reserved for the bedroom.

His lips pulled in a grimace. Egad, next he'd be spouting sonnets of the lady's fair skin. What mad spell had she cast upon him?

She sang, unaware that she'd captivated him with her intelligence, beauty, and now song. *"But the standing toast that pleased most . . ."* Anne tipped her head jauntily back and forth to the quick, staccato rhythm, as she continued; all the while she smiled through her singing.

At her infectious enthusiasm, he grinned. A grin that had nothing to do with seduction or passion or lust, but rather a smile that came from the joy of just being with *her*.

"The ship that goes . . ." Her playing increased to a frenzied rhythm. *"And the lass that loves a sailor."* She ended on a

dramatic flourish. Her cheeks a healthy pink, an, unfettered smile upon her lips, he was struck motionless wishing he was, in fact, a poet so then he could commit the memory of Anne Adamson to a page, forever immortalizing the spirited beauty. She dipped her head as their gazes locked.

A charged moment froze the room. The tick-tock of the ormolu clock marked the passage of time. A servant entered with the tray of tea and pastries, and set the world to spinning once more.

Harry stood, and clapped. "Brava, my lady."

Anne hopped up from her bench on a laugh, breathless. "Oh, do hush," she said, brushing off his compliment like a drop of rain upon her skin.

He reclaimed his seat upon the sofa and looked at this woman whom he'd thought he knew, whom he'd unfairly judged, and judged quite harshly. And looking at her, he was humbled by the truth of how little he or anyone else in Society, in fact, knew of her. For Society's opinion of Lady Anne as a vain, attention-seeking young lady, she neither wanted nor welcomed even deserved praise.

She hurried over and this time sat beside him.

He dipped his lips close to her ear. "You're remarkable, Anne."

She snorted. "And you're a flirt, Harry."

"Yes, indeed I am." He leaned over and tweaked her nose. "But I'm also a truth-teller."

She hastened to pour herself a cup of tea. He studied her precise, ladylike movements, surely perfected many years ago through lessons ingrained into her by a stern governess. Lady Anne Adamson evinced everything of a perfectly proper, English lady and was therefore everything he'd avoided since Margaret's betrayal. Now, however, studying her as he did, Harry found her to be far more than one of the insipid, colorless young ladies in the market for a husband. As though she felt his gaze on her, Anne glanced up. Her long, graceful fingers curled about the handle of the pale blue porcelain teapot trembled.

Ah, the minx wasn't immune to him after all, and masculine satisfaction flared in his chest.

Liquid splashed over her hands and splattered the edge the mahogany table. She set the teapot down with a firm thunk. "Blast and double blast," she hissed.

From across the room, her maid jumped up from her tucked away seat. "I'll see to an ointment, my lady." She fled as fast as if a fire had been set to the parlor.

Harry yanked out a handkerchief. "Here—" He snapped it open.

She drew her fingers back. "It's fine," she said softly.

His mouth hardened. Did she see herself as nothing more than an obligation to him? "Don't be daft." Did Anne not realize *she'd* come to mean something to him? "Let me see." He took her hands in his and turned over the injured digits. He cursed.

"It's fine," she murmured. The delicate skin of her three middle fingers bore the red, angry marks from her tea.

He popped the digits into his mouth, drawing the soft flesh deep.

The quick intake of her breath filled the quiet between them. The muscles of her throat moved up and down. He expected her to politely avert her gaze and draw her hand back. In the time he'd come to know Anne, however, he should realize she never did that which was expected. A little sigh escaped her lips. "That feels splendid." She leaned close to him.

Had anyone told him he'd be sucking upon a lady's fingers and there was nothing the least bit sexual in the act, he'd have laughed in the gent's face and proceeded to list twenty acts one could do with one's mouth and a lady's fingers. She somehow made him forget the rogue he'd been and turned him into a man he didn't recognize—one who wasn't solely fixed on tugging up Anne's skirts and making sweet love to her, but rather, one who wanted to know the little pieces that made Anne—well, Anne.

Harry pressed his eyes closed a moment. He drew her fingers out of his mouth and studied the reddened flesh. *This was very bad, indeed.*

Chapter 13

$\mathcal{H}$arry had been accused of doing many things that were the height of foolishness, and on more scores than he could count. He could even readily take ownership of any number of those foolish decisions. Agreeing to school Lady Anne Adamson on the art of seduction, however, was the height of all foolish acts to come before this. Though, staring at the collection of delicate, wire-rimmed spectacle frames spread out on his immaculate desk, he could admit this was certainly the second.

He picked up an oval pair and weighed them in his hands.

"They are a lovely pair," the doctor murmured.

Harry glanced at the seventy-somethingish doctor who'd served his family through the years. There were not many he could trust with such a delicate, such an intimate matter. "But how can I be certain she . . . ?" He flushed. "That is . . . a person might be able to see more accurately."

The older man swiped a hand over his mouth, and Harry suspected it was a meager attempt to conceal his mirth. "Er, well, this, uh . . . *person* . . . does not struggle to see things that are in the distance?"

I can see. I just cannot see so very well when I'm reading . . .

Harry gave his head a curt shake. "She . . . or, rather, *he*"— the doctor's lips twitched once more—"claims to have no difficulty seeing objects in the distance."

Harry set down the gold-framed spectacles and reached for another lighter, oval-shaped pair. He turned them over in his hands, imagining her as she'd been squinting desperately to make sense of the words on a page, words that had been about him and his actions the previous evening. Why should Anne care whether he'd been with another woman? Why, unless . . . she cared . . . And why did he want her to care? History had shown him the dangers in forming any emotional entanglements with a woman who'd pledged to wed a duke.

"And how blurred are the words when this"—the doctor coughed into his hand—"*person* is reading?"

Startled, Harry dropped the pair of spectacles. They landed with a soft clink upon the collection of other frames assembled before him. "Quite blurred," he said quickly. Unbidden, a smile pulled at his lips in remembrance of Anne with her copy of *The Times* and the indignant expression on her furious, heart-shaped face.

"My lord?"

The doctor's prodding jerked him from his senseless musings. Harry gave his head a disgusted shake and grabbed another pair. "Sh . . . *he* squints." He picked up a forgotten copy of *The Times* at the corner of his desk. He held it up and angled the pages away from him to display the angle. "Holds the page about here and squints." He demonstrated for the old doctor once more the extent of Anne's squint. "In this manner."

"Ahh."

That was it? Just "Ahh."

"Also tilts the page toward the light." He remembered her as she'd been, endearing and enticing in her innocent attempt to muddle her way through the reading of that page. Harry threw the paper down and reached for a third pair of the thin metal frames. "And can you help h—this person?"

The doctor's face settled into a very somber, very doctorly mask. "I would have a better gauge on just what is best for this"—he arched an eyebrow—"*gentleman* in terms of the actual lenses if I were to meet—"

"No."

"And assess—"

"Still no." Harry tugged his cravat. "This gentleman is quite busy. Quite," he added. A gentleman did not give a young lady gifts unless he was prepared to declare for her.

"I see."

A knowing sparkle lit the man's kindly blue eyes. Dr. Craven likely assumed Harry's delicate purchase was for a well-favored mistress. Nothing could be further from the truth.

And all the more dangerous for it. Harry, the Earl of Stanhope, did not call family physicians to his townhouse with a collection of lady's spectacles and have a pair commissioned; not for a respectable young woman.

Outside of expensive, extravagant, and emotionally insignificant jewels he'd purchased for mistresses through the years, he'd never gifted such a personal and meaningful item—to anyone. And yet, he wanted, nay, *needed* to make this purchase for Anne.

His mind shied away from the implications of this gift. He looked at the pair of spectacles he currently held. Silver, delicate. He weighed this pair in his palm the way he had the previous pairs. This frame would not be uncomfortable for the lady to wear. He held them up. Sunlight filtered through the drawn back curtains from the full floor-length windows. It reflected off the metallic rim. He imagined Anne in the spectacles and not much more. Biting back a groan at the enticing image, he shoved the pair toward Dr. Craven. "These will do."

Perfectly.

The doctor tucked them into the front of his coat. "I cannot promise the lenses will be completely perfect for the young . . . *person*."

"Do the best you are able." *Without seeing the lady.* Because if this intimate gift for the unwed Lady Anne was discovered by the *ton*, the young woman would be ruined as surely as if he'd been discovered with her in Lord Essex's conservatory that first night. "I imagine whatever you manage will be a vast improvement to what the la . . . *person* sees now while reading." Which was next to nothing based on Harry's earlier observation.

The physician stood up. He opened his mouth to speak but was interrupted by a knock at the door.

Renshaw, Harry's butler, opened the door and cleared his throat. "Lord Edgerton," he announced and backed out of the room.

Harry hopped guiltily to his feet. Heat crept up his neck as his friend entered the room.

The other man swept an entirely too-astute gaze over the room, lingering a moment upon the doctor, and then of course, the collection of spectacles still littering Harry's desk. He quirked a mocking eyebrow.

Harry silently cursed and gathered the wire frames into a neat little pile and handed the stack over to Dr. Craven who accepted the awkward bundle in his aged hands.

Dr. Craven executed a slight brow. "If that is all, my lord?"

"That is all," he said tersely. "Thank you," he added as an afterthought. The old doctor was hardly to blame for Edgerton's ill timing.

"I will bring them 'round as soon as they are complete, my lord."

"Splendid." And it would be a good deal more splendid if the other man took himself off. For the more he spoke, the more interest flared in Edgerton's amused eyes.

The doctor sketched another bow and then hurried past Edgerton and out of the room. He closed the door behind him with a soft click.

Harry propped his hip on the edge of his desk and folded his arms across his chest. "To what do I owe the pleasure of this visit?"

His friend scoffed. "Come now, can a friend not pay another friend a visit?" He didn't await an answer. Instead, he crossed over to Harry's sideboard and availed himself to a decanter of brandy and a crystal glass. He carried them to the front of the room and claimed one of the leather winged-back chairs at the foot of Harry's desk. Edgerton yanked the stopper out and splashed several fingers into his glass.

"By all means, help yourself," Harry said drolly.

"Indeed I shall." Edgerton raised the glass in mock salute and took a drink. He hooked his ankle across his knee and drummed his fingers along the edge of his boot. "Spectacles."

Of course he could not expect his friend would abandon all questions about Dr. Craven's visit. "Is that a question?" he asked, with a touch of impatience.

Edgerton took another sip and eyed him over the rim of his glass. "Never tell me you've begun taking on with a bluestocking mistress?" He shuddered. "Egad, you're becoming stuffy in your advancing years." Humor fled and he leaned forward. "Who is she?"

Harry gritted his teeth. "Who is who?" He didn't need the other man asking probing questions when all answers led back to Lady Anne Adamson.

Edgerton's brown eyebrows knitted into a single line and then he let loose a slow whistle. He gave his head a pitying shake.

Harry tightened his jaw. "What?" he bit out. He really didn't want to feed the other man's humor but really, what had merited Edgerton's pity?

"Why, they aren't for a bluestocking mistress, after all, are they?"

Somehow, Edgerton's words were a question that wasn't a question. Harry remained silent.

"They are for . . ."

Christ.

"A lady."

Harry went taut. In spite of a lifetime of friendship between them, he welcomed the idea of handing Edgerton a well-placed facer for his deliberate needling.

A sharp bark of hilarity exploded from his friend's chest. The other man laughed so hard, liquid drops of brandy splashed over the side of his glass. "Oh, th-this is rich!" He set his tumbler down on the edge of Harry's desk and dashed tears from his cheeks.

Harry drummed his fingertips upon his forearms. "I'm pleased you find this hilarious, though I must admit I can hardly fathom what—"

"Why, you've gone and purchased spectacles for a lady who I gather is *not* your mistress."

"You know I do not have a mistress," he replied automatically. *Bloody hell!*

Edgerton widened his eyes.

Why hadn't he insisted they were, in fact, for a bluestocking mistress, a lie far safer than the truth? He braced himself, knowing his friend well enough to know he'd correctly surmised the young lady's identity.

Edgerton reached inside his jacket and withdrew a crisp white handkerchief. He dried the moisture from his cheeks and then stuffed it back inside his front pocket. "By God, it's the Lady Anne."

Harry let his silence serve as an answer.

His friend snorted. "Though I suspect a young lady as vain as Lady Anne would not be seen in spectacles, even if the queen herself declared it the latest fashion trend." He chuckled. "Then, perhaps offer the lady a title of duchess and she'll walk herself upside down by her hands if she had to."

He balled his hands into tight fists at his friend's ill-favored opinion of Anne. *I'll not be destitute again, Harry. Not because I'm avaricious, as you've accused me, but because I knew the terror of lying awake and wondering what is to become of my family . . .*

Edgerton uncrossed his leg and rested his palms upon his knees. All earlier humor fled, replaced with a somber concern.

"I know what I am doing," Harry muttered before his friend could speak.

"Do you?" Edgerton asked. "Do you?" he pressed.

Harry looked away. As wrong as Edgerton's unfavorable opinion of Anne happened to be, in this regard, the other man was right. He really didn't know what he was doing; first agreeing to help Anne in her quest for the heart of a duke. And now, in this, buying gifts for a lady who wanted nothing more than the security, stability, and title she could find in Crawford.

"I saw you betrayed once by a grasping, avaricious, fickle creature. Lady Margaret was undeserving of you and so is this one, Stanhope."

Harry inclined his head. "I thank you for your concern." Edgerton had been a good friend to him these years. The best. "But it is unwarranted." He glanced over at the ormolu clock atop his fireplace mantle. "Now, if you'll excuse me. I've business to see to."

Edgerton eyed him skeptically. "Oh?" There were a million shades of doubt within that single-syllable utterance.

Harry shoved himself off his desk. "I'm meeting Lord Westmoreland on a matter of importance." He sketched a quick bow and abandoned his friend to his own devices.

As he took his leave, Edgerton's dangerous charges dogged his every thought.

Chapter 14

A whispery-soft spring breeze tugged at Anne's hair and freed a single ringlet. She brushed the strand from her eyes, her attention fixed on the same page she'd been attempting to read from *The Mysteries of Udolpho*. With a sigh, she conceded the futility of her efforts. Her inability to focus had little to do with the blurred words of the scandalous volume given her by Aldora, and everything to do with a too-charming Earl of Stanhope.

Anne tossed the book onto the ground and threw herself back upon the blanket. She flung her arms out beside her and stared up at the robin's-egg blue sky overhead and the smattering of orange and pink sun-kissed clouds from the early dawn.

For the briefest smidgeon of time, as Harry had held her fingers in his and tended her burned digits, she'd imagined he intended to kiss her again. She'd been so certain of it; she'd have wagered every last ribbon of her possession, which said a good deal, considering she'd sooner send all gamblers to the devil than join their ranks. The absence of that kiss only served to reiterate the importance of not wagering—funds, markers, or hearts. None of it.

Anne plucked at the thick blades of grass in the tucked-away copse. She raised a strand to her lips and blew the long green wisp. It fluttered and danced, and ultimately landed upon the earth. She grabbed the forgotten volume and held it overhead, determined to set Harry from her thoughts, determined to call forth the images of an entirely suitable, pleasantly handsome duke who smiled at the right moments and never, *ever* did anything as scandalous as try to kiss her.

Kisses intended mostly to silence her that did not reek of cardamom and brandy as Lord Ackland, but rather the hint of cinnamon and mint like a holiday treat. She groaned and knocked the book against her forehead. "Do. Not. Be. A. Fool, Anne Arlette Adamson." Not for one such as Harry, whose heart belonged to an unworthy lady who bore some lofty title and little else . . .

She shoved herself up onto her knees. Her heart dropped to her stomach. *Just as you, yourself will*, a niggling voice taunted. She remembered the harsher charges Harry had leveled at her and guilt hammered her breast.

Only, on the heels of that was her mother's recent warning about Harry. The rub of it was, Anne had spent years determined to not be the bitter, heartbroken woman her mother had evolved into over the years. She'd resolved to wed a perfectly respectable, staid, pleasantly handsome, unfailingly polite nobleman.

She flung herself back upon the lush blanket of grass and fanned the pages of her book. The gentle breeze wafted across her face. Harry, or anyone, could certainly construe her desire for a powerful, and powerfully wealthy, duke's hand as mercurial. Only after the string of mistresses held by Father, his betrayal of Mother and their family's security, Anne's girlish notions of love had been forever shattered—replaced instead with a calm practicality and a hope for love . . . nothing more than that: hope.

Then Aldora found Lord Michael Knightly who loved her eldest sister to distraction. Then Katherine had fallen madly in love with Jasper. And Anne had begun to believe perhaps, just perhaps, she too could know love, as well as the heart of a duke prophesied by a gypsy woman to the young ladies who wore the gold charm.

Anne touched the talisman about her neck. It really needn't be a duke. Why, he might be a marquess, a viscount, or even . . . an earl. Wistfulness swept through her. She'd barter her every last ribbon and all hope of the title of duchess for the man who wanted nothing more than to hold her heart, which flew in the face of her resolve to never be reduced to her mother's sorry state. Sometime between Lord Essex's conservatory and this very moment, her firm resolve to find security and stability as a formidable, wealthy duchess had slipped.

Harry's face danced behind her eyes and she forced his visage back. She pressed the spine of the book against her eyes. There were too many follies to count in wishing for anything more from him, to whom every woman bore the moniker *sweet*. She frowned. The least the ever-charming earl could do was to adapt something cleverer such as . . . "goddess of my heart," "keeper of my love" . . . anything but *sweet*.

No, to hope for anything more from one such as him would be tantamount to disaster. Determined to forget thoughts of Harry, she lowered the book closer to her face and squinted. She angled the page in attempt to bring the words into focus, damning her blasted vision. Hating the vanity of her mother and the haute *ton* that discouraged necessary pleasures . . . such as sight. *A gentleman never weds a woman in spectacles, Anne*, Mother had scolded on more scores than she could remember. Of course, Aldora had secured a happy, if less illustrious match, with a wealthy gentleman who loved her to distraction—spectacles and all. Mother pointedly ignored that reminder whenever Anne put it to her.

She stuck the leather volume out arm's length in front of her and deepened her squint in attempt to make sense of the words. A shadow fell across the early morning sun. She blinked as she registered Harry's towering figure. He stood above her, a grin on his firm lips . . . and all her earlier resolve weakened at the ease of his smile. "Harry," she greeted. "Whatever are you doing here?" She returned his smile from around the opened book.

He leaned over and plucked the tome from her fingers. "I came to see you."

Her heart fluttered wildly, even as she knew the dangers of that fool sensation. "You did?"

He nodded.

"How did you know where to find me?"

He winked. "I've my ways, love." He paused. "My footman bribed one of your maids."

A startled laugh burst from her lips. "You're incorrigible." However, warmth spiraled through her belly and fanned out, heating her through. He'd cared enough, wanted to see her enough that he'd sent a footman to find her maid to discover her whereabouts.

Then she froze. The air suspended in her lungs as his words registered. *All* of his words. In the span of a moment she'd become more than just "sweet" . . . she'd become his "love." And though a man such as Harry would never mean anything more by that endearment, warmth exploded into a fiery conflagration inside her heart, and spread out with a growing force through every corner of her being.

His next words snuffed out all hint of romantic musings faster than a strong night wind on a candle's wick. "It is as I suspected before," he murmured. "You cannot see."

Anne made no attempt at ceremony. "I can see." She made an unsuccessful grab at her book. "I just cannot see so very well when I'm *reading*," she muttered.

"Tsk, tsk." He held the book out of her reach. "Never tell me you are too proud for something as common as spectacles." He crouched beside her.

Her heart twisted. In the time she'd come to know him and appreciate the many erroneous assumptions she'd drawn about Harry, he continued to see her just as all Society did—an empty-headed, vain, *pleasantly pretty* young lady as the scandal sheets had labeled her upon her Come Out three years ago. "Give me that." Anne wrestled the book from his hands. He released it swiftly and she nearly toppled backward.

He tugged one of her strands of hair the way he might a bothersome sister and not the young lady he'd pledged to introduce to the art of the seduction. "Come, what's this? You've gone all serious, Anne."

"I'm not," she blurted.

Harry cocked his head. "Yes, I do say you seem rather serious. Your lips are pulled down tight in the corners, here." He brushed the backs of his knuckles along the corner of her mouth, and she leaned into his soft caress. "And you've got those same four lines at the center of your brow whenever you're pondering something."

Emotion clogged her throat. Harry knew her so well he could detect the subtle nuances of her body's movements. "No. You misunderstood me." No one ever looked close enough to truly see her. "I meant, I'm not too proud." She glanced at the copy of *The Mysteries of Udolpho* in her hands. Then, how many times had she forsaken spectacles at Mother's insistence, fearful she'd not make an advantageous match for the minute detail? "Or perhaps I am." Shame filled her as she confronted her own vanity; did she truly wish to have a husband who'd not permit her the simple pleasures of reading? Did she want to wed a man who'd be so shallow as to begrudge her the necessity of spectacles?

Before, she'd not thought it mattered so much. Stability seemed more important than all else. Now, other less-tangible dreams held a dangerous appeal that threatened the goals she'd carried these many years now. She braced for a rush of panic—that did not come. Harry studied her with intensity in his hazel eyes, saying nothing, his face set in an expressionless mask and just then she wanted to share the truth with him, when no one else knew it. Her gaze slid to a point beyond his shoulder. "Aldora wears spectacles."

Harry claimed the seat beside her on the grass. He stretched his long legs out in front of him as though reclining on a fine upholstered sofa and not upon the dew-dampened morning grass. "And?"

She lifted her shoulder in a shrug. "I'm just Anne."

"And you wouldn't be with spectacles?" Had his question contained a recrimination, she wouldn't have continued, but it didn't.

Heat flooded her cheeks and she spoke on a rush, needing him to understand. "I'm not seen as the intelligent one as Aldora or the sensible one like Katherine."

He quirked a golden eyebrow.

Her heart wrenched at the unwitting reminder of his attempted seduction of her twin. "But all my life, I've been the pleasantly pretty one, Harry." She lifted her palms. "If I'm not pleasantly pretty, then what am I?" Her mother and the world had been quite clear—she was nothing without being a pleasantly pretty English miss. Until Harry, she'd buried the truth even from herself—she wanted to be seen as more, appreciated for more.

She curled her toes with the truth she'd at last shared; sure he'd chuckle at her in that charming, affable, roguish way of his and not knowing if she could stand the pain of that. He passed his eyes over her a long while. He came up on his knees over her and claimed her chin between his thumb and forefinger. Anne braced for an onslaught of his amusement.

"Look at me," he demanded in that commanding, harsh tone that had probably been the demise of too many young ladies' good reputations. She looked up. "You will never be *just* anything."

Anne swallowed hard, as there amidst the copse with just the noisy kestrel overhead as her witness—Anne fell in love. She expected she should feel the race of panic in her breast. The impending sense of doom that would surely come in giving her heart to a man who no more wanted possession of the foolish organ than he wanted to attend Sunday sermon after a sinful night of debauchery. Later, she'd restore her mind and heart to rights. When the birds didn't soar about the pink-and-orange-tinted morning sky and Harry didn't study her with his hot, heated stare, she'd recall her mother's warnings and all the perils in loving such a man.

For now, she knew she loved him. Logic could come later.

"Close your eyes," he instructed.

Her lids fluttered closed and she tipped her head back to receive his kiss. The book tumbled from her fingers as she prepared to open herself up to the fierce invasion of his mouth. Wanting his kiss. *Needing* his kiss. And needing him. She needed him. Something cool and metallic touched her burning skin. Her eyes flew open.

He thrust her opened book into her hands. "Here."

She stared at the concise, clear words. Words that didn't blur together and require squinting in order to bring them into focus. She touched the wire-rimmed spectacles perched on her nose. "You gave me spectacles," she whispered.

He cupped her cheek. "And you're still as beautiful as you've always been, Anne," he said softly. Tears filled her eyes. He released her as if her skin had burned his palms. He nearly fell over himself in his attempt to put distance between them. "Egad, you're crying." He jumped up.

She tipped up the spectacles and dashed away the hint of moisture. "I am not," she said defensively.

He snorted. "You are."

Anne set the book down hard beside her. "I merely had something in my eye."

A muscle jumped at the corner of his eye, as though detecting the clear lie to her words. "I detest a woman's tears," he muttered.

She glared up at him, *detesting* his placing her into a category with all women. "Well, that is fine, my lord, because I don't make it a habit of crying." The last tear she'd shed had been when she'd made her Come Out and discovered the truth of her whore-mongering, wastrel father. After that, she'd decided no gentleman was deserving of a single salty memento. "And furthermore, if I *had* been crying, which I certainly was not," she added pointedly when he opened his mouth to speak, "tears of happiness are entirely acceptable."

He eyed her a long while. "No forms of tears are acceptable. Ever," he spoke with a resolute firmness. "They're merely a ploy used by women to wheedle their way into a gentleman's heart."

She folded her arms across her chest. Oh, the lout. Of course, she'd have the bad sense to go and fall in love with a gentleman who possessed an ill opinion of women and happened to be missing a heart. "I don't use tears."

He dropped to his haunches beside her. "A lady is better advised to use her mouth to entice a man than those crystal drops."

His words had the same effect as a powerful slap. They reminded her of Harry's fleeting presence in her life. She might love him, but she remained nothing more than a bothersome miss whom he'd generously offered to help, and merely because of her connection to Katherine, not out of any regard or concern for Anne, herself. The knife twisted in her heart. The muscles in her throat moved up and down with the force of her swallow. "Is this just another lesson, then, Harry?" For the first time since she'd enlisted his support, she realized Harry, the Earl of Stanhope, was, in fact, the one in desperate need of a lesson.

Tension snapped Harry's body erect, unnerved by the sudden realization—he'd not thought of the damned lessons on seduction once. Not when he'd had his footman find out from Anne's maid when he could find the young lady alone. And not when he'd come upon her in this tucked-away copse, like Eve in her garden of sin.

Except now, she'd mentioned the damned lessons and an ugly vision wrapped its tentacle-like grip about his vile musings—Crawford taking Anne's lush lips under his. Anne moaning as her blasted duke slipped his tongue inside and made love to her mouth the way Harry ached to worship her body.

Anne came up on her knees. "Should I touch a finger to the corner of my lips?" The tip of her index finger tantalizingly, invitingly stroked the edge of her mouth. She inched closer to him. "Or should I trail my tongue over my lips invitingly." The pink tip darted out and circled her lips, lingering on the plump flesh of her slightly fuller lower lip.

His heart thudded. "Where have you learned such a trick?" He'd kill the blighter who'd shown her such things. The role belonged to him alone.

She tipped her head. "Because it is wrong, Harry?"

Because it was right. *Too* right. And yet, wrong all at the same time. Desire flared inside him.

Her hand fluttered about her breast. She captured a loose, golden strand between her fingers and rubbed it along the modest décolletage of her gown. His breath left him. He'd had the pleasure of bedding some of the most inventive creatures on the Continent. Women of skill. Women who'd found pleasure in giving *him* pleasure. In this moment, he couldn't recall a single one of their faces, their actions, or even their names. He saw only Anne. He caught her to him. "Are you seducing me, Anne?" he whispered harshly against her temple.

"Is it working?" she asked on a sultry whisper.

"It is, love." He didn't recognize the garbled quality of his voice.

She tilted her head back, eyes closed, searching for his kiss. Harry lowered his head. Their mouths a breath apart, heat rolling off her body in waves. He claimed her lips in a gentle meeting. Anne leaned into him and Harry deepened the kiss, knocking her glasses askew. She moaned. The heady erotic sound shattered the quiet and penetrated the spell she'd cast upon him. He drew back, chest heaving with the force of his desire. He wanted to freeze this moment with her. Make Anne his in every way; in a world away from the reality of broken promises and the pain of betrayal. Away from the fear of losing—again.

Her eyes flew open. "Why did you . . . ?" Red blossomed on her cheeks.

He'd not lay claim to her body in this tucked-away haven, just a stone's throw from a possible passerby. He might be a bastard but there was still honor in him.

He adjusted her spectacles and then pressed a kiss to her forehead. "I'll not disrespect you more than I have here, Anne."

"You didn't disrespect me," she blurted.

Except he had. Each time he met her without a chaperone, he risked ruining her with his attention. He fought back a groan. If the *ton* could see the change she'd wrought upon him, they'd be laughing all the way to the betting books at White's to guess the date of his and Anne's impeding nuptials. Harry blinked several times. *Marriage?* He stumbled back.

Anne scratched at her brow. "Harry?"

Harry attempted to still the panicked beat of his heart, fearing this momentary lapse in sanity. Fearing it was, in fact, more. Only, it couldn't be. He'd not be so imprudent as to fall in love. He affected a lazy grin. "Come, Anne, even I'll not steal your virtue in Hyde Park." She'd chosen her duke long ago. And he'd chosen the safety of an uninjured heart.

She pursed her lips. "But—"

Harry tweaked her nose, killing the words that would follow. "I'll not chance someone stumbling by." This could never be anything more. Not with her. Nor any woman. "Then you'd be stuck with this old rogue for a husband instead of your duke." Yet, why then did a sharp pain twist inside him with the knowing that some other man would lay claim to her?

Anne passed a searching gaze over his face. "Is that what you'd have, Harry? Would you have me become his duchess?" Her question emerged haltingly.

He fisted his hands tight at his side as the image of her in the marital ducal bed rolled through his mind. He imagined a world in which Anne belonged to Crawford while Harry waited on the sidelines for a place in the wedded lady's bed. Only . . . knowing Anne as he now did, he knew she'd never give herself to another. Not after she bound herself to a man. She'd honor Crawford, or whoever the nameless, faceless gentleman who took her to wife in name, body, and spirit.

Harry dusted his hands over the front of his breeches. "No, Anne. *You'd* have you become his duchess." He sketched a bow and ignoring the question in her eyes, turned on his heel and left.

Wishing for the first time that he could be more than a shiftless bounder.

Chapter 15

*A*nne made it no farther than the foyer before her mother descended upon her like a hawk circling a poor field mouse. "Where were you, Anne Adamson?" Mother sailed down the sweeping staircase in a flurry of pale-peach skirts.

"I—"

Mother wrapped a hand around Anne's forearm and propelled her forward. "Your hair is mussed. Your skirts are wrinkled. And . . ." She jerked to a sudden halt and dragged Anne in front of her. Horror filled her eyes. "Are those spectacles?" she hissed. She plucked the precious gift from Anne's nose.

"No!" She grabbed for them. "They're merely to help me re—"

"By the queen and all her maids, if you say read, Anne, you'll not see another ball this Season."

This would be rather fine with Anne who, after two full Seasons and part of a third, had grown to detest the silly, nonsensical events. Anne slipped her glasses back from her mother's distracted hands and buried them into the side of her skirt.

"Oh, why, why must you have gone out and returned looking like you've"—Mother dropped her voice to a hushed whisper—"been doing inappropriate things in the grass."

She'd been so very close to doing all number of inappropriate things in the grass. Regret tightened in her belly. If Harry weren't so very honorable . . .

Her mother narrowed her gaze as though she'd gleaned her daughter's thoughts.

"I was reading, Mother," Anne said quietly. She may as well have said she'd been tupping a servant.

Mother's eyes went round in her face. "Regardless, there is no time to change your attire, to right your hair. He's been waiting." She took Anne's hand and tugged her from the corridor.

Anne cocked her head as they continued the brisk pace through the house. "He . . . ?"

Mother drew to a halt beside the drawing room. The Duke of Crawford stood at the empty hearth, hands clasped behind his back.

Oh. That *he*. Noting her sudden appearance, his broad shoulders stiffened. The fabric of his fine russet jacket tightened over his frame.

Mother rushed past Anne. She sank into a deep, deferential curtsy. "Your Grace, thank you ever so much for your patience. My Anne has a strong constitution and enjoys a brisk walk in the morning . . ." The countess continued to prattle on and on.

The duke shifted his hard gaze to Anne. His probing stare lingered a moment on the stained white hemline of her day dress. Anne tipped her chin as he returned his attention to her face. The ghost of a smile played about his lips, with unexpected amusement at her slight show of insolence. He bowed.

From the doorway, Anne dipped a belated curtsy.

Mother looked between them and Anne ventured the title-hungry countess even now planned the distinguished guest list and morning breakfast for some imagined wedding between Anne and the duke. She held her hands out. "Come forth, dear Anne. His Grace has come to visit you." Her high-pitched whiny tone and wild gesticulations were better reserved for a recalcitrant dog than a cherished daughter.

Anne winced. She threw a quick glance over her shoulder, eying a hasty retreat. When she returned her attention to the pair now studying her, she startled. And then started forward. She stopped wordlessly before the duke.

A beaming, white smile wreathed Mother's ageless cheeks. "Splendid!" She made her eyes go wide again in her best attempt at shock and surprise. "My goodness, wherever is Mary? Pardon me a moment while I retrieve Anne's maid."

Words of protest sprung to Anne's lips, even as her faithless mother rushed from the room. Ah, so this is what it felt like to be turned over for a bag of silver. Anne shifted back and forth on her feet. For weeks she'd considered how to bring this very man up to scratch. She'd risked her reputation and sought out the notorious Earl of Stanhope's assistance on the matter of seduction. Except, now, with the duke before her, all the reasons, wishes, and rationale behind a match with this man fled. She didn't want a duke.

Not this duke.

Not *any* duke.

She wanted far more than a duke.

She wanted Harry. Her eyes slid closed. *God in heaven what have I done?*

"I must admit, I don't usually find myself the recipient of shocked horror."

Anne snapped her eyes open at the duke's droll response. "Y-your Grace?" Her voice cracked.

The duke looped his arms behind his back and rocked back and forth on the heels of his gleaming black shoes. "Eager fawning, wide-eyed stares, but never shocked horror." Such words could have been construed as bold, ducal arrogance. Then . . . he winked.

And in that moment Anne realized the Duke of Crawford had a sense of humor. She smiled, suddenly, unexpectedly at ease. "Not horror," she assured him. She claimed the edge of the ivory embroidered sofa and motioned to the chair opposite her.

He flicked his coattails and settled into the gold-trimmed armchair. "Shock, then?"

Shock that had everything to do with a strikingly powerful, golden-haired gentleman, and nothing to do with this man. "Perhaps a wee bit of shock."

They shared a smile.

Relief surged through her as Mary discreetly slipped into the room. The maid sought out her usual chair at the far back corner of the large parlor. Anne supposed she should have welcomed the time without her chaperone. Except she hadn't. This man, a stranger, did not rouse the gentle ease that Harry's presence did.

The duke sat back in his seat. He folded his arms across his broad, surprisingly well-muscled chest. Hmm, she'd have imagined he'd be one of those padded gentleman. It seemed not. His lips pulled at the corner and her skin warmed with embarrassment. He'd clearly noted her study and most likely took it for interest. Which it was assuredly not. Though handsome, it would be nigh impossible to admire any other figure when Harry had taken her in his arms and all but made love to her.

Or had he made love to her?

She suspected there was an element of lovemaking to what had transpired between them in their tucked-away copse—

"I would trade my country holdings to know the reason for that delightful smile."

She jumped. "That would be rather a waste of your country holdings, Your Grace." And the end of her reputation if her actions this morning were discovered.

"Well, I have a good deal in terms of holdings, that it wouldn't be missed." At one time that would have mattered a great deal to her. Not anymore. "Why do I gather from your reaction that you seem wholly unimpressed by such a claim?"

Anne fiddled with the spectacles in her hands. Why, indeed? Why, when she'd craved monetary security above all else these nearly eight years now? Despite her family's and Society's ill opinion of her, she craved more than material possessions. She yearned for stability. Harry's grin flitted through her mind. And there was nothing stable in loving a man such a Harry. "Not at all," she said at long last. Long enough for him to surely note her pause and detect the certain lie there.

He leaned forward. The scent of him, sandalwood and spice, pleasant but *not Harry*, wafted about her. "May I speak candidly?" he said with a bluntness that surely came from someone in possession of his lofty rank.

She nodded. "I prefer candid to veiled, Your Grace."

That fleeting grin tugged at his lips and then disappeared, settling into a familiar, unsmiling mask of this man who seemed to fear expressions of mirth. Was it merely his station? Or had something happened to turn him so very serious? Her own girlhood had taught her that no one could truly understand what shaped an individual's past. "I'd ask for your hand if I thought you might say yes," he said quietly.

Anne blinked as his words penetrated her musings. "Beg pardon?"

He stretched his legs in front of him as though he'd asked for refreshments and not just hinted at an offer of marriage. "Marriage, my lady."

"But you don't know me," she blurted. Her heart drummed loudly in her ears, steady, loud, and hard; a painful staccato that threatened her with a devilish headache.

"I know enough to know you'd make a suitable duchess."

She frowned. That is what he'd base a marital offer upon? Her being *suitable*. Garments were suitable. Portions of the morning meals were suitable. Potential spouses were not.

"Most young ladies would be pleased by my words," he said with a bluntness she appreciated.

"I'm not most young ladies, Your Grace."

He inclined his head. "No. Which is why I'd make you my duchess. If I thought you might say yes," he added once more. Many marriages had begun from less. Most had begun from more. "Alas, I'd venture you'd toss away the opportunity to be my duchess for Lord Stanhope."

Her heart paused midbeat.

"You needn't say anything. It is written in every line of your face when he enters a room."

Heat rushed her cheeks. If she'd been transparent to this gentleman, a stranger, then surely Harry had noted her unwise interest. The duke's gaze fell to her mouth. *Smile with your eyes and your lips as one. A sultry, sweet smile, Anne. A smile that convinces a man he's the only one in the room . . .* She couldn't. Not even if a smile were to mean the title of Queen of England.

"But when you realize Stanhope won't make you his wife, then I'll have you."

He spoke as a man accustomed to having his wishes honored.

A knock sounded at the door, and Anne was saved from answering. She glanced toward the door, past the butler, to the commanding gentleman at the entrance. A light sensation lifted her heart at Harry's unexpected appearance.

Ollie cleared his throat. "The Earl of Stanhope." The old servant bowed and shuffled past the earl.

What is he doing here? Her heart kicked up a beat. With the speed of his earlier departure, she'd thought not to see him until he decided to impart the next lesson.

Only, Harry stood at the entrance of the room, his primal gaze lingering on the duke. Then, he shifted his attention to Anne. "My lady."

Anne rose quickly. Her skirts snapped about her ankles. She dropped a curtsy. "My lord."

An awkward pall descended upon the room. The duke stood. Tension fairly dripped from his formidable frame. He issued a stiff bow. "If you'll excuse me. I'll leave you to your visit." He held Anne's gaze. "I encourage you to think on what I've said."

Harry stepped aside as the duke made to take his exit. The two men eyed each other a long moment, and then without a word, the Duke of Crawford left.

Harry strolled into the room. Once again the familiar, affable, coolly elegant gentleman she'd come to know. "What was that about?" he asked on a lazy drawl.

She fisted her hands. How could he appear so unaffected by her nearness when he now consumed her sleeping and waking thoughts? "He expressed an interest in courting me," she said bluntly. Though his words had actually danced more around marriage than anything else. Something called that truth back.

He paused midstride. Then he completed the step. He continued walking until he came to a stop before her. "Oh?" he arched a golden brow.

"Mary," she called to her maid across the room. "Will you fetch my book?"

"Which book will you require, my lady?" The young woman sprang from her seat.

"Any book shall do."

The maid hesitated and then raced from the room.

Anne drew in a breath. She dug her toes into the soles of her slippers, making them so tight, the arches of her feet ached. She loved him. Against all better judgment. Against all her earlier convictions to never be one of his ladies in the conservatory. But then, in matters of the heart, things such as logic and reason ceased to exist and deep down, she believed his curt "Oh" concealed more than he wished to reveal.

Even if it didn't, she needed to tell him. She needed for him to know he owned her heart in ways Crawford or no other gentleman could. If she didn't confess her love and allowed him to think he meant no more to her than a lesson in seduction, there would never be even the hope of more. Not with him.

Harry affected an attitude of indifference. He glanced disinterestedly at the suspicious maid who hurried to do her mistress's bidding even as a volatile force thrummed through his entire being. A primitive urge filled him. A desire to drag Anne close, and brand her as his with a hot, furious kiss.

He captured the heart pendant around her neck between his thumb and forefinger. She'd enlisted his aid solely to win the heart of a duke and by Crawford's appearance and the lady's words, it seemed to have proven wholly effective. "It would appear your bauble has served you well."

She flinched as though he'd struck her.

Sheer madness had compelled him to visit. He'd taken his leave of her in Hyde Park just a short while ago. Yet, she'd managed to weave some captivating spell that drove back logic and the sense to avoid a woman like Anne. A woman who'd settle for nothing less than marriage . . . and in her case, a duke.

Just like Margaret.

Yet, at the same time, nothing like Margaret. Only now could he force himself to acknowledge that truth. Instead of finding comfort in the differences in the women, panic battered his insides. He preferred the Lady Anne he'd believed her to be this past year who would sell her soul for the title of duchess because then it would make the idea of losing her something he could survive. "You'll marry him, then," he said, his voice flat.

She placed her hand over his, stilling his distracted movement. "I don't believe I will."

Harry froze. He studied their connected fingers. "Why?" he demanded hoarsely.

She tilted her head back. The graceful column of her throat moved up and down. "I find I do not really want a duke after all, Harry."

Don't ask the question unless you're prepared for her answer. "Why?"

Her lids fluttered. "I rather find an earl would do quite nicely."

He sucked in a breath. "What game do you play?" he asked, his tone harsh.

Anne eyed him with gentle warmth that threatened to undo him. "There is no game, Harry."

For a long time, he'd viewed Anne as a selfish, title-hungry miss, who'd have Crawford at any cost. After all, isn't that ultimately what all young ladies craved? But now, for the first time, someone had chosen Harry . . . over a powerful duke.

Nay, not someone. Anne. She'd chosen him. And it scared the bloody hell out of him. *Christ. Set her away. Release her hand. Turn on your heel.* He could never be all she required in a husband, nor could he open himself up to trusting again. *Why not?* a voice needled. She could have Crawford, but she would throw him over—*for me.* "Anne," he said gruffly. But for her name, for the first time, in a very long time, words failed him.

"You needn't say anything." She gave him a small smile. "I do not expect a pledge of love or undying devotion." She wrinkled her nose. "Though a strong modicum of devotion would do." Her lips turned down. "That isn't to say I'd appreciate your conducting yourself in a roguish manner as you have these years now. I wouldn't. So in that sense, I'd rather you be devoted."

A quiet laugh rumbled up from his throat. "What are you trying to say?"

She looked him square in the eyes. "I love you, Harry, and I know it is the height of foolishness to entrust my heart to one such as you . . ."

At her innocent admission, a blinding panic filled him. The cynical Harry who'd first kissed her in Lord Essex's conservatory would have sneered at Anne's words of love. This new man, a stranger he no longer recognized, instead fixed on her last four words. *One such as you . . . ?* He rather detested the sound of that. Granted, the lady was, of course, accurate—it was madness to entrust any part of her to his unscrupulous hands.

God help him, though.

He wanted her. And perhaps this desire to hold her, to claim her, to make her laugh and tease her were transient sentiments that would fade in the days and weeks he came to know her. But for now, he could only focus on this over-whelming desire to make her his and drive away any thoughts she might still have of *pleasantly handsome, unfailingly polite, and wealthy dukes in possession of one of the oldest titles . . .* He searched her face, and more importantly, searched for words, but he could not promise her forever.

Harry opened his mouth and Anne jabbed him in the chest. "Don't look at me like that. As though you pity me," she clarified. "As though you're trying to find a sufficient response. I don't crave empty words from you." She held his gaze. "I'd have only the truth."

And yet, she deserved more than that. For all the times he'd scoffed at her selection of Crawford. The duke was, in fact, the better, more respectable match she deserved. Harry would always be a rogue. He dropped his brow to hers. "I don't know if I'll ever have the words you crave and assur-edly deserve, but I know I want you. And when I eventually do right by the Stanhope line, then I imagine a union with you would suffice." His lips pulled in a grimace. His declara-tion was not the heartfelt words any young lady hoped for. He'd not fill her ears with platitudes and falsities most young ladies hung their hopes and dreams upon.

"Suffice?" That low, drawn-out whisper would have been enough to raise terror in most men. She stuck another finger in his chest. "Did you say a marriage to me would . . . *suffice*?"

He flinched, recognizing the certain dangers when a lady tended to repeat herself in that outraged tone. He eyed the path of escape over her shoulder. Yes, he really should have a care. "What would you have me say?" He cared about her enough to not lie to her. "I thought you desired the truth, Anne, and I've given you that. What would you have of me? I've told you before, there is nothing left of my heart."

Her body jerked and he would have traded every single one of his holdings to call the words back, if for no other reason than to spare her this hurt. "No. You are indeed correct," she said huskily. "I'd not have falsity from you." Her eyes blazed with the force of her emotion. "I'll not have a man marry me because I'm suitable. My mother had my father because he sufficed."

He growled, not caring about being tucked into a neat little category with men such as her father, as effortlessly as she arranged her satin ribbons.

She gave a terse nod and stepped out of his arms. "Very well, Harry." She held a hand out.

Harry eyed the five graceful fingers warily, knowing Anne enough to know there was certainly more to that "Very well, Harry." He took her fingers in his.

Anne gave his hand a solid shake. She looked to the doorway. He followed her gaze to the wide-eyed maid who stood in the entrance, a leather book in her hands.

"Mary," she said. "Lord Stanhope was just leaving." She gave a toss of her loose, golden waves. With head held as high as the queen marching past her lowly subjects, she sailed past her maid and out of the room.

As Harry stood, staring after her, he couldn't rid himself of a sudden sense of foreboding that Lady Anne Adamson had launched an all-out battle.

Chapter 16

$\mathscr{S}$tanding in front of the bevel glass mirror at the corner of her room, Anne came to a very unexpected revelation. She might perhaps be just a bit more than a pleasingly pretty proper English miss, as the papers had labeled her during her first Season. Those same gossip columns had lamented that a placid English miss should find herself still unwed after a second Season. Now, she thought perhaps there was a bit more merit to Harry's claims on the art of seduction and beauty than she'd originally credited. Oh, that isn't to say she'd not trusted his judgment over hers in matters of . . . of . . . er, ensuring a person's notice.

She'd just not quite imagined how a single gown, a different coiffure, and a strategically placed strand of hair could transform someone.

Anne tilted her head and studied herself objectively as she tried to see the woman Harry might see that evening. If the lout left his clubs to attend a single one of the same soirees Mother had accepted invitations to. The diaphanous burnt-orange satin clung to her skin. A single thread of gold lined the daring décolletage. She touched the loose curl woven with a pale orange ribbon that dangled between the swell of her breasts.

Would he be indifferent toward the woman who employed the carefully taught strategies he'd given her this past week? Would he see her as a hellish termagant, as he'd called her on countless occasions? Or would he see in her a sufficient match when he . . . nay, *if* he ever decided to set aside his roguish ways?

"You are beautiful, my lady," her maid, Mary, breathed over her shoulder.

She caught her maid's shocked visage in the mirror. "Do you believe my mother will concur?"

Mary snorted.

Anne's lips pulled up in a humorless smile. "When do you venture she'll permit me to leave the townhouse after this display?"

"Perhaps next winter," Mary replied automatically. She held up the silver muslin cloak in her hands.

Anne presented her back and allowed the young woman to assist her into the garment. She fastened the hooks at her throat. Approaching her twenty-first year and midway through her third Season, certain liberties were afforded the young women who claimed the same unwed status. She squared her shoulders, feeling she imagined much the way Wellington had at Waterloo, and marched to the door. Mary pulled it open.

Anne concentrated on the soft pad of silver slippers upon the thin carpeted floor. She counted each step, in doing so she'd not have to consider Mother's inevitable outrage, but worse—the possibility that all her efforts tonight would be for naught. The scandalous measures she'd gone to, seeking out the most sophisticated, lauded French modiste and turning over every last coin of her pin money to have a stunning creation readied in such a short span of time.

She reached the top of the winding staircase. Her mother glanced up. "Hurry, hurry, Anne. The duke has surely arrived by now." She tugged on her stark-white evening gloves.

If Mother were to find out that the Duke of Crawford had mentioned marriage and Anne's name together and her daughter hadn't managed even a hint of joy or gratitude, she'd have Anne wed to cousin Bertrand as certain punishment.

As Anne made her slow descent, she gave thanks for the protective cover of her cloak. Her mother would have ordered her back abovestairs, to her chambers, and into a new, more suitable gown if she'd caught one glimpse of Anne's scandalous gown.

The butler pulled the door open. She smiled up at him as she trailed after Mother, onward to the waiting carriage.

The driver stood beside the black lacquer carriage. A footman assisted Mother inside, and then handed Anne up. She murmured her thanks and settled into the thick, plush, red-velvet squabs. The door clicked closed lending finality to her bold decision this evening. She swallowed hard, toying with the fabric of her cloak.

"I venture he'll offer for you soon, Anne," Mother said, with a smile to rival a child given the last cherry tart at dessert.

"Who, Mother?"

Her mother's eyebrows snapped together. "Do not make light of this, Anne. This is your third Season. And you were the one I'd imagined would have made a match within the first month of your Come Out." She patted the back of her head. "Though, if you manage to bring Crawford up to scratch, well then all will be forgiven."

Ah, yes, because she'd only served one purpose for the Countess of Wakefield—marriage to a lofty lord. Over the years, Anne's worth had been measured in the match she might make and not more than that. She bit back the stinging words on her lips. "Is my unwed state something that requires forgiveness?" she asked, her tone dry.

Her mother carried on as though she'd not spoken. "Oh, can you imagine my ultimate triumph over all those who've made snide remarks about your unwed state?"

Her stomach muscles clenched involuntarily. She'd not allowed herself to consider the unkind comments made after two failed Seasons—even if those "failed Seasons" had been in large part a decision she'd made. A desire for more. Once, the title of duchess, now . . . the love of a gentleman who didn't even believe in that emotion.

She pulled the curtain back and peered out at the passing streets. The irony of her situation didn't escape her. If anyone had told her a mere week ago that the Duke of Crawford would have courted her and spoken marriage, and she'd have rebuffed any interest on his part for Harry, the Earl of Stanhope, she'd have eaten every last one of her ribbons.

Now, she knew she wanted more than a duke.

And she was determined to not sit around waiting for Harry to realize she was more than *sufficient*. Her smiling visage reflected back in the windowpane.

I hope you are prepared to have your lessons used fully against you, Harry Falston, Earl of Stanhope.

He'd not seen her in three damned days. Which, in the scheme of time, wasn't altogether very long. Rather, a mere seventy-two hours. That somehow managed to seem like a bloody eternity. With Anne's profession of love, he should have run as far and as fast as his legs would carry him. Instead . . .

Harry scanned the crowded ballroom. He passed his gaze over a sea of blonde hair either a shade too light or a touch too dark, searching for the pale-honey tresses kissed with liquid sunshine.

"You do know Society has noted your interest in the particular lady," Edgerton drawled at his side.

"Go to hell," Harry muttered, dismissing his friend. When he'd handed Anne the truth those three days ago, he'd suspected she'd been wounded. He'd not, however, imagined she'd cut him from the fabric of her life as neatly as she'd snip the thread from an embroidery frame.

A servant came over bearing a tray of champagne. Edgerton retrieved two glasses. He handed one wordlessly over to Harry.

Harry took a sip and continued his search over the rim of his glass. And that was another matter entirely. Did Lady Anne embroider? He didn't know if the lady was proficient or whether she enjoyed it. He knew she tasted of raspberries and lemon. He knew the way her brow wrinkled with annoyance. He even knew the breathy little moans that escaped her lips when she came undone in his arms. But he didn't know the littlest pieces that together made Lady Anne and he intended to rectify that.

As soon as he found her.

He skimmed the hall. Where in hell was she? His footman had it on good authority from her tight-lipped maid the lady would be attending Lady Preston's. He took a long swallow of fine French champagne. Alas, it would seem it had come to this. He, the Earl of Stanhope, likening her hair to hues of gold and sunshine like a lovesick poet, and sending his servants to ascertain the lady's plans for the evening.

A buzz filled the crowded space, like a swarm of angry bees knocked from their nest. He ignored the overly loud whispers and continued his search.

Edgerton whistled. "Well, well," he murmured.

"What is it?" Harry asked distractedly.

"It would seem you, my friend, saw a diamond amidst paste baubles." He motioned with his nearly empty glass to the receiving line at the crest of Lord and Lady Preston's staircase into the main hall.

"What are you on . . ." He fixed his gaze on the arrival of a golden beauty draped in burnt-orange satin. The candles strategically placed throughout the ballroom cast a pale glow about her, lending an almost ethereal, otherworldly quality to the woman. ". . . about?" The air left him on a slow exhale.

Vaguely familiar, and yet . . . not. The slender, sweetly curved temptress had the look of a siren who'd just broke through fiery waters and climbed ashore. She fingered a loose blonde curl artfully arranged between the crevice of her delectable mounds of white flesh, calling Harry's—and every living, breathing gentlemen's—attention to the enticing décolletage. She stood, regally elegant, while introductions were made. She worked her gaze over the crowd, bypassing the interested stares trained on her by lustful lords and jaded rogues.

He willed her stare to his, willed her to forget every single last unworthy gentleman present. As though she sensed his silent beckoning, her pale-blue eyes collided with his.

A slow, inviting smile turned the corner of her lips. *Smile with your eyes . . . and your lips as one . . .* The air left him on a soft hiss. Ah, God, she was. With her lips, eyes, her every movement she smiled. *Lady Anne Arlette Adamson.*

Lord and Lady Preston's majordomo could have rattled off the name. Or mayhap the four words, her name, echoed around the chambers of his mind.

He held his glass of champagne out.

Edgerton accepted it with a cynical chuckle. "You've gone all moon-eyed."

Perhaps he had. She'd captivated him, mind, body, and soul.

Harry cut a quick path through the crowd. He shouldered his way past gentlemen determined to encroach on that which was Harry's but whose wits had been dulled by the mere presence of her. She hovered at the edge of the ballroom floor. The orchestra struck up the chords of a waltz. He quickened his step. So close.

Lord Rutland, rogue, reprobate, everything Anne deserved so much more than, sidled up to her. The same bastard he'd sparred with for Margaret's affections would now turn his lecherous sights upon Anne?

Harry growled. He'd meet the bastard at dawn once more, and this time it wouldn't merely be for the draw of first blood, but to the damned death. He nearly sprinted the remainder of the way. His footsteps beat an angry rhythm upon the Italian marble floor as he recalled her boast more than a week ago to enlist Rutland's support. He'd put his fist in the other man's face before he allowed him to sully her with his presence. Couldn't Rutland realize a woman of her wit, humor, and beauty deserved more than a jaded lord with a hard-edged smile?

He narrowed his gaze upon the couple as Rutland dared to touch the dance card dangling from her wrist. "I believe this set is mine," Harry barked as he came upon them, attracting rapacious stares from nearby lords and ladies.

Anne started as though startled by his sudden appearance, which was, of course, madness. Surely her body's awareness of him rivaled his own sense of knowing whenever she was near. Another seductive smile tugged at the corners of her lips.

He fisted his hands at his side. Where in hell had Anne learned such a thing? Then Harry blinked with the sick, slow realization—she'd learned every last seductive trick from him. Harry had schooled her—too well.

Rutland eyed Harry with an ice-cold grin. "Stanhope," he said, running a contemptuous glance over him. "The lady's only just arrived. Her dance card is as of yet—"

"Filled with my name," he bit out. If Rutland cared to debate the point, he'd gladly do it with his fists outside the fashionable ballroom floor. Harry held out his hand.

Anne eyed him a long while. His stomach roiled as a sudden, irrational fear coursed through him that she intended to reject his offer, that she intended to allow Rutland to put his lecherous hands upon her satiny soft shoulders and touch her waist and this, this would be so much different than the fight he'd waged for Margaret's affections. This would eat away at Harry like a fast-moving cancer.

She placed her fingertips in Harry's hand. He folded his around them and studied the interlocked digits a moment.

Home.

He guided her to the ballroom floor while Rutland glared after him. A primordial sense of masculine victory consumed him at Anne's clear decision. They took their positions at the rapidly filling ballroom floor. He settled his hand upon her waist and guided hers upon his shoulder. "You aren't to go near Rutland. I thought I'd been clear," he said, his tone brusque.

Anne arched a golden brow. "Come, Harry. Surely you don't care if I take Rutland or the Prince Regent himself as my partner."

Actually, yes. Yes, he did. He eyed her. She played some manner of game with him. And yet, he was still completely ensnared by her trap, unwanting and unwilling to shake free of her hold. The orchestra plucked the strings of a waltz. "You know, I despise the manner in which the men present eye you."

She pinched his shoulder. "Do you?" The teasing words, the slight pinch were more reserved for a bothersome older brother rather than a man who wanted to lay masterful claim to her. She touched the ribbon cleverly woven in that lone golden curl.

A groan built in his chest at the sweetly erotic gesture and then with all the force of the king's men riding into him it occurred to him. He narrowed his eyes. The little spitfire. The bold minx. Why, she'd used his own lessons against him. "You're seducing me, aren't you?" he whispered for her ears alone. Satisfaction flared in his chest. She didn't use her wiles upon her damned duke, but instead Harry.

She winked. "Is it working?" Bold as you please, for all to see, she winked at him.

"Yes." He'd never wanted another more than he wanted Lady Anne Adamson. He tightened his hold on her.

Anne's smile deepened. "I've been told I've learned from the most notorious rogue."

He angled her body closer to his. "The cad who'd dare teach a lady such scandalous tricks."

She tilted her chin up and whispered softly, "I would meet you, Harry."

If he were wise, he'd blithely ignore her request, continue waltzing her around the crowded ballroom floor, and then turn her over to her frowning mama's care. Alas, he'd not been wise in a very long time.

"I've heard told Lady Preston has rather splendid gardens," she continued.

The waltz drew to a finish. Couples around them politely clapped.

Harry studied the beautiful planes of her face knowing the perils in clandestinely meeting her. They danced with ruin. If discovered, they'd be forced to wed. "Perhaps those gardens require exploring, then." Some risks were worth taking.

Anne smiled, curtsied, and took her leave.

Harry stared after her swift-retreating form. There really was no helping it. He was a bastard.

"Have a care, Stanhope. You're staring," a low, surly voice growled from over his shoulder.

He spun. Lady Katherine's husband, the Duke of Bainbridge, stood, a familiar scowl fixed to his hard face. Harry gave a crooked grin.

"Wipe that damned smug smile from your face or by God I'll do it for you." The duke's lip curled back in a sneer.

For all of Katherine's influence in bringing the Mad Duke out of his self-imposed exile after the death of the man's first wife years earlier, the ugly brutish bear still seemed the boorish lout Harry remembered. Then, if a gentleman dared encroach upon the woman who was his wife, Harry would bloody the bastard senseless and then meet him at dawn.

"What do you have to say?" Bainbridge snapped.

The other man was a surly beast. "Bainbridge, a pleasure as usual," he lied. He still couldn't account for Lady Katherine's love of the fiend.

The duke's black glare nearly singed him.

"Wrong answer, then," Harry said with a sigh. "The next dance is beginning."

Bainbridge took a step closer. They earned curious stares from those around them. Society tended to remember when a gentleman tried to seduce another man's wife.

Harry held a hand up. "Please, rest assured, Bainbridge. I wasn't asking you to dance. Merely suggesting we continue this"—he arched an eyebrow—"er, discussion, elsewhere."

The other man registered the couples lining up around them for the next set. He spun around and marched from the ballroom floor, clearly, in his ducal arrogance, expecting Harry to follow.

Harry glanced around for a familiar blonde head. Alas, if his Anne, recently schooled in seduction, had been clear in her message—which she had . . . abundantly—she was even now in Lady Preston's prized gardens while he remained with Katherine's bear of a husband. "As much as I'd enjoy continuing our discourse, Bainbridge"—he'd far rather find Anne—"I'd—"

"You are to stay the hell away from my wife's sister."

Katherine's sister, as the cold, arrogant bastard referred to her, in fact, had a name. Her name was Anne and she was not defined by her connection to Katherine, even as the lady's family and Society believed it to be the singularly most important thing about her.

Harry firmed his jaw. He leaned close, his words intended for Bainbridge's ears alone. "You can go to hell."

The duke continued as though he'd not even spoken. "If you hurt Anne and through that hurt Katherine, by God I'll end you, Stanhope."

Harry suspected that threat had a good deal more to do with his whole attempt to seduce Katherine than anything else. He gave a curt nod. "Are we finished here?" he said with an affable grin.

If looks could kill, Bainbridge would have smote him with the fire in his eyes and probably eaten the ashes for an evening meal.

A loud buzz filled the ballroom. Knowing it would infuriate the other man; Harry directed his attention to the arrival of the guest who'd caused a stir at the front of the ballroom. He blinked. There was something vaguely familiar about the tall, voluptuous woman at the top of Lord and Lady Preston's stairs. She may as well have been any blousy widow he'd . . .

The air lodged in his lungs.

"What is it?" Bainbridge snapped.

Miss Margaret Dunn, now the Duchess of Monteith, had returned.

Chapter 17

*A*nne had done three small laps throughout the walled-in gardens, this little sliver of country a mere illusion in the grimy, crowded city streets of London. She paused beside a peony bush. A slight breeze stirred the flowers around her, catching them in a gentle night dance.

She shivered at the uncharacteristic cold and hugged her arms close to her chest. Perhaps he'd not come after all. Perhaps even in this, Harry—notorious scoundrel, unrepentant rogue—had demonstrated greater constraint than the notoriously impulsive Anne Adamson.

The moon's glow beamed down on a pale-pink bloom. She leaned forward and smelled the fragrant bud . . . and sneezed. Anne straightened, wrinkling her nose. It really was such a shame being unable to appreciate the full beauty of the bloom. A shadow fell over the illuminated flower and she smiled. Large hands came up, rested upon her shoulders. She straightened and leaned back into Harry's touch. And froze.

Her heart raced with panic as the scent of cheroot and coffee, unfamiliar and not at all Harry, filled her senses. A husky baritone whispered against her ear, "Hullo, love."

She'd been sweet, Anne, hellion, minx, and termagant to Harry. But only twice before had she been his love. Anne spun around and jumped backward. She knocked against the pink flowers. Her heart pounded loudly as she stared up at Lord Rutland. A hard, stone-cold smile turned the man's lips in feigned warmth, the only suggestion of gentleness in an otherwise harsh, angular face. "L-Lord Rutland," she stammered and sidled away from him.

A glint sparked in his brown eyes.

She frantically searched the gardens with her gaze.

"Are you perhaps looking for someone, Lady Anne?"

His faintly mocking question jerked her attention back to him. She shook her head and looked over his broad shoulder for sign of Harry. "Er . . . no . . . I merely sought some air." Panic built in her breast. Should anyone else come upon her and Lord Rutland, she would be ruined.

"Air?" Rutland murmured and advanced toward her.

She hastened back another step. "Er. Yes. Air. You breathe it." *Stop rambling, Anne.* The ghost of a smile played about his lips, which was really impossible. Men like Lord Rutland, who fought other men to first blood, did not smile. "It is particularly beneficial when it is extremely crowded or hot, which it was. Inside the ballroom, that is." He continued his forward approach. "Wouldn't you agree?" That gave him pause.

Lines creased his brow. "Wouldn't I agree about what? The need for air? Or that you're rambling?"

"Oh." Her knees knocked against a wrought iron bench. "Did I speak that aloud?" She had that nasty tendency when she was nervous. She shot another glance over his shoulder for Harry.

He stopped so close their legs nearly brushed. "You did, Anne."

Drat. She frowned at the sheer insolence of the man. "I didn't give you leave to use my Christian name." She should err on the greater side of caution, alone with this blackguard, but really he had no leave to go about using her given name.

He touched his thumb to her lower lip. She gasped and drew her hand back. He caught her wrist before her palm collided with his cheek. "Tsk, tsk. You shouldn't do that." He lowered his brow to hers. She shivered as the thick scent of brandy fanned her lips. "Unless I demand it. In which case you should do it quite hard."

She cocked her head. "Whyever would you want me to slap you?"

He froze, and then tossed his head back and laughed. The sound came rusty and hoarse as though from ill use.

She'd never understand gentlemen. Not a single one of them. Not her somber brother-in-law, Jasper. Not Harry in his many lessons. And not this stranger who spoke of welcoming a slap to his person. Anne shoved against his chest, but he was as immobile as Lady Preston's towering brick wall. For her efforts, a strand of hair fell loose from her expertly arranged curls. "Wh-what are you doing?"

"I'm going to kiss you, Lady Anne," his words emerged as a steely, satiny promise.

Her stomach lurched. "No." She shook her head. "No. No you are not." She slammed her fist into the hard muscles of his stomach and cried out. He grinned as though amused by her ineffectual attempt.

He lowered his head and she arched away not wanting his kiss. She'd already had loathsome Lord Ackland's tongue in her mouth. And then Harry. Now, she'd know no one else but Harry's kiss upon her lips. Certainly not Lord Rutland, the cad who'd dueled Harry for his ladylove, Margaret.

Anne slipped out from under his arm and all but sprinted toward the door. When Harry arrived, she'd have certain choice words for his rather delayed entrance and—She gasped when a strong arm closed around her waist, bringing her close.

"Do you know, Lady Anne, I never imagined when I followed you out here that I'd find our meeting so vastly entertaining."

She pulled his forearm. "I'm so very pleased to be able to *entertain* you, my lord." Her desperate attempt at nonchalance came out breathy with fear. Did he hear it? Did he delight in it? Somehow, she suspected it brought him perverse pleasure.

"I merely thought to sample the charms known by Stanhope."

"I assure you, there's been no sampling of charms." She pursed her lips. Well, that didn't sound altogether correct.

He tweaked her nose. "Do you know, I believe you're lying to me, Lady Anne?" The teasing gesture was so vaguely reminiscent of all the times Harry touched her so, Anne slapped at his hand.

He chuckled.

She shot a glance over the marquess's shoulder, searching out Harry.

"In fact, I'd wager you're out here even now awaiting a meeting with Stanhope."

"I'm not," she said a touch too quickly.

"And," he continued, the unholy glint in his eyes indicating he delighted in her unease, "I'd venture you've come to even love the earl." A mocking sneer wrapped about that supposition. He must have taken her silence for an admission. He tossed his head back and laughed, a chillingly empty sound that sent fear spiraling through her.

She yanked her arm, but he only angled her body closer to his. "What do you want?" she asked, proud of the steady deliverance of that question. Panic churned in her belly. If she were discovered with Lord Rutland, she'd be ruined and forced to wed the bounder—if a cur like him were even capable of honor. "I really must return, my lord. If you'll unhand me."

He pulled her closer and whispered as if his was the most delicious secret in the world. "Surely you wonder where your love is?"

She flattened her lips into a tight line to keep from responding to his deliberate baiting.

"Tsk, tsk. Poor Lady Anne Adamson. You've no idea how little you matter to him."

All her mother's warnings, Anne's own fears twisted about, magnified by the poison in his taunting words. "What are you speaking about?" she snapped.

"Come now, surely you know of his Margaret."

His barb hit like a well-placed arrow to her heart. She gave a toss of her curls, determined to conceal the effect his taunting words were having. "I believe she was your Margaret, as well."

His body went taut like a king cobra poised to strike she'd once viewed as a small girl at the Piccadilly Circus. "No," he spat. "She was always Stanhope's." A deep-rooted bitterness coated his words.

And for the fraction of a moment, she felt awash with guilt for deliberately hurting Lord Rutland. Instead of loathing, she felt a kindred connection to this man who loved another incapable of returning those sentiments. "I'm so sorry," she said softly.

A dull flush stained his cheeks. "You've never been anything more than a diversion," he lashed out ruthlessly. "I suggest you return to the festivities so you may see just why

Stanhope has left you out here alone. With me for your only company." He pressed a hard kiss to her lips.

Anne recoiled as revulsion turned her belly. And then he set her from him. He gave her firm nudge between her shoulders, sending her toward the garden doors.

The hard beating of her heart filled her ears and matched her fleeting footsteps. Her slippers skidded upon the moisture of the grass. She continued running, knowing if she were seen she'd appear a madwoman loose in the halls of Bedlam. When she'd reached the corridor leading to the ballroom, she patted her cheeks, smoothed her skirts, took a deep breath, and returned to search for Harry.

As she entered the ballroom, she expected the lords and ladies to eye her with charged accusations in their eyes, expecting someone to know Lord Rutland had cornered her. All the while his cruel words weaved around her mind, refusing to relinquish their tentacle-like hold as she sought Harry out. Surely there had been a reason Harry had failed to come to her. Surely he'd merely been deterred. Surely—

The din of whispers tugged at her attention. The *ton* moved as one, as their gazes swiveled to the front of the room.

Anne frowned and leaned around the edge of the wall to study the tall, willowy creature who'd captured their notice. With raven-black hair and a diaphanous gown that clung to a lush, perfectly curved figure, she'd earn the resentment of all ladies present and the admiration of all the gentlemen. Even in the darkest times for her family, Anne hadn't allowed herself that iniquitous emotion of envy. Her own struggles had taught her that one never truly knew the inner tumult carried by others. Still, the stranger possessed an ageless beauty it was not hard to be the slightest bit jealous of.

A figure moved beside Anne. "Where have you been?" her mother snapped.

"I tore my hem." The lie came easily. She returned her attention to the stranger at the front of the room. "Who is she?"

"Why, that is Her Grace, Lady Margaret Monteith."

There was something so very familiar in the name. Lady Margaret Monteith . . . Lady Margaret . . . Her mind slowed to a stall. Margaret.

As in Miss Margaret Dunn.

As in Harry's love.

As in her heart was breaking open and bleeding for all to see, if they weren't already focused upon the breathtaking creature that held Harry's heart.

"Oh, God," she whispered. At the unrepressed admission, her mother shot her a scathing look. Anne gave her head a shake, but the fog retained its hazy hold over her. She could not leave, and bury her head, a coward to the truth, so instead, she stood, witness to the horrific unfolding tableau. Of rival suitors who'd waged a duel. Of a long-returned love. Of a reunion.

Of a life that Anne did not belong to.

Lady Margaret searched the crowd with her piercing, catlike eyes and Anne knew as sure as she knew the count and color of every ribbon to her collection just who the woman sought, and also the moment her unwavering eyes found him.

Anne sucked in a shuddery breath. She watched, as though a voyeur to some other pathetic woman's publicly agonized pain, as Harry's love glided through the crowd. She didn't know what she expected. Perhaps the foolish naïveté that compelled her to read silly Gothic novels imagined Harry would turn his back, storm across the floor, claim Anne's hand, and publicly declare his love. Then, for any of that to happen, Harry would have to love her. And he didn't. As Lord Rutland had ruthlessly, yet accurately, pointed out, Harry had forever seen her as an empty-headed, pleasantly pretty miss, and not much more.

Lady Margaret stopped before Harry, so close their bodies brushed. Anne curled her fingers into the palms of her hands so tightly she left crescent marks upon her skin. A glutton to this agonizing pain, Anne continued to watch the reunion of two old lovers.

The magnificent creature eyed him with such familiarity, Anne felt the worst sort of interloper on their private moment. Theirs was an intimate connection that moved beyond mere lovers. The room swayed beneath her feet and she shot her hand out in search of purchase, finding it along the wall. Her throat worked spasmodically.

Did Harry still love her?

Of course he does, you ninny.

Heart cracking with each unknown word spoken between Harry and his Margaret, Anne forced her gaze away. Her agonized stare collided with Lord Rutland's stock-still frame. She stared blankly at him. The monster who'd held her outside a short while ago and threatened her very existence had seemed incapable of all feeling and emotion. Yet, studying him, agony bled through his eyes, so stark, so real she may as well have peered into a mirror.

He jerked his stare away from the reunited couple and inadvertently caught her gaze. Something honest and real passed between them; a bond shared by two people who would never be the choice of the one they truly loved. Then the moment faded as quick as it came.

Her mother leaned close and kept her tone low. "Have you gathered now, the exact identity of that woman? That, my dear, is the Duchess of Monteith. The woman who truly holds Lord Stanhope's heart." A viselike pressure tightened around her middle. Mother patted her hand, her next words indicating how greatly she misunderstood the reason for her daughter's upset. "You needn't be envious, Anne. You too shall become a duchess."

Why would Anne be a duchess? Ah, yes, then reality came crashing. The Duke of Crawford. The heart of a duke. Harry's role in helping her to ensnare him. A lump clogged her throat and she struggled to swallow past it.

Suddenly, Rutland's jibing made sense. He'd known. He had known Margaret had returned. Just as he'd known Harry would be so thoroughly bewitched he would forget poor Anne with her silly ringlets and her need for spectacles, waiting for him like a lovesick fool. Tears filled her eyes and she blinked them back, lest someone see. But then someone would have to notice Anne, and the *ton* had still not removed their rabid curiosity from the scene still unfolding before them.

"And this is the man you'd wear such a scandalous creation for," her mother said with disgust.

Humiliation burned like fire on her cheeks. "I didn't . . . I . . ." The words died on her lips. In this moment, stricken by the pain of Harry alongside his love, she couldn't muster even a false word.

"I've told you, Anne. The duke will make you a splendid match. A safe match."

Staring at Harry again, conversing with his black-haired beauty, Anne could admit to the vast appeal of wedding for safety. For then, you wouldn't know this mind-numbing agony of watching the man you loved on display for all polite

Society. Then you needn't know, and more, care that another had come before you, who'd mattered in ways you never would.

The woman, Margaret, a name somehow made her, made *this*, more real, brushed his arm with a hand.

Jealousy, green and vile with a life of its own, unfurled within her, but Anne continued looking on, just as the crowd did.

I am supposed to mean more to him. Only, he'd given her no indication that he either wanted or needed anything more with her. Quite the opposite, in fact. Rather, he'd been shockingly clear that Anne, a woman he called *sweet*, was no different than any other who'd earned that empty endearment from him.

Fool. Fool. Fool.

A small smile turned Margaret's lips. She eyed Harry through thick, smoky lashes.

She possessed the kind of beauty men fought wars for.

Yes. Yes, indeed, she did.

"I want to go home," Anne whispered.

When Harry had been a boy of thirteen, his mount had taken a jump too low. He had been tossed aground. Staring at Margaret as she reentered his life, like a ghost of a distant past, he felt much the same way he did that long-ago day. A loud buzzing filled his ears.

Tall and regal like a queen stood Margaret, now the Duchess of Monteith. Resplendent in a gold satin gown with black lace overlay, she peered out amongst the crowd. Still every inch as beautiful as she'd ever been, she bore but the faintest traces of the innocent young lady she'd been. The lines of her mouth, slightly harder, the set to her shoulders, stiffer.

His friend Edgerton sidled up to him. "I gather you did not know? Your Miss Margaret, I suppose she is now the *Lady* Margaret, has returned to London. Her old husband made a widow of her some months ago."

He shook his head. "No." After she'd wed, he'd not been presented with the constant reminder of her defection. She'd gone off to the remote corner of Northumberland and he'd been content to keep her memory buried there. In time, his, the *ton*'s, once-cherished memories of Miss Margaret Dunn faded.

Edgerton gave him a sideways look. "She's not even waited the requisite period of mourning before making her return. Why do you think that is?"

The hostess, Lady Preston, rushed forward to greet Margaret.

Harry registered the attention fixed his way by gossipy *ton* members. He rescued a flute of champagne from a nearby servant and took a sip damning polite Society and their sick fascination to hell. His life, his past, to bored nobles was nothing more than a momentary amusement for an apathetic lot. He stared on disinterestedly as Margaret wound her way through the crowd; her gaze scanned the room, searching, searching, and then finding him.

Standing at the side of the ballroom floor, Harry observed the *ton* part, and followed Margaret's deliberate walk. Her soft satin skirts danced about her ankles. She came to a stop before him. Her gaze lingered a moment on Edgerton. "Lord Edgerton," she murmured, her voice lower, more sultry than he remembered.

His friend's jaw tightened. "Your Grace," he drawled. It didn't escape Harry's notice that the other man failed to bow.

Her rouged-red lips twitched. She turned her attention to Harry. Her sultry brown-eyed gaze ran a path over his face. "Hullo, Harry," she whispered.

He bowed. "Your Grace," he said, stiffly polite. This woman, who'd broken his heart, who'd reduced him to an empty, hollow version of his youthful self, now stood before him.

He'd not allowed himself to think of her but with resentment through the years. In the earliest days of her marriage he'd relished the moment they'd once again meet. He would have mocked her union with the wizened, ancient duke and then given her the cut direct. On his worst days, he'd tortured himself with the reminder of her lush, generously curved frame. Now, staring back at her, it struck him just how her dark beauty paled to Anne's innocent light.

He made another stiff bow. "If you'll excuse me." He stepped around her. She touched his sleeve, staying his movement. The crowd gasped. He cast a pointed look at her gloved fingers. "Remember yourself, madam," he said with deliberate coldness.

Margaret pulled her hand back. "Forgive me," she said quietly. "Will you . . . ? I . . ." She glanced pointedly at Edgerton. "May we talk, Harry?"

"This seems like a rather ill choice of a meeting place," Edgerton said tauntingly. Then, after an insolent bow, took his leave.

Margaret shifted her attention to Harry. "Please. I'd speak to you." She looked momentarily to the couples assembling for a waltz.

"Whatever you care to say, you may do so here, madam," he said stiffly. He'd not partner her for a dance and he most certainly didn't care to meet with her alone.

"Very well." She sighed. "You'd have me humble myself here. I will. For you. I love you," she said, her words soft yet resolute. "I've always loved you. My marriage to the duke, my parents required it of me, Harry." She held her palms up beseechingly. "Surely you know you're all I've ever wanted."

All she'd ever wanted but not enough to fight for his love. He braced for the familiar rush of old resentment. That didn't come.

"I came out of mourning early for you."

He arched an eyebrow. "Am I supposed to be flattered, Your Grace? Grateful?" Did Margaret imagine she'd reenter his life and they might resume the courtship begun before life had jaded them?

She winced. "If my misery brings you happiness, know that I've spent the past eight years in hell, dreaming of . . ." Her voice grew husky. "Longing for you."

A twinge of pity tugged at him. She had her title of duchess, but he couldn't imagine there'd been anything pleasant in being wed to the ancient, doddering duke. And in that moment he realized, for all the pain she'd caused him, he didn't resent her. Sometime over the years, his love for her had died.

"In spite of what you believe, I don't wish for you to be unhappy, Margaret," he said, surprised by the truth of that admission. If he were still in love with her, perhaps she'd inspire grand sentiments of agony and old, youthful jealousies. And mayhap if she'd stepped into a different ballroom, a different soiree a mere ten days ago, before Anne had upended his life, this conversation would take a different course. Anne, however, had driven back all the bitter hurts and replaced them with a genuine, unfettered happiness.

"I read there is a woman." Pain hoarsened her voice. "Is there?" Tears filled her eyes and she blinked them away. "Tell me there is not," she pleaded.

Ah, she'd learned of Anne. A muscle jumped in the corner of his eye. He didn't want Margaret speaking of her; he preferred the smiling, teasing Anne, untouched by the scandal of his past.

She took his silence for confirmation. "Do you care for her?" Margaret asked with marked hesitancy.

Harry gave a curt bow. "Please excuse me, Your Grace." He certainly cared for Anne. What she meant to him exactly, he didn't allow himself to consider and most definitely not before the *ton*, and worse, before Margaret. "This is neither the time, nor the place." With that, he turned on his heel and went in search of Anne.

Chapter 18

From the corner of the parlor, Anne pulled back the curtain and peered down into the street below. She touched a finger to the sun-warmed windowpane.

She'd been expecting him if for no other reason than to make his apologies for abandoning her last evening, to Rutland's cruelty, no less. The greater likelihood was that Harry would call and ask to be spared of any further lessons with her. She swallowed painfully. This way he would be able to pursue his Margaret, a widow and free to therefore pick up where life had left them. Harry would be free to become the man he'd once been, before Margaret's marriage had turned him into a jaded, heartbroken rogue.

And Anne would never be anything more than a distant thought in his head. She pressed her eyes tight, dreading the moment he would arrive and all her happiness ended. With a shuddery sigh, she opened her eyes and stared blankly out into the streets below. The loss of Harry would force her to confront just what a liar she truly was. She'd told him she didn't expect a profession of love or his undying devotion, but God help her she did. Wanted it more than she craved food or drink or silly ribbons and mindless Gothic novels . . . even that blasted pianoforte played by the Westmoreland daughters.

She wanted him. *All* of him. And more, she wanted him to want her.

Anne bit her lip hard and winced. A rider pulled up on a magnificent chestnut steed. Her heart thumped madly and she leaned close. "Harry," she mouthed silently.

A young lad rushed forward to collect the reins. Harry handed them off, tossed the boy a sack of coins, and murmured instructions.

A shuddery sob escaped her lips and she buried it in her fingers.

Her mother's visage reflected back in the exposed glass panel. "Anne Arlette Adamson, come away from that window," she snapped from the doorway.

Anne ignored her demands. Instead, she pressed her forehead against the glass and peered down at him as he rapped on the door.

"He's come for no other reason than to end this madness between you, Anne," her mother predicted.

"I know that," she whispered, no longer lying to her mother or herself in the importance his presence meant to her. Somewhere along the way, he'd come to mean more than a lesson in seduction. Perhaps it happened when they'd been seated side by side at Lady Westmoreland's musicale. Or after one too many tweaks of her golden ringlets or Dibdin's songs or . . .

She didn't know the precise moment but at some point, Harry's happiness had come to matter more to her than even her own.

The door opened below and Ollie allowed the earl entrance. She pressed her lids tightly shut so that flecks of white light danced behind her closed eyes.

Mother touched a hand to her shoulder. "He is not worth this pain."

"He is," she whispered brokenly. He was so much more than the shiftless bounder he presented to Society. He was the sole person to look close enough at her to know she needed spectacles to read, and had taken it upon himself to find the most perfect pair, so that she might read to her heart's pleasure.

"Even if he comes here now, Anne, and does not break it off, then it is honor driving his actions."

She fisted her hands at her side. "Perhaps he loves me," she ventured, hearing the futility in her own hopeless words.

"I imagined your father loved me as well." The pity underscoring her mother's tone dug at Anne's insides. "He's no different than your father."

Anne spun around. "He is nothing like Father," she spat. She slashed the air with her hand. "Father was a wastrel, dishonorable, disloyal to his children, to you—"

"And your Lord Stanhope will be the same if you do not have the courage to set him free, Anne." Her mother took her hands. "Set him free," she implored with her eyes. "Do what I could not. Allow him his love. His *true* love," she amended, her words a thousand daggers upon Anne's wounded heart.

As if on perfect cue, a knock sounded at the door. The butler, Ollie, appeared. He cleared his throat. "My lady, the Earl of Stanhope to see Lady Anne."

Anne jammed the heel of her palms against her eyes, attempting to rid herself of thoughts of Harry.

"Anne, remember yourself," Mother scolded.

Ah, yes, the unpleasantness of showing the hint of real emotion. Anne forced herself to take a deep and slow breath. "Please tell the earl I'm not receiving callers," she said, the words so faint, Ollie, the ancient servant, cupped a hand around his ear.

"What was that?"

"Please tell the earl I'm not receiving callers," she repeated, and this time resolve strengthened her words.

Mother tossed her hands into the air. "Anne, meet with him and—"

"I will, Mother. Just not now." *Please, do not ask this of me. Allow me to do this as I will, at my own time, in my own way.*

Her mother gave a terse nod and left.

Anne waited for her mother to take her leave and then sprinted across the room to her spot beside the window. She peered down into the streets in time to observe Harry's exit. He beat his black hat atop his right leg and glared at the door, as though he could command the black panel to open and permit him entry. A broken laugh, more of a sob, escaped her lips. Then, Harry possessed enough roguish appeal to charm a door to open.

He stiffened and for the fraction of a moment she thought he might feel her gaze upon him. But then, the young street lad rushed over with the reins to his steed and Harry took them, mounted his horse, and left.

Anne buried her face into her hands and wept copious amount of tears. *Egad, I'm crying? I detest tears.* She cried all the harder in remembrance of that recent day in their stolen copse when he'd given her spectacles, and then shown her more pleasure than she'd imagined her body capable of.

Anne folded her arms about herself to still the tremors quaking her form. She sank down onto her piano bench and her back knocked against the keyboard in a discordant melody of agony and despair. What if her mother had been wrong, even as logic told her she'd not been? But what if she had? What if Harry had merely come to apologize and dole out another of his lessons, as she'd clung to the foolish hope of since early that morn?

"Fool, fool, fool," she choked out between great, big gasping sobs.

There were certain moments a person remembered in life. For Anne, she'd forever recall stumbling into Lady Preston's ballroom and witnessing the magnificent tableau presented; Harry in his golden glory and the willowy duchess with her thick black ringletless hair. And poor, pathetic Anne, no different than her mother longing for a man who'd never been, nor would ever *be* hers.

She brushed back the useless tears. Another knock sounded at the door. "What is it, Mother?" she said impatiently. She spun to face the doorway. "I've already told you I'll speak . . ." Her words faded into silence.

Ollie stood at the doorway, a contrite expression on his face. He cleared his throat. "His Grace, the Duke of Crawford, to see you, my lady."

Ah, Mother wouldn't turn away a duke if it meant saving her own life and the lives of all her children.

Her lips twisted in bitter remembrance of Mother's callous treatment of Katherine's husband, Jasper. Then, she tended to draw a proverbial line at dukes with a scandal to their name. She wrinkled her brow. Then, in thinking on it . . . it rather seemed Mother abhorred all manner of scandalous gentlemen, from wealthy second sons like Aldora's Michael, to Katherine's once heart-broken Jasper, to the Earl of Stanhope, to—

The duke entered the room, a bouquet of hothouse flowers in his right hand. He paused a moment. His eyes lingered upon her face and she dug her toes hard into the soles of her slippers, certain he could detect the surely swollen-red eyes. "Lady Anne," he murmured.

Anne shook her head, and remembered herself. She sprung to her feet. "Your Grace." She sank into a curtsy, dropping her gaze to the floral Aubusson carpet, looking anywhere but at him.

Her maid, Mary, slipped into the room, eyes downcast. She dipped a curtsy and then sought out her all-too-familiar seat. After three Seasons of Anne unwed, the poor woman had likely worn quite a place on the upholstered seat.

The duke moved farther into the room. He passed his intense gaze around the ivory parlor then trained his penetrating stare on her. "Are you well, Lady Anne?"

Which was the most polite, nondirect way of inquiring after her tear-reddened eyes. "Er, quite," she lied. His eyes said he knew it. From across the room, Mary coughed. Anne jumped, remembering herself. She rushed over to the duke and motioned to the sofa. "Please, won't you sit, Your Grace?"

Sit in the very seat Harry had occupied some days ago when he'd asked her to sing to him. There was something so very wrong in the duke sitting in . . .

The duke sat.

. . . in Harry's seat. A vise threatened to crush her heart.

His Grace extended the bouquet in his hands. "These are for—"

"Achoo!" Anne sneezed. For all the beauty of a flower, she'd never been able to breathe around a single bloom. Bitterness pulled at her lips. Yes, she'd never have made an ideal trysting partner for the Earl of Stanhope.

The duke fished into his pocket and withdrew a kerchief. He held it out.

"F-forgive . . . achoo!" Anne sneezed into the fabric neatly monogrammed with the initials *ADC*. "Forgive . . . achoo!" Oh dear, this really was rather inconvenient.

The duke's lips twitched even as Mary rushed over to take the flowers from him. She hurried from the room.

"My apologies," he said with a smile in his words. "I wasn't aware—"

"No apologies necessary, Your Grace," she assured him. "It is quite a bother." A frown replaced the austere duke's fleeting smile. "Not receiving flowers. Because it is quite lovely. That is, if I could breathe around them, it would . . ." She allowed the words to go unfinished.

"I find it quite endearing." Only, the hard, determined edge to his words hinted at a world-wary man who didn't find life endearing, let alone an unwed young lady's sneezing.

Anne directed her attention to the handkerchief. Had the Duke of Crawford entered the world a squalling, haughty baby with a frozen noble heart? Or had life invariably done what life invariably did, and shatter whatever innocence he'd carried? She felt his stare on her and reluctantly shifted her attention upward. She made to give the linen back but he waved his hand.

"Consider it yours, Lady Anne." Specks of silver danced in his blue eyes.

"Thank you." She studied the gold, monogrammed letters and angled her head, humbled by her own self-centeredness. She'd set her sights upon the duke, determined to have him as her husband . . . and yet she didn't know something as simple as his Christian name. Society referred to him as His Grace, the duke, the Duke of Crawford. It occurred to her that she, like the rest of the *ton*, hadn't bothered to consider him beyond his title. She touched a finger to the single *A*, wondering over the lone initial.

"Auric," he said quietly.

Her head snapped up.

"I gathered you wondered about the *A*."

"Auric," she said softly. A bold, unique name for one of the most powerful peers in the realm.

He shifted on his seat. "A rather unconventional name for an English lad."

She managed her first real smile that day as she imagined him as Auric, a mere boy being schooled on the future role of duke. Then her smile withered as she considered her own grasping attempts at his title. She plucked at the fabric of the monogrammed handkerchief. She didn't know the Duke of Crawford beyond their handful of meetings, but she'd already determined he deserved far more than to be desired for his title alone.

No gentleman deserved that.

No *person* deserved that.

He leaned over and placed his hand upon hers, his blue eyes filled with such intensity she looked down—and stilled. Anne studied his large hands, cased in buff-colored kid leather. She didn't imagine a duke to have such imposing hands, and more, she desperately wanted those hands to elicit all manner of delicious shivers inside. She wanted to burn from where their fingers met . . . and yet . . . Her eyes slid closed a moment.

Nothing.

Not a blasted spark.

Or shiver.

Or tingle.

Nothing.

"Marriages have been forged on nothing more than a matter of convenience, Lady Anne."

She jerked her stare back to his. "Your Grace?"

"I'd have to be a fool to not realize you prefer Lord Stanhope's suit to my own." He sounded bemused, and she'd venture it was hardly every day a young lady preferred the attentions of a roguish earl to a powerful duke.

She bit the inside of her lip, unsure how to respond.

"Yet, I find I want you. As my duchess."

Ah, there it was. The pinnacle of all her dreams realized. Only now did she realize those dreams belonged to her mother. They'd never been Anne's. And perhaps Anne was, in fact, the foolish, whimsical creature everyone had taken her for, because she craved love above all else.

Fool. Fool. Fool. Hadn't life taught her that most times, love wasn't enough?

"Why?" she asked.

He raised her fingertips to his lips and touched his mouth to the inside of her wrist. The intimate gesture felt like a betrayal of sorts to Harry.

"Why, Anne?" When one was a duke he could drop all formality and call a young lady by her given name. Even without permission. "Because you wondered about the *A.*"

"And you'd have me for your wife." She'd spent so very many days attempting to capture a duke, and yet so very little time in considering the best, most polite way to decline a duke's offer. She took a deep breath.

He placed his index finger upon her lips. "Think on it. Stanhope's past has returned and I suspect it impacts your future. Therefore, I'd like to claim that spot in your future, Anne. I don't require an answer now."

She knew so very little about the duke. No one truly knew a thing of this man or his past, and yet, she suspected he would make some young lady a wonderful husband. It didn't matter if she gave her answer now or two years from now. The answer would still be no. That young lady would never be her.

As he stood, to take his leave, she suspected he knew it as well.

Harry strode through White's, daring some foolish bastard to look his way. Since Margaret's scandalous reentrance into Society, his name, her name, their past, the question of their future had been splashed across every last scandal sheet. He yanked out the chair at his table and sat with his back to the club. A liveried servant rushed over, with a bottle of brandy and an empty glass. Harry reached for them. And then remembered Anne's damned father and shoved it aside. Instead, he picked up the empty glass and rolled it between his hands.

He'd paid her a visit earlier that afternoon, but he'd been politely, if coolly, turned away by the aged butler. Not receiving callers.

Harry growled. As though he were any other suitor and she was any other woman. Nothing could be further from the truth. Why, she was . . . hell, he still didn't know quite what Anne Adamson was or meant to him. It was enough to know fury roiled in his belly at being turned away from her front door.

He imagined she was cross with him for having failed to meet her in Lady Preston's gardens last evening. Any woman would be annoyed at having been abandoned with a scheduled meeting. Even as he'd ached to find the temptress in orange satin, her damned brother-in-law and then Margaret had cut off all hopes of seeing Anne, alone, removed from the gossipy *ton*. Anne had never struck him as a vindictive female. Yes, she'd made him want to gnash his teeth on more scores than he could count, but he'd never imagine she would turn him away.

He set the empty glass down with a *thunk*! He'd not truly allowed himself to consider what Margaret's appearance meant to him and Anne, because even now, he didn't even know what the hell he and Anne had, or were, if anything. What Harry did have the sense to realize, however, is that Margaret's arrival in London would inevitably impact his relationship with Anne. In the span of a single evening, he'd been forced to confront his past and try and sort out just where Anne fit into his future.

With Margaret's reentry into his life he'd at last found an unexpected sense of peace. The resentment and fury he'd carried had been the passionate response of a headstrong, competitive gentleman vying for her hand. There had been no real love there.

Anne mattered. She mattered in ways that no woman, not even Margaret, truly had . . . or ever would.

Could he wed Anne?

Could he, when after Margaret's betrayal, he'd sworn to never give his heart to another?

Tension knotted in his stomach. Since his first meeting with Anne, she'd vowed to capture the heart of a duke and Harry had done his damnedest to teach her just how to land not just Crawford, but any gentleman's notice.

He swiped a hand over his eyes. Could he humble himself before her, in the hope that she would invariably choose him? Choose him, when there was another more titled, more proper choice?

"You look to be in need of company," a haughty, now hated voice drawled.

He glanced up at the more titled, more proper choice. The illustrious Duke of Crawford didn't wait for a response. Instead he slid into the vacant seat opposite Harry. And the pressure in Harry's gut tightened. The last thing he cared for was company. Particularly with the man Anne had set her sights upon.

Crawford gestured to the brandy. "May I?"

Wordlessly, Harry shoved the unused glass across to the other man. Someone should make use of the fine spirits.

A servant rushed forward and the duke waved him off. "Believe it or not, I can manage opening my own bottle and pouring myself a glass of brandy." His dry humor, as crisp as autumn leaves, gave Harry pause.

He preferred the image of lofty noble who considered himself well above the lesser lords and ladies. He preferred that image because he'd rather hate the man Anne would have as her husband, in her bed, the man who'd place his hands upon her breasts, and bring her pleasure, and—

"I just visited with Lady Anne."

Harry's leg jumped in an involuntary reflex. The duke caught the opened bottle before it toppled over. "Did you?" Harry managed to squeeze past tight lips. She'd turned him away but received the duke. "And how is Lady Anne?" *Of course, she sent you away, you blasted fool. You've served one purpose, to school the lady in the art of seduction.* He'd apparently succeeded beyond even his expectations.

The duke took a sip of his brandy. "Quite well."

Quite well. And here he'd spent all of last evening awake, well into the early morning hours, fearful Anne had been wounded with Margaret returning and calling his attention away from their arranged meeting.

Fool. Fool. Fool.

"I'll speak bluntly, Stanhope. I intend to wed the young lady."

Harry stared, unblinking, at the duke's throat. It would create quite the scandal if he dragged the other man across the table by his meticulous cravat and beat him within a breath of oblivion. Harry, however, had weathered far greater scandals. "Do you?" he asked with a deliberate yawn. "And does the young lady know of these intentions?"

"She does," Crawford said quietly.

Another image slipped into his mind. Anne taking Crawford's kiss, and laughing about Harry, the poor sod who'd grown to . . . He forced his mind to a screeching halt, not allowing himself to consider just what he'd grown to do exactly.

The duke took another sip. "I brought the lady flowers and spoke quite plainly of my intentions."

Flowers. His lips pulled in a derisive smile. The bastard knew her so little he didn't even know the small details that made Anne, Anne. He didn't know she sneezed at the mere sight of a bloom.

Crawford passed his glass back and forth between his hands. "Though it appears the lady has a sensitivity to flowers."

It would also appear her damned duke had gleaned that particular detail. He now knew her husky contralto, and likely her sultry laugh, and . . . Harry tightened his grip upon the edge of the table, digging so hard, his fingers were sure to leave crescent indents upon the immaculate surface.

"Why don't you say what it is you've come to say and then be on your way?" Harry snarled, all out of patience with the other man and his veneer of politeness.

Crawford set his glass down. He laid his elbows upon the table and leaned over, all hint of friendliness gone. "May I speak plainly?"

He gave a brusque nod.

"The lady will make me an excellent duchess."

Harry's empty stomach churned with nausea.

"There is nothing you can give her that I cannot. Perhaps with the exception of a broken heart, that is." The other man ran a condescending stare over Harry. "I'm the better man." He leaned back in his chair. "I suspect you know that, and will allow me to do the honorable thing where Lady Anne is concerned."

Harry clenched his jaw so tight, pain radiated up to his temple as a tumult of emotion swept through him. Hate burned violent and strong, threatening to consume. Hate for Anne's having involved him in this scheme. Hate with himself for caring for her when he'd pledged to never care again. And hate for Crawford—for being right.

"Oh, come, now, Stanhope," the duke scoffed. "No need to act affronted. You're a rogue," he said flatly. "A shiftless cad. Then, I gather you know exactly what you are, which is why you'll also realize I am, in fact, Lady Anne's best option." He shoved back his seat and stood. "Now, if you'll excuse me."

Harry stared after the duke's swiftly retreating form, damning him to hell for being correct.

Chapter 19

*H*arry suspected that after Margaret's unexpected return, the woman who'd broken his heart should occupy his thoughts. And yet, since the Duke of Crawford had taken his leave earlier that afternoon, Harry hadn't been able to rid himself of thoughts of the other man's visit.

He stared blankly out at the sea of faces, the waltzing couples, not truly seeing anything. He dimly registered Margaret at the opposite end of the ballroom. He yanked his attention away from her and searched the crowd for the woman he truly wished to see.

His friend Edgerton strolled over with two glasses of champagne. He handed one to Harry. "I see Rutland has wasted little time," Edgerton murmured.

Harry glanced up in time to see Rutland cut a path through the ballroom floor. He stared dispassionately on as his old rival for Margaret's affections, a man he'd nearly fought to the death for the right to her, made his way to the young duchess. Odd he should feel nothing. Not even the faintest stirrings of regret, jealousy . . . just a detached disinterest in these two people who owned a piece of his past and shaped him into the bastard he'd become. Rutland paused before Margaret and bowed. The crowd caught and held a collective breath in anticipation of the lady's reaction. The duchess placed her fingertips in Rutland's hand and allowed him to kiss her fingers.

"I heard you had a visitor at your club today."

Bloody Crawford. He'd love to send the arrogant bastard to the devil.

"Vying for a young lady's hand." Edgerton shook his head pityingly. "A bit of history repeating itself, one could say."

"One could not say," he snapped, despising the eerie similarities that had cost him first Margaret, and now, his greatest loss—Anne Adamson.

"He's better off with her, Stanhope," his friend continued, following Harry's unspoken thoughts. "She's an empty-headed, pleasantly pretty miss, who desires nothing more than the most advantageous match."

Harry curled his hands into tight balls and fought the urge to bury his fist into Edgerton's face.

"Do you know what I believe?" the other man went on, clearly having no idea how very close Harry was to laying him out.

"No." Nor did he care about his friend's opinion just then. With each word Edgerton uttered, the idea of delivering a well-aimed facer became more appealing.

"Take your Margaret. Avail yourself to the pleasures of her body," he urged with a trace of annoyance. "Everyone saw the lust in her eyes, Stanhope. Take her. And once you tire of her, be done with the lady. Just as you would any other widow." He jerked his chin across the room. "And leave that one to Crawford."

Harry followed his friend's movement. The sight of Anne sucked the breath from his lungs. He'd not seen her in but a day and it was too long. Her expertly arranged, gloriously free tresses hung about her shoulders giving her the look of a woman who'd discovered sin and delighted in it. A lone ribbon woven through one errant strand hung between her breasts. Ah, she was an excellent study. He wished she'd been a horrid student. Wished she'd failed miserably. Instead, she glided down the stairs with the grace to rival all the queens in Europe. Her eyes searched the crowd and he allowed himself to foolishly believe he was, in fact, the one she sought.

Katherine sidled up to her. Strange, he had ever favored Anne's sister. Now, the duchess seemed a dull shadow to Anne's effervescent beauty. She whispered something close to Anne's ear. Even with the space of the ballroom between them, Harry detected the imperceptible stiffening of Anne's bared shoulders. She gave a curt nod and then followed Katherine off.

He cursed as he lost them in the crowd of bodies.

"You've the look of a lovesick swain etched upon your face," Edgerton whispered. "By God, man, I'm trying to help you."

Harry straightened the lapels of his jacket. "Go to hell, Edgerton," he said, tiring of his *friend's* sage advice.

"Hullo, Harry. I've been waiting for you all evening."

His body went taut, wishing it had been an altogether different woman waiting for him. "Have you?" He turned and greeted Margaret with frigid coldness. "If you'll excuse me, there is someone I need to speak with."

And the desire to find Anne had nothing to do with Margaret or revenge . . . and everything to do with Anne.

"What do you see?" Katherine whispered up to her husband. More than a foot taller than Anne and Katherine's heights of five feet two inches, Jasper skimmed the crowd.

Anne's heart paused at the unholy glint in her brother-in-law's eyes. "What is it?" she asked, reaching for his sleeve, and then drew her fingers back.

He brusquely shook his head. "Nothing." The curt, one-word utterance told an entirely different tale.

Anne arched up on tiptoes and craned her neck.

Her sister pinched her arm. "Do behave, Anne. You'll attract notice."

She ignored her prudent warning and scanned the ballroom in search of Harry. Her heart tripped a beat as she spied him. He stood, a glorious, golden god beside a lush fertility goddess. Anne sank back on her heels, a hopelessly empty feeling spiraling through her.

"I'll kill him," Katherine muttered. Her catlike eyes narrowed into thin slits. "Oh, the bounder, coming this way."

Anne's heart kicked up a beat. She clutched her sister's forearm. "Is he?" Then, the crowd parted for Harry's tall, well-muscled frame as he continued his forward course, in her direction. She knew her mother spoke the truth and inevitably there would have to be a good-bye between her and Harry. For now, all she knew was him. A lazy smile played about his lips.

Oh, how she'd missed him. He stopped before the small trio that represented Anne's family. He inclined his head. "Bainbridge."

For a moment, Anne suspected her brother-in-law might not return the greeting. She held her breath, but then Jasper sketched a short, if insolent, bow. Katherine glared at Harry.

He seemed wholly immune to her sister's displeasure. His gaze remained fixed on Anne while the crowd's laughter soared above the crescendo of the lively country reel.

"Lord Stanhope," Katherine said in a cold tone Anne had come to know of their mother but never her twin.

"Kat," he replied absently, in a way that snapped Jasper's eyebrows into a single, menacing black line.

Anne fisted her skirts at the unwitting reminder of the ignominious beginning to Katherine and Harry's friendship. If her sister didn't love Jasper to distraction, then she would have been the Adamson sister who'd earned a place in Harry's bed. And Anne wouldn't know Harry in this beautifully intimate way. She'd never know this man who saw in her a clever woman with actual thoughts beyond the fabric of her gowns. How empty her life would have been, if there'd never been Harry.

The dancers erupted into a bevy of applause as the country reel drew to a close.

She looked away. And how much emptier it would be when he ultimately wed another.

Harry glanced down at the dance card about Anne's wrist. "Will you do me the pleasure of partnering me in the next set?"

Ignoring her sister's pointed look, Anne placed her fingertips upon his sleeve and allowed him to draw her out onto the floor as the orchestra plucked the opening strands of a waltz.

"I missed you last evening, Anne," he murmured as they took their places amongst the other dancers.

If it weren't for the insolent grin on his cynical lips she might believe him. She looked to a point beyond his shoulder, ultimately finding the lush widow. The woman stood eying them with such pain dripping from the depths of her eyes, Anne forced herself to look away. "Did you?" she said tightly.

He applied slight pressure to her waist. "Never tell me you were displeased with me?"

She fixed her angry stare upon the expert lines of his white cravat. This was all a game to him. Margaret's reentry into his, and subsequently, Anne's life. The *ton*'s morbid fascination with the small scandal. All the while he'd met with his former love, Anne had fended off Lord Rutland's vile advances.

"What, nothing to say? Were you this silent with Crawford earlier this morn? After you'd sent me away."

Her eyes flew to his. A hard glint reflected in their depths. "How . . . ?"

"How did I know about Crawford?" he correctly finished her question. "I've my ways, sweet."

She gritted her teeth. "I'd ask you not to call me sweet, Harry."

"Particularly if you are to become the Duchess of Crawford," he said, his words taunting.

She would never be Crawford's *anything*.

Anne said nothing. She'd not give Harry the satisfaction of baiting her, not when she was the one suffering so.

He pulled her body closer. She wanted to shove him away, remind him of the rules of propriety, but more she longed to feel his body close to hers. Harry dipped his head. "I gather our lessons are at an end," he said, close to her ear.

He might as well have taken a blunt dagger and thrust it into her breaking heart. Anne dropped her gaze to his cravat shamed by the truth; she'd broken the promise he'd required of her in Lord Essex's conservatory. "I gather you're indeed correct," she said, her voice a near whisper. She'd fallen hopelessly in love with him.

"Will you meet me, sweet Anne?"

Fool that she was, she'd steal this one final moment with him, for herself. "Where?" So someday, when she was miserable and alone, she'd recall there had been a gentleman who'd made *her* heart race, even as his heart had belonged to another.

"In the conservatory." Her eyes slid closed of their own volition. Of course. The conservatory. "Will you?" His husky whisper brushed her skin. Like any other one of his scandalous widows and unhappily wed ladies.

She managed a jerky nod and mourned the ending of the waltz that signified the beginning of the end of her and Harry, the Earl of Stanhope. "Meet me, after the next set." The harsh, unyielding command belonged to a man accustomed to women falling at his proverbial feet, for the pleasure of his touch. They parted. He with a curt bow. She with a stiffly polite curtsy.

And then for the first time in ten days, moved in opposite directions. Away from one another.

Anne spied Katherine and Jasper; their bodies leaned close, a soft smile on her sister's blushing cheeks. Anne halted, feeling like the worst sort of interloper upon their intimate exchange. With wooden steps she changed direction and wandered back to her spot beside Lady Cavendish's potted fern, staring blankly at the green plant. How very unusual, to have a fern in the midst of a ball. She touched a finger to a green leaf, wondering if she didn't meet Harry just now, would they continue on as they had for the past ten days? She drew her hand back, and gave her head a clearing shake. She'd been fool enough where Harry was concerned, giving her heart to him when he could never love her in return.

With wooden steps she skirted the edge of the ballroom floor. Of course, no one would note her furtive movements, her inevitable disappearance. They had only been interested in the old scandal brought to life for the voracious appetites of hungry peers. The pad of her slippers nearly silent upon the thin, carpeted corridor. She followed the crimson red path. Absently, she thought of the many scandalous trysts Harry had engaged in. How had he known where the conservatory was from the garden from the library?

He must be quite practiced, indeed. Why—A startled shriek escaped her as a horribly familiar, flawlessly beautiful figure stepped into Anne's path.

The Duchess of Monteith picked Anne apart with her eyes, and Anne knew the moment the woman lifted her vivid brown gaze up, that she'd found her lacking. Suddenly, feeling very silly in her modest ivory skirts when the other woman in her dampened satin sapphire evinced the beauty men penned sonnets for.

When it became clear the duchess had little intention of breaking the awkward silence, Anne sank into a deep curtsy. "Your Grace," she murmured. "Forgive me, I was just—"

"You are Harry's current lover, aren't you?" Anne flinched, feeling as though she'd been kicked in the stomach. A malevolent gleam lit the sparks of green in her eyes and for a moment all hint of beauty was lost in the ugliness of a woman made bitter by life . . . and jealousy. "I've read of you," She paused and flicked her gaze over Anne's person. "And the others dear Harry has been with."

Anne flinched but then took a steadying breath. This mean-spirited shrew would not cow her. Beauty aside, she couldn't fathom what Harry saw in one such as this. "I'm no one's lover, Your Grace. *I'm* a lady."

Her black eyebrows knitted into a single line. Fury sparked in her cold gaze.

"If you'll excuse me," Anne said again.

It was one thing to give Harry up to this foul creature, quite another to needlessly take the woman's abuse.

"I gather you're off to repair your hem?"

The mocking words slowed Anne's step.

Do not look back, Anne Arlette Adamson. Do not give her the satisfaction.

Then, her sister had always deplored the rash decisions made by her. She turned back around.

"You may have your champagne in the conservatory. Ah, surely you didn't think you were special," the duchess jeered, clearly seeing the shock in Anne's expression.

"No. No, I did not think I was special." She'd known all along just how much she meant to Harry.

Nothing at all.

"Go have your champagne, Lady Anne, and when you're done, he'll come back to me. Because he loves me." If those last four words had been biting and cruel they'd have hurt a good deal less. But the matter-of-factness of that pronouncement burned like acid thrown upon an open wound.

"Just as you love him?" Anne shot back. Fury licked at her insides and she embraced it, finding strength in the heated emotion. "You loved him so much you threw away his heart and the opportunity to be his in every sense of the word. And for what? The title of duchess." She passed a condescending glance up and down the woman's perfect form, and then shook her head, repulsed by the mere sight of her. "You never deserved him." And yet, he would forever be hers.

The woman blanched, in apparent shock at Anne's boldness. "I'll not answer to you for the mistakes of my past, Lady Anne." She spoke in a stoic calm. "Know that I've never stopped loving him and I intend to win back his heart."

"I'm sure that will be some consolation after the manner in which you betrayed him." She dipped a final curtsy. "Now, if you'll excuse me, I should really see to my . . . hem." Anne snapped her flawless skirts and started down the hall. All the while the duchess's stare bore a hole into her back. When she turned right down another corridor she leaned back against the wall, and sought support from the solid plaster. She pressed a hand against her wildly hammering heart.

She'd never before realized how vastly different she was than the Harry, Earl of Stanhopes of the world. She'd spoken to him of seduction with a child's naïveté and yet, in truth she did not fit into the malicious, grasping world that belonged to him and all the widows and lovers he'd taken before her.

She peeked around the wall and found the duchess at last gone. She briefly thought about returning to the ballroom and abandoning this clandestine meeting. "You're a fool, Anne," she muttered under her breath and started in search of the conservatory.

A short while later she'd turned down another long corridor and at last found the blasted room. Before her courage deserted her, she pressed the handle and stepped inside. "Hullo," she called into the quiet.

Hullo, Lord Stanhope . . .

The memory of Lady Kendricks in her dampened gown in an altogether different conservatory weaved its way about her consciousness. She strolled over to the long worktable.

And froze.

Two crystal champagne flutes.

That appeared to be what *she* would now throw away her respectability and sense of decency for.

Anne picked a glass up and for the first time in her twenty years sipped of the forbidden French liquor. She then downed it in a long, slow swallow, delighting in the liquid fortitude that worked its way through her suddenly warm being. The moments ticked by, with the loud hum of quiet blaring in her ears and she stared into the now empty glass. One crystal bead clung to the inside rim of the glass. Anne stilled, and then touched one trembling finger to the lonely drop.

She loved him. She loved him with a strength that terrified her. The same depth of emotion that had surely broken her own mother's heart. And yet, even with her love for him, she couldn't forsake either her pride or her virtue. If she did this thing, if she allowed Harry to lay claim to her body as she longed to, knowing all the while he belonged to another—then what would she be?

Large, sure hands settled upon her shoulders. Her lids fluttered closed. "I can't do this, Harry," she said with the same regret surely known by Calypso when being forced to free her Odysseus. "I shouldn't have come."

"I'm ever so glad you did," a loathsome voice said against her ear.

She dropped the glass. It shattered upon the mahogany table. Crystal shards sprayed her skirts. Lord Rutland's lips brushed her ear and she cringed. "Unhand me, you . . . you bastard," she hissed. Her heart thumped painfully.

Lord Rutland chuckled.

Gooseflesh dotted her skin at that mirthless, cruel sound. The implications of being here, alone with the merciless Lord Rutland sank into her with a growing dread. She struggled against him. "I'll be ruined if I'm discovered with you." She attempted to slip out from under his powerful grip.

He held firm. "Never tell me you didn't think of our last kiss."

How could she ever think of another kiss, imagine another embrace after Harry? She jammed her elbow into his stomach. "No. I really haven't," she said with a bluntness that elicited another one of those steely smiles.

Anne ground her heel upon his instep. "Unhand me," she ordered again. Last time she'd managed to elude the marquess, but really the truth is more he'd set her free. What if he held firm? One passerby and she'd be ruined. The pebble in her belly grew to the size of a boulder and churned painfully.

He shifted her in his arms. "Rest assured, I've no intention for *us* to be discovered together, my lady," he drawled in that condescending tone she'd come to expect.

The conservatory door opened and her heart sank somewhere in the vicinity of her toes. "Anne?"

She pressed her eyes closed.

Harry.

Chapter 20

*I*t took a moment for Harry's eyes to adjust to the dimly lit conservatory. A cloud drifted over the half-moon in the inky-black night sky bathing the room in temporary darkness. Then the cloud passed and a black haze of fury descended over Harry's vision.

Until he drew his last breath, he'd forever remember the vile sight of Rutland with his arm wrapped loosely about Anne, his lips against her skin. He'd detested the idea of Lord Ackland forcing his kiss upon her at a masquerade, but witnessing this horror robbed him of rational thought until he knew the manner of madness that saw men shut behind the walls of Bedlam.

"You bloody bastard. Release her or I vow I'll cut your hands off and stuff them down your throat," he snarled, feeling like a caged beast unleashed in the wild.

Rutland grinned, a cool, vindictive smile that never reached his eyes. "Do you know, I think I won't. Not yet, anyway, Stanhope."

Harry strode forward. "What is this about?" Before he'd dueled him to first blood. This time would be different. This would be to the death and he'd relish putting a bullet through the blackguard's heart.

Rutland flashed another taunting grin. He kissed Anne's cheek. Even with the space between them, Harry detected the faint shudder of her fragile body. He growled and leapt forward, but Rutland placed Anne between them, a form of shield.

Harry fell back. He'd sooner sever his own leg than see Anne come to hurt. He'd wait for whatever game Rutland now played to run its course. When it did, he would pounce on him like the loathsome pig's flesh he was.

"Do you know, I'd never have taken Lady Anne as a true beauty," Rutland remarked as casually as if he spoke of the evening's weather. "But you did. Didn't you? Oh, not immediately. Why at first, you saw the same vain, silly girl all the *ton* did." His smile deepened as one who knew the hell he wrought and relished in it. "But you managed to look past her empty head and silly ringlets. Didn't you?"

A spasm of pain contorted Anne's face.

Harry's gut clenched. *Do not listen to him, Anne. Even if the words were once truth, I was wrong. So very wrong.*

Rutland licked his lips like a wolf about to devour its prey, and in this case the game he toyed with was Anne, a woman whose happiness had come to mean more to Harry than even his own. "You see, you should take care when arranging your trysts. As a rogue, you should know to verify your privacy, Stanhope."

An icy chill stole down his spine. "What are you on about?" he barked. Even as a horrible sense of realization sank into his brain, and with a numbing dread he knew the other man's words before they even left his cold lips.

"Imagine my surprise when Lady Anne arrived to meet you." He chuckled. The force of his coarse laugh shook Anne's slender frame. Her waxen grey skin indicated she also knew very well the direction of Rutland's next words. "How did you describe her?"

"Passably pretty," Anne supplied on a broken whisper.

"Ah, yes. That is correct. Or to be precise . . ."

. . . though you are passably pretty, I couldn't even begin to drum up interest enough to help you . . .

"I couldn't even begin to feign interest to help you," Rutland finished.

Wrong, Rutland. You're wrong. I remember every last, blasted word I leveled at her. Harry looked to Anne. He held her pain-filled gaze. Surely she knew everything had changed. That the moment she shook his hand and sprinted out of the gardens, she'd ceased to be the termagant who tormented him and had since then become the spirited beauty who'd captivated him.

"Pleasantly pretty, empty-headed Lady Anne Adamson desiring a lesson on seduction to . . ." He quirked a chestnut eyebrow. "To what, did you say, my lady?" He whispered against her ear. "To bring a duke up to scratch. Crawford?" Rutland trailed a finger down the line of her jaw, marking her with his evil hands.

Anne pressed her eyes closed.

Oh, God, he wanted to wake from this bloody nightmare. His and Anne's exchange, their real first meeting, forever tarnished by Rutland who'd watched as a voyeur to their private discussion.

And he'd heard all.

Dread sat like a rock in his stomach. Rutland could ruin her if he so wished. And by the vindictive flecks in his brown eyes, he wished it.

The force of Anne's trembling loosened one of her golden locks. Rutland caught it between his fingers and made a show of studying it. "Imagine my honor in being named a prospective tutor to instruct you, Lady Anne."

A black glare flashed in her eyes. "I'd never deign to so much as converse with a snake such as you," she hissed.

Pride flared in Harry's chest. His brave, courageous Anne was stronger than most men. Then Rutland raised her strand of hair to his nose and inhaled. Fury nearly blackened Harry's vision. She belonged to him. Even the lemon and honeysuckle scent of her. He'd come to know even the faintest hint of sweetness that clung to her . . . and now Rutland knew, too. "What the hell do you want?" he bit out, taking another step closer.

Rutland tipped his head, as though he'd forgotten Harry's presence. He grinned. "I want what always belonged to me. What should have been mine," he said in a flat, emotionless tone that chilled Harry through. He shoved Anne.

Harry caught her against him and folded her in his arms. She buried her face in the crook of his shoulder and trembled like the delicate rose bushes in the cool night wind.

The marquess jerked his chin at Anne. "You're going to ruin her."

Harry snapped his eyebrows together. "What are you on about?"

Rutland dropped a bow. "Oh, and Lady Anne? Please send my best to your sister, the Duchess of Bainbridge." Another dark smile that failed to reach his eyes turned his lips up slowly. "We had a most interesting conversation just prior to this *delightful* exchange." With those cryptic words, he took his leave.

Perhaps if Anne were not shaking against him, silent, when she was never short of words, he'd have been able to piece together whatever rhyme the other man spoke in. He willed his rational mind to sort through it all, but could not separate from the stinging rage of Rutland's treatment of her. Harry tightened his hold on her and she turned her cheek against his chest, as though seeking warmth.

Harry tipped Anne's chin up. "Did he harm you?" Loathsome images of Rutland caressing her lean frame wrapped about his mind and refused to relinquish their tentacle-like hold.

"No," she said quickly.

"Did he touch you?" If Rutland had dared put his vile hands upon that which belonged to him, he'd kill him quite gladly.

She shook her head once. He'd come to know her so very well that he detected the hesitancy in that movement. "It doesn't matter, Harry." The resignation in her tone dug at him.

He took her by the shoulders. "It does matter," he said angrily and then gentled his tone. "It *does* matter, Anne."

She jerked away from him. "He knows. He knows all." She began to pace, the frenetic movements indicating the very thin thread she had on her control. "My mother, my sisters through the years have insisted that one of my madcap schemes would ultimately result in my ruination." Her words broke on a shuddery sob. "But this . . ." She stumbled to a halt and stared sightlessly at the doors through which Rutland had just departed. "This I'll never recover from."

Harry steeled his jaw. He'd see Rutland in hell before he allowed him to destroy Anne's reputation. "I'll wed you." He blinked, not knowing where the words came from.

Anne swung back to look at him. Her eyes round like moons. "Why?" Her voice was so whisper soft he strained to hear.

His palms dampened and he rubbed them along the side of his breeches. Why, indeed. He settled for the least complicated response that didn't require much further thought on his part. "I'll not see you hurt. I will give you the protection of my name."

A spasm contorted her face. "What of your heart?" Her gaze slid to a point past his shoulder.

His mouth went dry, a loud humming filled his ears. He closed his eyes desperately wanting to be the man she deserved. "Anne . . ." He began. "Are you asking me if I love you?" His mind stalled at the implications of that question and more, his own feelings for Anne. He'd protected himself against hurt for eight years now. Margaret's reentry into Society only served to remind him of the dangers of entrusting oneself to a woman's fickle hands.

With sad eyes, Anne searched his. She touched her fingertips to his lips, cutting off the inadequate words. "If you must ask it as a question, then I don't need any answer but that." The muscles in her throat bobbed up and down. "You don't need to say anything." Apparently, in his silence he'd said enough. A woeful smile played about her mouth. "I'll not have a husband who'd wed me out of a sense of obligation."

His body jerked reflexively. She'd reject his offer. With the realization of that, a panicky terror gripped him. *Say something, you fool. Give her the words she desires. Give her the words she deserves.* "It wouldn't be borne of obligation, Anne. I enjoy being with you. You make me laugh. You'd make a sufficient partner." *Isn't it more than that, though?*

A desperate giggle bubbled past her lips and she shook her head slowly. "Oh, Harry. You'd do just as well with a loyal pup than a wife, if those are your requirements."

He tried again. "Anne," he said gently. "We are happy together." In the days he'd spent with Anne, he'd found more happiness than he'd ever known in all his thirty years. His mouth went dry, fear holding back the words that would splay him open before her. He'd offered all of himself once before. He could not humble himself again.

Seeing the determined tilt to her chin, Harry realized that nothing he could or would say in that moment would convince her of the rightness of his suit. He, the Earl of Stanhope, who'd no intention of settling upon the future countess any time in the near or even distant future, had spoken to her of marriage—and she'd very clearly rejected him. Then, his offer had been more an afterthought, one made out of obligation. Anne surely craved more than that . . .

A dark, niggling thought worked its way about his brain. *Mayhap it's not that she'd rather be ruined. Mayhap she still longs for the title of duchess.* He stomped over and took her by the arms. "Look at me," he commanded, his tone harsh and angry. "You'd rather be ruined?" *Than accept a union we can ultimately find happiness in?*

She boldly met his gaze and in the clear depths of her blue eyes he saw the truth—she wouldn't wed him. In that moment, his past converged with his future as he recalled a different woman, a different rejection. Her shoulders moved up and down on her slow inhalation. "I'd rather—"

"Good God, Anne!"

Their gazes swiveled to the entrance.

Horror churned inside his shocked being at the untimely arrival of Lady Katherine, the Duke of Bainbridge, and Anne's mother, the Countess of Wakefield.

Harry stared numbly back at the trio glowering at him. The horrified betrayal in Katherine's eyes registered. Once upon a lifetime ago, he'd attempted to seduce her. And yet, he believed he'd proven himself a true friend to her. Only, the sneer on her lips indicated that she viewed him no different than the rest of the *ton*; as a self-serving rogue who'd placed his own desires before that of even her sister's reputation. Unable to bear the sight of her abject disappointment, he glanced to her husband. Fiery rage filled the duke's eyes, and Harry suspected the presence of the ladies was the only thing keeping him from storming the conservatory and pummeling Harry within an inch of his life.

Anne nudged him and he realized too late, he still held her. He released her with such alacrity she stumbled. Harry cursed and quickly steadied her.

The countess gasped, burying the sound in her hands.

Bainbridge's eyes narrowed into black slits.

Harry yanked his hands back and took a step away from her.

The duke advanced. Hell, with Napoleon and his plans for France, the British hadn't needed Wellington or Nelson; they merely had needed this single, hulking figure advancing on the French and Boney's efforts would have been halted before the French emperor could have uttered *world domination*.

"Bainbridge," he said calmly, directing his attention to the gentleman who'd detested him since their first meeting. "This is not how it appears," he said.

"Oh, and how does it appear?" Bainbridge snarled.

He opted for honesty. "As though I'm seducing her."

The countess cried out.

Bainbridge lunged for him and he danced out of the other man's reach. Perhaps honesty had not been the wisest course.

Anne's mother held a hand out. "Anne, come here now," she said, in the tone a nursemaid might use with a recalcitrant child.

The duke gnashed his teeth. "Get her out of here," he said to his wife.

Anne shook her head and remained fixed to the spot. "Jasper, don't," she said quietly. "It is as Harry says. This is not at all as it appears."

"Harry?" the countess snapped that one-word question, a name teeming with fury.

Color blazed to life in Anne's cheeks. "It can be explained."

"I'm certain it can," Katherine finally spoke, her seething tone indicating no answer he gave would ever be sufficient.

You're going to ruin her. He swiped a hand over his face.

"I anticipate your visit first thing in the morning," the duke said between clenched teeth.

It was on the tip of his tongue to keep from telling the other man to go to hell. He opened his mouth, but then something in Anne's eyes killed the words. No gentleman cared to have his hand forced, not even if it was for the delicate, beautiful hand of Lady Anne. He gave a curt nod.

The duke spun on his heel and marched from the gardens, clearly expecting Anne to follow. She hesitated a moment, alongside her mother.

What a blasted fool he'd been in agreeing to help Anne. Her reputation now in tatters; and Harry forced to do the right thing, even as she longed for her duke. He dragged a hand through his hair. What an ignominious beginning to a marriage.

She stretched a hand out. "Harry," she said softly. Anne's fingers fell back to her side and she fisted her skirts; her white-knuckled grip upon the fabric the only indication of her upset. Her brother-in-law spoke quietly, the words lost to the distance between Harry and Anne. She gave a tight nod. Katherine took her by the hand and tugged her from the conservatory with the duke and Countess of Wakefield following suit.

Harry stood there long after Anne had taken her leave. It was only a matter of time before Rutland divulged the secrets that would ruin Anne.

His brave, spirited Anne had been adamant that she would not marry him and yet surely with the immediacy of the moment behind them, she'd inevitably realize they had no recourse but to wed. His palms went moist at the thought and he brushed them against his breeches. As much as he'd considered himself a bastard these years, it would appear he was a good deal less than he'd ever imagined, for he'd sacrifice his freedom to protect Anne from scandal.

His mind suddenly moved with lightning like speed, as it all began to make sense.

Rutland's plan.

Margaret's return.

Anne's ruin.

The careful timing of her family's arrival.

Rutland would have her ruined to free Margaret for his attention. Anne had been nothing more than a pawn to advance Rutland's selfish desires.

In the end, Anne would pay the ultimate price, her good name, her reputation, so the ruthless Rutland could at last claim Margaret.

If only the bastard had bothered to ask, Harry would have told Rutland he was welcome to her. The moment Anne had slipped into Lord Essex's conservatory, all other women had ceased to matter.

And on the heel of that staggering realization was the dawning truth . . . he did not feel compelled to offer for Anne out of obligation. He wanted her because he could not imagine his life without her.

For the first time that evening, Harry smiled.

I love her.

Chapter 21

$\mathscr{S}$ince Anne had entered the Duke of Bainbridge's carriage behind her mother and sister, shock had robbed her of words. Her sister's regret, her mother's shame, tangible and painful, ravaged her conscience. And yet, for the life's worth of bad decisions she'd made where Harry was concerned, she'd do nothing differently. She loved him. Loved him with a hopeless, helpless passion that defied logic and reason and baubles that promised one the heart of a duke. She braced for the impending barrage, and when it came it was fast and volatile like a summer lightning storm.

"Whatever were you thinking?" Mother cried. "I've warned you time and time again about the earl." She leaned across her seat. "You insisted you'd no interest in him."

"I lied," Anne whispered. Pity fairly seeped from her sister's eyes and Anne glanced away, detesting the sentiment.

"That is what you'd say to me? You lied?" Mother jabbed a finger in Anne's direction. "You've been ruined. A young lady is *never* permitted to be alone with a man. And a man such as Stanhope, no less."

"No one knows, Mother," Katherine said softly.

Sweet, supportive Katherine who'd always sought to protect Anne from herself. "No one knows. Isn't that correct, Anne?" A twin look passed between them. The unspoken language that only they two understood. Just as Anne would sacrifice everything and anything for her sister, so too would Katherine do anything within her means to spare

Anne pain. And now, she sought to protect Anne from their mother's wrath.

However, sometime between Lord Essex's conservatory and this moment Anne had changed; grown from the carefree, whimsical miss to a sensible woman who finally knew there were consequences to her actions.

"Anne?" her sister said, a plaintive note in that one-word utterance.

She was no longer a child to be protected by her sisters.

Anne's silence served as her answer.

Mother buried her face into her hands. "I'd had such grand hopes for you. I'd indulged you in your first Season and didn't truly begin to worry until your second Season. Now this?" She wept noisy tears that transported Anne back to the long-ago day she'd come upon Mother sobbing about the rumors that had circulated during Anne's Come Out regarding her late husband's infidelity.

"Perhaps we can still right this." Katherine looked hopefully to her husband. "Isn't that right, Jasper?"

Envy tugged at Anne's breast. She'd trade anything and everything to have another person with whom she could unburden all the woes and fears she carried. What a vastly less lonely world it would be for her.

"Lord Rutland knows," she whispered, knowing the temporary reprieve Katherine sought on her behalf was just that—temporary. Rutland knew all . . . and soon the entire *ton* would know.

A muscle ticked at the corner of her brother-in-law's eye.

Rutland, notoriously ruthless in all matters, wouldn't hesitate to shred Anne's reputation.

Then her mother murmured perhaps the truest words she'd ever spoken. "This *cannot* be undone."

Anne folded her arms about herself and hugged tight remembering Harry's pledge to do right by her.

"He will wed her, Mother," Katherine said in a gentling tone one might reserve for a fractious mare. "I'm certain of it."

Anne didn't doubt he'd sacrifice his own happiness to protect her from Rutland's scheming. Everything she'd known of Harry before these past ten days had changed so very greatly. The man she'd once taken as an ignoble libertine was honorable, valiant, and all things good.

"Wed her?" Anne cringed at her mother's high-pitched squeal. "Wed her? I'd have her sooner wed"—she slashed the small space with a furious hand—"any number of gentleman than that shameless rogue."

Anne retreated within herself. She sat, more a voyeur than an actual participant in the discussion her mother and sister proceeded to have about her life. She dimly registered the remote pity in her brother-in-law's usually hard stare.

Marriage . . .

Harry . . .

No choice . . .

She wanted Harry with everything and anything she was. Anything and everything she would ever be. Anne drew in a shuddery breath. She could not have him this way. "I won't wed him." Her whisper-soft admission cut into the frenzied discussion.

"I don't see that you have a choice." The gentleness in Katherine's tone was nearly Anne's undoing.

"The *duke* will certainly not have her now," Mother spat, bitterness dripping from her words.

Anne glanced out the window. She'd not allow Harry to be forced and bound to marry her out of some misbegotten sense of honor. Not when she'd been the one to force him into the role of tutor. If he'd spoken of love, or in the least, a desire to wed her, she'd have embraced marriage to him. But he hadn't. She'd asked why he'd wed her, and he'd answered truthfully.

Tears filled her eyes and she blinked them away. Foolish, foolish drops.

The carriage rocked to a slow halt before her townhouse. Jasper didn't wait for the servant, but instead leaned over, and flung the door open. He leapt to the ground and handed first Katherine down, and then Anne.

She hurried inside, wanting the solace of her own chambers.

Her mother's sharp voice called after her. "Anne, you are to await for me in the parlor."

Alas, solace would have to come later. Much later.

She all but sprinted past Ollie, who stood with the door opened. Her slippers were silent on the Italian marble and she gathered this was much how Joan of Arc had felt when being marched up the gallows. Her lips twisted. Then, Joan of Arc wouldn't have been fool to make the collection of mistakes Anne herself had. She entered the Ivory Parlor and clasped her hands, wringing them together, her mind curiously blank.

Footsteps sounded at the door. She drew a steadying breath. "Mother, I know what you intend to say."

Katherine entered the room. Her husband hovered just outside, allowing the sisters a brief moment of privacy. "I certainly hope you've something vastly more original and slightly more reassuring than *that* to begin your discussion with Mother." Her sister's droll words, a clear attempt at easing the tension, did little to cut through Anne's inner turmoil.

She rocked back on her heels. "Katherine," she said tiredly. "You should go." Had word begun to circulate even now, throughout ballrooms and parlors all over London? After all, when one knew . . . all knew. Her heart quickened as the implications of her actions, and all Rutland knew of her and Harry, truly sank into her mind.

"Oh, Anne, what have you done?"

If Katherine's tone had been the bothered, I've-come-to-expect-this-of-you one she'd adopted through the years, it would have been so much easier than the agonized disappointment in her younger sister's words. She firmed her jaw. "I don't expect you to understand."

"Harry, well, I expect such outrageous behavior of him." Katherine shook her head, sadly. "But you?"

"It wasn't Harry," she said firmly.

Katherine's brow wrinkled. "What do you mean? I saw him, Anne. I saw his hands on your person. I—"

"I propositioned the earl, Kat. I made him a scandalous proposal and asked him to help me win the Duke of Crawford's heart," she uttered that last part on a shamed whisper.

The air left Katherine on a slow, elongated breath. "My God."

Her lips twisted wryly. No, not even the Lord himself could help with this.

She pressed ahead, determined for Katherine to know the truth. "I threatened to seek out Lord Rutland's help if he didn't agree, and so he did." Because he was good and honorable, far more honorable than Society gave him credit for.

Her sister rocked back on her heels, silent.

And now, for his efforts, he'd be forced into marriage, and she had little doubt he'd do right by her. Just as her father's heart had belonged to another, so too would Harry's. Tears filled her eyes, but she blinked them back. Oh, God. For all her fears of becoming Mother and all her efforts to avoid that same, sorry, broken fate, with her actions she'd gone and carved out a future that would turn her into just that person she'd striven her whole adult life not to be. She could not. Would not . . .

Katherine broke the silence. "Why would you . . . ?" She steepled her fingers and pressed the tips to her mouth. "This is about that blasted pendant, isn't it? The—"

"The heart of a duke, yes." Her lips twisted. Only now, she realized how very grasping, how very shameful her efforts had been. She'd once imagined a match with a distinguished, powerful duke posed as the ultimate triumph over her parents' miserable existence. In the end, she'd found she wanted nothing more than that honorable, respectable match—except she wanted it with Harry, and no other.

Katherine said nothing for a long while. She sank back into a chair. "Oh, dear."

Anne thought "Oh, hell" would better suit the current situation, but she supposed "Oh, dear" would also suffice.

"And Lord Rutland discovered your intentions," she said to herself.

Anne toyed with her skirt. "Discovered my intentions." And would ruin her for it.

Katherine's eyes slid closed. "Oh, dear."

Their mother chose that opportune moment to make her entrance, sweeping past Jasper, and advancing deep into the room. She glared Anne into silence. "I've tolerated your headstrong spiritedness through the years. I've forgiven your lack of marriage for three Seasons. This, however, I cannot forgive."

Katherine sprang to her feet. Ever the protector, she placed herself between Anne and their mother's vitriolic attack. "Lord Stanhope aside, Mother, we shall find Anne a perfectly suitable husband." She turned an optimistic smile on her sister. "Why, you'll have the heart of a handsome, young, affable duke," she said using Anne's innocently hopeful words from more than a year ago when they'd traipsed over the ice at the Frost Fair.

"No gentleman will have her." Mother held Anne's stare, and she knew before the words left Mother's lips what would be required of her. "You know what you must do, Anne. I'd expected it would be Katherine, but it must be you."

The resignation in Mother's tone raised the stirring of panic within her belly. Revulsion snaked through her being at the prospect of marriage to Mr. Ekstrom. Anne sank into the edge of a nearby seat. "I know." Did that garbled whisper belong to her?

Katherine's head whipped back and forth between them. "I don't understand."

Anne considered the stocky Bertie Ekstrom with his sausage-sized fingers and leering gaze. She managed words past the lump in her throat. The heart-wrenchingly beautiful lessons Harry had given her on seduction, their stolen interludes, all of it would be the complete ruin of her. Always considered the passionate, flighty sister, she prided herself on maintaining her composure in the face of the horrible life in front of her. "I have to wed someone, Katherine. I cannot simply trust Lord Rutland will not someday divulge the scandalous information he discovered."

"That is the first sensible decision you've made since you began carrying on with that outrageous rogue." Icy scorn coated Mother's words.

Her sister ignored their irate mother and looked momentarily to her husband who remained at the door as a manner of sentry. A look passed between husband and wife. Again, an almost painful envy coursed through Anne at the shared connection. He gave an imperceptible nod.

Katherine's brown eyes formed wide circles in her face. "No," she breathed. "Not—"

"Don't," Anne implored, not needing, and certainly not wanting the words uttered into existence.

"You'd have her wed vile Mr. Ekstrom," Katherine hissed.

"I'd see her married and protected while you'd see her ruined," her mother spat.

The two women stood, locked in a silent battle of the wills. Mother had once sought to wed Katherine to their cousin. With her quick wit and bold courage, she'd instead put an offer of marriage to the Duke of Bainbridge, thus saving herself from Mother's maneuverings. However, Anne was long past saving. She knew that. Her guardian would know that. And if Rutland had his way, everyone in polite Society would soon know it, too.

Katherine broke the impasse. "I'll see you a spinster before I ever see you wed that vile toad," she said to Anne, never taking her eyes from their mother.

The countess narrowed her eyes. "I shall speak to your uncle first thing in the morning, Anne. After his shameful lack of regard for my marital aspirations for Katherine"— Katherine's eyebrows dipped—"I'm sure he'll at least have sense enough to see to the necessity of a union between yourself and Mr. Ekstrom."

The bottom fell out from Anne's stomach as her mother's words somehow made this hell all the more real. She managed a jerky nod.

"Splendid." Mother gave a pleased nod. "The matter is settled. I'll meet with my brother tomorrow morning and he'll see to the arrangements with Bertrand." She swept out of the room as though she'd spoken on mundane matters such as the London weather and her latest modiste, and not Anne's grim future.

Katherine glowered at Anne. "I forbid you from wedding him."

What her sister failed to realize was that it didn't really matter who Anne wed. Mr. Ekstrom may as well have been the Duke of Crawford who may as well have been Prinny himself. None of them were Harry. The irony wasn't lost on her. Always regarded as selfish and self-serving, Anne would relinquish Harry, and in doing so, lose the only man she would ever love.

"We shall simply find you a husband." She motioned to Jasper who still remained by his post at the doorway. "After all, I found one."

A broken laugh bubbled past Anne's lips. She took Katherine's hands and gave them a firm squeeze. "Oh, Kat, don't you see you can't fix this. You were right through the years. I was headstrong and unwise and now I'll pay the price." The ultimate price, marriage to Bertrand Ekstrom. The threat that had dangled first over Katherine, and then Anne, would be realized.

Her sister shook her head back and forth. "I cannot believe that," she said, with a fool's optimism. Anne marveled at the great shift that had occurred. Long considered the fanciful, foolishly whimsical twin, Anne had somehow altered roles with her practical, logic-driven sister. Katherine appealed to Jasper. "Surely there is something we can do?"

He looked to his wife and said tersely, "Stanhope."

Anne was remarkably low on options. Ruin. Harry. Vile Bertie Ekstrom. Options that would salvage her reputation, that was. Her throat worked. She could not wed Harry. Would not. Not under duress. Not because he'd been forced into a union with a wife who would merely *suffice*. In time, he would grow to hate her and she'd become an empty, bitter shell of a woman just as her mother had been . . . and still was, even long after Father had died. All the while she'd sit from the sidelines as Harry longed for another, loved another he could not have. No, that she could not do. She took a steadying breath. "The decision is mine, Katherine."

An almost pitying look wreathed the harsh, angular planes of her brother-in-law's face. She cocked her head at the crack in Jasper's hard veneer. But for the clear love he carried for his wife and sweet son, Maxwell, she'd never bore witness to a single show of emotion from the austere duke. Until now. "Rutland," she whispered aloud.

Katherine and Jasper stared at her questioningly.

Anne pressed her fingers against her temples and rubbed her fingers in slow, circular motions. "I need to speak with Lord Rutland." Any man who'd stood to the side and watched on as though his heart too was publicly breaking was not wholly a monster.

"No," Katherine said, her lips a flat line of disapproval. "Enough of your schemes, Anne."

Only, she'd witnessed Rutland's despair. "I must speak to him." She scrambled forward in her seat. "Rutland will—"

"Rutland is a despicable bounder," her sister said bluntly. "Tell her," she said to her husband. Her eyes narrowed at his silence. "Tell her, Jasper."

"I believe, perhaps, it might be beneficial to speak to Rutland," he said quietly. He still clearly believed Harry to be a worthless cur, and likely saw the imagined perils in Anne wedding one such as the Earl of Stanhope.

"Thank you, Jasper," Anne said softly.

Katherine leaned over and took Anne's hand in her own. "I'm disappointed Harry would meet you as he did and compromise your reputation, but Anne, you've been ruined. Ruined before one, may as well be ruined before all. Surely you must see the folly in choosing one such as Mr. Ekstrom over Harry?"

Anne pressed her eyes tight, remembering his laugh, his teasing, the moment he'd placed the delicate wire-framed spectacles upon her nose in Hyde Park. Until the day she drew her last breath, Harry would hold every last sliver of her now broken heart. She loved him enough to set him free.

"Anne?" her sister prodded.

"He . . ." She didn't know how much Katherine knew of Harry's past and would not betray the pieces she had of him. "He loved another, and I'll not come between that." She pulled her hand free and shoved to her feet. She would not become their mother. Of course, she could not say as much. Katherine knew nothing of Father's infidelity, so in this, Anne would protect her.

"This is madness." Katherine stood. "*Madness*."

"Do you believe Harry loves me?"

Her sister fell stonily silent, her lack of response more resounding than any answer.

A sad smile tugged at her lips. "No, I did not believe so, either."

Katherine held her palms up. "I don't know if Harry is capable of loving anyone." Katherine was wrong. As much as her sister knew of Harry, she clearly didn't know of the love he'd carried for Margaret. She crossed over to Anne. "I trust he'll marry you," she said quietly.

How could her sister with such a beautiful love with Jasper believe Anne could ever, *would* ever enter into a union that had been orchestrated by the vile Lord Rutland? "I'll not have him that way." She'd have him in a loving marriage or not at all.

"You'd rather wed that toad, Bertrand Ekstrom?" Katherine glanced to her husband. "Say something, Jasper."

His response was lost to Anne as she wandered to the window. She peeled back the curtain. In spite of the warmth of the night, a chill stole through her.

Katherine's face reflected in the crystal panes. Her brown eyebrows stitched in a single, suspicious line. "What are you thinking, Anne?"

She touched her forehead to the cool windowpane as her mother's previous threats of and for a marriage to Mr. Ekstrom and the inevitability of her ruin blended into one perfectly horrific resolution. A lone carriage rumbled down the darkened street. "I can't marry him."

"Bah, of course you can!"

Anne shook her head. "No." She turned back around. "I can't." Harry would do the honorable thing and wed her. But it would never be for the right reasons. Ultimately, in protecting her and denying himself the one woman he truly loved, he would bind himself to Anne—forever. That was the kind of gentleman he was.

Katherine took a step toward her. Fire lit her eyes. "As infuriated as I am with Harry for helping you in your foolish plan to win the heart of a duke, I know him well enough to say he would never"—she took another step closer—"*ever* allow you to wed Bertrand Ekstrom. Never," she added for final measure.

Anne captured her lower lip between her teeth. No, her sister was, as usual, correct. She began to pace. In the morning, Harry intended to meet her guardian.

"What are you thinking?" her sister asked.

Anne ignored her and continued her frantic pace. Perceived by all of polite society as an unrepentant rogue, in actuality Harry possessed more honor, integrity, and respectability than all of the peerage combined. Even as he didn't love her, he would marry her. No, he wouldn't stand idly by while she wed Mr. Ekstrom. Perhaps ten days ago Harry would have flatly rejected marriage to Anne. Then, he'd viewed her as a young lady who . . .

She drew to a slow halt and blinked.

"What is it?" her sister prodded, her tone sharper.

Anne shook her head slowly. If he still saw her as nothing more than a title-grasping miss, then he'd not do this thing, and cost himself his every happiness.

A knowing glint flashed in Katherine's eyes, a sudden understanding, that only came from a sister who'd been dragged along years of foolish schemes. "What are you planning?"

"He won't be happy with me," she said in an entreating tone, willing her sister to see. She sucked in a shuddery breath. "He loved her."

Her brother-in-law averted his gaze, silent through the sisters' exchange.

Katherine cocked her head at the sudden shift in conversation. "Loved who?"

"Lady Margaret Monteith."

Understanding lit her sister's brown eyes. After all, the *ton* was well-aware of the scandalous young widow's reentrance into Society. But then she gave her head a quick shake. "That doesn't matter."

A pained laugh escaped her. Her sister was all things loyal. "I don't want him to marry me because he's been forced to. He will resent me for denying him his true love and I will resent him for loving another." And in that, she would become her mother. She had to set him free and the only way to do so was making him hate her. Again. Her heart twisted with a bitter pain. Considering the loathing he'd carried for her this past year that should prove rather an easy task to accomplish.

Katherine jabbed a finger in her direction. "Anne Arlette Adamson, by God I've seen that look in your eyes more times than has ever been good for either of us."

Anne looked down. All her life, she'd been rash. She'd moved through life without ever truly considering the consequences of her actions. Rutland's discovery and subsequent threat had shown her belatedly the dangers of such recklessness. She picked her head up. "There will be no more schemes," she said softly, assuring her twin. *After this.*

Anne looked to Jasper. He stood, laconic as usual, hands clasped behind his back.

"Jasper, there is a favor I would put to you."

He inclined his head. "You need but ask."

"I need you to arrange one additional meeting tomorrow."

He quirked a black eyebrow.

She drew in a steadying breath. "Following my meeting with the Marquess of Rutland"—her throat closed up—"I'd like to see Lord Stanhope. Alone."

Chapter 22

*S*eated in the corner of the 8th Duke of Bainbridge's spacious office, Anne glanced for surely the hundredth time at the long-case clock across the room.

"He's not due 'round for another fifteen minutes," Jasper called from his place at the mahogany desk, head bent over his ledgers.

She played with the precious pair of wire-rimmed spectacles. "I know that," she felt inclined to point out.

He dipped his pen into the inkwell "Do you?" he asked, taciturn as usual. He continued to work away.

She very well knew the time Lord Rutland was scheduled to meet with Jasper. Just as she knew the time of his meeting with Harry. She'd lain awake until the morning sun peeked across the horizon going over exactly what she'd say, drawing on every last negative perception everyone and anyone had ever possessed of Lady Anne Arlette Adamson.

As she'd stared down at her untouched breakfast plate she'd convinced herself she could carry through with her plans, because she loved Harry, even when he could not love her, loved enough for the both of them. Loved him enough to do that which was truly selfless.

She tapped her feet on the hardwood floor. Jasper picked his head up and gave her a pointed look. She continued to beat the hasty, staccato rhythm upon the floor. "Do you believe I can reason with him?" She toyed with the spectacles in her hands, running her finger over the delicate frame.

"I believe if you cannot, I can," he said in the low, hoarse voice that had terrified her since their first meeting. In other words, he'd find some way to silence Rutland.

A knock sounded at the door. Anne dropped her spectacles. They fell with a soft clink upon the hardwood floor. She surged to her feet as the butler opened the door. "Your Grace, the Marquess of Rutland to see you."

In walked the man who'd see her ruined, bold as if he owned the office, really quite an impressive feat considering her brother-in-law had every last single lord and lady in London quaking in his presence.

Jasper remained seated, in a blatant statement of disrespect.

The butler closed the door quietly behind Rutland. "Bainbridge," he said, a cruel edge to that terse greeting. "A pleasure, and of course a surprise. To what do I owe the honor of this unexpected meeting?" Though, he, Jasper, and Anne all knew there was nothing surprising about this meeting. Well, with the exception of her forgotten figure in the corner.

She took a step forward. "My lord."

Lord Rutland's tall, well-muscled frame went taut and he turned stiffly to face Anne. "My *lady*," he said, the two-word greeting faintly mocking.

She ticked her chin up a notch. "I'd speak with you." she said before her courage deserted her and she begged Jasper to handle the loathsome fiend for her. But with all she'd planned for the day, this was certainly the least difficult task she'd undertake.

Jasper stood. "I'll be right outside the room," he murmured. He fixed a frosty glare on Rutland that would have had most other men quaking. Instead, the sinister lord inclined his head with icy amusement in his dark eyes. Jasper closed the door with a soft click. She suspected he hovered at the other side, prepared to storm the room and take Rutland apart if she simply whispered it.

Anne smoothed her palms over the front of her skirt. She eyed the impassive gentleman. He'd earned a reputation amongst the *ton* as a black-hearted fiend, whose presence was accepted amongst fashionable Society for his old, distinguished title. "My sisters believed my efforts in speaking with you today were futile." Surely a man who'd loved so passionately was still capable of some good?

He spoke on a lethal whisper. "And what do you believe, Lady Anne?"

She managed a weak smile. "You wouldn't be here if I felt that was the case, my lord." She took a step toward him, and another, and another. He remained rooted to his spot, his expression a blank mask. "I've thought a good deal about . . ." Her cheeks warmed. "About your discovery. That is, my meeting with Lord Stanhope." She furrowed her brow. "Er, well, them both really." He quirked a chestnut eyebrow, that very human gesture transforming him from monster, into someone quite . . . human.

Anne started at the sudden revelation that for all his coldness and legendary escapades, he really was quite a handsome gentleman. Good, human was indeed preferable to the fire-breathing, jagged-toothed dragon she'd made him out to be these past days.

She imagined he hadn't always been the merciless man who'd threaten to destroy a lady's reputation; imagined he'd been so very different before Lady Margaret.

One of those familiar hard smiles played at his lips.

She flushed at having been discovered studying him so.

"My lady?" he whispered, an invitation in his words.

Anne wrinkled her nose. Did he truly imagine she would desire *him*? Oh, the arrogance of men. "I have not called you here for . . ." She clamped her lips shut, not finishing that bold supposition.

The first flash of amusement flared briefly in his eyes. "Then why am I here?" he asked, that flinty look in place once more.

"Er, yes, well, right." What could she ever say to a jaded, broken man like Lord Rutland to make him see? She took another breath. "I've thought of nothing else since our"— she averted her gaze—"*meeting*, last evening."

"Is that what we are to call it?" he mocked, calling her attention back once more.

She gritted her teeth, not rising to his baiting.

He folded his arms across his chest. "And?"

"You'd have me wed Harry for what purpose? So you'll be free to your Lady Margaret?" A muscle jumped at the corner of his eye, the sole indication she'd been correct in her supposition. "I thought about it a good deal last evening."

"Undoubtedly," he said, coolly mocking.

She carried on as though he'd not spoken. "You'd force me to wed Lord Stanhope and there is nothing that would bring me greater happiness than having him as my husband. And I thought about that well into the morning hours. I thought about how very happy I could be." She held his gaze. "Only, do you know what I realized, my lord?"

"What was that?" the response came as though dragged from him.

"I don't doubt he'd do the honorable thing and marry me if for no other reason than to save me." So, in this, she would save him, even at the expense of her own name. "I realized even as I love him, if I allowed you to force us into marriage, the time would come, now or in the future, when he'd grow to resent me. Perhaps even hate me." She closed her eyes a moment. That she could not bear. "I would forever remind him of the woman he could not have." She folded her arms across her chest and rubbed warmth back into her limbs. She'd rather have no marriage than the bleak, empty existence her own mother had known. "I'll not marry him," she whispered. "Not like this." And so, not ever.

He froze, unblinking.

Anne slid her gaze to the forgotten pair of spectacles, a splendid gift from a man who would never be anything more than a memory. She wandered over and stooped to retrieve them. "They are beautiful, aren't they?" she murmured, more to herself. With the delicate spectacle frames in hand, she stood, and carried them over to the window. The slight crack in the brocade curtains cast a narrow stream of sunshine through the opening. It reflected off the metal frames and painted the opposite wall with a magnificent display of shimmering light. She held the gift given her by Harry up to that streaming ray of sunshine, appreciating the light refracting off the metal. "Do you know something?"

"What?" he asked, voice gruff. The slight widening of his eyes indicated he'd surprised the both of them with his question.

She gave him a small, gentle smile. "I spent the whole of my life told if I wore spectacles I'd never make a proper match." She managed a laugh. "So I didn't wear them because I thought they might detract from my *pleasant prettiness*." She shot him a wry look over her shoulder at those words he'd hurled at her last evening, and then returned her attention to her spectacles. "I thought I was protecting myself, only now I think of all those wasted years . . . not seeing. Yet with these"—she held the slight pair up—"small and so very insignificant . . ." The muscles of her throat moved up and down with the force of her swallow. "They changed me." She met his gaze. "They helped me see differently." The kind of person she was. The kind of person she *wanted* to be. They'd helped her see more clearly. About *everything*. "Sometimes one simply needs a little help bringing life more clearly into focus. Don't you agree, my lord?"

A muscle jumped at the corner of his mouth, and she knew the hard, but not unintelligent, Lord Rutland knew exactly what she said, knew she spoke of the jealous rage that had blinded him all these years. He cursed. "You won't wed him?" he asked at last.

She shook her head. "I won't." What had he expected? That she would have some sage words to ease the heartache he'd known.

"You'll be ruined," Rutland shot back.

Anne lifted her shoulders in a little shrug. "Yes." She paused. "But only if you allow it."

As though unsettled by her accusatory stare, he strolled to the edge of Jasper's wide mahogany desk. He propped his hip at the edge and continued to study her through thick, hooded lashes. Which was, of course, madness. Ruthless Lord Rutland wasn't unsettled by anyone or anything.

She walked toward him, coming to a stop at the leather winged-back chair. "You'll have your Margaret at any cost." Anne passed a searching gaze over his face, seeking a hint of warmth, some emotion other than this immobile mask. "Only, what you'll find is what I already know. She'll not love you for what you've done. She'll resent you because you've robbed her of her heart's happiness." Anne had witnessed the unadulterated love and longing in the other woman's eyes. She took another step. "You'll inevitably make a decision to ruin me to advance your own gains." She tipped her chin back. "But know this, my lord. You'll not have Margaret at the expense of mine"—and more importantly—"and Lord Stanhope's happiness."

He narrowed his eyes. "You would . . ." Would. Not—will. ". . . be cast out of Society, shunned by your friends and family. You'd sacrifice all that?"

"I would," she said, her answer automatic. "When you love someone"—as she loved Harry—"you'll sacrifice anything, *even* your own happiness, if that brings them true happiness." She glanced at the toes of her slippers, suddenly reminded of how very inadequate she'd always been with words. "If I were my sister Aldora," she said softly, "perhaps I would be more eloquent." Certainly enough to not mention happiness twice in the same sentence. "Or if I was my sister Katherine, I could speak to you with logic and clear reason, deterring you from your goals." She shrugged. "All I can do is appeal to the man you surely once were before your Lady Margaret."

Silence blanketed the room. He said nothing for so long she suspected he might simply stride from the room and close the door behind him, her words forgotten. "I was never a good man," he said at last, his words flat and emotionless.

"I don't believe that," she said quietly.

"You believe wrong, then."

Anne passed the spectacles back and forth between her hands. "Well, then. There is nothing else I can say." Now her mother would know the truth, the truth her family had been good enough to keep from the overdramatic countess until this particular meeting. She stuck her fingers out, the gesture so very reminiscent of her first meeting with Harry.

"What are you doing?"

"I'm thanking you for having come and at least considered my request. You'll do what you think is best."

"And you think my decision is a poor one," he tossed back, ignoring her hand.

She let her fingers fall to her side. "Undoubtedly."

The marquess caught his square jaw between his thumb and forefinger. He rubbed his chin contemplatively, then stopped suddenly and cursed. He shoved off the desk and started for the door.

Her heart pounded wildly and she was filled with an almost physical urge to call out and beg him to change his course. For everyone's low opinion of her, however, she'd never been called a coward.

He spun around. "Stanhope's a bloody fool," he growled.

She cocked her head.

He spoke between gritted teeth. "Your secret is your secret."

Her heart kicked up a frantic rhythm. "I don't understand." She touched a hand to her pounding heart, besieged by hope.

"I'll not divulge you and Stanhope's"—he spat out Harry's name as though spitting out a vile epithet—"secret."

Anne sank back on her heels under the enormous weight of relief. "Th—"

"Do not thank me," he snapped.

She closed her mouth.

He turned to the door and then wheeled around to face her yet again. "You are not empty headed, my lady. Quite the opposite."

And that was the instant Anne realized the cold, hard exterior he presented to the world was nothing more than a facade. In his brown eyes, she detected a glimmer of the man buried deep inside the wary, broken-hearted marquess.

Then the stiff, brittle set to his lips masked all momentary warmth. "Oh, and Lady Anne?"

"Yes, my lord?"

"I do wish Stanhope had turned you away. It would have been my pleasure to school you in the art of seduction." He touched the brim of an imagined hat, opened the door, and . . . nearly collided with Harry. Jasper stood, stoic at his side.

Harry froze, his mouth fell agape at the appearance of Lord Rutland. The two men eyed each other for a moment, two savage beasts warring over terrain. In a way, they had been for eight years. In a way that didn't truly have anything to do with Anne and everything to do with Margaret, Duchess of Monteith.

Lord Rutland ran his flinty gaze stare over Stanhope. "A pleasure as usual, Stanhope." Mockery lined that curt greeting. Without a bow, he took his leave.

Jasper motioned Harry forward. "Anne." He gave her an indecipherable look and then closed the door with a soft click leaving her alone. With Harry.

Harry stared after Rutland's swiftly retreating form then swung to face Anne. "What the hell did he want? Has he threatened you?" He advanced forward. Anne backed away. From him? What in hell was Bainbridge thinking allowing her to meet with that reprobate? "Why were you alone with Rutland?" His voice came out an angry snarl he barely recognized.

Anne toyed with a single, deliberately placed strand interwoven with an orange ribbon. She continued to edge backward. "The duke was so good as to arrange a meeting between us," she said, her voice breezy. "It is, after all, essential that Rutland say nothing about what he observed." If she believed Rutland to do the honorable thing with their secret, then she was a good deal more naïve than he'd ever believed. She swept her arms wide. "Come in, dear Harry. Do come in. Please."

He furrowed his brow. "Why are you speaking in that manner?" The faint stirrings of unease unfurled in his belly.

Anne laughed, the sound like clear tinkling bells. "Oh, Lord Stanhope." She snapped her skirts. "You scoundrel, you know you shouldn't curse in front of a lady." She dropped her voice to a scandalized whisper. "Imagine the shock."

Harry beat a hand against his leg. "Are you flirting with me, Anne?"

She tittered behind her hand and danced backward, until her lower back knocked against the duke's solid desk and she spread her palms on the surface behind her. "Oh, come, Lord Stanhope," she fluttered her thick, golden lashes. "We've moved well past flirtation."

He strode forward and stopped, a mere handbreadth between them. "What is going on?" This shallow creature did not bear even a hint of resemblance to Anne. "Why am I suddenly Lord Stanhope?" And why did he crave the sound of his name upon her tempting red lips? Anxiety roiled like a rapidly brewing storm inside him.

Anne gave a flounce of her luscious golden curls. "You were *always* Lord Stanhope. Our relationship has been clear from the very beginning."

He raked his trembling fingers through his hair. "What are you on about?" he asked, his voice gruff. He held a hand out. "Is this about Rutland? I've already plans to speak with your mother after my meeting with Bainbridge. You'll not be ruined." He'd slice off his own hand before he allowed Rutland to destroy her reputation.

Some emotion flashed behind Anne's eyes. Grief, shock, agony, together as one. Then gone as her lips curved up in the corner as she smiled with her lips and eyes as one . . . as he'd instructed her. She eyed his fingers a moment, and then her lips pulled back in a sneer.

Harry staggered backward. His Anne did not sneer. She wasn't even capable of such hardness.

"Oh, Lord Stanhope," she said in a self-aggrandizing way that made him grit his teeth. "Surely you know you needn't offer for me?"

"I want to," he said, his answer instantaneous, born of truth. After she'd taken her leave last evening, after she'd coolly, if politely, rejected his offer, he'd realized he wanted her. Not merely because he sought to do right by her. "Mayhap not ten days ago, or a week, but now, I'd wed you."

Her long, graceful fingers toyed with a single curl. "Oh, Harry. Poor, poor, Harry." She shook her head. "Never say you've come to"—she widened her eyes—"*care* for me?" Those handful of words dripped with pity.

"What are you doing?" Disbelief crept into his question.

With the enthusiasm of a child who'd just won at a game of spillikin, she clapped her hands together once. "I'm relieving you of your duties, Lord Stanhope. You've served your purpose." A victorious glimmer lit her eyes.

His mouth went dry. "What?" The one-word question emerged hollow and empty.

"My plans to secure the title of duchess." She giggled. "Do pay attention," she chided, slapping his fingers teasingly. With a whispery-soft sigh, she fingered the golden heart pendant around her neck, an innocently sensual movement learned under his tutelage "You thought it silly, I'm sure. The prophecy told by an old gypsy that whatever woman wears it—"

"Will earn the heart of a duke." He fixed his stare on the small, golden bauble. In this way he didn't have to see the cool mockery in her eyes.

"Yes, yes, exactly!" She giggled. "And I truly *would* have settled on an earl, Harry. If I had to, of course. Which I do not. Have to settle, that is."

He flinched, silently begging her to stop, begging her to tell him this was all a cruel jest. But he'd not begged Margaret and he'd not beg Lady Anne Adamson.

"The duke," she went on, each word a dagger in his belly, "well, it was one thing when he expressed an interest, quite another when he called with a specific offer."

She clasped her hands in front of her, the grip so tight, her knuckles were white.

Why were her knuckles white? "I don't understand," he said numbly. The world shifted under him and he sought purchase atop the leather winged-back chair. "You said you loved me." His voice rang hollow.

Anne again giggled. "That was before he all but offered for me, silly." She waved a hand. "Before you would have sufficed but now . . . oh, can you believe it, Harry?" A dreamy glimmer lit the blue irises of her eyes. "Soon, I'll be a duchess." She dipped a curtsy. "I wanted to thank you for the invaluable lessons, my lord. Every time I'm referred to as Your Grace, I promise to think of you."

Harry's heart wrenched, the pain so great it threatened to cleave him in two. This betrayal on Anne's part so very much worse than Margaret's defection. Anne had restored his hope, given him reason to laugh again, and God help him, made him love her. His mouth went dry. "This is a jest." He could not believe it. Anne was supposed to be different. Not ruthless. Not calculated. Sweetly serene and spirited and honest . . .

The bright, easy smile on her lips dipped. She stilled and held his gaze with her own. "This is no jest, my lord. This is very real." She held her hand out. His gaze fell to the wire-rimmed spectacles. "I mustn't wear these, of course. A duchess cannot be seen in s-spectacles." Her voice broke and numbly, he picked his head up. A paroxysm of grief contorted her face. The subtle expression so very brief he must have imagined any regret he saw there. She cleared her throat. "Here." She pressed them into his hand.

Harry stared blankly down at a gift he'd toiled over. Yet again, he'd made a bloody fool of himself where a young lady was concerned. He balled his fingers into a fist. The spectacles bent under the intensity of his grip. He lightened his hold lest he break the lenses and with his other hand absently he rubbed at the spot in his chest where his heart used to be. He could not believe he'd been so very wrong. Not about her. This woman, he didn't recognize. "Anne," he tried again. "I'll protect you from scandal. You needn't—"

"Tsk, tsk. My, how arrogant you are. Do you imagine this is borne of my love for you? It is not," she said firmly. "This comes from the sole reason I sought you out in the first place. You've served but one purpose. And now, well, now you've fulfilled it." She worked the ribbon free of the lone golden curl. "There will always be ribbons and spectacles, though," she said.

As Harry stared at her, it was as though the veil had lifted and he saw the same self-centered, grasping minx he'd first taken her for more than a year ago. The hellion, the vixen. The woman who'd claimed his heart. And now, the woman who'd *broken* his heart. He flexed his jaw and yanked the ribbon from her fingers. "I am glad I was able to assist you in your endeavors, my lady," he said stiffly. He crushed the ribbon in his fist. "If you'll excuse me," he said with a short bow.

He didn't even remember crossing over to the door until she called out to him. "Oh, Lord Stanhope?"

He paused, staring dumbly at the wood panel, begging for her to point her eyes to the ceiling as she was wont to do, and say she merely teased. "That is my favorite ribbon. Treat it with care."

And all hope withered and died in his chest. He wanted to hurl it at her title-grasping, deceitful face. He yanked the door open and left without a backward glance, her burnt-orange ribbon a forever reminder lest he forget the perils in loving.

Chapter 23

Anne suspected the pain of letting Harry go would always be with her. But now, nearly one week later after sending him away from Jasper's office, she suspected her heart would always be a useless, deadened organ that could never be mended.

"You have to get out of bed, sweet."

Anne pulled her knees to her chest and stared blankly out the window at the night-darkened sky. "Don't call me sweet." The pillow she clutched to her mouth muffled her words. Once upon a lifetime ago, Harry had called her sweet. Then, she'd craved the endearment, love from his roguish lips. Now, she'd settle for sweet, hellion, termagant. Anything to hear his voice again. She pulled her arms closer to her chest. Oh, God. She could not bear this.

"Very well. You have to get out of bed, Anne." Katherine picked up the wrinkled copies of *The Times* that littered the bed and dropped them into a heap upon the floor. "I'm worried about you. Mother is worried about you."

"Mother is not worried. She's angry." Livid, if one were being truly accurate. Anne had agreed to wed Mr. Ekstrom; she'd not agreed to smile her way through his offer, and the inevitable union. She curled deeper into herself.

"Yes. I'm sure there is merit to that." Katherine stroked a soothing circle over Anne's back. "But you can't simply lay abed reading copies of *The Times*."

She wasn't reading *The Times*. She was squinting hopelessly through them, scouring the blurred words for hint of Harry's name, for some indication of how he spent his days . . . and worse . . . his nights. She needed her spectacles.

More . . . she needed *him*. Tears filled her eyes.

"Oh, Anne," Katherine whispered and lay down behind her. She folded her arm across her older sister the way she had when they'd been small girls. "I'm so sorry you've been hurt. I'd take it away."

"I know," Anne said and borrowed support from her twin. She knew, because she would barter her very soul for Katherine's own happiness. "Do you see him?" The words emerged halting past her dry lips. Her sister hesitated. Anne felt it in the way her body stiffened and the prolonged pause, and knew. She closed her eyes tight because did she truly wish to know?

"You've always known he was a hopeless rogue, Anne." Katherine spoke with such gentleness, her meaning clear as if she'd bluntly stated the truth—Harry had begun carrying on with his ladyloves.

Knowing did not make it any better. When he'd whispered against her ear and perched her spectacles upon her nose, she'd managed to convince herself she meant more to him.

She'd believed he would go to his Margaret and that thought had shattered her, but this, knowing he'd become the same Harry meeting his scandalous ladies in conservatories with two crystal champagne flutes wrenched at her insides.

She'd lashed at herself in the six days, twelve hours, and handful of minutes since she'd fed him every worst perception he'd ever carried of her. She'd forced her eyes to make sense of the words in the gossip sheets . . . and had seen enough to recognize his name linked to any other number of widows and scandalously wed ladies.

In the end, Harry had proven himself to be . . . well, Harry. And there was little consolation in knowing her lies had wrought the transformation upon him once more, because ultimately all he'd revealed was how little she'd meant to him.

Which really wasn't all that fair, considering *she'd* set *him* free. Tears filled her eyes. She blinked them back.

Katherine sat up. "You need to make an appearance at some event, Anne. Society has noted your absence."

Inevitably she would. At her betrothal ball. Anne rolled onto her back. She flung a hand over her eyes. "I don't care." In the past, polite Society's singular interest on Lady Anne Arlette Adamson would have mattered.

"I'm not leaving," Katherine said, firming her jaw.

Guilt needled at Anne. Each morning, Katherine had come and stayed with her, nearly throughout the day. Her sister had fashioned herself as something of Anne's protector through the years. Everyone had believed Anne in need of saving. She'd never have imagined the only one who could save her was in fact the single gentleman she'd taken to be a rogue and scoundrel.

"You are going to the Vauxhall Gardens masquerade tonight."

"I'm not." With its secret paths and illuminated groves, it posed the perfect place for trysting couples. Harry would undoubtedly lead one lady or another down to one of those trysting places.

Katherine hopped to her feet in a flurry of greenish-blue diaphanous Grecian skirts. She made a splendid Amphitrite, the goddess of the Mediterranean Sea. Her lips pulled. Unlike her, with her foolish shepherdess costume. Of course Harry would have always preferred one such as sophisticated Katherine to Anne and her silly golden ringlets. "But you always love a masquerade, Anne," her sister said, pulling her back from her self-pitying musings. Katherine hurried over and picked up the costume set out by her maid earlier that evening. "Tell me you don't long to don this splendid garment."

The world, twin sister included, still saw Anne as a young lady fixed on nothing more than the fabric of her gown or her attire for a silly masquerade. "I don't long to don that splendid garment," she mumbled. *Harry hadn't.* He'd seen her as a clever woman with real thoughts inside her head.

And I let him go.

Agony knifed at her heart, once again.

"You're going." She crossed over and threw the wispy, silken confection at Anne. Her mouth tightened. "I'm fetching your maid and you're putting the damned garment on. I'll sooner eat this costume than see you pine for the Earl of Stanhope. Do you understand me?" The impassioned response burned her sister's cheeks red.

Quite clearly. Anne's guilt intensified at her sister's clear displeasure with Harry. Katherine and Harry had been friends long before Anne. Back when she had identified him as a scoundrel and cad, Katherine had confided in him and embraced his friendship. Until Anne had gone and ruined that, too . . .

"Don't be foolish. You are my sister," Katherine snapped, clearly interpreting her twin's private musings.

The door opened so swiftly Anne would wager her every worldly possession the maid had been waiting outside in the hall. Her sister handed the costume off to the young woman. "My sister requires assistance." She sailed to the front of the room. "This is not finished, Anne. And do not tarry, we've a masquerade to attend."

A short while later, Anne wound her way through the long corridors and down the winding staircase to the foyer. Her mother and Katherine stood in costume, quietly conversing. An uncostumed Jasper, with arms folded behind his back, glanced up. He murmured something to his wife.

Katherine glanced upward. Pleasure lit her eyes. "Splendid, Anne. You look just splendid. Doesn't she?" She jabbed her husband in the side.

Jasper grunted. "Yes, indeed."

Her mother studied her with a critical eye and frowned. "You look pale," she said bluntly.

"I have a mask on," she murmured when her slippered feet touched the floors.

"Only partially." Mother's lips tightened. "Oh, this will never do. The *ton* will take one glimpse of your swollen eyes and wan complexion and know you're pining."

Anne spun on her heel. "You're indeed correct." And Mother was largely incorrect on most scores. "I shouldn't attend."

She placed her foot on the bottom step when Katherine settled her hand on her shoulder. "You're going." She firmly steered her back around.

Ollie, the family butler, threw the door open, anticipating her sister's efforts. Katherine took her by the elbow and guided her outside and onward to the waiting carriage. "Trust me, you'll feel a good deal better when you are there."

She very much doubted that.

Lord Edgerton's amused chuckle cut into Harry's silent ponderings. "You've consumed nearly an entire bottle of champagne, Stanhope."

Harry downed the contents of his sixth glass, polishing off, as his friend predicted, an entire bottle of fine French brew. He managed a lazy grin and held the empty glass up in salute. "Indeed." He scanned the crowd at Vauxhall Gardens purposefully.

After he'd taken his leave of the grasping, self-centered brat, Lady Anne Adamson, a week ago, he'd expected word of her betrothal to the Duke of Crawford to break as the latest source of gossip. In the first days, he'd taken care to avoid any polite Society event where he might see the shameless creature who'd broken his fool heart. He'd resumed his all-too comfortable life, returned to the Forbidden Pleasures. Except, all his attempts to bury himself in some nameless, faceless creature who didn't have blonde hair and blue eyes, a creature who still haunted his thoughts, had proven futile. In the end, he'd not touched a single woman.

And so, he'd reentered polite Society, fully prepared to see the little flirt—the flirt *he'd* schooled. Fortunately, they seemed to be now moving in very different social circles. The little viper.

His lips pulled in a sneer, teeming with cynicism and contempt. Even as he'd thought himself prepared for the duplicitousness of a female's lack of faithfulness following Margaret, he'd still allowed Anne to wheedle her way into his thoughts, and worse, his dammed heart. And what had he gotten for his efforts? A reminder as to why the only thing the female form was good for was as a receptacle for a man's lust. He plucked another glass of champagne from a costumed servant. He took a long swallow and looked around.

Edgerton shot him a sideways look. "Are you searching for anyone in particular?"

"No." The lie came easy.

His friend snorted. Even if his laconic response didn't ring with any truth. "I told you the lady was to be avoided," Edgerton said unhelpfully.

"Would you like me to congratulate you on being correct?"

His friend took a sip of his champagne. "Certainly not. Just reminding you so that when you inevitably see the heartless wench, you take care to not make a cake of yourself."

Again. The sole word missing from his friend's warning.

His searching gaze collided with a fair Aphrodite. The trim Greek goddess touched a finger to the corner of her lip invitingly. The curls, more brown than blonde, didn't have the same sun-kissed effect of a particular young lady's golden silk tresses.

He paused, narrowing his eyes . . . and then looked away.

Another woman, with familiar raven-black locks, sidled up to him. "Hullo, my lord." She touched her expertly manicured fingers to the latch of his thick, black cloak. "A highwayman," she murmured. Taller than most men of his acquaintance, the lady leaned up. Her breath fanned his ear. "You may steal whatever jewels I possess, my lord," she whispered invitingly.

Harry glanced at the scantily clad Cleopatra through the slits in his black half-mask. With her ample hips, sweetly rounded buttocks, and generous breasts, she was a veritable lustful feast. His for the taking.

She sauntered away, crooking one perfectly manicured finger in his direction, inviting him forward.

Take her, then. Lead her off to some tucked away corner, lift her golden skirts, and plunge all your frustration into her warm, willing body.

He took a step forward.

I'd like you to teach me how to seduce a man . . . Anne's words whispered around his tortured mind.

And he retreated. The woman's plump red lips formed a moue of displeasure, and she moved on to some other less dead inside lord.

"You're a fool," Edgerton said with an exasperated sigh.

Harry closed his eyes a moment. Anne had ruined him for anyone else.

Edgerton whistled. "I do say this is a deal worse than the broken heart you nursed over Lady Margaret."

"Go to hell," Harry muttered and took another sip.

"Will you at least speak of it, then?" Edgerton asked quietly.

"What would you have me tell you? That the lady merely needed me to entice the Duke of Crawford. She sought nothing more than a tutor who'd help her garner Crawford's affection." He'd known all along what Anne's purpose in seeking him had been, only in the days he'd come to know her, he'd allowed himself to forget the more than a year of needling and annoyance. Instead, he'd come to appreciate her humor, quick wit, the inner beauty Society failed to see . . .

Lies. All of it.

Edgerton stiffened. "Ahh, it would appear the shepherdess has arrived to fleece other poor, unsuspecting gents of their hearts." His mouth formed a hard, flat line.

Harry's body went taut as he followed his friend's distracted wave to the demure shepherdess in frilly skirts. Until he was an old, doddering lord who didn't recall where he'd placed his monocle, he'd forever recall the sight of those golden ringlets piled high atop her head. She tapped her staff upon the gravel path and scanned the costumed crowd. For an infinitesimal moment, he allowed himself to believe he was the someone she searched for. And not Crawford.

Her sister Katherine whispered something against her ear. The ghost of a smile played about Anne's red, bow-shaped lips and he cursed himself for the inherent weakness inside that made him long to cross over, rip the gauzy mask from her face, and make love to her deceitful mouth.

As though his wicked thought burned an awareness into her, she squared her creamy-white shoulders and continued her search. Their gazes collided.

The din of chatter and the orchestra's distant strands faded into nothing more than background noise . . . *You've served your purpose* . . . Her cruelly mocking words weaved around his mind and he touched the slip of fabric buried inside his coat, pressed against his heart, a forever reminder of Lady Anne Adamson's faithlessness. He raised his glass in mock salute.

Color flooded her cheeks and she dropped her stare to the ground, but not before he detected the trace of hurt.

He scoffed. A heartless, title-grasping wench like Anne was incapable of being wounded.

From across the stretch of lawn, Katherine glared at him. He bowed low at the waist. If looks could kill a person, he'd have been flayed to bits by the fury in her once friendly eyes. She snapped her skirts and presented him with her back.

Just another thing destroyed by Anne's cruel hands; not only his heart, but his friendship with her loyal, devoted sister.

"Look away, Stanhope," Edgerton murmured at his shoulder. "Neither of those ladies is worth your time or efforts."

Katherine had been. Her sister, well, Anne had not, nor would she ever be worthy of his time and efforts and yet, he could not ignore this tangible pull between them.

A familiar, loathsome form materialized behind Anne. The bastard, in his arrogance hadn't even deigned to wear a costume. The Duke of Crawford called her attention away and capturing Anne's fingers, he bowed over her hand.

Harry tortured himself with the blush that climbed her neck and cheeks, a blush she surely summoned on will alone. *Fleecing hearts, indeed.*

"One viper for another," his friend muttered. Harry followed his stare to the approaching Athena in pleated Greek skirts.

Lady Margaret stopped before them. "Hullo, Harry," she greeted, her voice thick with emotion.

He cast a glance over her delicate shoulders and found Anne's focus on his exchange with Margaret. Relishing the momentary flash of regret that flickered in her eyes, he raised Margaret's hand to his lips. And this time, he allowed her to drag him away from the reminders of his greatest mistake in life.

As he followed her down the dimly lit gravel path, he registered a pair of eyes trained on his back. It was foolish to imagine it was Anne. She'd been quite explicit in her feelings for him and her aspirations for Crawford.

"The Lord Stanhope I remember was always full of humor and quick to speak," Margaret murmured, pulling him back to the moment.

"Fighting a duel for a young lady who then chooses an old letch tends to make a gentleman more cautious." But not cautious enough to know better than to give his heart to Anne.

Margaret paused beside a towering fountain. Fireworks lit the sky in hues of red and orange, illuminating the bubbling water. She stared down silently as though searching for words. "I spent nearly eight years regretting my marriage, Harry. I thought I might be happy with the title of duchess," she confessed.

Just as Anne. Only Anne's duke would be *pleasantly handsome, unfailingly polite, wealthy, and in possession of one of the oldest titles* . . . His gut tightened. "And you've not been happy in eight years?"

She toyed with the fabric of her skirts and gave a curt shake of her head. "No. I've not been happy," she said tersely.

He expected he should find some sense of victory in her misery. Only, with time he'd found he'd not truly loved Margaret. A young gentleman's arrogance and the battle he'd waged with Rutland for the lady's affections had driven him more than any real sentiments of love. He'd failed to realized that—until Anne.

"You don't love me," she whispered, the words bearing traces of shock and pain.

He said nothing.

"I believed at Lady Preston's ball your treatment of me was driven by jealousy and old hurts. But it wasn't. Was it?" She turned to face him. Her lower lip trembled, indicating there was, in fact, more depth to the capricious woman who'd walked out of his life. Still, he felt no stirring of emotion, no desire for more with her. Lady Margaret belonged to his past. "You've come to care for another."

No. He didn't care for Anne Adamson. He loved her. Even with her betrayal, he would *always* love her.

Margaret caught her lower lip between her teeth.

"I'm sorry, Margaret," he said simply. Finding that he truly meant it.

She folded her arms across her waist. "Is it . . . ?" She hesitated. "The Lady Anne Adamson?"

Even though Anne didn't deserve any loyalty from him, he'd not betray the memory of her with this woman.

When his silence confirmed that he'd not share Anne's identity, she sighed. "I can't imagine she deserves you, Harry."

His jaw tightened. No, she didn't and yet, she'd forever hold his heart—whether he wished it or not.

Margaret's lips turned up in a wistful smile. She leaned up on tiptoe and pressed her lips against his cheek.

A gasp cut into their private exchange. He glanced over Margaret's shoulder. Twin sisters, foils in every way, stood at the end of the path.

Fireworks shot into the sky, illuminating their faces. Katherine singed him to the spot even as Anne swayed against her sister. A momentary expression of grief ravaged her cheeks. Which made little sense. Anne had been quite clear in her feelings for him. Or rather her lack of feelings.

He raised Margaret's hand to his lips and pressed a kiss to her knuckles. Anne's skin took on a sickly pallor and then she presented him her back. Katherine eyed him with such loathing he shifted on his feet, feeling like a properly chastised child. She said something to Anne.

Margaret frowned. "I gather she is in fact the young lady who captured your heart."

He clenched his teeth, giving Margaret his attention.

"That was rather poorly done of you, Harry," she chided.

"Yes. Yes it was," he agreed and swiped a hand over his face, tortured by the memory of Anne's pale cheeks and horrified eyes. It shouldn't matter that she'd been wounded by his meeting Margaret. She'd proven herself faithless and fickle.

And yet, it mattered.

Chapter 24

*K*atherine guided Anne with a military precision that could have afforded her command of the King's army away from the loving tableau presented by Harry and his Margaret.

Oh, God.

"Breathe," her sister muttered, lips unmoving.

Pain rolled through Anne in vicious waves, one after the other. She blinked back tears, blurring her vision. The joyous, ribald laughter sounded throughout the grounds punctuated by the overhead burst of fireworks. "I cannot stay," she rasped out.

Her sister gave her forearm a hard, reassuring squeeze. "I'll find Mother."

Anne jerked free of her sister's hold and took her by the arms, earning rabidly curious glances from nearby peers. "Please." She begged with her eyes, needing to be spared her mother's continual disapproval and angry stares.

Her sister gave a terse nod and gently guided Anne's arms back to her side. "Wait here. I'll gather Jasper." She hesitated.

"I'll be fine," she lied. She would never be fine again.

Katherine lingered, recognizing the words Anne left unspoken. Then, that was just part of being a twin. That inherent sense of knowing. Wordlessly, she turned on her heel and strode through the crowd, boldly striding past those who sought a word with the Duchess of Bainbridge.

Anne hovered, feeling undone and exposed. She cast furtive glances about. Yet, for the way in which her heart now splintered apart, broken and useless, the members of polite Society moved about with gaiety, merry with drink and the *pleasure* of the inane amusements. Anne remained invisible.

A prickle of awareness stole down her spine. She stiffened and turned, seeking out the source of that unease.

Harry studied her, alongside his splendorous duchess. That icy blackness in his flinty expression chilled her. Then, he smiled. A dark, emotionless smile that sucked the breath from her. He returned his attention the flawlessly perfect duchess. And Anne was forgotten, once more.

Oh, God, this is too much.

A restive panic filled her and sucking in a gasping breath, she hurried away. *Away from Harry and Margaret.* She quickened her steps, sidestepping lustful lords. *Away from all I've lost.* Anne moved in a near sprint. *Away from his steely contempt.* She slipped inside a skillfully tended maze of towering hedges and ran deeper into the hidden trails. Yet no matter how fast or far her legs carried her, she could not rid herself of the agonized memory of Lady Margaret layering her tall, regal frame against Harry's. Or the two of them as they'd slipped away. Most likely stealing off to some other hidden trysting corner where he could worship the other woman's mouth the way he'd once kissed her.

Kissed her like she was the only lady in the entire kingdom. *Fool. Fool. Fool.* Her gasping breaths gave way to a sob while her slippers were soundless upon the dampened grass. As though she could ever match his Lady Margaret. *In beauty.* She wrenched her mask off. *In elegance.* Her heart pounded hard with the exertions of her efforts and the pain of her musings.

Her toes collided with a large rock and a gasp of pain escaped her. *In grace.* She pitched forward, hard on her knees. "Oomph!" The air left her on a whoosh. She attempted to stand and bit back a curse as pain radiated up her leg.

Anne sank back down and lifted her skirts to inspect the swollen flesh of her ankle. She gently probed the nasty area and winced. Blast and double blast. She should have never come. Then she wouldn't have seen Harry and his perfect Lady Margaret. And she wouldn't have fled like a silly ninny in attempt to be free of the sight of them. Anne sighed. And she certainly wouldn't be sprawled gracelessly on her derriere like a real shepherdess. She let her skirts flutter back into place and lay on her back. She tossed her arms wide and stared at the glittering stars in the black London night.

The irony of life not lost on her. Over the years, her sisters, Society, everyone had taken her as nothing more than a self-serving, selfish young lady who placed her own personal desires before all else. And here she lay, humbled by the loss of her own making, born of the greatest sacrifice she could have or would ever make.

"It appears you've lost your sheep, my lady."

Anne sat up quickly. Her heart hammered at the unexpected interruption. She peered up at the long, towering, muscle-hewn frame of Harry, Earl of Stanhope. Her heart slowed and then picked up its fast rhythm. "Hello, my lord." Was he intending to meet his Lady Margaret? A hysterical half-sob, half-cry bubbled past her lips at the idea of having stumbled upon their clandestine tryst.

A cold smile tugged at those once tender lips. "I gather I've intruded on your assignation with the duke. Forgive me, I do know the inconvenience of having my trysts interrupted by bothersome people I'd really rather do without," he said, confirming her earlier suspicions.

Anne recoiled. She curled her fingers into the soft patch of earth as his deliberate taunting words ravaged her heart. He might see her as a cruel, title-grasping miss who'd toyed with his affections, but she'd done this for him. She angled her chin up. "What do you want, Harry?" she asked quietly, finding little solace in her sacrifice.

He wandered closer. A faint breeze caught the fabric of his black cloak. It snapped wildly against his legs as he paused above her. His grin, that cold, patently false one, widened. "I must admit, you look quite fetching after an evening's tryst."

An evening's tryst? She wrinkled her brow. What was he on about? She widened her eyes as the truth settled slowly into her mind. By God, he thought . . . he believed . . . *she* met a lover?

Anne narrowed her eyes. She knew she'd sent him away quite deliberately believing all the worst about her. But really, was his opinion so very low? Or was it because that is the exact exchange she herself had interrupted? The tender reunion between two lovers, stealing a moment for themselves until Anne and Katherine had the misfortune of stumbling upon their exchange.

"Will you not say anything, Anne?"

She folded her arms across her chest. "Thank you," she said pertly.

"Crawford?" He quirked an eyebrow. As though he had a right to know the imagined gentleman she'd been . . . doing . . . doing *that* with.

She gave a flounce of her curls. "Oh, it . . . was just splendid," she said on a breathless laugh. That is, if one considered a bruised ankle and injured derriere splendid. "*Quite* splendid," she added for good measure, because this was at least preferable to watching him kiss Lady Margaret Monteith.

A dark look passed over his harshly beautiful face.

Anne shoved herself up onto her elbows. Harry shot a hand out. She eyed his long, tan fingers a moment and then placed her hand tentatively in his. Not because she craved his touch. No, not that at all. Rather, because she needed assistance. The whole business with her ankle, and all.

He retained his hold. "You always did have beautiful fingers."

She remembered back to a day not long ago when he'd drawn her fingers soothingly into his mouth. "Er . . ." She cleared her throat. "Thank you." That seemed like a rather odd compliment. She held her hand up and tried to note what it is he might admire in the five digits but failed to see anything unique in them.

He tweaked a golden ringlet. "Tsk, tsk, ringlets, again." The jeering edge of his tone grated along her skin.

"Yes," she said, dropping her gaze to the green grass. She'd never wear her hair loose and down about her shoulders. Not again. It would forever remind her of how he favored it.

"Indeed, perfect for a shepherdess gathering the hearts of dukes throughout the kingdom."

She gritted her teeth at the icy condescension in his heartless charge. She found solace in knowing that for his ill opinion of her, she didn't give a fig about the heart of a duke; that the only heart she longed to gather close and forever hold was his. "Have you sought me out to taunt me, Harry? Does this make you feel better about yourself?" It made her hate this man she didn't recognize.

A small squeak escaped her as Harry drew her close. He hooked an arm around her waist and ran his palms over the curve of her hips. "Ah, Anne." He lowered his lips close to hers. Her lids fluttered and she leaned up, wanting—"Sweet, beautiful, and treacherous Anne."

But for those last two words, she could almost believe he still cared for her. Anne wanted to push him away, tell him to go to the devil. But she wanted *him* more.

She would wed Mr. Ekstrom at her mother's insistence, but before she did, she would know what it was to be well and truly loved. She longed to know the true madness that compelled women into the conservatory for Harry's attention. And she would give herself to him so that for her first time, she knew magic and splendor and not responsibility or necessity. No other decision would truly be hers, but in this, she'd be mistress of her own fate.

Anne leaned up and kissed him. He froze, as though shocked by either her body's nearness, or perhaps it was the boldness of her actions. Then, he groaned. His mouth closed over hers again and again. Harry gentled his hold about her waist. He parted her lips with his tongue. Their mouths met in a furious dance of longing and regret.

And she kissed him. Kissed him as she knew she never could again. Kissed him when she knew it was wrong as he belonged to another, however, she would never be able to give him completely up, at least not where her heart was concerned.

In his life, Harry had made love to some of the most inventive, sinfully beautiful creatures in England. He'd had French mistresses and eager widows. Not a single one of them had caused this fiery burn as Anne did. She roused a grand passion and desire. He wanted to set her away, burn her with the ferocity of her desire, a desire he roused, and then leave so he might avail himself to a woman who desired nothing more than a quick tumble in the gardens. So then, mayhap he might forget what Anne made him feel, think, experience . . .

Harry trailed feverish kisses along the side of her cheek, down her throat, laving her neck. He nipped and sucked at the flesh marking her and uncaring that she'd return bearing his love bite.

Anne's head fell back. "Harry," she pleaded.

"You still want me. Don't you, sweet?" he rasped. He worked the bodice of her gown lower, exposing her cream-white breasts to the cool night air. The pink-tipped breasts puckered from the chill. He lowered his head and drew a nipple deep into his mouth. He stole a glance up at her.

Her mouth hung open and desperate gasping pants escaped her.

Harry lowered her to the ground. "Crawford can never give you this." Desperate fury punctuated his words. He'd leave his impression with her, make her writhe with knowing all she'd given up when she'd chosen her damned duke. "He will make you his duchess, but he'll never make your body sing like I can." He reached for the hem of her ruffled skirts. Sweat beaded the top of his brow and he looked at her. Skin flushed, curls disheveled, breathless moans escaping her lips. God help him. "I cannot do this." He didn't recognize the garbled, agonized voice as his own.

She blinked up at him, dazed. "Harry?" A question hung in that one word, his name.

He rolled off her. Anne deserved more than being tumbled like a strumpet in Vauxhall Gardens. He stared at the twinkling stars overhead. They mocked him with their shimmering brightness. With a groan, Harry laid his forearm over his eyes. Who'd have imagined that he, Harry, 6th Earl of Stanhope, was . . . honorable?

Goddamn it.

The soft whoosh of delicate skirts and the crinkle of muslin ruffles split the quiet. Lemon and berry, a sweet, enticing scent flooded his senses. Anne touched a hand to his chest. "Why did you . . . ? Don't you . . . ?" Her unfinished question teemed with disappointment.

Perhaps if the words she'd uttered had been demanding and worldly he'd have shoved her back down and made hard and fast love to her as he ached to do. Only, the trace of innocence reminded him that even as he wanted her, he could not take her and certainly not in this manner like she was a common whore. If he did this thing, he'd hate himself forever. "I might be a bastard, Anne, but I'll not take your virginity." That honor and privilege would belong to Crawford. Bile climbed in his throat and he feared he'd cast up the accounts of his stomach.

She slipped her hand into his and squeezed. He lowered his arm and looked at her. "Even if I want you, too?" A desperate glimmer set the silver specks of her eyes aglow. She lowered her lips close to his. It took every last vestige of his control, but Harry turned away. Her kiss grazed his cheek.

He set his jaw at a stony angle. "I'll not merely be the man who soothes the ache betwixt your legs." He wanted more of her than that. Not without marriage. And she'd been abundantly clear of her marital aspirations.

She flinched as if struck.

Harry shoved back guilt. She'd been the one to cut him from her life. He'd not be made to feel guilty for rejecting her. Not when he made the greatest sacrifice in preserving her virtue for another. Ah God, this would kill him.

He stood, carefully tucking his shirt back into his breeches and rearranging his cloak. Wordlessly, he held a hand out to her.

She eyed it for a moment, and then her glance slid off to a point beyond his shoulder. "I'll stay here."

Rutland's actions nearly a week ago blared as a loud reminder of the perils of leaving her. "I won't leave you without a chaperone."

A hard, ugly smile wreathed her face, a smile so patently not Anne, it chilled him. "I'm not your responsibility."

No. She was not. She'd been quite clear in who . . . or rather, *what* she desired. Crawford's bloody title. He lowered his hand. "Good-bye, Anne."

"G-good-bye." The moon's glow shone down upon her heart-shaped face; the crystal tears filling her eyes nearly undid him. "Harry?"

He froze when she called out to him. *Please tell me you want me. Tell me I matter more than Crawford and his damned dukedom.*

"I'm not marrying the . . . that is . . ." She cleared her throat. "I am to be wed." His heart turned to stone inside his chest and with every stammered word, she chiseled away at each piece until it crumbled into a pile of rubble in her pliant hands. "I'm marrying . . ." The crucial end to those words faded into silence. "I just thought . . ." She looked away. "Good-bye, Harry." He strained to hear that final pronouncement.

He exited the gardens and stopped, setting himself as a sentry until she took her leave. A display of fireworks lit the sky in burnt-orange and crimson-red hues. He wrenched off his mask and tossed it aside where it fluttered about in a night breeze and then landed in a heap.

Harry raked his hands through his hair. Oh God. She was to be married. To the duke. His stomach roiled. She would wed another. Bed another. Give another children.

I want you, Harry.

He pressed his eyes closed. She wanted him, even as she'd take another man as her husband. She wanted the pleasure of his embrace and nothing more.

The sight of her, broken and shattered, penetrated the horror of her revelation. He began to pace, grinding the gravel under his booted feet.

We'll always have ribbons and spectacles.

The crowd's merriment in the distance came as if down a long empty corridor. He fished around the front of his cloak and withdrew a familiar orange scrap of fabric.

He turned the cherished item over in his hands, passing it back and forth between his fingers.

With the exception of one burnt-orange scrap . . .

"Ah, there you are, friend."

The memento given him by Anne fell from his fingers. Harry bent to retrieve the scrap of Anne's past. "What the hell do you want, Edgerton?" His voice came out as a nasty growl, but he was in a foul mood and wanted to be free of this damned place . . . and his confounded thoughts about Anne.

"I was concerned about your sudden disappearance."

"Have you fashioned yourself as my nursemaid now?"

Apparently undeterred by Harry's snappishness that evening, Edgerton spread his hands in front of him. "I'd merely imagined with the word that has begun to circulate, you might benefit from some drink and company."

"With the word—?" Harry's heart thudded to a slow, staggering halt. Anne and Crawford. He dragged a hand across his face. "What the hell are you on about?" Invariably, he knew, as surely as he knew the letters of his name that Edgerton in some way referred to Anne.

He quirked an eyebrow. "According to the whispers of gossip, it would seem your Lady Anne is to be wed."

Harry crushed the orange ribbon in his hand. Ah, hell. He'd known it was coming and yet Edgerton may as well have taken a claymore and cleaved him in two.

"That is hardly the interesting bit," his friend continued, not comprehending Harry's very thin grasp on control.

". . . a mere miss . . ."

He loved her.

"Hardly in line with the grasping . . ."

He could not live without her.

". . . a beauty, but no grand beauty . . ."

Harry wanted to throw his head back and rail like a savage beast. He examined the ribbon in his hand.

. . . *They claimed every last blasted scrap of satin. It will forever remind me of the perils of love . . .*

He eyed the fabric so long, seconds passed into minutes, which may have passed to hours. Edgerton's words ran together as one. And his heart pounded hard, even as his tumultuous thoughts sought to make reason to that which he'd not allowed himself to consider before now.

Why would she give him this ribbon? Why, if he meant nothing to her? Why . . . ?

"Certainly capable of making a better match than . . ."

He went stock-still as the truth crashed into him with the force of a fist being plowed into his midsection. The breath left him on a slow exhale. He looked at the satin frippery as Edgerton's voice droned on and on; a ribbon, the sole precious strip Anne had clung to when her entire world had fallen apart. She'd given it to him. As a parting remembrance. And he'd been so enraged, believing the absolute worst of her, that he'd not allowed himself to see the truth . . . until now.

". . . even Lady Anne deserves more than being wedded to a depraved bastard like Ekstrom . . ."

I love her.

He—Harry blinked. "What?" he asked, the raspy one-word utterance seemed to belong to another. Surely he'd heard his friend wrong. It had sounded as though he'd said she was to wed—

"Bertrand Ekstrom." Edgerton waved a white-gloved hand. "A cousin, it would seem. Next in line behind the . . . Christ, Stanhope, where are you off to? I imagined you'd want to know . . ."

His words trailed after Harry as he charged back into the Vauxhall maze, onward. His breath came in great, gasping spurts from the force of his emotion, and he staggered to a halt. Anne stared wide-eyed up at him, in the exact spot he'd last left her. "Anne . . ."

"Harry . . ." her broken whisper ravaged him. She shoved herself up on her elbows. "What are you . . . ?" She cocked her head. "Why are you staring at me like that?"

"Why are you still on the ground?" he shot back.

For a moment, the past week melted away and she was the sweet, smiling Anne he remembered. She sighed and gestured to her ankle. "I fell."

"When?" He dropped to a knee beside her and pulled back her skirts.

"Earlier. I . . . what are you doing?" She shoved her gauzy shepherdess costume down.

He pushed it up once more and probed the skin in search of a break.

She swatted at his shoulder. "Harry, you shouldn't . . ." She winced when he touched the bruised flesh. "I was going to suggest your actions were improper, but now I'd ask you to stop because it's really rather unpleasant." She wrinkled her brow. "Which I suspect is because I've gone and injured it."

"Yes. It is sprained." He shoved her skirts down and cursed. "You were going to allow me to leave you here?"

"You shouldn't curse."

His lips twitched. "That's all you'd say?"

She screwed her mouth up. "It's really not at all appropriate."

Ah, God . . . I love you. Why was I so afraid to admit that to you before now? He studied her face, more precious to him than his own. She'd deserved those words from him. Long ago. Another firework illuminated the sky, bathing her face in a pale glow. He reached into the front of his cloak and fished out the small, metallic frames he kept close to his heart. "Here." He perched the spectacles on the bridge of her nose.

"What . . . ?" She touched her fingertips to the frames almost reverently. "I don't understand."

"You need them, Anne. They help you to see."

"To read," she corrected, taking them off. She dropped her fathomless gaze to the pair.

"Though I suspect it is I whose vision has been significantly impaired, Anne."

"You'd have my spectacles?" she asked, perplexity under-scored her question.

He snapped his gaze to hers. "It was because of me. The morning in Bainbridge's office."

She folded her hands into fists, clenching them so tight the blood drained from them and they stood a splash of white in the dark night.

Agony lanced his heart. "You believed I . . . that Marga-ret . . ." The words went unfinished at the confirmation in her tear-filled gaze. She'd released him of any and all obli-gation toward her, so he could be free to pursue Margaret. Even as it had portended her own ruination. "Oh, Anne," he said achingly. He reached for her.

She batted his hand away. "I don't want your pity, Harry." The words eerily reminiscent to those uttered another time in their tucked-away copse at Hyde Park, when she'd pro-fessed her love and he'd not managed even a hint of the dec-laration she deserved. "And I'll not come between you and your Miss Margaret . . . the duchess."

"I don't love Margaret." Loving Anne as he did, he could now recognize that in his youth, he'd looked upon Marga-ret with the same reverence one might a prized piece of artwork—to be admired and coveted, devoid, however, of the emotional connection he shared with Anne. No, he didn't love Margaret. Perhaps he never really had.

"You don't?" A single crystal teardrop slid down Anne's cheek.

"No, you silly woman." He captured the moist bead with his thumb.

"A-and I'm not crying," she said, her words breaking.

"Of course you're not." He caught another teardrop.

"I'm not," she insisted, "and not simply because you d-detest tears."

He'd always seen a woman's tears as a ploy to manipulate. Seeing his proud, dignified Anne battling back all show of emotion reminded him of just how erroneous he'd been—about so many things. Mostly the things he'd thought he'd known about her. He gathered her close. Anne stiffened in his embrace and then the tension seeped from her. She went soft in his arms. "You silly, silly fool," he managed on a ragged whisper.

She shoved against him. "That is hardly endearing. You're supposed to be a rogue with all manner of wicked words to entice a lady. I'd imagine not a single one of your ladies would care to be called a—"

"I don't care a jot about any other woman. Surely you must know that?" Her lids grew shuttered. He'd not managed a single thought of anyone—except her. He touched his lips to her closed lashes. "Surely you realize there is just you. That there has only *been* you since you stole into Lord Essex's conservatory and stole my heart."

"N-no." Her lips trembled. "I-I did *not* know that."

"I've been a fool."

"Yes. Yes you have." Anne sucked in a shuddery breath. "Though my mother claims it is I who has been the fool." She discreetly brushed at her tears, wrenching his heart all the further. "She reminded me of the pain in being wed to a man who would always love another."

With her cynicism, the countess had shaken her daughter's faith in Harry and her confidence in her own self-worth. God, how he abhorred the woman. The sole worthwhile thing she'd done in her life was the gift of Anne she'd given the world. "Look at me, Anne." His harsh command forced her gaze upward. "I could never betray you."

"The papers have said you've begun carrying on as you had before . . . me . . . before us . . ." Her throat worked.

His lips twisted wryly. "I couldn't even begin to feign interest in another. You've ruined me for all other women, love."

The tremulous smile on her lips illuminated her face. "Have I? I don't believe you've ever said anything so . . ." Her words trailed off. "Love," she whispered. She touched a hand to her heart. "You called me love."

He blinked. "Why, yes, I believe I did." He took her lips in a slow, soft caress. "I imagine that is vastly suitable when a man loves a woman as hopelessly and helplessly as I love you." He lowered his lips to hers yet again.

Anne drew back. "Are you teasing me, Harry?" She looked at him through hooded eyes. "If this is some wicked—"

He took her mouth under his and the feeling of coming home washed over him. The meeting of lips an aching reunion. She wrapped her fingers about his neck and held him in place. The metallic spectacles crushed against the back of his head as she returned his kiss, kissing him as though there was no other place she'd rather be but here, in his arms.

Anne drew back. She dropped her gaze to his cravat. "I'm to wed another."

His heart thudded to a momentary halt. "Who?" he demanded, loving her so much he willed the unspoken name to be the pleasantly handsome, unfailingly polite, and wealthy duke she'd always desired and not the wicked reprobate, Ekstrom.

"My cousin, Bertrand Ekstrom."

He strained to hear the faint whisper. Ekstrom. His gut clenched. He'd hoped Edgerton's words were no more than a gross rumor circulated by a gossipy *ton*. Harry touched his fingers to her chin, forcing her gaze back to his. "Bertrand Ekstrom?"

Her fingers curled around the spectacles and he placed his hand upon hers, until she lightened her grip. "That is what I said," she spoke between gritted teeth.

"Hardly a duke. Why?" he demanded gruffly.

Her shoulders lifted in a slight shrug. "I didn't think it really mattered."

He sank back on his haunches. "Not matter?" Not matter when her search for a duke had brought her into his life in the first place? Not matter when she'd sent him from her life, cruelly throwing her desire for a duke at him? He'd imagined there could be no greater hell than imagining Anne wed to Crawford. He'd been so very wrong. This, the idea of her married to Bertrand Ekstrom, that foul deviant, shredded him inside. He loved her so much that even as it would kill him, he'd see her with her pleasantly handsome, unfailingly polite, and wealthy duke . . .

On the heel of that was the quite humbling, if staggering, truth. She'd rather wed Bertrand Ekstrom than him. And because it made little sense when rolling silently around his mind, he said, "I offered for you, yet you'd rather wed Ekstrom than me?"

A pretty blush colored her cheek. "Certainly not. Though I'm sure he's"—five lines wrinkled her brow—"er, perfectly pleasant."

"You're wrong," he said flatly. "He's a bastard." She was far too innocent to know the depth of Ekstrom's depravity.

"You're not wedding him." He'd kill the bastard before he allowed the other man to take her to wife.

A blonde ringlet fell over her eyes. She blew it back, then a frown pulled her lips down at the corner "That is rather high-handed of you. You can't simply determine who I might and might not wed."

"In this matter I can. I just did."

"It's not your concern whose offer I've accepted."

Accepted as in she'd already agreed. Knots tightened his stomach. He took her chin firmly between his thumb and forefinger. "I love you," he said again, needing her to realize his life was inextricably intertwined with hers, forevermore. "*You* are my concern, Anne." She'd become far more than the annoying termagant from long ago.

She jerked her chin out of his grip. "Because of Katherine." Yes, in the beginning he'd merely agreed to assist Anne out of a sense of loyalty to Katherine. Intending to protect the maddening vixen from herself. "I assure you, there is no need to—"

"Because of you." He pierced her with his stare. "Surely you know how much you've come to mean to me." Silence met his pronouncement. He scoured her with his gaze. Ah God, she didn't. She had no idea how much she'd shaken his roguish world, changed him, ruined him for all other women. He wanted no one else but her. Only her.

"Anne Arlette Adamson!"

They glanced up as Katherine and her husband entered the maze. "By God, Harry. You cad!" she spat.

Anne shook her head frantically. "It is not how it appears, Katherine. I fell."

The fight drained out of Katherine. "Fell?" She raced over. "Oh, dear."

Forced apart by the sudden, and unwelcome appearance of Anne's family, Harry stood. He scooped Anne into his arms and reluctantly passed her over to the waiting duke. Bainbridge wordlessly accepted her. Promptly dismissing the other man, Harry looked back to Anne. "This is not over." With that he spun on his heel, and took his leave.

Chapter 25

$\mathscr{A}$ nne bounced Katherine's baby up and down on her knee. Snorting laughter escaped Maxwell's lips. "You sweet, sweet boy." She smothered his chubby cheeks with kisses until his laughter doubled.

Katherine and Jasper exchanged a look as though they feared Anne had gone mad and was one bumpy cart ride away from a trip to Bedlam. "I do say you seem rather, er . . ."

She looked to her sister expectantly.

"Er, happy. You've not been happy in so very long. And you're giddy like a debutante who's just attended her first ball."

Anne nuzzled her cheek against Maxwell's. "Your mean mama, being so very rude to your aunt."

Mother glanced up from her embroidery. "I daresay this is a vast improvement from the morose creature you've become. You should be wearing a perpetual smile considering the extremely magnanimous gesture on Mr. Ekstrom's part."

A sad little smile played about Anne's lips and she buried it in her nephew's cheek. From over the boy's crown of brown curls, she caught Katherine studying her with suspicion-laden eyes. Anne winked. And the bond shared as only twin sisters could passed between them. Her sister's narrow gaze deepened.

A servant appeared at the doorway and ankle still sore from last evening, Anne struggled to her feet. Her heart hammered wildly at the sudden interruption and then promptly sank.

The footman rushed over with a silver tray bearing a missive. He carried it over to the countess. "Leave it on the table, would you?" Mother murmured, not taking her eyes off the crimson rose upon her frame.

Anne sat back into her seat, her gaze wandering over to the clock. He'd said whatever was between them was not over and she'd imagined he intended to call.

"Ma-Ma-Ma-Ma." Maxwell's soft babbling commanded her attention.

"You want your mother, do you? What about your poor aunt?" She feigned noisy tears and noisy giggles erupted from the boy's lips.

Another knock sounded at the door. And Anne knew with the same intuitiveness that had driven her to seek out Harry in the first place for her madcap scheme to catch a duke, he'd arrived.

Ollie cleared his throat. "The Earl of Stanhope."

The embroidery frame slipped from Mother's hands and landed noiselessly on the Aubusson carpet at her feet. "What is this about?" She jumped to her feet in a flurry of bombazine skirts.

Harry stood, impossibly tall, devastatingly elegant in a sapphire-blue coat and fawn breeches.

Anne awkwardly shoved herself to her feet even as her sister rushed over to take Maxwell, a suspicious glower trained on Harry. Jasper stood and placed himself beside his precious family, touching a hand to Katherine's shoulder.

His face an impenetrable mask, serious as she'd never remembered him, Harry bowed. "My lady," he greeted her mother with all the charm that had earned him the reputation as rogue.

Alas, Mother had long ago learned the perils of a charming gentleman. "You dare come here?" She looked to Jasper, the glint in her eyes indicating she expected him to toss the earl out.

Anne sank into a deferential curtsy. "My lord." She furled and unfurled her hands into fists, an attempt to calm her racing heart.

Harry held her stare, heedless of her family's presence. His thick, hooded gaze indicated he knew the exact path her thoughts had wandered and he reveled in it. He wandered deeper into the room.

"You, my lord, do not have leave to enter this parlor. Of all the insolence. My daughter is to be married and you are a . . . a . . . rogue!"

Harry's smile faded. He walked boldly by the outraged countess and the fiercely glowering duke, and dropped to a knee beside Anne. "I'm afraid your mother is indeed correct, Anne."

Her heart paused and the hope she'd carried since that gravel path in Vauxhall Gardens died. A viselike pressure squeezed about the organ that would forever beat for him. "Then why are you here?" she whispered. Still, for the agony of this moment, so very glad he was.

He took her hand. "You didn't allow me to finish." He stroked his thumb over the sensitive flesh of her palm. "I was a rogue. A scoundrel." Harry held her gaze. "Not anymore, Anne." Hope flared to life with the implications of his words, his bold touch. "I was a shiftless bounder until you slipped into Lord Essex's conservatory, seeking me out—"

"You slipped into Lord Essex's conservatory to meet him?" Katherine and Mother's voices united in shock.

Anne buried a half-sob, half-laugh in her fingertips. That first meeting with Harry had been the least scandalous of all the things she'd done with him.

"I love you, Anne." She sucked in a breath, and her family's presence fell away under the depth of emotion in his eyes. "I love everything about you. I love your husky contralto, but would love you if you possessed a light, lyrical soprano singing voice." He captured one of her loose curls between his fingers. "I love your golden ringlets."

"Remember yourself, my lord!" Mother's outrage went unheeded.

Anne touched her left hand to the side of her face, brushing back a loose curl. It fell stubbornly over her brow. "You claimed they were silly," she whispered, ignoring her mother as she should have for years now.

Harry reached up and captured the strand. He gently tucked it behind her ear. "I've been an unmitigated ass, too blind to see true beauty until you donned those small spectacles opening both our eyes." Emotion thickened his voice.

Tears clogged her voice, strangling her words. "They're for reading."

He stroked her cheek. "Ah, Anne. Don't marry Ekstrom. Marry me." His next words drowned out her mother's shocked gasp. "I would wed you with your family's approval, but even if they will not give it, I'd ask you to wed me anyway."

Anne looked down at their interlocked hands, a desire to take all that he now offered. She pressed her eyes closed and drew in a slow breath. When she opened them, she took in the rugged planes of his square jaw, the slight cleft in his firm chin. "If you were to wed me, to save me from Mr. Ekstrom, the time would come when you resented . . ."

Harry raised her hands to his mouth, and the words died on her lips. "This is not about me saving you." He kissed first one, then the other. "This is about you saving me." He released one of her hands.

"This is most improper, Lord Stanhope!" Mother cried.

Harry ignored the countess's fervent outburst. He reached inside the front of his jacket and withdrew a small packet. "You are the only woman I wish to have. I love you, Anne Arlette Adamson, and I would have you for my wife." He pressed the vellum into her hand.

She glanced frantically at the blurred words and then searched around. Katherine rushed forward with Anne's spectacles. She accepted them, struggling to open the frames and maintain her grip upon the sheets in her hand.

"Here," he murmured. Harry took them from her trembling fingers and placed them on her nose.

The countess stalked across the room. She stopped beside them, her skirts snapping wildly about her ankles. "You've no right to such familiarity where my daughter is concerned!"

Anne read several lines and her heart kicked up a quick rhythm. Her gaze flew to Harry's.

"What is this?" her mother sputtered. She snatched the marriage license from Anne's fingers and read, her eyes huge circles in her face. She crumpled it in her palm. "Impossible! Why, why my daughter is to wed the honorable Mr. Ekstrom."

Harry held Anne's stare as he spoke to her mother. His jaw tightened. "Your daughter is *not* wedding Ekstrom." He looked to Anne. "Marry me, Anne."

Anne closed her eyes. After her discovery of Father's betrayal, she'd foolishly believed she knew what she needed—in a husband, life, love. Material gain and a powerful connection was to come before all else. Only, with Harry, she'd found how very little she'd known about life or love. He'd shown her. He'd opened her eyes to all she longed for . . . all she needed. *He* was all she needed. She opened her eyes. "I—"

"You needn't marry either of them, Anne," Katherine said quietly.

Anne opened her mouth.

"Marry *him*?" She winced at her mother's high-pitched shriek. "She is to wed Bertrand Ekstrom." Then, in a very un-countess-like display of rage—she stomped a foot.

The duke continued past his mother-in-law's antics. "Indeed, Katherine is correct. I'd agree that you shouldn't feel compelled to wed." He peered down his hawklike nose at Harry. "Either of them."

Harry fished something out of his jacket. Her gaze fell to the orange ribbon dangling between his fingers. "This reminded you of everything you lost, Anne. Take it back now, take it as a reminder of what you'll always carry. My love. My fidelity. My—"

"Yes," Katherine and Jasper spoken in unison.

"No," the countess cried out, burying her face in her hands.

Three pairs of eyes swiveled to the fiercely frowning duke who'd made little attempt to hide his dislike of the other man. He tugged at his lapels. "That is, if you'll have him."

Harry gave a slight nod and the duke returned the gesture, as a silent, unspoken truce passed between them.

Mother scraped her disapproving stare over Harry. "There is an agreement already reached. The scandal would be disastrous. Furthermore, he will break your heart. He is a philanderer, a rogue, and rogues cannot be reformed."

Fury spiraled through Anne and she took a step toward her mother. "He is not *him*."

Her hand fluttered to her breast. "What are you—?"

"He is not Father," Anne said with steely strength underscoring those words.

The older woman's skin turned waxen and she sputtered. "H-he is—"

"A good man," she interrupted. She slid her hand into Harry's. "An honorable man." *A man who will never betray me.* A man who would care for his children. And always place his family first . . . because he loved Anne in ways Father had never loved her mother. To say as much would devastate the other woman and for that, Anne fell silent.

Harry cleared his throat and she looked to him once more. "If you'll marry a bounder such as me . . . Even as I don't deserve you. Even as you'd be better with damned Crawford—"

A little hiccuppy laugh emerged more as a sob from her lips. He still did not realize he was all she wanted, all she'd ever wanted. "Are you trying to convince me to wed another? Because if you are, it's really not well done of you, Harry."

He stroked her cheek. "I love you, Anne. Marry me."

Four pairs of eyes looked intently back at her. She leaned up on tiptoes. "Yes," she whispered. And pressed her mouth to his.

Four days later, in the presence of Mother, her brother, Benedict, and Anne's sisters, Aldora and Katherine, along with their families, Anne found herself in the most unlikely of places. A rueful smile pulled at her lips as she glanced around at the pink, red, and peach rose bushes. But then, not all that unlikely if one knew Harry, the Earl of Stanhope.

A disapproving vicar beat the small black leather book in his palm, which she suspected was the beginning of a rather hastily thrown together ceremony.

"Are you having second thoughts, love?"

She jumped at Harry's teasing whisper. She gave her head a shake and stole a glance at her family. Her sisters waved, matching smiles on their faces. "Of course not," she assured him. Though . . . She stole a glance at her mother. *Mother* certainly appeared hopeful her daughter would march from Lord Essex's prized gardens and leave Harry standing there at the altar . . . well, an altar of flowers anyway.

The vicar fanned the pages of his book.

She winked. "My mother on the other hand . . ."

A bark of laughter escaped Harry and the vicar dropped his Bible. He bent to retrieve it, muttering something about reverence and bold, hastily thrown together ceremonies. Anne took this for clear disapproval with her and Harry's not waiting the requisite period of three Sundays to have the banns read.

Anne schooled her features in a semblance of piety. Even as her husband-to-be stifled a yawn. Her shoulders shook with the force of her amusement. "Achoo!" Harry withdrew a kerchief and handed it over.

"Shall we begin?" the vicar began and glared at Anne for doing something as impolite as sneezing before he launched into the service. "Dearly Beloved, we are gathered together here in the sight of God, and in the face of this congregation, to join together this man and this woman in holy matrimony, which is an honorable estate . . ."

Anne glanced across the Marquess of Essex's infamous conservatory.

The old lord's loud whisper cut across the vicar's recitation of her and Harry's marital vows. "I do say, quite unconventional. A pleasure, nonetheless, just an unexpected pleasure," the wizened gentleman rattled on to the Duke of Bainbridge. "Not every day a couple wants to be married in my gardens. Not that I can blame them," he said on a rush, lest anyone present believe the man disparaged his own well-tended space. Her brother-in-law kept his gaze directed to the front of the room, wincing as the Marquess of Essex carried on. "It must be my prized peonies."

Anne looked up at Harry and they shared a smile.

"I knew the gardener was well worth the sum he demanded," Lord Essex said with a pleased nod, eyeing the small cluster of people and the vicar in his conservatory. "Or I supposed it might have been my rose bushes." His brow wrinkled. "Then, there are the prized hibiscuses. Brought from Africa you know, they are. All very exotic. Er . . . Africa, and the flowers, that is . . ."

The Marquess of Essex's ramblings reached Anne once more . . . "Achoo!" . . . as did the scent of one of those prized, exotic hibiscuses. Harry fished out a second handkerchief and handed it over. She blew her nose noisily into the fabric.

The vicar glared at her in response, clearly taking slight to her inability to control the flurry of sneezing.

It really was quite inconvenient that this was the place they should have first met.

"Achoo!" She buried the sneeze into Harry's kerchief and grinned up at him.

He returned her smile.

But there was no more perfect place for them to be wed. Her mother continued to glare in their direction. Even if Mother quite disagreed.

". . . Thirdly, it was ordained for the mutual society, help, and comfort, that the one ought to have of the other, both in prosperity and adversity. Into which holy estate these two persons present come now to be joined . . ."

"I'm going to try my hand with the azalea bush," Lord Essex said noisily. A muscle ticked at the corner of the duke's right eye, and Katherine's lips twitched with silent amusement. "They say the soil acidity affects the color of the bush. What are your thoughts on that, Bainbridge?"

"Nonexistent." The duke's curt response did little to dampen the other man's enthusiasm.

Anne's lips pulled with amusement and she spoke from the side of her mouth. "Do you think Lord Essex knows the truth?" she whispered to Harry.

He lowered his head. "The truth?"

The vicar glared them into momentary silence. He resumed the ceremony. Her mother sat stiffly beside Lady Essex, wincing every time the white-haired woman mentioned the words "prized peonies."

"And what truth do you refer to, love?" he repeated on a hushed whisper.

She waggled a brow. "That it was really two glasses of champagne that first called you to this space."

Ignoring the glowering vicar, Harry leaned close. His breath fanned her ear. "Ah, then you would both prove wrong, Anne. It wasn't the peonies or the champagne that led me here."

She cocked her head. She'd rather thought it had been the champagne and scandalous activities business. "It wasn't?"

The vicar's monotonous voice droned on with the ceremonial vows. "I require and charge you both, as ye will answer at the dreadful Day of Judgment when the secrets of all hearts shall be disclosed . . ."

Harry brushed his knuckles along her cheek. The vicar stopped midsentence. A mottled flush splotched his cheeks. Harry ignored the man's displeasure with his improper touch, his gaze trained on Anne. "How can you still not know? It was only you that brought me here, love. It was only you," he said, his voice rough with emotion.

Warmth filled Anne's heart as her love of this man spiraled out, in a burning conflagration of heat that could never destroy her. Harry made her stronger, and better, and . . .

"If it is all the same to you, may I continue?" The vicar's angry whisper cut into their exchange.

Harry waved a hand lazily about. "Proceed."

Anne smothered a giggle with her palm. Her thirteen-year-old brother, Benedict, however, made little attempt to conceal his mirth. He laughed quite boldly in his seat beside Aldora's husband, Michael. Mother leaned over and pinched him on the arm. He winced and shifted in his seat with all the embarrassment of a boy on the cusp of manhood who'd been properly chastised before a series of observers.

"Henry Richard Falston, 6th Earl of Stanhope, wilt thou have this woman to thy wedded wife, to live together after God's ordinance in the holy estate of matrimony? Wilt thou love her, comfort her, honor, and keep her in sickness and in health; and, forsaking all other, keep thee only unto her, so long as ye both shall live?"

Harry raised her hand to his mouth and brushed his lips over her knuckles. "I will." Her throat worked under the force of emotion in his hazel eyes. "There is no one I want but you, Anne," he added, his voice hoarse.

The vicar cleared his throat, and glared at Harry for daring to add anything to the sacred vows. "Anne Arlette Adamson, wilt thou have this man to thy wedded husband, to live together after God's ordinance in the holy estate of matrimony? Wilt thou obey him, and serve him, love, honor, and keep him in sickness and in health; and, forsaking all other, keep thee only unto him, so long as ye both shall live?"

She blinked back tears. "I'm not crying," she whispered. But then a blasted drop fell. Followed by another.

"Because you don't cry," Harry said solemnly.

Another tear. "Precisely."

"Anne?"

"Your vows," Benedict shouted from his seat. The family frowned at the boy and he shifted. "I was merely reminding her," he mumbled and slouched lower in his chair.

Anne's cheeks warmed and she gave her head a shake. "Er, yes, indeed." She looked at Harry and held his gaze. "I will. Love you and honor you, and forsake all others," she amended. She jabbed a finger into his chest. "But you aren't ever to do anything as horrid as fall sick and leave me. Do you hear me, Harry?"

His lips twitched with what she suspected was mirth. "What of obeying me? Do you intend to obey me, love?"

"We shall see." She paused. "I'll most likely be deplorable at the whole obeying business." A loose golden ringlet fell across her brow.

Harry brushed the strand back. Seriousness replaced the gentle teasing in his eyes. "I will never leave you. Ever."

The vicar cleared his throat. "Now that we've quite addressed the matters of my lord's health and constancy, may I conclude this service?" There was something faintly beseeching in that question, so Anne took pity on the older, grey-haired gentleman and remained silent through the remainder of the proceedings.

". . . by joining of hands; I pronounce that they be man and wife together. In the name of the Father, and of the Son, and of the Holy Ghost. Amen."

Just like that, Anne Arlette Adamson became the Countess of Stanhope.

"Just lovely, absolutely beautiful!" Lady Essex cried.

Anne's mother seethed in silence, a clear indication of just how beautiful she saw this particular day. A pang of regret struck. Her mother would never accept the love Anne had for Harry.

"I imagine the wedding breakfast prepared by your mother should be quite enjoyable," he drawled close to her ear.

Father's betrayal, however, belonged to her past. Anne smiled at Harry—her husband. *He* was her future. "Indeed, it should."

As Harry gathered with the loquacious, excited lot that was Anne's family for his and Anne's wedding breakfast, all his earlier suspicions had indeed proven correct, but certainly not in the manner he'd imagined. Seated beside Anne, listening to her laugh alongside her two sisters and younger brother, the feast really was quite—enjoyable.

"I daresay Lord Essex will brag about the brilliance of his gardens that brought a couple to wed in his conservatory for the remainder of his days," Aldora said on a laugh.

Anne smiled over the rim of her wine glass. "He'll certainly never imagine it was something as shocking as—"

The countess's eyebrows shot to her hairline. "Anne," she snapped.

Anne's grin widened. "Harry's love of the exotic hibiscus."

The three Adamson ladies dissolved into a fit of laughter.

Benedict scratched his brow. "What is it?" He looked to his new brother-in-law. "I say, do you have a thing for Lord Essex's flowers? I've never known a gentleman to love gardening."

Harry inclined his head. "I have a love of all things magnificent." He winked. "Particularly your sister."

The young boy groaned and slapped his hands over his ears to drown out any other possible words.

Harry chuckled and slipped his hand under the table to find Anne's fingers. He took them in his and gave a faint squeeze. She looked at him and solemnity drove back his earlier teasing. The chatter of her siblings blurred with the conversation between Lord Michael and the Duke of Bainbridge. He ran a searching gaze over her face. Had there been a time when he'd truly not found her beautiful? There was no one more glorious than his wife.

"What is it?" She dabbed her napkin against her mouth. "Is—?"

He fished around the front of his jacket and withdrew a long, narrow box. "Here," he said quietly. Anne dropped the crisp linen and accepted the gift. She looked to him questioningly. "Go on," he urged.

Anne slipped off the top of the box and then gasped. She looked from the necklace within and then back to him. "Oh, Harry," she whispered. She gently removed the gold strand and ran the tip of her finger over the five-carat ruby heart.

Harry took it from her fingers. "May I?" he murmured.

She angled her head in response. He appreciated the long, graceful stretch of her neck and brushed his fingers caressingly over the tempting silken softness of her skin. "I imagined you'd no longer have need of the heart of a duke necklace, and thought to replace it with the heart of your earl." He clicked the clasp shut. "Just so that some lofty duke doesn't take it into his head to spirit you away from me."

Anne touched her hand to the blood-red ruby. "Oh, Harry," she whispered. "Surely you know no one could take me from you."

He tweaked her nose. "With the exception of your cousin, the loathsome Bertie Ekstrom, who nearly succeeded?"

She pointed her eyes toward the ceiling. "Well, but for horrid Mr. Ekstrom, I'm only yours."

"What's he given her?" Benedict shouted and leaned over, squinting. It would appear another Adamson sibling was in need of spectacles. The boy wrinkled his nose. "I'll never understand a lady's fascination with jewelry."

Lord Michael Knightly cuffed the boy under the chin. "Some day you will, Benedict."

Lady Aldora glared up at her husband. "I never had need of jewelry."

"Nor I!" Katherine intoned, with equal indignation. She looked to Bainbridge, a challenge in her brown eyes. Her husband, the duke, had sense enough to say nothing on the matter.

Harry inclined his head. "I imagine each of you had need of some jewelry."

The Adamson sisters' three furious stares swung toward Harry.

He gestured to the collection of gentlemen seated about the table. "Why, if there had been no certain pendant, I don't imagine there would have been a Lord Knightly." He looked to Bainbridge, who he'd entered into a truce of sorts with. "And Katherine would have no Bainbridge."

"And I would not have you," Anne said quietly as Harry's pronouncement spurred some level of debate amongst the table of individuals who clearly held all manner of different opinions on the heart of a duke necklace.

Harry returned his attention to his new wife. "Ahh, there you are wrong, Anne." He brushed his lips over hers. "You always had me. Just as you always will."

Anne's throat moved up and down and from across the table, the ladies present released a collective sigh. He looked momentarily at his recent mother-in-law and detected the softness in her usually bitter eyes. She eyed Anne seated alongside him, and a wistful smile played about her lips, lending the first real warmth he could remember in the usually cold woman.

As though feeling his attention on her, the countess stiffened. She squared her shoulders and met Harry's gaze. They looked at one another a moment. He the man who'd been determined to have her daughter at any cost, she the mother who'd have rather wed Anne off to a horrid, lecherous second cousin. Something passed between them. She nodded her head once, and then shifted her attention to the babe on Katherine's lap.

"Do you have any regrets, Harry?" Anne's soft question pulled him back to his new bride.

He leaned closed. "I do." She stiffened. Harry placed his lips close to her ear. "I regret that this meal is not over so I can have you alone."

Anne lowered her voice. "Then you are not alone in those regrets, my lord." She winked.

He fought back a groan. And suddenly what had once been a rather enjoyable breakfast meal became an interminable affair.

Chapter 26

$\mathcal{L}$ater that evening, at last free of her family and enconsced in her new home, Anne giggled. She stuck her arms out, searching for purchase from behind the blindfold her husband had placed over her eyes. "Is this another one of your lessons on seduction, Harry?" She laughed again as he guided her by the forearm.

"Hush, love," he scolded. "There are no more lessons." He paused. "Well, perhaps there are some additional lessons, but none of which pertain to you learning to seduce *another* man."

"As if I would ever want another . . . ouch . . ." She grunted as he steered her into some piece of furniture or another. Her hip struck a solid piece of . . . well, something. "You are quite a horrid guide."

"Forgive me." Amusement threaded his half-hearted apology.

"Humph. Are we almost there?" she muttered. They'd arrived in Harry's townhouse, nay *their* townhouse, nearly two hours ago. She'd changed into a modest nightshift and waited expectantly for him to come and make love to her, at last.

Alas . . . she grunted . . .

"My apologies," Harry murmured once more as he steered her into what might have been a sideboard. It felt like a sideboard. "Just a bit further." He stopped, bringing Anne to a halt. "Here."

She reached for the cravat he'd secured about her eyes, but he stilled her movements. "Just a moment, love."

A fluttering sensation filled her belly. Her heightened senses registered the slight scrape of a chair being dragged over the hardwood floor. He guided her into a seated position and the backs of her legs knocked against a bench.

Harry loosened the folds of his cravat and tossed it aside. "Here."

Anne blinked as her eyes struggled to adjust in the dimly lit room. She looked about the grand parlor. High, sweeping ceilings and resplendent in gold, the parlor may have belonged in the king's palace. She'd never truly considered where Harry made his home. The space was extravagant. The gold upholstery of the sofas lush and finer than most owned by her family, even before all their goods had been carted off by the creditors. She registered Harry's gaze trained upon her. "It is beautiful," she murmured.

Harry knelt at her feet. "Not the room, love." He guided her around in her seat. Anne's heart froze as her fingers collided with a much-loved, familiar instrument. And then the organ inside her chest thudded wildly. She touched a reverent finger to the *AA* carved alongside the Wedgewood cameo.

Anne looked wordlessly to him.

He caught a golden ringlet between his fingers. "I spoke to Westmoreland some time ago," he said. He continued to rub the lock between his thumb and forefinger. "After you told me about the Westmoreland girls playing your pianoforte, I couldn't leave it there. Not knowing that someone else played what belonged to you."

Tears blurred her eyes and she blinked them back. A single drop slipped down her cheek. This gift was about so much more than simply a material possession. It was about a link to her innocence, stolen by the profligacy of a shameful parent.

Harry caught it with his thumb. "Even if I couldn't have you, Anne, even if you wed Crawford, I needed to know your pianoforte was cared for." His voice grew hoarse. "I'd rather it sit here unused, out of tune, with me holding onto this sliver of you. Touching the keys you once touched—"

Anne kissed him. She kissed him as he'd taught. Kissed him as she'd longed to since that first meeting in Lord Essex's conservatory.

Harry froze and then claimed her mouth with his. He pulled her into his arms, swallowing the small, startled squeak that escaped her lips. With a remarkable ease, he turned around and marched the same path they'd walked a short while ago, upstairs, effortless and . . . "Oomph." He collided into a wall.

A breathless laugh escaped her as he cursed and then strode quickly through the magnificent townhouse; down the long corridors, up the stairs, three doors down, to his chambers. He paused and pressed the handle. He shoved the door open and carried her inside.

Harry kicked it closed with the heel of his boot. He set her down in a way that her body slid down his. "Look at me."

She suspected if he spoke in that commanding, silken whisper, she couldn't very well deny him anything. She met his gaze.

He cupped her cheek. "You once came to me and asked me to teach you the art of seduction." He placed his lips against her temple. "Tonight, I'm going to teach you the art of seduction." He moved his lips on a determined path, caressing her cheek, her nose, the corner of her mouth. "I'm going to teach your body how to sing." He trailed his lips lower. "I'm going to caress you until you aren't capable of a single word." He palmed her breast.

"I . . ." She fought to muster words to tell him she was very nearly there.

"I'm going to love you until you are capable of nothing else but feeling."

She drew in a shuddery breath. "Harry?"

He lowered his brow to hers. "Yes, Anne?"

"Get on with it then, already." The words hadn't even left her mouth when he'd swept her into his arms and carried her over to the massive four-poster bed at the center of the room. He carefully laid her down and came over her.

She shoved herself up on her knees and appreciated the moment he disrobed before her. He shrugged out of his elegant black jacket and tossed it aside. His white shirttails followed suit. Her mouth went dry at the sight of his broad, muscular chest, dusted with a sprinkling of tightly coiled golden curls. She caressed him.

He groaned and encouraged while Anne trailed her fingers over the flat nipples that puckered under her attention. Harry sucked in a breath. He gently undid the fastenings of her robe and tossed it atop a heap of rapidly growing garments. He reached for the hem of her nightdress.

She pulled away, more aware than ever before of the vast difference between her and the voluptuous, scandalous women to come before. "Don't," he commanded when she folded her arms across her chest. He pulled the nightshift over her head and dislodged her arms. Silence reigned. She shifted, her body heated with embarrassment at Harry's silent perusal. She kicked him with her toes.

He winced. "What was that for?"

"You aren't doing anything." And then mortified heat promptly coursed through her body at the bold-sounding words. "That is . . . What I'd meant to say is—"

He kissed her into silence.

She moaned and reached her arms up about his neck. "Must you always do that?" she managed to rasp as he came down over her and trailed his lips down her neck. "Must you . . . ?" He closed his lips over the turgid peak of one breast and she cried out. He drew the fortunate nipple deep in his mouth and sucked. *Oh you must. You really must.* Anne's hips shot off the bed and he lowered his hand between her legs. Harry found her center and proceeded to work her with his clever fingers.

She tugged at his hair and forced his attention to her other breast. Hardly fair to leave one so horribly neglected . . . *ohhh* . . . "Harry," she cried out as he slipped another finger inside her. "I'm . . ." Going to shatter into a million shards of nothing.

"Yes?" he asked, his gruff tone hinted at the thin shred of control he retained.

And somehow that empowered Anne and filled her with a wanton desire to show him the same pleasure he now showed her. She reached between them instinctively and stroked her hand over the swell in his breeches.

Harry groaned. He shifted away and she moaned in protest at the loss of him, but he merely shed his breeches and tossed them aside.

Her mouth went dry and she stared unblinking at the enormous shaft stretched eagerly toward her. "What are you going to do with that?" she blurted. Because the much-needed lesson given her that morning by her two sisters seemed vastly more daunting and . . . quite impossible.

Harry grinned. He took her hand and guided it to his manhood. His smile faded as his flesh leaped involuntarily at her gentle caress.

Anne's reservations slipped aside as she explored his body. She ran her fingers over the length of him then took him in her fist and worked him. Up and down. Up and down. Harry's head fell back and he arched into her hand.

"Ah, God, you need to stop, love." His voice came out garbled, desperate and pleading, and hot desire flooded her center at the sight of him finding his pleasure at her hands.

She continued to work him and her efforts were rewarded when he reached between them and found her center once more. Then Harry shifted his weight atop of hers. He braced himself upon his elbows and thrust a knee between her legs. "Forgive me, Anne," he whispered.

She brushed back the moisture from his brow with a tremulous hand and gave him a soft smile. "There is nothing to—" Her eyes flew wide as he thrust deep inside her. "Bloody hell," she gasped. She gave his shoulders a nudge. "That is quite not well-done of you, Harry," she charged as pain throbbed at her center.

He remained frozen above her, his eyes clenched tightly. A faint muscle ticked at the corner of his mouth and her annoyance fled in the face of Harry's tenderness. She touched his cheek until his eyes opened. "It will be all right, Harry," she promised. She couldn't be absolutely certain of that, but . . . She frowned. "Are you laughing at me?" His shoulders shook and it certainly appeared as though he were. She gave him another nudge. "How—?"

Her words ended on a breathless gasp as he flexed his hips and began to move inside her and all the earlier discomfort melted away to be replaced by the most exquisite, desperate rightness of his loving. His strokes grew deeper, longer, and she arched her hips aching to know . . . something . . . that her body would know once it found it. Harry's brow remained furrowed as if in deep concentration as he thrust inside her. Again. Thrust. And again. "Oh, dear, Harry." She bit her lip.

"Yes, love, come for me."

She wanted to. She really wanted to. Except she feared if she plunged over the precipice she now clung to, she'd dissolve into a puddle of nothingness she could never recover from. Then he stroked her center. "I love you, Harry," she whispered and then shattered in a fiery explosion of color and light.

Harry groaned and poured himself into her; his hot seed flooded her center and she wanted the moment to go on and on. Their cries blended together in a sweet song until he collapsed atop her. His chest heaved up and down from the force of his release.

Anne folded her arms about his broad back and stroked her fingernails lightly over his sweat-dampened skin. A smile played about her lips. "That was quite splendid."

He rolled off her and carried her with him, pulling her into the curve of his arm. "Indeed it was." He touched a finger to her lips. "I love you, Anne," he whispered, raising her hand to his mouth. He kissed her wrist. Delicious shivers raced from the point of contact and spiraled throughout her body. He fixed his gaze on the heart pendant he'd gifted her that she now wore about her neck. "I know you desired the heart of a duke. I know Crawford, or any other duke, would have made you a better husband and yet, selfishly, I could not live without you."

How could he possibly believe that? She swallowed hard. How could he not realize he was all she wanted? All she'd ever wanted? Losing him to Lady Margaret would have sucked the very soul from her and left her a wispy shell of a creature who'd once loved and lost. Anne touched her fingertips to his cheek. "Oh, you silly man. Surely by now you realize?"

Emotion roughed his voice. "Realize what?"

A smile played about her lips. "How could I have ever wanted Crawford, when I have more than a duke?"

He touched his brow to hers. "And what is that?"

She brushed her lips against his. "I have you," she whispered.

The End

Heart of a Duke series

continues with

The Love of a Rogue
Loved by a Duke
To Love a Lord
The Heart of a Scoundrel
To Wed His Christmas Lady
To Trust a Rogue
The Lure of a Rake
To Woo a Widow
To Redeem a Rake
One Winter With a Baron
To Enchant a Wicked Duke
Beguiled by a Baron

Turn the page for an excerpt of *The Love of a Rogue*!

Chapter 1

London, England
Spring 1815

The day Lady Imogen Isabel Moore had made her Come Out almost three Seasons ago, she'd taken the *ton* by storm.

Not, however for any reasons that were good.

One glass of lemonade held in trembling fingers, one graceless misstep, and an inconveniently situated Lady Jersey in the hallowed halls of Almack's had placed Imogen in polite Society's focus. At the time, that moment with the glass of lemonade had proven the most disastrous of her then eighteen years. In a single night, she'd shocked polite Society . . . and also earned the attention of the gloriously handsome William, the Duke of Montrose.

With a sigh, Imogen glanced down at the copy of *The Times*.

The D of M, recently wedded, had returned to London . . .

She skimmed the details of the article. *Hopelessly in love. Devoted . . . Love at any cost . . .* Imogen tossed the newspaper aside, where it landed with a thump upon the mahogany side table.

He'd returned. The gloriously handsome golden duke with his glib tongue and winning smile and his black heart. And he'd returned with his wife—Imogen's, younger by a year sister, Rosalind. Or, the Duchess of Montrose, as she was now properly titled.

"Never tell me you are melancholy again."

A gasp escaped her and she spun around so quickly, a blindingly bright, crimson curl slipped free of its chignon and tumbled over her eye. In a flurry of noisy, blue bombazine skirts, her mother swept into the room. "Mother," Imogen greeted with a weak smile for the parent who'd merely been happy that one of her daughters had secured the duke's title. None of the rest had mattered. "I'm not melancholy," she added as an afterthought. Egad. Her lips pulled in a grimace. That faithless, roguish duke she'd imagined herself in love with had turned her into one of those dreadfully miserable types to be around.

Mother came to a stop before her and wordlessly brushed the errant, hideously red curl back behind Imogen's ear. Narrowing her eyes like a doddering lord in need of his monocle, she peered at Imogen.

Imogen drew back. "What is it?"

"I'm looking for tears. There are to be no tears. Your sister is happy and that should bring you happiness and . . ." Her mother launched into a familiar lecture; a nonsensical lesson on sibling loyalty expected of Imogen when her own sister had been anything but. ". . . you will take the *ton* by storm." Those hopeful words brought her to the moment.

An inelegant snort escaped her, earning a hard frown from her mama. "I did take the *ton* by storm, Mother. Remember? There was the whole incident with the lemonade two," nearly three, "years ago." That defining moment that had brought the Duke of Montrose into her life and into her heart.

That blasted glass of lemonade.

Her mother waved a hand about. "Oh, do hush, Imogen. That is not the manner of storm to which I refer." Alas,

Mother had never been capable of detecting sarcasm. "You shall go to events and smile and find a gentleman."

"I found a gentleman," she took an unholy joy in pointing out. "The Du—"

"Would you have had him wed where his heart was not engaged?" That handful of words struck like a well-placed barb.

Ah, so her mother had become something of a romantic. "Indeed, not," she squeezed out past tight lips. Greed for a duke tended to do that to a title-grasping mama.

"We shall find you a powerful, titled nobleman and then you shall be blissfully happy. Just as your sister." Another well-placed mark. If her mother weren't so very flighty, Imogen would have believed her words were intended with deliberate cruelty. A startled squeak escaped her as her mother claimed her cheeks in her hands and squished Imogen's face. "I promise this shall be your last Season as an unwed lady. We shall see you attend all the most popular events and dance with all the most eligible bachelors." All of which sounded utterly dreadful. With a smile, her mother released Imogen and spun on her heel.

Her mind raced. Surely even her flighty mother knew that anything and everything the *ton* discussed would not be Imogen's suitability as a match, but the scandal surrounding her name. "But—" Her protestation trailed off as her mother slipped from the room. From the corner of her eye, the open copy of *The Times* stared mockingly at her. With a curse unfit for most gentlemen's ears, she swiped the newspaper and carried it over to the window seat. As she claimed a seat, Imogen scoured the page for other poor souls who'd already earned the *ton*'s attention this Season.

Lord AE, the notorious Lord Alexander Edgerton, has taken up residence at his scandalous clubs and gaming hells.

Well, that was hardly news. She scoffed. Lord Alexander Edgerton, her dearest friend Chloe's brother, had earned a reputation as quite the scapegrace. A rogue. A scoundrel. In short, another Duke of Montrose.

The young duke had, at one time, been an outrageous, scandalous gentleman most mamas would turn their noses up at. Until a distant relative had gone and died making him the unlikely new duke . . . and suddenly perfect marriageable material for all those protective mamas.

Imogen threw the paper aside once again and turned her attention to the window, studying the passersby below. There were certainly worse things than having your betrothed sever the contract just three days before the blessed wedding. It was a good deal harder finding those worse things when one's betrothed broke your engagement—to marry your sister. Imogen desperately tried to call up those worse things.

She could . . .

Or there was . . .

Imogen sighed. Nothing. There was surely nothing worse than this.

A soft rapping at the door cut into her musings.

Imogen knocked her head against the wall. "Go away," she murmured to herself. She didn't want company. Certainly not her harebrained mother. Another knock. She was content to become one of those outrageous spinsters who brought their wildly attired pups to fashionable events and earned furious amounts of stares from—

Another knock. "My lady . . ."

Oh, bother. "Do come in," she bit out, not taking her gaze from the carriages rattling along the London streets below.

The butler cleared his throat. "Lady Chloe Edgerton to see you."

Imogen spun about. Her best friend stood in the doorway, a wry smile on her pretty face.

Imogen dangled her legs over the side of the seat. "Chloe," she greeted with far more excitement than she'd felt for anything or anyone since the broken betrothal. She'd been wrong. There was one person she'd care to see.

"Imogen." Chloe swung her reticule back and forth.

The butler discreetly backed out of the room and pulled the door quietly closed.

"I gather you've heard the news," Imogen said without preamble. She'd never been one to prevaricate.

Chloe tipped her head. "The news?" She tapped her hand to the center of her forehead once. "Ah, yes, silly me. Did you mean about Lord Whetmore's horse nipping Lady McTav-ishs's shoulder? Quite scandalous really."

Imogen appreciated what her friend was doing. She really did. Her shoulders sank and she returned her attention to the window. It was hard to be happy when your sister had so betrayed you and your betrothed had humiliated you. Even a best friend who'd boldly challenged all your nasty enemies at finishing school didn't have much of a chance in rousing you from your melancholy.

Chloe sank beside her in a flutter of ivory skirts. "I do hate seeing you like this," she said quietly, setting aside her matching ivory reticule.

Imogen mustered a wan smile. "And I hate being like this." Nobody preferred a gloomy, despondent crea-ture. Then again, her betrothed clearly hadn't preferred her happy and loquacious. So really, who knew what one wanted, after all?

A dandy in garish, canary-yellow knee breeches and a lady in like color chose that awful, inopportune moment to glance up. The couple in the street widened their eyes and stared openly at her.

Chloe reached over and drew the curtain completely closed. "Busybodies," she mumbled.

With a scandal that was as great as Imogen's, even the rare few who didn't partake in gossip now bandied her name about.

"It will get better," her friend said with a confidence Imogen didn't feel. Chloe leaned over and patted her hand. "Why, I daresay you are better off without one such as him."

"Polite Society does not agree," Imogen said, a wry smile on her lips. With his golden-blond Brutus curls and his grinning countenance, the Duke of Montrose's company was desired by all—including her sister.

Chloe squeezed her hands. "Look at me."

Imogen lifted her gaze.

"You are better off without him." Chloe wrinkled her nose. "Why, I heard Mama say he's quite a rogue and not at all proper."

Yes, breaking a formal arrangement to wed your betrothed's younger sister certainly spoke to that truth. Imogen curled her hands into tight fists. Though for one considered to be a rogue, he'd hardly demonstrated an amorous intention toward Imogen. Embarrassment turned in her belly.

"You wouldn't want to marry him. Not when he's proven himself inconstant. You deserve more than that." Chloe paused and when next she spoke, she did so in hushed tones. "Don't you remember what you confessed at Mrs. Belton's?"

Ah, yes, Mrs. Belton would not be pleased by this very public shaming of one of her students. For purely self-serving reasons, of course. After all, a headmistress's reputation was bound to the ladies she turned out into the world.

Chloe nudged her in the side.

Imogen grunted. "Love. I said I'd wanted to make a love match." She'd believed she loved William and, worse, believed he'd loved her, too. What a naïve fool she'd been. A young girl so desperate for that emotion in her life, she'd convinced herself of foolish dreams. And yet, a shameful, pathetic sliver of her soul still longed for that dangerous, painful emotion.

"You do remember." A wide smile wreathed her friend's face. "Splendid." Chloe glanced about, as though searching for interlopers. She reached for her reticule and fished around inside the elaborate, satin piece. "I've brought you something," she said, dropping her voice to a conspiratorial whisper.

The faintest stirring of curiosity filled Imogen; any sentiment beyond the self-pitying, pained fury she carried was a welcome emotion. Chloe withdrew a shining gold chain. The sun's morning rays filtered through the crack in the curtains and played off the small heart pendant. Imogen studied the light reflecting off the glimmering heart. "It is beautiful," she murmured.

"Here, take it," Chloe prodded. She pressed it into Imogen's fingers. "It is yours."

"I couldn't." Imogen made to push it back.

"It belonged to Lady Anne, the Countess of Stanhope."

Imogen blinked several times. "What?" she blurted. The young lady, courted by the powerful Duke of Crawford, then betrothed to her cousin, had quite scandalized the *ton* when she'd abruptly ended her engagement and wed the roguish Earl of Stanhope. In fact, it had been the last scandal to shock the *ton* . . . until Imogen. "How?" She couldn't string together a coherent thought. The faint stirrings of unease rolled through her. Oh, dear she didn't care to know the extent her friend had gone to obtain the piece.

"Lady Anne is married to Alex's closest friend, Lord Stanhope. It was nothing to speak to the woman."

Oh, please let the floor open up and swallow me whole. "You didn't." She dropped her head into her hands and shook it back and forth.

"I did." Chloe nodded excitedly. "You see," she spoke in such hushed tones, it brought Imogen's head up. "The necklace," she nodded to it, "is the same one worn by her sisters and a handful of their friends. It is fabled to land the wearer the heart of a duke and as you've already had a duke, you'd instead want one of those noblemen, but this time, his heart as—"

Oh, please, no. "You did not speak to her." Shame curled Imogen's toes.

Chloe paused, mouth opened, thought unfinished, only confirming Imogen's suspicions. "She was entirely gracious." Imogen winced. "And understanding." She flinched again. "And more than happy to gift you the heart pendant." Chloe wrinkled her brow. "Or rather, give me the pendant to pass along to you." An uncharacteristically somber light filled her dearest friend's eyes. "I just want you to be happy once more."

So much so that she'd unknowingly humiliate Imogen before a stranger. Imogen sighed, not knowing if she should laugh or cry.

Chloe claimed her hands and gave them a squeeze. "You will find the gentleman who is your true love. I promise." Through the years, Chloe had been the more practical, logical of them when it came to matters of the heart, swearing off that emotion for herself while allowing, even supporting, Imogen in that dream.

Imogen hardly recognized this young woman who spoke of magic and pendants and dreams of love. With a sound of impatience, she shoved to her feet, her fist tightened reflexively about the chain. "This is about more than love."

Imogen began to pace. Chloe had never been accused of being a hopeless romantic. Unlike Imogen—or rather, Imogen had been, until life happened and showed her the folly in giving her heart to another. She increased her frantic movements. "It is about being respected, inspiring devotion and dedication in another." Feats she'd failed miserably at where the Duke of Montrose was concerned.

Her friend hopped up and placed herself in Imogen's path. And then she said the only two words Imogen had longed to hear since the whole public shaming heaped on her by her disloyal sister and fickle betrothed. "I'm sorry," Chloe said softly.

That was it. Imogen just wanted someone to not make excuses or worry after the scandal and how Society looked on it. She wanted someone to care about her and that she'd been hurt.

Imogen mustered a smile. "He did have fetid breath."

A sharp bark of unexpected laughter bubbled past her friend's lips. "And he was entirely too tall." She shuddered. "We shan't find you a tall gentleman like him."

"And handsome," Imogen supplied, feeling vastly better for her friend's devoted teasing. "He was too handsome." Which is why her grasping, self-centered sister had first noticed him. The familiar stirring of fury turned in her belly. And she embraced it, far preferring it to the kicked and wounded pup she'd been since the unhappy occasion. Determined to set aside the still fresh betrayal, Imogen threw herself back into her friend's game. "He drinks too much brandy." His breath had stunk of it whenever he was near. "I shan't ever wed a gentleman who touches even one glass of liquor."

"Splendid." Chloe gave a pleased nod. "You are quite grasping the spirit of this." She lowered her voice. "I've heard from my brother that His Grace has a wicked penchant for the gaming tables."

Imogen had little doubt just which brother Chloe spoke of. Not the respectable Marquess of Waverly but rather Lord Alex Edgerton, known rogue, skirt-chaser, reprobate, brandy drinker. Another gentleman all ladies would be best served to avoid.

Chloe clapped her hands once, jerking Imogen's attention back to her. "You're woeful again." A stern frown turned her lips down in the corners. "You must focus on how horrid and horrible and all things awful he is."

"Er. Yes, right." Except she'd run out of insulting charges to level on his miserable head. She stopped pacing so quickly, her satin skirts fluttered about her ankles. Though in truth, as hurt and humiliated as she was by his betrayal, she truly was better knowing the man's true character before she'd gone and wed him.

"I have an idea," her friend put in tentatively, which was all show. There was nothing tentative about Lady Chloe Edgerton.

"Oh?" Imogen asked dryly. Too many troublesome scrapes at Mrs. Belton's Finishing School had begun with those four words.

Chloe beamed with Imogen's interest. "Now that you have this necklace," she gestured to the chain in Imogen's hand, "you shall find a gentleman. And make him fall hopelessly and helplessly in love with you and His Grace will be outrageously, wickedly jealous."

"That is your plan?" She'd long adored her friend for her cleverness, however, this was an ill-thought-out idea on the lady's part. What was the use in making William jealous? "That will not change anything where Montrose is concerned."

Her friend plucked the necklace from her fingers. "Nor should you want to change anything, silly," Chloe murmured.

"Here, turn around." Before Imogen could protest, Chloe spun her about. She settled the chain about her friend's neck and fiddled with the clasp. A soft click filled the quiet. "There," she said, turning Imogen around once more. "I'll have you know," she gave a toss of her blonde curls, "that was not my plan." A slow, mischievous grin turned her lips. "You rejoining Society was . . . is," she amended, "my plan."

Imogen had retreated from *ton* events after The Scandal, as Society had taken to referring to it. Those drawn out syllables the *ton* used to set it apart from other scandals. Imogen sighed. "I've little interest in entering Society." Alas, now that Rosalind had wed her duke, Mother's wedding plans were at an end, and she'd turned her sights once more upon Imogen. "I intend to wait until the scandal isn't so—"

Her friend's snort cut across the remainder of those hopeful words. "Oh, Imogen," she said gently, taking her friend's hands once more. "This scandal shall remain until some other foul lord goes and does something outrageous that captures their notice. I shan't allow you to bury your head in shame. Not when you haven't done anything wrong." Fire snapped in her blue eyes. "Is that clear?" Imogen opened her mouth to respond but Chloe gave a pleased nod. "We shall fill your days! There will be shopping trips and we'll take in the theater, and various balls . . ."

As her friend prattled on, Imogen groaned. All those options were about as appealing as being tasked with plucking out each strand of hair on her head, but most particularly any visits to Drury Lane. "Not the theater." There she would be on public display like one of those Captain Cook exhibits at the Egyptian Hall. She was brave. She was not that brave.

"You'll have me," her friend said, accurately interpreting her concerns. "The sooner you make your appearance and show the *ton* you'll not be cowed or shamed by them and miserable Montrose, then the sooner they shall move on to some other poor creature."

Imogen shot her a look.

Chloe had the good grace to blush. "Er . . . not that you're a poor creature."

Imogen tapped a finger to her lips. Insult aside, if she was being honest, it really wasn't an altogether awful plan. In fact, it was quite a brilliant one.

As though sensing victory was close, Chloe added, "Furthermore you'll be spared your mother's matchmaking for the Season."

Yes, Mother had begun to speak of the Marquess of Waverly with an increasing frequency. After all, by Mother's thinking, if one couldn't have a duke, she may as well aspire to a marquess. "Very well, I shall go." After all, the alternative would be to flit from one event to the next with her married sister and her beaming mother and the faithless Duke of Montrose for company.

"Splendid!" Chloe said, with a clap of her hands. "My brother Gabriel will accompany us. No one will dare slight you with the fierce Marquess of Waverly at our side."

Envy tugged at Imogen. Through the years, her own sister had been at best rude and condescending, and at worst, deliberately cruel, mocking the flame-red curls Imogen had been cursed with. She would have traded her left index finger to know the loving friendship Chloe had with her siblings.

With an energized stride, her friend started for the door. She paused at the threshold and spun back once more to face Imogen. "Prepare yourself, Imogen Moore. You are going to take Society by storm."

Not again.

Other Books by Christi Caldwell

Historical Romances

Lords of Honor Series
Seduced by a Lady's Heart
Captivated by a Lady's Charm
Rescued by a Lady's Love
Tempted by a Lady's Smile

Scandalous Seasons Series
Forever Betrothed, Never the Bride
Never Courted, Suddenly Wed
Always Proper, Suddenly Scandalous
Always a Rogue, Forever Her Love
A Marquess for Christmas
Once a Wallflower, at Last His Love

Sinful Brides Series
The Rogue's Wager
The Scoundrel's Honor

Standalones
'Twas the Night Before Scandal
The Theodosia Sword

Contemporary Romances

Danby Novellas
A Season of Hope
Winning a Lady's Heart